**"What the hell are you doing?" he demanded, looking
tough and clearly ready to prove it.**

And that's when her brain kicked back into gear and reminded her of her situation. She was in a strange house. In a
strange *bathroom*, out in the middle of nowhere, surrounded
by rugged mountain peaks and more snow than she'd ever
seen.

And she was staring at a furious, naked guy. "Um—"

"Who the hell are you?"

"I—" She glanced at the neon-pink vibrator in her hand
and felt every single brain cell desert her.

"Get out."

Yeah. On that, they were perfectly in sync, thank you very
much. She might have a secret weak spot for an edgy, difficult bad boy, but she absolutely did not have a weak spot for
being stupid.

Whirling, she dropped the vibrator and ran.

The Novels of Jill Shalvis

Aussie Rules
Out of This World
Smart and Sexy
Strong and Sexy
Superb and Sexy
Instant Attraction
Instant Gratification
Instant Temptation

Anthologies Featuring Jill

Bad Boys Southern Style
He's the One
Merry and Bright

Published by Kensington Publishing Corporation

JILL SHALVIS

Get a Clue

KENSINGTON BOOKS
Kensington Publishing Corp.
www.kensingtonbooks.com

ISBN-13: 978-1-61773-788-6
ISBN-10: 1-61773-788-7
First Kensington Trade Edition: September 2005
First Kensington Mass Market Edition: January 2008

eISBN-13: 978-1-61773-789-3
eISBN-10: 1-61773-789-5
Kensington Electronic Edition: May 2015

10 9 8 7 6 5 4

Printed in the United States of America

One

Never agree to marry a man because he has potential.
Men are not like houses; they do not make good fixer-
uppers.

— Breanne Mooreland's journal entry

It took her a while, but eventually Breanne Mooreland realized she had a naked man in her shower. Normally that would be the icing on a double-fudge chocolate cake, but in today's case, where she'd already had more failures than she could face, it felt like the last straw.

Consider her the camel, back broken.

In the interest of sanity—hers—she pretended to be fine as she dropped her small carry-on bag to the chair by the bed and stepped to the closed bathroom door. "Um . . . hello?"

Nothing but the sound of water hitting tiles. She glanced around the bedroom, exquisitely decorated in rustic wooden-log furniture and soft, fluffy, equally exquisite bedding with pillows piled higher than Mt. Everest. Just what she and Dean had ordered for their honeymoon.

That she was on said honeymoon alone caused her throat to tighten, but she'd cried bucketfuls on the plane and had promised herself no more pity parties.

But, of course, that had been when she'd merely been stood up at the altar in front of two hundred of her closest friends and family members. Before she'd gotten on the plane from hell all by her lonesome, where the turbulence had been so bad she'd had to stay seated between a three-hundred-pound

Louisiana woman crying, "Oh, Lordy, Lordy, have mercy—save us, Jesus!" and an Alaskan fisherman who smelled as if he'd kept some of his daily catch in his pockets.

Thinking she'd hit rock bottom—oh, how wrong she'd been—she'd gotten off the plane to discover that the rest of her luggage had never made it from San Francisco. That landing in the rugged, unpredictable Sierras in the middle of a snowstorm was equal to being shaken *and* stirred. The storm had only increased in severity since, so that the Jeep that had driven her to her "secluded, exclusive, fully staffed manse on the lake" honeymoon house could barely even get down the narrow, windy roads.

Breanne had distracted herself on the terrifying drive by pulling out her Palm Pilot and opening her journal. There she had her life—her hopes, her dreams, her failures, everything. Her last entry, made on the plane: *No more failures.*

Ha! That was going to be tricky, as she tended to make bad decisions. Maybe she wasn't enough of a giver. Maybe she just took, took, took. Maybe concentrating on others more would somehow turn the tide for her. Yeah, that's what she'd do, she'd give back. Do favors. Perform public service. Try harder at work, where, granted, she slaved over the books for a large accounting firm, but with an attitude.

She knew being the baby of a large family allowed her to fly beneath the radar. Even with her older brothers looking over her shoulder, she'd sought out trouble like a moth to the proverbial flame, beginning back in elementary school, where her sharp tongue and naughty pranks had regularly gotten her into hot water. By middle school she'd switched from pranks to boys, having developed an early fascination.

Of course, her mother always put it more simply: Breanne was drawn to the wrong type—jobs, friends, it didn't matter. Even men. Especially men. Hence, being stood up at the altar—for the third time.

On second thought, chances were she needed more direction than "no failures," so she added: *And especially, no more men.*

That's when her driver had begun four-wheeling up a narrow private road lined by tall pines covered in so much snow they looked like two-hundred-foot ghosts, swaying in the wind. On either side of them was a dramatic drop as they rose in altitude with every mile. Hues of peach, pink, blue, and purple colored the sheer granite escarpment of the Sierras through the falling snow in the deepening dusk.

Finally they'd maneuvered down a long, steep driveway, stopping in front of a beautiful log-cabin mansion. The backdrop should have been a private alpine lake, but the ascending dark and thick precipitation kept it from view.

"Here you go." The driver had reached over and opened her door instead of getting out and coming around for her.

She supposed she couldn't blame him; night was nearly upon them, and there was at least three feet of white, fluffy snow all around. She ruined her new suede boots just by hoofing it to the front door, clutching her only possession, her carry-on bag. She felt a little awed at how fast it was getting dark, and at the utter lack of city lights—or any lights, for that matter.

As she'd raised her hand to knock, a blast of wind pummeled her, plastering the snow from face to toe, going in her mouth, stinging her eyes, snaking like chilled fingers down her cashmere, open-necked sweater. Gasping for breath at the shocking cold, she staggered around to face her driver, intending to ask him for help.

He was gone.

As she contemplated the aloneness of that, a small streak rushed out from the corner of the house and practically across her feet, ripping a startled scream from her.

Then the streak *howled*. A coyote.

The sound had the hair on the back of her neck rising as she stumbled back against the door. *Don't panic, coyotes don't eat humans. Probably.* Hugging herself, she felt very alone.

Alone, alone, alone . . . the word echoed in her head in the voice of her mother, who was certain her troubled youngest child would never marry, would never bring forth grand-children into the world to spoil, and therefore would never amount to anything.

Shrugging that off—no more pity parties!—Breanne eyed the house. It certainly looked impressive with mounds and mounds of white snow pressed against the base, more white stuff falling, and the sky ominously dark and foreboding. In-side, there was supposedly a huge stone fireplace, a Jacuzzi tub, a sauna, a mini movie theater with an entire library of DVDs to pick from, and much, much more, including her own discreet staff for the week.

A honeymooner's delight, right? Dean had claimed to be excited. A shame he'd not been as excited about showing up for the wedding.

No one answered her second, desperately desperate knock, which for an instant perpetuated the hope that maybe she'd been cast in some sort of new reality show called *Torture the Bride.* Any second now, the director would yell *Cut!* and then, in a *This Is Your Life* moment, Dean would pop out and laugh at her for falling for it.

Only there was no camera, no Dean, laughing or other-wise, nothing but snow in her face, making her eyes water, her lips cold, raising goose bumps over every inch of her flesh.

Oh, and let's not forget the coyote, still howling in the dis-tance with his friends, discussing eating her for dinner.

Forget *polite.* She opened the unlocked front door and gaped in awe at the interior of a most impressive house. She stepped inside the foyer that stretched up to the second story—and came face-to-face with a moose.

Just a head, she told herself, *mounted on the wall.*

Slowly, purposely, she let out the air that she'd nearly used to scream. "Definitely not in Kansas anymore," she whispered. There was also a wood mirror with shelves, each holding glass lamps that sent soft light across shiny, hardwood floors. In complete opposition to the "warm" feel of the room, the air itself danced over her, icy cold.

"Hello?" she called out, trying to stomp the snow off her clothes. Not much of it budged, happier to stick to her every inch, making her wet and miserable.

There was a reception area with a small pine desk, and a sticky note there that read:

> *Newlyweds get the honeymoon suite, complete with accessory package. Room is open and cleaned.*

Well, damn it, she might not be a newlywed, but she was still getting that honeymoon suite, charged as it was to the rat bastard Dean's credit card. She just hoped the suite was warmer than the foyer, because she could make ice cubes in here.

Clutching her small carry-on, which held only her makeup and two extremely naughty negligees that had been meant for her wedding night, she walked to the base of the huge, wooden staircase that slowly curved and vanished up into the second floor, with several big potted plants lining the way. More glass sconces along the wall lit the area so that she could see into the fading daylight. It was an Old West, cabin-style interior, beautifully and tastefully done.

But no one appeared, and she hadn't heard a sound. Along with the daylight, much of her bravado deserted her. She didn't relish the idea of being here alone tonight. *"Hello?"*

She didn't know what the check-in procedure was, but she wondered if the huge storm had sent the staff members running for their homes in town, a one-horse place called Sunshine, of all things, a good ten miles back down the curvy, surely now snowed-in road.

They'd probably left the door unlocked for their guests, never even considering she'd be alone.

But alone she was. *Thanks, Dean.*

Knowing from the brochure that the honeymoon suite was on the second floor, she reached for the banister and began to climb the stairs.

"Anyone here?" she called out again at the top, stopping to pant for air. Damn altitude. The landing looked down to an open, large room below, rustic and cozy, with two forest green and maroon sofas shaped in an L, a large leather recliner, and throw rugs dotting the floor. It looked far more inviting than the cold, silent hallway where she stood, shivering like crazy from her wet clothes, and maybe nerves.

Then she realized she *did* hear something—running water. Proof of life! Hugging herself, she followed the noise, past three doors on the right and left, all of which appeared to be bedrooms.

The hallway walls had old photographs of the Wild West on them: cowboys, wagons, old mining towns. At the end of the hallway, she stopped in front of a set of double wooden doors.

The honeymoon suite?

Hoping so, she stepped inside. That's where she found the log bed, so high she'd need a stool to climb up on it. The bedding was white down, with bear-and-moose pillows, and looked so scrumptiously warm she nearly sank into it. There was a matching armoire and dresser as well, also done in pine logs. The ceiling was open-beamed, and a work of art all by itself. The stone fireplace—not lit, darn it—and floor-to-ceiling windows finished off the room, the windows revealing that the day had fled completely now.

There was a goodie basket on a chair for the honeymooners: body paints in every flavor, a package of edible underwear, and several books on the pleasures of massage and touch therapy, including *How to Make a Woman Come Every Single Time*.

Too bad Dean wasn't here. He could use that one.

There were other fillers, too: body lotion, bath oils, a brand new vibrator in neon-pink and shaped just like a penis she'd once seen that had a terrible curve to the right. She picked it up and took a good look at it, trying to picture the designers of such an item sitting around a table and deciding on the angle of the curve. She considered herself adventurous and fun in bed, but she couldn't imagine Dean figuring out a way to make good use of this. Gee, guess it was a good thing he wasn't here . . .

It penetrated her addled brain that the shower was still running.

Odd. Surely the housekeeper wouldn't be in there . . . Curious, a little unnerved—and if she let herself think about all that had happened to her since she got out of bed that morning, she could add *crazed* to the list—she stepped over a pile of wet clothes on the floor.

Huh?

Turning back, she crouched down to look at them, trying to get a clue as to who was in her shower. Levi's, original fit, size 34x36. Hmm. Tall and lean. There was also a white Hanes Beefy T-shirt, size large, and a soft blue chambray overshirt, both smelling good enough that if she hadn't given up men, she might have pressed her face against the material and inhaled.

But she *had* given up men. She'd written it in her journal and therefore it had become law.

He didn't wear underwear.

Why the hell *that* intrigued her, she had no idea. Rising, shivering because her clothes had become iced to her skin, she knocked on the bathroom door.

Whoever he was, he had the radio on; she could hear the broadcaster talking about the storm of the century—

Storm of the century. That couldn't be good. Pressing her ear to the door, she heard other disturbing words, such as "No one is going anywhere, folks" and "I hope you're all

stocked up on whatever you need, because this one's a doozy."
At that, she twisted the handle on the door and pushed it
open.

The bathroom was as amazingly detailed as the rest of the
house. Even through all the thick steam, she could see the
stunning granite countertops, the raw wood-framed mirrors,
the small overstuffed day couch, the old-fashioned brass fix-
tures—

And yet another gift basket, filled with more goodies. She
looked at the vibrator she still had in her hand. What else
could she possibly need? Well, besides a new groom, that is.
A shame they didn't come a dime a dozen in a gift basket
such as this, selection ready.

The shower took up one full corner, all in clear glass,
etched with the outline of the Sierras, which in fact did nothing at all to hide the tall, leanly muscled man standing in it.

Naked.

Gloriously so, she might add. The water sprayed out of
four different rain heads, massaging over him. He had his
back to her, and what a fine back it was: broad, ropey shoulders, sleek, strong spine, smooth and tanned until, low on his
narrow hips, his tan line abruptly ended.

He had a fabulous, mouthwatering butt, and Breanne
took a moment to wonder at the man who wore a bathing suit
in the sun but not underwear beneath his jeans.

Water sluiced off him, and soap, too, and then, as if God
had decided to bestow one tiny little favor on her shitty, rotten day, the guy dropped the soap.

Breanne held her breath. Would he—

Yes. Yes, he would.

Bending for it, blissfully unaware that there were a pair of
very curious female eyes on him, he clearly didn't even consider his modesty. Every muscle in his body flexed as he
doubled over, legs slightly spread, offering her an eye-popping
view of his—

Oh, my.

Lifting her hand, she furiously fanned air to her face, because the front of him lived up to the back, and how. She wondered how old he was, thinking that body couldn't be more than thirty, which was only two years older than herself. In any case, she stood there, rooted to the ground, her own wet misery forgotten, mouth hanging open, drool pooling, eyes locked on the backs of his well-defined thighs.

And what was between them.

But then suddenly he whipped around, staring at her through the glass for one beat before shoving open the shower door, allowing steam and water to pour into the room as he glared at her with an ominous, thunderstruck expression on his face.

More than thirty, she thought inanely. Probably, given those laugh lines bracketing his unsmiling mouth, and startling sky-blue eyes, at least thirty-five.

Not that age mattered, with a majorly heart-stopping body like his.

"What the hell are you doing?" he demanded, looking tough and clearly ready to prove it.

And that's when her brain kicked back into gear and reminded her of her situation. She was in a strange house. In a strange *bathroom*, out in the middle of nowhere, surrounded by rugged mountain peaks and more snow than she'd ever seen.

And she was staring at a furious, naked guy. "Um—"

"Who the hell are you?"

"I—" She glanced at the neon-pink vibrator in her hand and felt every single brain cell desert her.

"Get out."

Yeah. On that, they were perfectly in sync, thank you very much. She might have a secret weak spot for an edgy, difficult bad boy, but she absolutely did not have a weak spot for being stupid.

Whirling, she dropped the vibrator and ran. She ran like hell through the open bathroom door, slamming it behind her to give her an extra second on him.

He'd told her to get out, so chances were that he wasn't planning on chasing her, but she'd rather be safe than sorry. She hightailed it through the bedroom, leaping over his clothes, moving more quickly in her ruined boots than she'd moved in . . . well, a very long time.

Behind her the bathroom door whipped open.

Oh, God.

He was in pursuit and he was quick.

With a startled squeak, she sped up, thinking no one back home would believe she could ever move this fast, not even to save her life.

"Wait!" that low, almost gravelly voice called out. *"Who are you?"*

Stopping to chat seemed like a bad idea, so she kept moving.

Her only problem was, she really had nowhere to go.

Two

Cooper Scott stood butt-ass-naked, freezing cold and dripping wet in the bathroom doorway, holding the vibrator his
mystery guest had just dropped. Bad enough that he'd quit his
job, shocking everyone he knew. Bad enough that he wasn't
getting laid, now that he'd sent a pretty woman screaming
like a banshee into the night.

A woman carrying a vibrator.

He could still hear her, pounding down the stairs in those
ridiculous, towering high-heeled boots that were all for show
and had absolutely no practicality.

Who would wear such things to the Sierras at the onset of
winter, in the middle of an insane storm like the one they
were facing?

He had no idea, but he supposed, as she was in his house,
he needed to find out. Well, not *his* house, exactly, but his
rented vacation house.

And a stunning one at that.

His brother James had sent him here with strict orders to
"get his shit together," not mentioning that the place was at
least ten thousand square feet of pure luxury. Log-cabin style,
it had gorgeous mahogany flooring, pine trim, soft, buttery

interior walls filled with rustic prints and old-time equipment such as hare-bone snowshoes and antique wooden skis.

But if the decorating was glorious, old western style, the
actual appliances were state of the art, with everything placed
and designed for ultimate comfort. He had a week to live in
style here, a week in which he'd intended to do nothing but
ski his brains out and maybe find a pretty ski bunny to keep
him warm at night.

And, as James had ordered, "get his shit together."

As long as he avoided thinking, he was good. All he
wanted to do was recover from the job that had nearly sent
him to the loony bin, and figure out what the hell to do with
the rest of his life.

No sweat.

He'd gotten here from San Francisco via his truck, which
was probably buried in the driveway by now. The drive had
been treacherous at the least, and given how the snow was
still coming down, he doubted he could get off the mountain
if he'd wanted to. But the staff that was supposed to greet
him had been nonexistent, the house cold as an iceberg. He'd
found the heating control and cranked it, but as yet, nothing
had happened.

He'd taken a hot shower anyway, intending to start a sizzling fire in all the fireplaces he could find, but instead had
been interrupted by a woman watching him soap up. Hoping
she was one of the promised staff members, maybe someone
who could cook—God, he was starving—he grabbed a thick,
plush white towel from its neat pile on the granite counter.

There had been all sorts of toiletries laid out for him on
the countertop, including a basket filled with condoms in
varying sizes and colors, which had amused him earlier.

How long had it been since he'd needed a condom?

Too damn long, he knew that much.

Towel around his hips, he stepped into the bedroom just
as the lights flickered. Perfect.

The electricity was going to go. Then he could be cold, wet, starving . . . *and* in the dark.

Another power surge, making the lights dim with an odd hum, and from somewhere below came the sound of a thud and low cry. Dropping the towel, Cooper grabbed his jeans, jamming first one leg and then the other in, hopping as he made his way out into the hallway, still shirtless and barefoot.

Up here at an altitude of sixty-five-hundred feet, daylight didn't slowly fade, but vanished in the blink of an eye, and today had been no exception. Full darkness had fallen. Any starlight was muted by the heavy snowfall, so the three overhead skylights and the wide range of huge windows in the rooms below were useless.

The lights were flickering nonstop now, offering only a sporadic glow from the wall sconces lined up in the empty hallway. "Hello?"

No answer. Of course not. What had seemed like a beautiful, welcoming house in the daytime suddenly didn't seem so welcoming. Still, he wasn't alone, he knew that much. He might be close to a nervous breakdown, but he wasn't seeing things.

He reached for the banister, just as the lights stopped flickering and went out completely.

"Don't panic, don't panic," Breanne whispered to herself. She'd flown down the stairs and across the hardwood floor at the base of the curved staircase, thankful for the lighting, stingy as it was, because she wasn't happy in the dark. That went back to the days of too many brothers, and too many times they'd happily tortured her. Once she'd even been locked in a closet and left there by accident.

But she was a grown-up now. "You're tough," she said out loud. "You're impenetrable." She wondered where Scary But Gorgeous Naked Guy was.

Coming after her.

At the thought, she tripped over her own two feet and went sprawling face-first across the shiny floor.

That's when the lights went out.

Then, from up above somewhere, she heard footsteps.

For years her brother Danny had been telling her she needed an exercise regime, some sort of weight training to give some tone to her body, and she'd always shuddered at the thought because she and exercise mixed like oil and water.

Now she wished she'd paid attention. Kickboxing, taebo, karate . . . Hell, *anything* aggressive would have been nice.

In the complete dark, she pushed herself up off the floor, breathing like a lunatic, probably looking like a deer caught in the headlights. Only there were no headlights, nothing but an inky blackness that had her stomach falling to her toes.

No groom.

No electricity.

Stuck in a house with a naked guy.

Screwed.

She was a self-proclaimed city girl, she reminded herself. Feisty and independent, not easily cowed or intimidated. Give her a scary downtown alley with a drunk leaning against the wall, or an obnoxious construction worker blocking her path any day. Anything but the big, open, scary, dark space where the unknown waited just out of sight. Bears, spiders, coyotes . . .

Oh, and a gorgeous naked guy with a low, sexy voice in her shower.

Maybe people found gorgeous naked men in their showers all the time out here. Maybe it was a way to greet the newcomers. Maybe . . . maybe she was delusional because her day had gone so badly.

She slipped her hand in her pocket and gripped the comforting weight of her cell phone. Normally she'd have mace there as well, but who'd have thought she'd be needing any on her faux honeymoon?

Pulling out the phone, the digital display lit up, providing a tiny, welcome bit of light. No bars, though, which meant no reception. She actually shook the thing, as if that would help. She'd heard about this, of course, and she'd seen the "Can you hear me now?" commercials, but having grown up in a city where people walked around with their cell phones permanently attached to their ears, where there were no mysterious pockets of low reception, she'd never had this problem.

Hell of a day to experience it now.

She should never have gotten out of bed, should never have donned that lacy white wedding dress she'd loved, never gone to the church to marry a man simply because it had seemed like a fun, exciting thing to do, and because her mother had suggested this was her last chance to get it right.

And she sure as hell wished she would stop falling for "I love you" when what a guy really meant was "Do me, and also my laundry, while you're at it."

She shivered again. Or maybe that was *still*. Her clothes, still wet and extremely cold against her skin, had stuck to her, probably steaming because despite her bone-deep chill, she'd also begun to sweat in sheer terror.

And then she heard it, a sound from behind her in the dark.

Just a slight scrape on the floor, which could have been a rat, a mere creak in the wood, or . . .

A footstep.

Oh, God.

Ballsy or not, this experience was quickly growing beyond her. She stumbled forward and fell into the front door. Grasping the handle, she wrenched it open.

Icy wind and snow greeted her, blasting her in the face, sliding down her collar. To add insult to injury, the horizon was pure black—no city lights, no stars, nothing but a velvety darkness. Still, propelled by fear, she took a step forward.

And sank up to her thigh.

Once when she'd been little, her grandma had given her one of those snow globes of San Francisco. Shake it up and it snowed down over the city.

In fact, it did snow in the city. Once in a blue moon. During those times the wind would slip in from the shore, chopping and dicing at any exposed skin. But in those rare events she simply stayed indoors. There was lots to do inside: hang out with friends, seduce a boyfriend, drink something warm . . .

But today was a whole new kind of cold. And this fluffy, powdered-sugar kind of snow, thick and currently up to her crotch . . . she'd never seen anything like it. Too bad she'd dressed for a chilly day looking at the snow from the *inside*.

Torn between sinking into the snow, never to be heard from again, or facing the dark, terrifying house, Breanne stood there in rare indecision for exactly one second, during which time another gust of wind hit her, sending her backwards a step, onto her butt in the doorway. More wet cold seeped through her denim.

Quickly scrambling to her feet, she fought the wind and slammed the door shut, then whirled around and flattened herself to it, blinking furiously, trying to adapt to the dark.

But there was no adapting, especially when out of that inky blackness came a low, almost rough masculine voice. "Hello?"

Oh, God. That didn't sound like Gorgeous Naked Guy. Biting her lip to keep quiet, hands out in front of her, she tiptoed toward the reception desk where she'd first seen the note about the honeymoon suite. There'd been a phone there . . . Her fingers closed over it.

Teeth chattering in earnest now, she lifted the receiver to

her ear, ready to call . . . she had no idea. It didn't matter; she'd take the Abominable Snowman, for God's sake.

No dial tone.

Okay, this wasn't happening. This couldn't really be happening. She'd stepped into some alternate universe—

She heard a click, and then a small flare of light appeared, and a face, floating in the air.

Breanne clapped her hands over her mouth to hold in her startled scream and pressed back against the wall as if she could vanish into it.

Once for Halloween she'd gone into a haunted house with a group of friends, smug and secure in the fact that having grown up with brothers, she couldn't be frightened. And indeed, her friends had all screamed their lungs out while she calmly walked through, her mind rationally dismissing each scare. Oh, that was just a CD of scary sounds. And there . . . just a skeleton—fake, of course. And that dead body swinging overhead? With all the blood? Just ketchup.

But this was real. Her hollow stomach and slipping grip on her sanity told her that. And while she really wanted to remain cool, calm, and collected, her heart threatened to burst right out of her chest, even as she registered the truth.

The floating face wasn't really a floating face at all, but a man holding a flashlight up beneath his chin.

Not Gorgeous Naked Guy.

No, this man was the same height but stockier, and in his twenties. He wore a hoodie sweatshirt over a baseball cap low on his forehead so she could only see a little of his face, but what she could see was overexaggerated by the beam of the flashlight, giving him a dark, almost Frankenstein-like glow that had her breath backing up in her throat.

"It's okay," Frankenstein said to her. "The phones go out all the time."

Oh, okay then. She'd just forget about the panic barreling through her at the speed of light. Her plan was to at least look calm. Get what info she could. "What about the electricity?" she managed, as if asking the time that tea would be served.

After that, she hadn't a clue.

"Yeah, that's new," he admitted, and shrugged as if to say he had no idea.

"Are you . . . the manager?" she asked, hoping the answer was "Yes" and not "No, I'm your murderer."

"No. The manager is . . . temporarily indisposed."

He didn't look so much like Frankenstein at all, she saw when he lowered the flashlight and his hood slipped back, revealing straight black hair to his shoulders, dark skin suggesting a Cuban descent, black eyes, and a long scar down one side of his jaw. "So who are you?" she asked.

But he'd already turned his back on her and was shining his light into the vast cavern that had been the great room before the lights had gone out. "I'll start a fire," he said, moving in that direction. "You should change your wet clothes."

She'd happily strip out of the sweater and jeans that had turned to sheets of ice on her body, but the two sexy nighties in her carry-on didn't have enough material combined to warm a gnat. "Are you going to tell me who you are?"

There was a snap, then a quick flare of light as he held the match to some kindling inside the huge stone fireplace. The resulting glow highlighted him from head to toe. He was built like a linebacker, wearing baggy jeans at least three sizes too big and low enough to reveal equally baggy boxer shorts. His sweatshirt strained across his shoulders as he glanced back at her, those dark, dark eyes of his landing on hers. "I'm Dante. The butler." He shoved up his sleeves, revealing heavy tattooing on both forearms, making him look more like a rapper than a butler, but what did she know about being either?

"Where were you when I first arrived?" she asked, trying

to control her shivering but having no luck. Instead she continued to tremble, mixing up her innards like a shake.

"Yeah, sorry about that," Dante said.

"There's someone in my suite."

He gave a palms-up gesture. "A mixup with reservations. Don't worry."

Oh, okay. She wouldn't worry, then. *Not.* Unsatisfied with the vague answers, she stayed where she was in the doorway, still freezing, wondering what the hell to do.

"You going to get any closer to the heat?" her thug butler asked.

Heat. Her entire body craved it more than her next breath, but there was still the matter of the Naked Guy and his status, and much as she didn't want to be *alone* in this house of horrors, she really, *really* didn't like the idea of being here with these guys, either.

"Suit yourself." With a shrug, Dante faced the burgeoning fire, holding his hands out as if he was cold, too.

On the other hand, Breanne thought, if these guys were going to hurt her, it was probably best that she be warm so she could fight back, right? But before she could move, from above came the unmistakable sound of footsteps coming down the stairs. Breanne tipped her head back, but in the dark couldn't see. "Um, Dante?"

"Relax," he said from his perch by the fire.

Sure. She'd just relax. *After* she died of nerves. From the stairs, a pair of bare feet emerged, then denim-covered legs, long and tough with strength.

Her heart jolted unexpectedly into her throat. She knew those legs; she'd seen them with water and soap raining down the length of them. They'd been tanned and well defined, as if he used his body for more than sitting behind a desk balancing other people's checkbooks for a living as she did.

And he didn't wear underwear.

The unbidden thought caused an inane hot flash. All those male . . . parts, nestled against the denim.

Naked.

She began to sweat some more but didn't bother to say a word to Dante, because if he told her to relax again, she was going to come unglued.

Then a bare chest materialized, still gleaming from the shower, but no less jaw-dropping for it. She already knew the guy had a nice body, muscular without being beefy, lean without being scrawny.

His belly was ridged, carved into a six-pack she envied, since sit-ups were something she occasionally thought about but never actually did. He had a very light smattering of hair between his pecs that narrowed into a line down his belly that vanished into the loose waistband of his jeans, like an arrow toward the hidden prize—

He held up his hand, and in it was . . .

Oh, God.

The neon-pink vibrator, glowing in the dark now.

It was following her, stalking her, all the way down the yellow brick road to hell.

Naked Guy—not quite naked now—came the rest of the way into view, and unerringly turned his head in her direction, and though it was dark in the shadows where she stood, she knew his eyes landed right on her.

He had an odd awareness to him, as if he could see in the dark. As if he knew exactly what was going on around him at all times, a skill she'd never mastered in the best of times, to which today absolutely did not belong.

He also had the look of a man thinking things—things that, even with fear coursing through her, made her face heat and other parts tingle.

He smiled grimly, a lopsided smile that did nothing to dull the fact that he was amazing to look at—and terrifying, all at the same time.

With a pathetic little whimper, Breanne pressed back closer to the wall, swallowing hard, trying to decide if that had been an anticipatory "all the better to eat you with" smile . . .

Or simply a trick of the flickering firelight.

Three

Note to self—give serious thought to becoming an alcoholic.

—Breanne Mooreland's journal entry

Cooper took the last step and came face-to-face with his voyeur for one brief flash before she backed up into the darkness. All around them it closed in, except for the low glow of light from the fireplace—and, of course, from the vibrator.

Then he caught a movement and tensed as a shadow to his left materialized into a man.

"Welcome," the man said in utter contradiction to his urban street clothes. He eyed the vibrator in Cooper's hand but whatever his thoughts were on a guy wielding a vibrator, he kept them to himself. "I'll get some candles."

"Who are you?"

"Dante, your butler," he said, without a hint of laughter, indicating he was serious.

A butler? Cooper watched Dante vanish into the darkness. He'd been dressed more like any of the punks he'd encountered over the years on the job, but if the punk had candles to share—

"Unbelievable."

This from the woman somewhere in the dark, beyond him in the foyer.

Turning, Cooper located her faint outline against the foyer

windows. She had sunk to the floor, her back to the glass. There was a low-light digital display in front of her face, and she appeared to be entering something into a handheld digital device.

"No groom," she muttered as she entered. "Flight from hell. More snow than the Arctic Circle. A serious lack of electricity. Oh, and a gorgeous naked guy."

Cooper blinked. Gorgeous naked guy? *Him?* As bad as things had been lately, he'd take it.

"Next up," she said, thumbs furiously hitting the keys. "Is getting knocked off on your honeymoon."

Cooper held up the glowing vibrator to see her better, filling in some of the details he'd only caught glimpses of before. She had long, wavy hair, most of it in her face, and huge, wide eyes. Hard to tell if she was pretty, but something about her grabbed him. Her sweater was pink, snug to her full breasts, and she was damn cold if the hardness of her nipples meant anything. As he moved closer, she gasped.

"No one's getting knocked off," he said softly.

"Easy for you to say." She was shivering out of control. "You're not the one facing death."

"Neither are you."

She lowered her digital unit. "I really, really wish I hadn't come."

She was scared, shaking with it, and probably chilled to the bone. Knowing how she felt, he crouched in front of her. Because he'd come running when he'd heard her cry out he was still wearing only his jeans, so he raised his hands to show that while he might be half-naked, he was harmless, forgetting for a moment that he held the glowing vibrator. "You dropped this."

This got him a vehement head-shake. "Not mine," she said firmly.

"But I saw you—" He broke off at the look of horror on her face. "No? Hmm . . ." Knowing damn well she'd dropped it, he pretended to ponder the ownership as he turned the thing over in his hands. It turned on, humming loudly into the silent foyer.

This drew another gasp from her, so he tried to turn it off, but only succeeded in cranking it into high gear, and it nearly vibrated right out of his hands.

"Oh, for—*here*." Snatching it out of his hand, she turned it off and then stood up, jamming the thing into her back pocket. "Who are you? Not the butler—there's already one of those."

"Cooper Scott." He left out the unemployed loser part as he straightened. "You're right, I'm not another butler. I'm a guest. And you're . . . ?"

"In the twilight zone," she said, peering uneasily into the dark around them.

"So in your twilight zone, you watch people shower?"

Without the glow of the vibrator, he couldn't see her expression clearly, but could feel the heat of her embarrassment. "I didn't intend to intrude on your privacy," she said primly. "I just didn't realize what you were doing."

"You didn't realize that when someone's standing bareass naked in the shower, rubbing soap all over their body, it means they're taking a shower?"

Her glare practically lit up the dark.

"Let me give you a helpful hint," he said. "Knocking on a closed door is a good thing."

"And let me give *you* a hint." She punctuated this with a poke to his chest. The contact of her finger with his bare flesh shocked him, and given the funny hitch to her breath, it startled her, too. "Stay out of other people's honeymoon suites."

"What?"

Jerking to her feet, she jammed her Palm Pilot in the bag strung over her shoulder. "You were showering in *my* honeymoon suite."

"No. *I* rented this house. Well, my brother did, but it's mine for the week."

She crossed her arms over her chest, plumping her full breasts up and out. She wasn't tall, maybe up to his shoulder, but her jeans and sweater clung to her body, revealing she was quite the package. "Wrong again," she said indignantly. "The place is mine, bucko."

"Bucko?"

"I forgot your name."

He stared at her, wondering how it was he felt both annoyed and . . . alive, extremely alive, a feeling he hadn't experienced in too long. He had no idea what she'd look like in the light of day. He had no idea what she really looked like in the dark, either, other than a nice set of curves with sparks of temper coming from her general direction, but it didn't matter. She was as annoying as hell, even if she did think he looked good naked.

She was also shaking like a drowning poodle. Fact was, he was damned cold himself, with no shirt and no socks. "Cooper," he said with a sigh. "My name is Cooper. And you're . . ."

"B-Breanne," she said through her chattering teeth.

"Look, Breanne, the fire is crackling now. Move closer to it."

"Why?"

He sighed again at her wariness. Had he done that, or was she just defensive and cranky all on her own? "Because you're turning into a popsicle." He put his hand on her arm, shocked at how chilled she really was. Her sweater was thin, wet, and nearly iced over, her skin beneath just as bad. "Didn't anyone ever tell you that you need to wear a coat in a snowstorm?"

"It wasn't snowing in San Francisco. Or on the plane. Or in the airport."

Another violent shiver wracked her and he ran his hand up and down her arm, trying to give her some of his body heat. "What about when you left the airport?"

She stared at his bare chest, though he figured that was just her way of avoiding eye contact. "Lost my luggage."

"You've lost your groom *and* your luggage?"

"Yes." Behind her temper was a sadness that got to him. "And I hate the dark, too."

He looked at her for a moment, wondering at the urge to touch her, to open his hand, spread his fingers and stroke her skin. "You're having a hell of a bad day all around, aren't you?" he murmured.

"You have no idea."

"Come here."

She went absolutely still, only her eyes cutting once again to his bare chest. "Why?"

Besides being wary and cold, she was a suspicious thing. And looking as she did, all disheveled and shockingly sexy for it, he could understand she had a good reason to feel that way. He could practically see her heart pounding at her ribs, and her belly rose and fell too quickly. *She was afraid of him.* That cut deep, as he'd spent most of his life helping people not to be afraid. "I'm not going to hurt you. I promise."

"Like I'd take your word," she said bravely, but then let him tug her out of the foyer and into the great room. The flames were roaring now, lighting the place with a soft glow, showing off the inviting leather couches.

But the woman just stood there stiffly, arms still wrapped around herself, shuddering with her chill. Her long, wavy hair was the same color as her eyes—expensive whiskey. She had a light smattering of freckles across her nose and cheeks, and lips that were soft and full. *Made for kissing* came the inane thought.

"You're staring," she said.

And for smart-mouthing. "You're cold. Come warm up."

She just shivered again, continuing to hug herself. He knew those clothes had to be damned uncomfortable against her skin, molding her figure, which happened to be a nice one. Not chunky, but not thin, either.

Just right for holding onto. Not that he'd ever been choosy when it came to women. Hell, he hadn't had the opportunity to be choosy, not with his job that had taken up every second of his last few years.

Yet another full-body shudder wracked her and he nearly reached for her. The stupid hero in him.

Ignoring him completely, she moved closer to the flames, leaning in, revealing her backside, and the vibrator glowing from the pocket.

"That butler guy . . ." She glanced over her shoulder and caught him grinning. "What?"

"Nothing." To swipe off the grin, he had to look away from the vibrator peeking out of her pants. "Go ahead. The butler guy . . . ?"

She narrowed her eyes. "He said the manager was temporarily unavailable. But as soon as he shows up, he'll tell you. This place is mine for the week."

"Look, I hate to argue with a lady who's already had a pretty fucked-up day—"

"—then don't."

"—but you're wrong."

"Not about this."

He might have said more, but instead frowned as it occurred to him that her teeth were in danger of rattling right out of her head. "Hey." He put his hand on her arm, which was even icier now than it had been. Beneath his fingers he felt her tense enough to shatter, and he lifted his other hand as well, holding both her arms. She was shaking so hard she nearly shuddered free, so he tightened his grip slightly, trying to hold her steady. "You really need to change your clothes."

She tried to twist away, but newly concerned, he held onto her, sucking in a breath when her hair brushed his own chilled skin.

"Trust me," she said through her rattling teeth. "Given what I have in my carry-on, I can't change."

"You have nothing?"

"Not exactly nothing." She stopped trying to break away from him and looked at her fancy boots, the kind that were made for muddying up a man's brain, not for real use. Her hair fell forward, again against his chest. Normally he loved a woman's hair teasing him there, but these strands were frozen. He sucked in another breath and waited for her to speak.

"Just . . . honeymoon stuff," she said softly.

Everything she'd said finally clicked in. "Are you really on your honeymoon? Alone?"

"Well, the tickets were paid for, weren't they?"

"What happened to your husband?"

"No husband. He never . . . we didn't—" Taking a step back, she lifted her head, eyes proud. "He didn't show up, all right? And there was no use sticking around to face the sympathy and barely masked glee that being dumped at the altar brings." Another violent shiver followed this statement, along with a very disparaging sigh.

Cooper swore softly, softening in spite of himself, and he pushed her into a large leather recliner. It was entirely possible she'd actually had it rougher than he had lately, and that was saying something. "No big deal. I have plenty of clothes upstairs. I'll be right back—"

She bounced back up so fast she nearly cracked his chin with her head. "Really, don't bother yourself. I'm fine."

"But I have a bag right upstairs."

"Honestly, I'm good . . ." She glanced around her. "No reason for you to have to go upstairs."

He took in the white around her eyes, the way she gripped

him tight, as if maybe he was the lesser of all the evils of her day. "You're scared."

She let out a laugh. "No."

"Just say it. You don't want me to leave you alone down here."

"Ridiculous," she muttered.

"Ridiculous? You're afraid of the dark, remember?"

"Not afraid, exactly. Unhappy with it."

"And it was only my imagination that a few minutes ago you were looking at me as if I might be a murderer?"

"Or a serial rapist." Her lips were still blue as her teeth chattered from her chill. "B-but I've since decided you're probably neither."

"Gee, thanks."

"Now you're just the guy standing between me and my honeymoon suite." More bone-crunching shudders wracked her, appearing to start at her roots and end at her toes. "My w-warm honeymoon suite."

Once again he ran his hands up and down her arm, truly alarmed for her now. "You were up there," he said, maneuvering her closer to the fire. "You know it's not any warmer than the rest of the house. At least not yet."

She didn't answer that but looked horribly dejected at the thought.

"Okay, listen," he said. "You can come *with* me upstairs, or you can wait here. Either way, I'm going to get us both something more to wear."

She plopped back into the chair and sent her chin to the heavens. "I'm not budging."

God, she was stubbornness personified. And frustrating. And somehow, also, inexplicably adorable. "Suit yourself, but I'm going. I'm getting you a change of clothing and me some socks and a shirt, and then I'm starting a fire up there so I can hit the sack."

"Not my sack, you're not."

Had he thought her adorable, even for a second? "I'll be right back."

He left her and loped up the dark, dark stairs, feeling his way along the hallway toward the bedroom, thinking the only way he'd want her in his bed was with a gag over that lovely, full, smart-ass mouth.

The image alone began to warm him up.

Four

I'd tell him to go to hell, but it just so happens I'm stuck there and don't want to have to see him every day.

—Breanne Mooreland's journal entry

Breanne watched Cooper walk away and concentrated on breathing through her panic. There was also the fact that the firelight gilded his broad shoulders and sleek back, highlighting the worn Levi's that fell low on his hips, intimately cupping his tush, which she had to acknowledge was absolutely worth intimately cupping.

He had a way of moving, and a way of taking in his surroundings as he did. *Intensely aware*, she would have said. As if he was a predator.

And maybe he was.

Gulp.

Then he vanished entirely, was simply swallowed up by the dark house, the only person she really had in this Alice-in-Wonderland place. Too proud to speak up, she sat there, heart in her throat, staring into the dark, gaping doorway that she couldn't see beyond, wondering what, or who, else besides Dante was out there.

A loud thump came from nowhere, and she leapt to her feet. The vibrator fell to the floor. Sweeping up the still-glowing thing, she clutched it to her chest as the thug/butler came back into the room.

Dante's hood was low over his face, but he carried a tray

with two steaming cups of something, and suddenly she didn't care if the beefy, scary guy was Hannibal Lecter, he had something *hot*.

"Here," he said, and handed her one of the cups with surprising grace for a tough, built guy who looked as if maybe he wore a cape and wrestled in his skivvies for a living. Or whacked kneecaps.

She stared at the offering, thinking of every bad movie she'd ever stayed up too late watching. Not only was she the stupid heroine alone in the house with two potential bad guys, she was about to be poisoned—

"If I was going to do something to you," he murmured, "it wouldn't be poisoning your drink."

She looked up at him and caught a surprising flash of humor in his eyes. "Are you laughing at me?"

"Nah, that would be rude." He pushed her mug toward her mouth. "Drink. You're shivering so much you're making *me* cold."

"Fine." At least she'd die warm. She tucked the vibrator back into her waistband, grateful he hadn't made fun of her makeshift flashlight. Then her fingers closed around the ceramic mug, and at the blessed heat of it, she nearly burst into tears. "What was that noise before?"

"What noise?"

"I heard something bump. Or crash."

Dante turned away, his wide shoulders completely blocking the fire's warmth for a moment as he set the other mug down on the small table by the couch. "I dropped something. Drink before you freeze to death."

Or something to death, anyway. She sipped and, despite herself, moaned aloud at the frothy, thick, melting chocolate on her tongue. "Oh, my God."

"Good?"

"Amazing."

"Shelly made it, the cook here. She had water going on

the stove before the power went out, luckily. I'll tell her you like it."

Eyes closed, Breanne sipped some more, savoring the heat of it as it slid down her throat. Lifting her head, she went to smile at her mysterious butler, meaning to ask about the rest of the invisible staff, but he was *gone*.

Without a sound.

Yikes. Real or Memorex? She'd have sworn she'd imagined the whole thing—except she was holding the hot chocolate. Lord, she was losing it here. She looked around uneasily, the only sound the crackling of the flames and her own heartbeat echoing heavily in her ears. No sign of her hooded, right-out-of-a-thriller butler.

Or, for that matter, Gorgeous Naked Guy.

She sucked down more of the hot chocolate, wishing it was liquid courage, then stood and moved closer to the fire. She was tired of shaking, and damn tired of being wet and cold, so she tugged off her iced-over sweater. That left her in just a white tank top, and, crouching down before the flames, the warmth of the flames danced over her torso and arms, and she wished she could shuck out of her wet jeans, too.

"Miss me?"

Whipping around, she faced one tall, dark, and slightly attitude-ridden Cooper Scott. Still sockless and shoeless, he smiled grimly, and she did her best not to drool or stare.

His gaze touched on the sweater she'd spread across the mantel to dry, then swiveled back to her standing there in her little white tank top. She'd worn it because it sucked her in and pushed her out in all the right places, and because after competing with Dean's cell phone and long hours at work for months, she'd decided *no more*. She'd wanted to make sure he noticed her tonight, every inch of her.

Too bad Dean hadn't told her that *he'd* also decided *no more*. No more *her*. Now she was standing there, probably looking like a coed after a wet T-shirt contest.

Cooper's gaze lingered on her chest for a beat before lifting to her face. He didn't say a word, but jaw tight, dropped a duffel bag at her feet. In that oddly graceful and yet utterly masculine way he had, he hunkered down and began to go through it, the long, sleek muscles of his back and shoulders bunching and releasing with his every movement. "I couldn't see upstairs," he muttered. "Or I'd have—Here."

She reached for what he offered, a dark pair of plain sweat bottoms. Elastic around the ankles and the waist. He tossed her another dark item as well, a matching sweatshirt.

Her job in the accounting firm required her to dress up on a daily basis, which was amusing given that in school she'd never met a math class *or* a dress she'd liked, but years later she'd developed a taste for both.

Sweats hadn't figured much in her life. But then again, this wasn't her life, this was some alternate universe she'd stumbled into. So what if the sweats were going to make her look both short *and* fat; this was about survival, not looking good. Or so she told herself. "These are too long."

"Roll 'em up."

Spoken like a man who'd probably never given his appearance a single thought. And why should he—she'd seen him naked. He had *nothing* to hide, not a damn thing.

"Hurry up," he said, and for a split beat his gaze dropped, running over her body. Specifically, her nipples, which could surely cut glass. "You're turning blue." He straightened and took a step toward her, maybe even to do it for her, and suddenly hurrying seemed like a good idea. She pulled the sweatshirt over her head; then, with her arms still up, she paused. Holy smoke, the inside of his sweatshirt smelled good, like . . . like rough-and-tumble man. She stood there and inhaled some more, thinking they ought to bottle this smell—

"You okay in there?"

She yanked the sweatshirt into place. "Fine. Just got stuck for a minute."

"Uh-huh." His expression said he knew exactly what

she'd been doing, but he sat on the floor without a word and pulled on socks, then running shoes, making her realize she wasn't the only one freezing.

And yet he'd seen to her comfort first. That did something she hadn't expected—it tugged at her.

Whoa. Stop the lust train. *Had she already forgotten?* No more men. Not even tall, built, bossy ones with an oddly thoughtful nature. *Especially* not even tall, built, bossy ones with an oddly thoughtful nature!

His hair, fawnlike with its myriad colors, stuck straight up in spots. Probably because she'd gotten him out of the shower and he hadn't had time to so much as comb it. His shoulders were still bare, and wide enough to withstand a lot, she'd bet.

He covered them up with a T-shirt he pulled from the bag, and then added a thick black sweater that looked deliriously soft and warm. "Better," he sighed, then leveled his eyes on her. The firelight gleamed over his chiseled features, reflecting in his eyes. There was so much intensity there. And heat. Looking at her like that, he seemed impossibly handsome, and far too sexy for her own fragile frame of mind.

"Change your pants," he said, and turning his back, jammed his hands in his pockets. "Hustle."

His sexiness forgotten, she shook her head even though he couldn't see her. "I'm not going to change right here."

"You're going to go somewhere else to do it? Into the dark house and maybe an even darker bathroom? You with your phobia of the dark?"

Damn. Good point. "Okay, but don't peek."

"Because you didn't peek at me?"

Did he always have to be right? "What about Dante?"

With a long-suffering sigh, Cooper moved around the couch to the huge double doors that led to the hallway and foyer. Shutting them, he turned back to face her, waggling his finger in a circle as if to say, *Go ahead.*

Breanne crossed her arms tighter over herself and shifted

her weight from one frozen foot to the other. "Why can't you be on the *other* side of the door?"

"So you can lock me out and away from the flames? Don't think so."

Another good point.

"You're stalling, Princess."

Princess? She'd show him princess! If she could move without trembling like a baby, that is. Since she couldn't, she just stood there in a rare moment of indecision, feeling oddly close to tears.

"Just do it," he said, sounding tired. "This place is supposed to be some sort of exclusive hideaway, famed for its privacy." Pushing away from the doors, he came close again, but then turned and faced the fire, holding out his hands to the flames. "Plus, I don't think Dante's exactly eager to have us demanding to know what the hell happened, booking two guests at the same time. He's probably in hiding."

Maybe. Another shiver shook her body. Her jaw was sore from all the chattering her teeth were doing inside her head, and she felt so weary she could have curled up into a tiny ball in front of the fire and slept for the rest of the week.

"You done yet?"

"*No.*"

"*Jesus.* Just do it, would you?"

She reached for the zipper on her jeans. "You always this patient?"

"It's a special gift."

"Betcha it gets you a lot of women."

"Yeah, they're beating down my door."

In direct conflict with those confident, cocky words, he hunched his shoulders, stretching the sweater taut across the muscles there as he stared into the fire.

She didn't have the time, nor could she spare the energy, to wonder about him, but she did. "Are you married?"

A rather harsh laugh escaped him. "No."

"Committed?"

"No."

With or without the attitude, she imagined he did have women beating down his door. It was all that disheveled hair calling to a woman's fingertips, that come-sin-with-me expression, those drown-in-me blue eyes.

And then there was the rest of him, which would have a weaker woman begging him for a distraction from this cold.

But she wasn't weak, and she had enough problems at the moment. She didn't need to be courting more. Hitching his oversized sweatshirt up to her chin to see, she reached for the zipper on her jeans, trying like hell not to inhale the delicious scent of the soft material again. Eyeing him carefully, she began to peel the wet jeans off her hips, not an easy chore because they'd practically iced themselves to her skin. She had to do the shimmy shake, and finally, *finally* got them to her knees, stopping to adjust her wayward panties.

Cooper turned around.

"Hey!" she squealed, crossing her hands over her tiny scrap of white satin—worn for the rat bastard Dean.

Cooper ran his gaze from her undoubtedly wild hair to his own sweatshirt stuffed up to her chin, exposing her belly button piercing and the panties that hadn't been meant to cover much, and didn't. "I figured fair's fair," he said very softly.

Five

Literally caught with her pants down, Breanne stood frozen
to the spot, unable to move or even breathe. In that horrible
beat of time she became painfully aware of how she must
look, sweatshirt high, pants at her knees, her barely there
bikini bottoms askance . . .

Cooper's deep blue eyes sparked, *flamed*, and the oddest
thing happened to her. In spite of everything, a little ball of
heat swirled low in her belly.

She had to be delirious. From the cold. From exhaustion.
From her life sucking big-time. Awkwardly she hopped again,
trying to pull her jeans back up, but they weren't going anywhere. Then she made one too many hops and caught her
boot heel on the hem of the jeans. Waving her arms wildly,
she struggled for balance.

Cooper merely stepped forward and caught her.

Fine. He could help her and she could die of mortification
later.

But he didn't help. He put a hand to the middle of her
chest and gave her a little push, making her fall gracelessly
to the couch. Once again, the pink vibrator hit the floor and
rolled to a stop at his feet.

They both stared at it for one beat before Breanne tried to bounce back up.

"*Stay*," he commanded.

Oh, no. *Hell, no.* She scissored her legs, meaning to kick him, either in the chin or the nads, she didn't care; she was going to take him down. *Now.*

But he just laughed low in his throat, and then again when she struggled to karate-chop him with her legs caught together by her own jeans. *Laughed*, as he crouched beside her, a big hand on either of her thighs and said, "Give in, Princess."

"I never give in."

Holding her down with ease, he reached for the fallen vibrator, lifting it up. The obnoxious thing still glowed neon-pink. "Never say never." Then he grinned at her in the firelight, looking just like the devil must look in the dead of winter with no one to torture. "This thing keeps showing up. Maybe you should claim it."

"It's *not* mine!"

"I don't know . . . earlier you were gripping it like it was your long-lost best friend." With a flick of his wrist, he turned it on.

The low hum filled the air, and with it came a buzzing in Breanne's ear—the sound of her brain coming to boiling point.

"Ready for use," Cooper said, suggestively waggling it in her face.

"Good." She struggled to get free, trying not to think about the picture she was presenting him with. "You can shove it up your—"

"Oh, no," he said. "Ladies first." He dropped the thing to the couch next to her, where it rumbled against the soft, buttery leather while he slid his hands down her legs to the jeans pooled between her knees.

"Don't even *think* about it," she choked out.

But he wasn't only thinking about it, he was doing it, fisting his fingers into the wet denim and yanking them past her knees to her ankles, where they caught on her boots.

His gaze met hers, intense and raw, and along with it a heart-stopping heat.

Did he have to pack such a sexual energy? She felt her entire body clench with a punch of shocking yearning.

"High-heeled boots," he murmured. "Ever so practical out here."

She stared down at the top of his head as he worked on stripping her. Her little triangle of white satin had not only slipped sideways, it was now riding up into parts unknown. She'd had a bikini wax two days ago—again for the rat bastard Dean—and judging from the very soft, very rough sound that escaped Cooper at her movements, he'd caught an eyeful up close and personal. "If I wasn't so tired," she murmured, sagging back, suddenly exhausted, "I'd kick your ass."

"Next time," he said, trying to untie her boots. The laces were iced. "I guess you were all prettied up for the honeymoon."

No. She'd prettied up for herself, to feel sexy, but she was not going to argue with a man when her pants were around her ankles; when she had a vibrator bouncing on the couch next to her, taunting her; when she had bigger worries, such as her panties, and what they still weren't covering. Shoving the sweatshirt down as far as she could, which was to the tops of her thighs, she leaned forward to hurry the process along.

While she worked on one boot, Cooper continued to work on the other, his fingers managing to work faster and far more efficiently than hers. His bowed head was close enough to her thighs that he could have lifted his head and drunk his fill, but he kept his gaze on her boot, pulling it off, pushing her hands aside, then removing her other as well. Finally he hooked his hands into her jeans again and peeled them away. Her legs were pink and mottled from the cold, and when his knuckles brushed against her, she flinched. Without a word he stood, once again turning his back to her, staring into the fire, looking a little more tense than he had a moment ago.

"A little late now," she muttered, pulling on the sweat bottoms.

He didn't respond to that.

"Done," she said, and stood.

Only then did he turn back to face her, his gaze sweeping from top to bottom, taking in the way his sweats looked on her. The only sign of strain was a tic in his jaw. "You want the couch in front of the warm fire?" he asked. "Or the cold honeymoon suite? We can start you a fire there."

She couldn't concentrate with the vibrator continuing to hum and jump on the couch, but she knew she didn't want to go further into the depths of the dark house. With an annoyed sound, she reached for the vibrator, desperate to turn it off.

Cooper beat her to it, turning it off himself before handing it back. "Keep it. You never know when you might need a friend."

She rolled her eyes, but the thing provided a tiny bit of light so she grabbed it. Plus, given that she was off men, it might be sooner than later before she'd need a friend of the battery-operated variety.

"'Night," he said with an irritating, knowing smile. He began to walk away.

"Wait!" When he turned back to her, she had to come up with something to say. "We . . . can't both really stay here."

He just raised a brow.

"And I think you should be the one to leave," she said, lifting her chin.

"Why me?"

"You said it yourself—I had a bad day."

"Hell, Princess, I've had a bad year, and you don't see me whining about it."

She wondered how bad was bad, and if it could possibly match hers.

"You want to trudge out in the snow and try to get into town?" he asked.

With the coyotes, bears, and God knew what else? "No. I thought . . ."

"That I'd do it." He shook his head. "I was here first."

"That's gentlemanly."

He laughed. "Yeah, well, you're not stuck out here in the middle of nowhere, in the storm of the century, with any sort of gentleman."

For some insane reason, that caused another flicker of heat to spiral through her.

Which proved it, really. She *had* lost her mind.

"We both know the roads are closed by now," he said. "And I for one am not snowshoeing into town. In fact, I'm not going anywhere."

"This is not how it was supposed to be," she said softly.

"No kidding. But shit happens, and we deal with it. Now are you going to pick a spot, or am I?"

There weren't many people who'd argued with her. Not her four older brothers, or the father she'd long ago wrapped around her finger. Fact was, she'd been getting her way since birth.

Aside from her family, the other men in her life had also let her get away with just about anything. Her first fiancé, Barry, had spoiled her rotten. Even Dean, King of Rat Bastards—whom she hoped had choked on his own tongue—had never so much as crossed opinions with her, but that was probably because he'd been too busy.

So the fact that this strange man was not only quarreling with her, but telling her how things were going to be, surprised her into momentary silence.

"Nightie-night, Princess," he said.

She looked around and once again panicked at the thought

of being alone. Damn him, but he truly was the lesser of two evils. "Wait!"

He turned back, propping up the doorway with a shoulder as if he didn't have a care. "Yeah?"

She opened her mouth, but her pride ran away with her good sense. "Nothing." She casually dropped to the couch but something must have given her away, whether it was the sudden panic pumping her heart loud enough to wake the dead, or the renewed tension that gripped her body, because he sighed. "Are you going to be okay?"

Was she? She wished she knew. Alone, she'd go back to obsessing about spiders and coyotes and bears, but if he stayed, she'd have new things to obsess about . . .

Still, he'd stuck by her side, even helped her when she'd needed it, and hadn't once thrown it in her face as any of her brothers might have.

Not that he was remotely brotherly . . . And yet he'd had her at every disadvantage and he'd not tried to press himself on her in any way.

"Breanne?"

Even more unnerving, she liked the sound of her name on his lips. "Seriously, I'm fine. Don't give me another thought."

"No?"

"No. I certainly won't be giving you one." *Liar, liar, pants on fire*.

He looked at her for a long moment, then pushed away from the doorway, moving toward her like a long, lean cat totally at ease with himself, confident that he was at the top of the food chain. He had a nice gait, the kind a woman could watch all day if she was admitting such things. Which she wasn't. *Besides, she'd given up men*. His toes touched hers, then he crouched down, his face level with her belly.

Push him away, her feminist brain demanded.

Pull him close, her body countered.

"You're not going to give me another thought at all?" he

asked silkily, and she knew damn well he was purposely invading her space.

She managed to shoot him a smile that she'd perfected before she'd ever left her crib. It was an I'm-fabulous, I-couldn't-be-better smile, an I've-got-the-world-by-the-balls smile. "Nope. Not another thought."

Reaching out, he settled a long finger to the base of her throat, where she imagined her pulse was about to leap right out at him. "So then what's this?" he murmured.

Only a moment ago it had been unease, even fear about her situation here, until he'd touched her.

Now it was arousal, plain and simple.

What kind of a woman was aroused by a perfect stranger? "Nothing but a physical reaction," she informed him.

"Ah." His fingers stroked over her racing pulse and then again. In the glow of the fire, his expression was one of curious intent as he watched the path of his fingers. "Because you're scared."

"I'm not scared."

His lips curved slightly. "Then what?"

Damn it, he'd caught her. "I'm tired and hungry and still cold."

"And that's making your heart pound?"

"Sure." They were so close his exhaled breath warmed her breasts through the tank and sweatshirt, so close that she could see his eyes weren't a solid azure blue at all, but had flecks of midnight dancing in them, holding secret all his thoughts.

He shifted then, his big, warm hand lightly cupping her throat, skimming to her shoulder and down her arm before gliding back up again in a gesture that could have been meant to warm. And it might have, if he'd been her brother or her father.

And she did get warm. Hot, actually. But something else as well, something far more.

"Still cold?" he murmured.

"Um, no. Thanks."

"No problem." His gaze dipped once again to her pulse. "It's still racing, Princess. How come?"

"Don't know."

"Want me to guess?"

Her pulse sped up even more. "No!"

"Because if you were still cold, or even afraid, we have an easy solution."

"Really? What's that?"

"We share this fire."

"You mean with you on the floor and me on the couch?"

His gaze didn't waver. "No."

Damn if her nipples didn't go happy at his low, rough voice. And other reactions occurred as well: her thighs tightened, and between them came a deep tingle. "We're perfect strangers," she reminded herself as well as him. "I'm not sleeping with a perfect stranger. I'm supposed to be sleeping with my husband."

"But there is no husband."

"*Good night*, Cooper."

"Yeah." He sighed, then shot a hopeful look at her carry-on. "You don't by any chance have any food in that bag of yours, do you?"

"No." *Just two sexy nighties*. "But Dante brought you a hot chocolate."

"Great. Hot chocolate." With one last stroke of his finger over her throat, he grabbed the mug and left, shutting the doors behind him.

Breanne let out a slow, careful breath and sank back. The man was potent, she'd give him that. But he was also domineering, and just alpha enough to make her want to scream.

And yet . . . and yet there was more. She didn't know what, and told herself she didn't want to. Curling up into a ball on the couch, she stared into the flames while the weight of the day began to drag her down, along with her eyelids.

But the problem with relaxing, even marginally, was that everything came back to her, beginning with being left at the altar.

How could she not have seen that coming? Seriously, her radar should have at least blipped a warning, but she'd gotten nothing.

She'd met Dean at work. As an investor for one of the companies her accounting firm handled, he'd sauntered by her cubicle, stopping to smile at her. Other than his most annoying habit of humming Elvis tunes at inopportune times—such as when he made love to her—he'd had a suave sophistication she hadn't been able to resist, even knowing he was a player. Foolishly, she'd let herself go for it, and for some reason that had always mystified her, he'd reciprocated.

But everything he'd ever told her—such as those three words, I love you—had turned out to be a lie.

And here she was. Alone. She looked around the large room, into the far corners and the shadows there, managing to convince herself she was fine. She'd even started to relax, at least enough that her muscles didn't ache. And then—

SNAP!

At the loud crack, she fell off the couch and landed on all fours, eyes wide, heart ricocheting off her ribs as she searched the room.

Just the fire crackling. Forcing herself to laugh, she climbed back up on the couch and let her eyes drift shut again. Everything was good, she was going to stay good—

A soft creaking sound had her leaping to her feet. She tried to tell herself she was still fine, but that was hard to believe as she watched the handle on the double doors turn. "Who—who's there?"

The door slowly opened, revealing the large, dark cavern that was the foyer.

"Cooper?" Her heart hit her throat. "This isn't funny."

A small, blond woman appeared. Mid-twenties, maybe, with a petite frame and a sweet, angelic smile. "Sorry. Did I wake you?"

Was she kidding? Who could sleep in the haunted horrors of the honeymoon house? "No."

"Oh, good. I'm Shelly, the cook. I came for the mugs I sent here with Dante." She came further into the room, passing Breanne's empty mug, heading directly toward the fire, where she held up her hands. "Darn, it's cold between the kitchen and here." She laughed. "Some storm, huh?" She wore dark jeans and a soft-looking white turtleneck, her blond hair neatly pulled back in a ponytail. "And welcome, by the way," she said with a smile when she caught Breanne staring. "I hope you had a nice trip here."

Her honest, hopeful expression seemed so completely innocent, Breanne found she couldn't say what was on her mind, which was *Are you kidding me?* "Uh, yeah. Nice."

With a sigh, Shelly moved away from the flames, scooping up the mug. "You're on your honeymoon, right?"

Breanne felt her smile congeal. "Yes. Alone."

"Oh." That startled her. "So the wedding, it went . . . badly?"

"You could say so."

"I'm sorry," Shelly said with true regret. "And now this huge, unbelievable storm . . ."

"Until you got here, I was trying to convince myself this is all a bad dream."

"You poor thing." Shelly sat down on the couch next to Breanne. "Did you get your heart broken?"

The question, coming from someone Breanne had known all of a minute, should have irked her. It should have, at the very least, brought her great pain. Instead, she leaned back on the sofa, nothing but exhausted. "Maybe it's been a little stepped on," she finally admitted. "But not broken, no."

"Good, then you can try to enjoy your trip in spite of him.

You don't need a man to have a good time." Shelly laughed at herself. "That's what my mom always told us, anyway. I don't really have a lot of experience to go by."

Breanne blinked at the easy familiarity with which Shelly had spoken. Breanne had family, coworkers. Friends. But truthfully, most were men. Girl talk had never really been her thing. "I don't know what I was thinking to do this, to come here alone. It was stupid."

"Oh, you're going to enjoy yourself, I promise you. And someday you'll find another man. A better one."

Been there, done that, bought the T-shirt, thought Breanne. "Would you know where I could get a few blankets?"

"Of course—I'll get them for you. But first, I came to bring you into the formal dining room."

No way was she going to be lured anywhere in this dark, haunted house. "I think I'll just stay here, thanks."

"I was spooked when I first got here, too," Shelly said kindly. "This place scared me to death."

"But not anymore?"

"Well . . ." Shelly hugged her enviable petite body for a moment, running her hands up and down her arms as if chilled. "I got used to it," she finally said. And then smiled. "And anyway, you're not alone in your fears. We all feel a little off tonight."

"We?"

"Me, and the rest of the staff."

"How many of you are there?"

"There's five of us. Myself, Lariana, Patrick, Edward, and Dante." She stopped with a faraway look in her eyes and sighed dreamily. "You've met Dante."

This pretty, innocent little thing was sighing over the hooded butler?

At Breanne's baffled expression, Shelly let out a laugh. "He's thrilling, isn't he?"

How about terrifying? "He's . . . something."

"He doesn't say much, but when he does, he's just so smart, so kind. And funny, too. I just think he's the sexiest man alive, don't you?"

"I didn't get to see much of him," Breanne said tactfully.

"I know, I'm sorry." Shelly's smile was tremulous, making Breanne realize the cook was just as nervous as she was. "All this dark is getting to me. It makes me talk too much. I should go finish my chores before I get myself into trouble with the boss."

"Speaking of that," Breanne said, "do you know where the manager is?"

"Edward?" Shelly lifted a shoulder. "I'm not sure, exactly. He's usually scarce at this time of day. You let me know if you want any of the extras, okay? We have massages and a few other spa treatments available. How about some mud therapy?"

Breanne could never relax through anything like that, not under these circumstances. "Maybe some other time."

"Aromatherapy? We use oils—it's lovely, really. Or you can swim in the indoor pool by candlelight. Oh! I could make you a lobster picnic when the electricity comes back on. And if you want me to book you for a helicopter tour when we get the phones back, or anything else like that, just let me know. For now I've got candles going in the dining room so it isn't dark there. There's food, too."

Breanne's stomach growled.

"See? You're hungry. Come."

"Will Edward be there?"

"Um . . ." Shelly fingered the mug. "I don't know."

At some point Breanne had begun to warm up, except for her bare feet. If she wanted food—which she absolutely did—she had no choice but to slip back into her high-heeled, wet boots. Ugh. "How come I didn't see any of you when I first got here?"

"Sorry about that. But food will help take the edge off

your travels. Then, in the light of day, everything will be okay."

The travels had been the least of Breanne's worries. She would happily take yet another horrendous flight, seated between a *dozen* stinky fishermen this time, if only she could erase the entire day from existence. But there was no magic genie in sight, and Shelly held the doors open, gesturing Breanne out first.

She peered into the dark, dark hallway and swallowed hard.

"Come on," Shelly coaxed. "I met the other guest on the stairs and redirected him. Cooper, right? He's there already." Shelly said this as if his presence should entice her.

Instead her stomach took a little dip, though truthfully it might not have been fear but an unwelcome sizzle of excitement.

"He's waiting for you," Shelly said.

"Oh, goody."

"Have you spoken to him? He's really nice."

"I've given up men for Lent."

"Are you Catholic?"

"No." She shook her head. "It was a joke. A bad one, sorry. Truthfully, I've discovered I have questionable taste in the male species, and I'm taking a break until I better hone my judgment."

"Well, that's a shame. He's cute."

Cute? Puppies were cute. Babies were cute.

But big, bad, sexy Cooper Scott was not. In fact, he was the furthest thing from cute she'd ever seen.

Which didn't explain that sizzle of excitement one little bit.

Six

Cooper sat in the vast formal dining room, at a table longer than his entire condo. He looked out floor-to-ceiling windows that revealed a black, endless night filled with the glow of white snow.

A small pixie of a blond woman named Shelly had seated him, after appearing out of nowhere when he'd been heading toward the stairs. Dante had lit the myriad white candles along the window ledges that she busily set out. She was pretty, with a sweet, giving, almost naive smile, and yet nothing within him revved like it had when he'd been sparring with Breanne.

As irrational as it seemed, given that she was the opposite of every fantasy he'd ever had, he was insanely fascinated by the irritating yet sexy-as-hell woman.

Maybe it'd been the way she'd looked at his naked body. Or how she'd reacted to the vibrator: like a starving student and a scared Bambi-in-the-headlights, all at the same time. Now all he wanted was to get her to look at him like that again.

Because that was an unsettling thought, he concentrated on Shelly, who was neat and tidy, cute, and smelled like onions and seasoning. She had his mouth watering at the promise of something good to eat.

While he waited, the snow kept falling in long lines of white that were mesmerizing. He'd been told by Shelly that in good weather, he'd be able to see all the way to the far shores of Lake Sunshine, though tonight he couldn't even see the dock that was supposedly only twenty yards from the house.

Nothing but snow and more snow, and he figured one thing was certain: the skiing would be out of this world. Assuming it stopped coming down long enough to clear the roads so he could get to the lifts.

He knew if Breanne had her way, he'd be leaving at dawn, but that wasn't going to happen. But then again, neither was her honeymoon, so she could just relax. This place was plenty big enough for the both of them.

He heard a click-click-clicking, and knew the sound. It came from a pair of ridiculously high-heeled boots, squeaking from all the water they'd absorbed.

Breanne.

A/K/A Princess.

And though he knew exactly what she looked like—good Christ, the thought of her with her pants around her ankles and those barely there panties giving her a world-class wedgie would most definitely highlight his fantasies for the rest of his life—when she entered the room, she stole his breath.

Her hair had dried in long waves around her face. Her makeup, if she'd ever worn any, was gone. And though she walked like a princess, she still wore his sweats. A princess in sweats and fancy, expensive boots, with her chin up, only the clasping of her hands giving her away.

"You're squeaking," he said.

She sent him a cool gaze, then looked around, taking in the exquisite ceiling molding and incredible casement bay windows. "I'm also underdressed for this room."

"Oh, no," Shelly said, coming in behind her. "No one has to dress for dinner. This isn't an inn—it's your private house for the week. You dress as you want."

"Not exactly *private*," Breanne noted dryly, her gaze cutting to Cooper. "But it's a good thing about the dress code, because my luggage is gone."

"Oh, dear. You *have* had a rough day," Shelly said in sympathy.

Cooper wasn't sorry. He had hopeful visions of her having to go all week in only her underwear—

"How about I see what I can round up for you in the morning?" Shelly offered, crushing Cooper's dream as she left them alone.

Breanne stood just inside the room, seeming as if she'd run if she only had somewhere to go. At the very least she was going to sit in the chair farthest from him, which was approximately miles down the room. To avoid that, he rose and pulled out the chair right next to him.

Breanne hesitated, but then came close, until once again he could see the wild, almost frantic beat of her pulse at the base of her neck.

"You still afraid?" he asked.

"Of course not."

"Cold?"

"Haven't we already had this conversation? No."

"Then . . ." He lifted his hand and stroked his thumb over her throat. He wasn't really sure why, except the strangest thing had happened when he'd touched her before. He'd felt a spark, from deep inside where he hadn't felt anything in too goddamn long. And he wanted another.

And another.

His brother had been fussing over him for months to get the hell out, take a leave, relax, just be, before he landed in the psych ward. Cooper had finally caved and gotten the hell out.

He'd quit.

And he still hadn't felt any better. Hadn't felt *anything*.

Until tonight.

Breanne encircled her fingers around his wrist and that inner spark leapt to flame. "*Cooper*."

"Breanne." *Don't shove me away. God, don't.*

Shockingly enough, she didn't, and for a long moment they stood just like that, eyes locked, her fingers over his.

"You keep touching me," she whispered.

He knew it. He had her soft skin imprinted on his brain already.

"If you keep it up, I'm going to—"

"What?"

Still looking into his eyes, she chewed on her bottom lip. "Something."

"Anything you want," he murmured, and smiled grimly when, with a sound of great vexation, she tossed his hand from her and stalked around the table—click, click, clicking—strutting as if she wore something straight out of a fashion magazine rather than his sweats. In fact, just the look of her hips sashaying with attitude turned him on.

He was in bad shape if riling and baiting her like this was the most fun he'd had in too long.

On the other side of the table now, she pulled out her own chair, shooting him a smug, superior smile.

"I think you're crazy about me," he said.

She sputtered. "You're delusional. You—" She broke off whatever insult she'd been about to fling his way as Shelly came back into the room with a bottle of wine. She was followed by Dante, who set down a large tray at the head of the table.

Shelly beamed at the butler-who-didn't-look-like-a-butler. "Thanks, Dante."

He didn't smile back. "You're welcome."

Shelly arranged the plates between Cooper and Breanne, one filled with an assortment of breads, another with luncheon meats and cheeses, and a third with fruit. "I feel so bad," she said, her smile still in place, but a bit wobbly now as she clasped her hands in front of her. "Edward insists on a gourmet meal, and I really did spend the day making up roasted chicken with asiago polenta and truffled mushrooms, but then the power went out, the oven flicked off—" She sounded close to tears. "It didn't finish, and now . . ." She lifted her hands helplessly.

"No worries," Cooper said. "I'd eat anything tonight and be happy."

"Really?" Shelly asked anxiously.

"Absolutely."

"Me, too." Breanne gave Shelly a smile of her own, one Cooper hadn't seen, which meant it was real and full of warmth. He almost did a double take, struck by how it softened her face, removing all lines of sarcasm and bite.

Had he thought her not classically beautiful? He needed his eyes checked.

"Thank you for serving us at all," Breanne said sincerely to Shelly.

"Oh, but it's nothing like how it should be," the cook told them, still twisting her fingers.

"You did the best you could," Dante said. "We all know it. Stop worrying."

She shot him a tremulous smile.

Dante jammed his hands in his pockets.

Breanne got busy, sliding some cheese and grapes on her plate. "The best thing I make is reservations, so for me, this is great."

More relaxed now, Shelly laughed as she picked up the empty tray. "Then you just wait until tomorrow. I'm going to spoil you both rotten."

Breanne paused, a grape halfway to her mouth. She set it down and looked at Cooper expectantly.

He knew what she wanted him to say, that tomorrow there wouldn't be two guests, because he was leaving. Instead, he just smiled. He wasn't going anywhere.

Dante moved to Shelly's side and took the tray from her hands. Shelly gazed up at him as if he were a god. Her god.

Cooper wondered what it'd be like to have someone look at him like that.

Not coming close to duplicating the expression, Breanne sent him the evil eye. "One of us is leaving tomorrow," she said to Shelly.

Dante shook his head.

"No?" Breanne asked. "Why not?"

"The roads aren't cleared and no one's going to be able to get to them until the storm passes, which is supposedly no time soon. We're all trapped here."

"Where do you sleep when you're stuck like this?" Breanne asked.

"Oh, don't worry about us," Shelly said quickly. "There are servants' quarters we can stay in. You won't even know we're here." Leaning in, she began to pour the wine, first for Cooper, and then for Breanne, who scooted her chair back to make room for Shelly. At the odd scraping noise, Breanne looked down, then carefully lifted a sliver of glass. "Yikes. Something must have broken in here."

Shelly stared at the glass without moving.

Dante reached in and took the shard. "No harm done," he said, then took the bottle of wine from Shelly's fingers, set it down on the table, and directed her from the room.

Silence reigned.

Cooper looked at Breanne.

She pretended not to notice.

"So we're stuck," he said, making her face it. "Might as well relax about it." He hoisted his glass of wine in a toast. "What do you say?"

She stared at him, then lifted her glass as well, downing the contents in a few gulps before reaching for the bottle.

"You might want to slow down, Princess," he warned. "You're at altitude now, and that's going to go straight to your head, fast. Drink some water so you don't get dehydrated."

She bared her teeth and growled.

He laughed but lifted his hands. "Just trying to help you avoid getting hung over."

"I could avoid a hangover entirely by just getting drunk and staying there," she said miserably, and when he laughed again, she picked up a grape and looked as if she was considering chucking it across the table at him.

Arching a brow, he silently dared her, enjoying being distracted by her frustration. The woman must burn up more stress calories a day than the president of the United States.

Or at least as many as he did at work when adrenaline was flowing and—and that no longer mattered because he'd quit. He'd walked away and had become unemployed. Funny that he'd forgotten, even for a second.

He was just getting into his cheese and crackers when another set of footsteps came down the hall—not light like Shelly's, nor rubber-soled like Dante's. These were heavy, hard, and clinked and rattled with every step.

"What's that?" Breanne whispered, eyes wide.

Step, clink. Step, clink.

"Not a what," Cooper said, "but a who."

"That isn't Shelly or Dante."

"No," he agreed.

The footsteps came closer.

Step, clink.

Step, clink.

With a sudden gasp, Breanne rose to her feet, running around the table in those silly heels, directly at Cooper. He reached to pull out the chair next to him for her, but as she reached the corner, her heels slipped and she flew into the home stretch.

It was all he could do to catch her, but catch her he did. Her hair stabbed him in the eye, caught on his jaw, and even went into his mouth, but his brain had locked on the fact that her warm, soft curves were trying to crawl up his body. Her breasts were mashed against his chest, her legs entangled with his. He liked it all, but then again, it'd been so long since he'd had any action, he'd have liked just about anything.

Then an extremely tall, extremely lean shadow filled the doorway with indistinguishable features. "Sorry," the shadow said in a heavy Scottish accent. "But has anyone seen me bloody flashlight?"

Still in Cooper's lap, Breanne froze.

The shadow stepped further into the room. The candlelight caught him, revealing nothing more than a mere mortal man, possibly thirty, wearing a tool belt from which swung a hammer, a wrench, and an assortment of other tools.

Hence the clinking.

Cooper threw an amused look at Breanne, who remained utterly still for one instant before she blew out a short breath and struggled like a wildcat to get out of his lap.

But because he was a sick, sick man, Cooper used his superior strength to hold her against him before craning his head toward the man in the doorway. "No flashlight, sorry."

"Well, fuck me," Scottish said, and scratched his head. His red hair stood straight up. "I'm trying to get the generator up and running, straightaway."

"That'd be good," Cooper said.

"Power lines are down all over the bloody place. It'll be days and days with no electricity if I don't get the generator running."

Breanne looked horrified. "*Days and days . . . ?*"

"Aye. Well, off I go, then." With another scratch of his head, Scottish walked out.

Step, clink.

Step, clink.

"If I call him back here," Cooper whispered in her ear, "will you crawl up my body again?"

"Oh!" she spit out. "You are so not a nice man!"

"Are you sure? Because a minute ago you couldn't get enough of me."

"Let me up!"

Enjoying not only the squirming, but the lovely, warm feel of her butt rubbing against his crotch, Cooper did no such thing.

"I said, let me go!"

Grinning down at her, he easily held her against him. "Not until you say 'thank you, Cooper, for saving my life.'"

"You didn't save my life!"

"But you wanted me to."

She stared at him. "I can't believe you can walk through a door with your head as swollen as it is."

And it wasn't the only thing on him swollen, either. Her fidgeting was having another effect on him entirely, and given the way she went suddenly still, she knew. *"What do you have in your pocket?"* she demanded.

He let his grin speak for itself.

She ground her teeth together. "You. Are. Impossible."

"You're the one wriggling around." But careful to mind her knees and where she put them, he let her go.

Jerking to her feet, she yanked down on the sweatshirt, which fell to her thighs and covered too much of her.

His own fault, but it didn't matter what she wore because he knew what lay beneath—a thin white tank top sans bra that outlined her breasts and mouthwatering nipples in such a way that he'd nearly swallowed his own tongue. And then there'd been those tiny panties—

"Whatever you're thinking about," she said shakily, backing away to walk back around the table to her chair. "Stop. Stop it right now."

"Why?"

She reached for her glass of wine, her hand shaking. "Because I'm on my honeymoon, remember?"

"You didn't get married today, remember?"

"Yes. I do remember that part," she said softly, face averted.

Ah, hell. He was an ass, especially since he knew how she felt. He'd also once had a woman walk away from him.

Only at least he'd seen it coming. Annie had chafed long and hard beneath the impossible hours Cooper had put in on his job. She'd broken under the strain only six months before he had, but she'd been long gone by the time he'd been free.

It no longer mattered, though, because he still deeply resented how she'd never accepted that part of him. In fact, few had. "Look," he said more gently, "consider it this way. The guy's an idiot for letting you get away."

She snorted her agreement and poured herself more wine.

"And anyway, in the long run, he did you a favor."

"Yeah? How's that?"

"He left you free to take advantage of the next best thing to come along."

She regarded him for a long moment, her bitterness and sadness draining away, replaced by a reluctant smile. "You know, just when I think you're part of my worst nightmare, you go and say something almost human. And definitely profound."

He smiled and lifted his glass in a silent toast.

"Days and days," she murmured again after another long sip. "Can you imagine?"

"It could be worse."

"How?"

"You could be stuck here with your ex."

She rolled her eyes. "You're very helpful tonight."

"I try." He dug back into the cheese and crackers, and was well on his way to filling his rumbling belly when something hit him on the nose and landed on his plate.

A grape.

"What was that?" he asked.

She looked it over. "I believe it's a grape."

"I can see that, smart-ass. I'm wondering why it was bouncing off my nose."

"Gee, I haven't a clue." Looking as if she felt a great deal better, she rose. "Good night," she said loftily, and grabbing her plate and the bottle of wine, headed toward the door, where she'd undoubtedly go sit in front of the warm, toasty fire while he climbed the dark stairs and had to light his own and wait for it to heat the room, hoping it did so before his balls froze off. "'Night," he muttered, watching her curvy little bod practically quiver with her superiority. "Sleep tight. Oh, and . . ." He paused for effect. "Don't let the monsters bite."

Her step faltered but she recovered, and with that pert little nose thrust high, kept going.

Seven

Don't expect a man with a hard-on to be able to think;
he doesn't have enough blood to run both heads.
                              —Breanne Mooreland's journal entry

Breanne kept her nose in the air until she left the formal dining room and found herself in the dark with nothing to guide
her except for a faint glow from far down the hallway.

The fire from inside the great room.

Or so she hoped, anyway. She wished now she'd brought
that vibrator as a flashlight instead of leaving it on the couch.
Standing there all alone with the huge mansion surrounding
her, the corners and far reaches unknown, she felt her belly
quiver unpleasantly. "You're a big girl," she whispered to
herself, and holding her plate and bottle of wine, took a tentative step toward the orange glow. "A big girl who's calm in
the face of adversity." Another step. "A big girl who doesn't
believe in haunted houses or monsters—"

Something creaked, probably just the house, but she jerked
as if shot, then thought, *the hell with this*. She burst into a
run, her wet boots squeaking, wine jostling, grapes flying,
skidding to a halt just inside the great room. Panting, she
shut the doors, then leaned back against them.

In front of her, the fire crackled. The downy-soft leather
couches looked inviting. Perfect for snuggling up on a night
like this. She pushed away from the doors and headed toward them.

Halfway there, the doors opened behind her, and with a startled gasp she whipped around, dropping both the plate and the bottle of wine.

"Just me," Shelly said quickly. "Sorry."

Right, just Shelly. Because there were no boogeymen or monsters anywhere in this house.

Shelly crouched down to help pick up the dropped plate. "You okay?"

"Sure." Except now the wine had spilled. She really could have used the rest of that bottle. "Sorry about the mess."

"Don't worry about it. It's not my usual fare, anyway. Trust me, once the power comes back on and I feed you, you'll think you've died and gone to heaven."

"I'll look forward to that." She looked up when another woman appeared in the doorway.

"Breanne, this is Lariana," Shelly said. "She's the maid here."

Lariana was not petite like Shelly or average like Breanne, but a tall, curvaceous, exotic creature, the kind women envied and men killed for. She wore tight black trousers and a white Lycra satin blouse with the top and bottom buttons undone, emphasizing her tiny waist and huge boobs. These were thrust forward due to her five-inch stiletto heels that had Breanne both envious and wincing at the thought of being on them all day long.

"Welcome," Lariana said. She had a beautiful Latin complexion and dark hair piled up on top of her head, with long strands artfully drifting free. She was incredibly beautiful and yet somehow also incredibly intimidating at the same time. "I have a warm bedroom for you upstairs," she said to Breanne, her voice soft, cultured, and slightly accented. Though she couldn't have been more than a few years older than Breanne, she spoke with far more elegance and grace.

Feeling sloppy and out of place, Breanne tugged at Cooper's sweats. "Did the heat kick on? We have electricity?"

"No," Lariana said regretfully. "But I started a fire for you in an upstairs bedroom."

"Which means no freezing to death tonight," Shelly said. Her smile faded at a long look from Lariana. "What? That's good news, right?"

Lariana didn't roll her eyes, nothing so obvious, but Shelly still looked chastened. "Yeah, um . . . How about that snow, huh? Crazy stuff."

Lariana shook her head and moved through the room, scooping up Breanne's wet sweater and jeans, holding them up with two fingers as if they were dirty instead of just wet. "I'll get these washed."

"Oh, no, that's not necessary," Breanne said, feeling as if she should have cleaned up for the maid.

"It is part of your service." Lariana's expression was perfectly even, and perfectly lofty. "Where is your groom?"

"He's . . ." The hell with it. "He dumped me." She waited for some sign of superiority from Lariana.

But the maid dropped her icy expression immediately. "Men are such scum," she said with feeling. "Bottom feeders. Every last one of them."

"Not *every* last one," Shelly said quietly. "Some are good."

"Take off the rose-colored glasses, Pollyanna," Lariana said.

"So I'm hopeful—so what?" Shelly lifted her chin. "She'll find another man. A *better* one."

"No, thank you," Breanne interjected. "No more men."

"Ever?" Lariana asked, intrigued.

"Ever."

Lariana didn't look convinced. "They *are* scum, but once in a while, they are good for a *few* things . . ."

Breanne picked up the vibrator, waggled it. "Anything that this can't take care of?"

Shelly gasped, but Lariana burst out laughing. "I have extra batteries, when you need."

Shelly looked scandalized. And desperate to change the

subject. "I still can't believe Edward messed up and booked two of you for the same week." She tossed a big log onto the fire. "He never messes up."

Lariana snorted her opinion of that, and when Shelly looked at her, more unspoken communication passed between them. "I need to get back to the kitchen," Shelly said.

"You do that." Lariana moved to the fireplace. "You can't just add a piece of hard wood, Shelly—it'll die. You have to put in some kindling, too."

Shelly ignored her and joined Breanne by the couch. "Don't let her intimidate you while I'm gone," she whispered as they both watched Lariana handle the fire like a pro.

"She is pretty intimidating," Breanne admitted.

"It's all an act. You should have seen her the last time Edward yelled at her. She cried."

"Edward yells at you guys?"

Shelly laughed, but there was no humor in the sound. "Just remember, she's human. I mean, she's sleeping with Patrick, for God's sake."

"Patrick?"

"Our fix-it guy."

"Does he clink spookily when he walks?"

Shelly grinned. "Aye, mate, that he does," she said in perfect imitation of Patrick's accent.

Breanne looked back at the cool, classy-looking Lariana poking at the fire and tried to picture her with the tall, skinny, almost gangly, redheaded Patrick. "Are you *sure?*"

"Oh, yeah."

Lariana rose, and with Breanne's clothes over her arm, moved toward the door, picking up the carry-on as well. "Please follow me, Ms. Mooreland."

"Breanne," Breanne said, but Lariana was already gone.

Unless she wanted to say good-bye to her bag and everything in it, she didn't have much choice but to follow Lariana out into the pitch-black hallway. Ahead of her, the maid moved quickly and briskly, her heels tapping as she pulled a flashlight out of nowhere to light their way.

They came to a fork in the hallway.

"Down that way is the movie theater, with thousands of DVDs to pick from," Lariana said, sounding like a tour guide. "On the other side is the gym, complete with sauna and indoor pool, and if you want, Shelly is also an excellent masseuse."

"I don't think I'll be staying long enough to enjoy those things," Breanne said, not having missed Cooper's non-committance about leaving. If he didn't, she would.

"Are you going to let a bottom feeder ruin a perfectly good vacation?" Lariana asked coolly.

"It's not just that. I just . . . don't think I should have come."

"Did this almost-groom of yours cover the costs of being here?"

"Yes."

Lariana smiled coldly. "Then you should enjoy it."

They took the stairs, this time without the comfort of the light sconces casting a warm glow over the hardwood floor and interior walls. The flashlight lit the way but didn't do much for Breanne's mental health, as it created as many shadows as it chased away. At the top, Breanne was breathing erratically, and wasn't at all sure it was just the altitude bothering her.

Lariana opened the first door on the right. Her thin beam of light revealed an open-beamed ceiling and hardwood flooring with several throw rugs. There was a stone hearth, lit, crackling cozily. The four-poster, raw wood, tiered bed had a matching dresser and an oval mirror hung over it. Lariana moved to the dresser, on which was a tray with lit candles. She carried a few to the two wide-framed windowsills, the dark glass revealing nothing but black sky.

"There's a down comforter," Lariana said, pointing to the fluffy cover folded at the foot of the bed. "There's also an attached bathroom that's shared by the bedroom on the other side, but that bedroom is empty."

They both looked at the closed door. Breanne was half hoping the maid would open it and check for the boogeyman, but she wasn't about to ask and apparently Lariana wasn't much of a mind reader. "There aren't any baskets of accessories in there, are there?"

Lariana didn't blink. "Did you want a basket of accessories?"

"No!" Breanne said, thinking about the pink vibrator she'd left downstairs. "I'm good."

"Well, then. I'm going to make sure our other guest is comfortable. Good night."

Their other guest. One sexy, irritating Cooper Scott, who was right now all cozy in *her* honeymoon suite.

The moment Lariana cleared the doorway, Breanne locked the door. Then she stood there, looking around. Feeling alone. It occurred to her that if Edward hadn't screwed up, Cooper wouldn't even be here. She might be even more alone.

She was glad she wasn't, a fact she'd admit out loud only upon threat of death, and maybe not even then.

Braving the bathroom, she brushed her teeth and moisturized her face. A silly thing to do while in the haunted house of terrors, but the routine made her feel better.

Moving back into the bedroom, she glanced uneasily at the candles. There were five of them, three burning very low already. Would the other two last until daylight, and if not, what would she do?

One thing was certain, the next time she traveled, she was leaving the sexy nighties at home and packing a flashlight. And chocolate. And alcohol.

Lots of it.

Even though the room had indeed warmed up nicely, she climbed into the bed still fully decked out in Cooper's sweats.

The bedding was lush, thick, and combined with the fire, she was cooking in less than two minutes. Swearing softly, she got out of the bed and went to her carry-on, pawing through it as if by some miracle she might find something else to wear. No such luck. She pulled out the siren-red teddy she'd gotten at her shower. See-through lace, high cut on the thighs, nearly nonexistent over the breasts, it hadn't been made for sleeping, that was for sure. It'd been made for her groom to say, "Looks great, baby, now take it off."

And just like that, self-pity welled up hard and fast, swelling her heart, filling her throat so that she could hardly draw a breath. She'd managed to keep it all at bay for hours and hours, but now there was nothing distracting her but her own pathetic thoughts.

Somehow she'd screwed everything up. Again. Truthfully? She'd blown just about every opportunity she'd ever been offered. With only so-so grades in high school—she'd thought grades didn't matter, she had Barry, ha!—she'd ended up at a junior college, with no idea of what to do with herself. She'd made her way through a string of go-nowhere jobs, and also a string of go-nowhere men, including fiancé number two.

And then Dean had come along.

She'd found him smart and cool under pressure, two traits she greatly admired because she wished she had more of each. With a single smile he'd swept her off her feet, despite the warning voice deep inside that said he wasn't the one, that said he didn't love her the way she wanted to be loved, that said she'd only get hurt in the end.

Her inner voice had been right. He *hadn't* been the one, he *hadn't* loved her the way she'd wanted to be loved, and she *had* gotten hurt.

Or at least humiliated.

Tossing aside the red lace, she reached for her Palm Pilot and made a new entry.

To Do list:

1. Live down expensive wedding that didn't happen
2. Find new job so you don't have to ever face Dean again
3. Hurry on #2 because you're broke due to #1

She read the words, then nodded and tossed the thing back in her bag. Now that she had a plan, maybe she could sleep. Sure, she'd have to face the mess that was her life in the morning, but not before then.

Still too hot, she pulled out the second nightie, a creamy white silky camisole and short set, made of staggeringly expensive silk. The top had spaghetti straps and dipped low between the breasts, and the bottoms uncovered more than they covered, but they'd be soft against her skin, and wouldn't itch.

Double checking the lock on both the bedroom and bathroom doors was a small gesture that made her feel marginally better as she stripped out of the sweats, and then her still-damp tank and panties. She put on the silk pj's that had been meant for show only, which was ridiculous when she thought about it. Surely women ended up being ditched on their honeymoons with some regularity. You'd think they'd make these things more practical.

She slid back into bed. Given how badly her life had gone today, and the new and unknown path she'd be taking from this day forth, she'd figured she'd lie there forever, stressing and obsessing, but the minute her head hit the soft, giving pillow, she sighed again, and drifted off . . .

She was standing at the back of the church wearing her gorgeous wedding gown as she peeked in at the large, restless crowd waiting for her nuptials. They were beginning to murmur, wondering about the groom's absence. Some pitied her, some merely nodded to each other, agreeing that she probably deserved what she'd gotten.

Her father, tall and stern and serious, looked at his watch for the hundredth time. Her mother's white, pinched face, strained with tension, forced a smile her way.

Breanne forced one in return, because a Mooreland never allowed a situation to get the best of her.

Even when that situation was seriously kicking her ass.

He wasn't going to show.

Crying in the church wouldn't do, so instead she turned tail, ran out of the church, and grabbed a cab. Mercifully, this was a dream, so it shifted forward then, in fast-forward past the horrendous plane ride, directly to the honeymoon house.

Suddenly she was dressed in her red teddy, walking toward a lovely four-poster bed. Only this time, a man waited in it, and her heart surged joyfully. She wasn't alone after all—she had a groom! How lovely of the house to come with a groom.

He sat up with a sexy grin, reaching for her, his eyes hot and hungry, his hands warm and sure. Cooper.

Cooper?

Whoa. Laughing at herself, Breanne opened her eyes and came back to reality.

Which was a dark face leering over her.

She stared at it for one heart-stopping moment before it sank in. *No longer dreaming.* Someone was actually leaning over her. With a terrified gasp, she fell out of the bed and scrambled toward the door—

And ran face-first into it.

Hitting her butt on the floor, she shook off the daze and the pain, and leapt up again. *Don't look back.* Fumbling, terror stuck in her throat, she yanked on the handle, belatedly realizing it was still locked. Somehow she managed to release it, then hauled the door open, heading down the hallway, her only thought being to get away—far, far away. She could have screamed and brought the staff running; logically she knew this, but there was no logic in her half-awake brain at the moment.

Besides, she didn't want Dante, with his beefy, scary mystique, or Shelly with her perpetual cheer. She didn't want Patrick with his spooky walk, or Lariana's quiet disdain— she'd had enough to last her a lifetime, thank you very much.

All she wanted was comfort.

The direction she ran for startled her almost as much as the scary face hanging over her bed had, but she'd face that later.

She sprinted directly toward the double wooden doors at the end of the hallway and burst into the dark room of the honeymoon suite, where a possibly far bigger predator lay than the one she was running from.

Cooper Scott.

Without pausing, she took a flying leap onto the high mattress. As she landed, bouncing twice, Cooper sat straight up with a muttered, *"What the hell?"*

Nearly sobbing with a relief she didn't quite understand and didn't want to, she launched herself at him, hitting him square in his gorgeous chest.

"Oof," he said, and caught her.

Eight

*When climbing the ladder of life, don't let boys look up
your dress!*

—Breanne Mooreland's journal entry

Out of breath, Breanne burrowed in closer to a warm, strong
Cooper as his arms came around her. "I was asleep—" she
began.

"Me, too." He said this in a voice she hadn't heard from
him before, rough and husky and . . . sweet. "But this is better. Much better. What are you wearing?"

"No, you don't understand—" Her words choked off
when he slid his hands down and cupped her butt, squeezing, kneading. "I got too hot. I locked the door to strip—"

"Mmm," came from deep in his chest as he pressed his
face to her throat. "I like the stripping part."

"And then I thought I was dreaming. Maybe I *was* dreaming—"

"About me?" he asked hopefully, opening his mouth on
her neck, sucking on a patch of skin.

"Oh, my God." She fisted her hands in his hair and pulled
his head back. "You're not listening!"

"Sure I am. You stripped."

"*Is every single penis-carrying human the same?*"

"Yeah." He went back to work on her neck.

Her eyes crossed with lust. "I'm having a crisis here!"

"Sorry," he said with dubious regret. "Go on."

"It's just that I don't know how he got in—"

"Wait." He tightened his grip on her and pulled back to see her face. "This isn't about you coming here for a slumber party, is it?"

"No!"

"Damn." He sighed, but sounding extremely alert now, he gave her one of those long, studying looks that did something funny to her belly. "Finish."

Somewhere in the back of her mind she realized he was once again shirtless, but as he was still holding her, that was only a bonus. "I saw a face leaning over me—" Just saying it brought it back. "*Leering*—" She squeezed her eyes shut. "I didn't know what to do, so I—"

"Jumped me." He held onto her when she might have wriggled free, but truthfully, she didn't want to get away.

Even awkwardly sprawled over the top of him, she could feel the easy strength in his body, the delicious heat, and then there was the disconcerting fact that he smelled better than the most expensive chocolate, better than coffee on a freezing morning, better than *anything* she'd ever smelled, which was really damn unfair.

The room had seemed pitch-black when she'd first entered in her blind panic, but her eyes had slowly adjusted. He had candles in a tray on the dresser, too, though there was only one left burning, just a small flicker of light in the huge room.

He brushed her hair from her face. "Did you really see a face, or did you have a dream about a face?"

"I really saw a face." At least she thought so. "When I opened my eyes, someone was leaning over me."

His sharp gaze swiveled to the door, which she'd left wide open. "Wait here."

"What?" She scrambled to her knees when he set her aside and rose out of the bed, wearing . . . *nothing*.

Absolutely nothing.

"Oh, my God," she said, staring, mouth open.

Perfectly at home in his own skin, he walked to his bag on a chair and took out a pair of sweats.

The man had the best ass she'd ever seen. She was still staring when he pulled on the sweats, and oh, baby, how they fit. Low on the hips, snug to his fabulous physique . . . if she hadn't been so afraid, she might have pretended to be. "You can't go! What if it gets you?"

He glanced back at her, and even in the dark, with the grim mood hovering over them, she caught his vague and brief amusement. "Don't worry, Princess. I can handle myself."

"But . . ."

Without bothering to tie the sweats, he moved to the door, ready to defend her world.

"Cooper? I'm sorry I called you a jerk earlier. You're not."

A brief smile touched his lips. "Yeah, I am." He nodded toward her. "Stay."

Right. Stay. Normally just the word would awaken every ornery, defensive bone she had, but she wasn't going anywhere. Not when she'd slid beneath his blankets and yanked them up to her chin, absorbing the incredible body heat he'd left behind; not when she'd been struck dumb and mute by the incredible protective gesture he'd just given her, whether he'd meant to or not.

Not when God knew what was out there, waiting.

At that thought, she clutched his blankets closer, frozen to the spot. *What had she sent him into?* If something happened to him, she'd never forgive herself. She should go after him, she should . . . do as he said and stay because he seemed more than capable of taking care of himself, and, in fact, more than a little dangerous in his own right.

Just the way he'd left the room, without drama or a need to show off, proved that.

She'd grown up with testosterone all around her, but typically her relationships with her brothers had been about torture. That is, their torture of her. The few times she'd needed any sort of rescuing or protecting, she'd done it on her own.

The men she'd been with had been more of the same. In the time she and Dean had been together, she'd rescued *him* quite a few times—from his boss, from other women, from his family.

He'd not returned the favor even once.

Which brought her back to her past decisions, and how she'd always made the wrong ones.

But no more.

It didn't matter how attracted she was to Cooper. When he got back—*if* he got back—she'd thank him, and then go back to sleep.

Temptation averted.

If only she could avert her tendency to screw up just as easily.

In another part of the house entirely, a shadow flattened against the wall as Cooper moved down the hallway.

Sweat beading.

Heart drumming.

Too close, way too close. If he'd so much as turned his head—

But he hadn't. No one had. No one saw.

No one ever did.

In the suite, Breanne waited. And waited. Going more and more crazy as the minutes ticked by.

Any time now, she thought. Any time now, Cooper would saunter back in, casually edgy, astonishingly sexy, laughing at her because he'd seen nothing. Yeah, any minute now.

And when he did, she was going to grab him and never let go—screw going to sleep. She was going to thank him, even though she didn't expect him to understand. She was going to—.

"Hi, honey, I'm home." Cooper swaggered back into the room, a vision in his sweat bottoms and nothing else, bringing life back into the place with just his presence.

"What did you find?" she demanded.

"Nothing." He crossed the room until his knees bumped the mattress. The candlelight danced over his sinewy chest, over that flat, rippled belly she wanted to touch, over his powerful thighs . . . and the intriguing bulge between them that kept captivating her gaze and holding it against her will.

"Nothing but a dark house," he said softly, in a voice that suggested he knew where her thoughts had just gone and liked it.

She forced her gaze up. "You went into my room?"

"I went down to the great room. Didn't see a thing." He frowned. "Not even your stuff. You weren't sleeping down there dressed like that," he realized.

She looked down at herself. The gossamer-thin silk clung to her breasts, just barely covering her nipples. Snatching the covers back up to her chin, she avoided his smirk that said it was too late—he'd already gotten an eyeful. "Lariana made me move upstairs to a bedroom," she murmured.

"And then you changed."

"I told you, I . . . got hot."

A fleeting smile touched his mouth at that. "Babe, you're always hot."

She was always hot?

"Which bedroom?" he asked.

She was always hot? "Uh, back to that *hot* comment. I thought I was a pain in your ass."

"Yeah, well, you can be both. You can be a hot pain-in-my-ass, how's that? Which bedroom, Princess?"

"Coming up the stairs, it was the first door on the right."

"Okay, hang tight."

"Wait!" No way was she getting left behind again. She

leapt out of bed, but a look at the way his gaze heated and she nearly dove back beneath the covers. She crossed her arms over her breasts. "Do you have a shirt I can wear?"

"No."

"Yes, you do. You have a big bag—"

"Do I look stupid enough to cover you up twice in one night?"

With an exasperated sigh, she tugged the sheet free of the bed. "Men are dogs," she muttered, wrapping herself up.

"Wuff, wuff," he said. "Come on, let's go find your boogeyman."

That slowed her steps, reminding her why they were doing this. Someone had been in her bedroom, someone had wanted to scare her or worse, and all she had for protection was a sheet and this man. She sneaked a sideways glance at his tall, leanly muscled form. That odd sense of awareness he had shimmering around him, coupled with the intensity he could get between the flashes of ridiculous guy humor, made her admit that low as her opinion of men was at the moment, if she had to depend on one even temporarily, she hadn't done too shabbily.

However, she'd long ago learned that the more good-looking a man was, the fewer his actual life skills. "You're not a pencil pusher," she guessed.

He looked startled. "Pencil pusher?"

"Accountant."

He let out a low laugh. "No. I'm not an anything pusher."

"What do you do?"

"Nothing at the moment."

Not exactly comforting. "But you think you can keep us safe if it comes right down to it?"

He gave her a funny look. "I think I can manage."

Glancing uneasily toward the door, she nodded, having no choice but to trust him. " 'Kay, then." Her voice wavered only slightly. "Let's go."

"Hey." Stepping close until their thighs bumped, he reached

out and slowly, purposely, stroked a finger over her hairline, across her temple, ostensibly to tuck a wayward strand of hair behind her ear. She didn't buy that, though, not with the way he was looking at her, as if maybe he was starving and she was a twelve-course meal, as if maybe he could gobble her up in one sitting.

Odd how that made her knees wobble, as did the way his own breathing wasn't any more steady than hers. "What are you doing?" she whispered.

"Comforting you." His fingers stroked their way over her throat, then further down, taking the sheet with them, to her shoulder. "Is it working?"

She slapped his hand away. "I'm fine."

"Sure?" he asked in that voice that melted her brain cells at an alarming rate. "Because I have a lot more comfort in me."

Damn her wobbly knees anyway. She locked them into place, along with her jaw. *No more men!* "Positive," she said through her teeth, afraid to let her mouth stay open for too long because God-knew-what would pop out of it, probably something like "Take me now, please."

"You can wait here, you know," he said.

"I'm going with you."

He studied her for a long moment, and she got the impression he saw far more than she wanted him to. "Suit yourself, then," he said.

"Oh, I will. I always do."

Wasn't that just the problem.

Nine

People who think they know everything are annoying to those of us who do.
                    —Breanne Mooreland's journal entry

As they left the bedroom together, Cooper surprised Breanne by taking her hand, leading the way. The hallway was every bit as dark as she remembered, and though she was no longer cold, a shiver shook her.

Cooper pulled her to his side, sliding an arm around her. She might have protested, but there was something incredibly protective, even possessive, in the gesture, and she was feeling just weak enough to need both.

She couldn't see a thing, but Cooper didn't seem to have the same problem, leading them unerringly to the bedroom she'd just vacated. Once inside the doorway, the glow from the candles on the dresser lit the room.

Cooper put a hand on her shoulder and gently squeezed, which she took to mean "stay," and then he walked through the room, checking the bathroom—which was *un*locked—the closet, under the bed, and even under the mountain of down bedding.

When he turned back to her she expected to see amusement, or perhaps even annoyance, but instead he looked quite intense. "I don't see anything."

He hadn't said she was crazy, or that she had an imagination she needed to turn off. He simply believed her. "Thank you," she whispered around a suddenly tight throat, fighting a sudden urge to hug him. "I'm just losing it. I can sleep now."

"Are you sure?"

"Very. Thanks."

Looking not quite happy with that, he again lifted the covers, this time for her, in a silent invitation for her to get back beneath them.

He was tucking her into bed. The sweetness of that didn't escape her, but her feet just wouldn't take her to the bed.

"Breanne?"

"Yeah. I'm coming."

"See, that's the thing," he said, watching her very carefully. "Your feet aren't moving."

"I know. Maybe if I give them a minute."

He dropped the covers and moved toward her. Reaching up, he entwined his fingers in her hair at the nape of her neck and tugged lightly, tipping her face up to his. "You don't really want to sleep in here, do you?"

She started to nod yes, but ended up giving a slow shake of her head. *No.*

"Back to the couch?" he asked.

Another shake in the negative.

"You can have the suite—you know that, right?" he asked.

This time she nodded.

"Is that yes, you want to switch rooms with me?"

She bit her lower lip.

His gaze dropped to the movement. "I'm going to need words here, Princess."

"I don't suppose you'd mind hosting a sleepover?"

His eyes flamed.

"I meant the platonic kind of sleepover," she said quickly. "Ah."

The "ah" was loaded, and the air felt charged as he looked at her. "What if you can't control yourself?" he finally asked, his fingers still in her hair.

"I think I can."

An almost smile curved his lips. "Sure?" He had fine laugh lines fanning out from the corners of his mischievous blue eyes, and looking into them, she thought, *God help me, I'm not.* "Don't flatter yourself." She backed away from him and grabbed her bag.

Before she could sling it over her shoulder, he took it and slung it over his instead, then held out his hand. He waggled his fingers, waiting, and when she slipped her hand in his big, warm one, he smiled at her. It was a kind smile, not mocking her fear or her antics of the night, and she felt herself want to smile back.

No more men.

Oops. Almost forgot. Damn, how easy was she? One smile and she'd been just about to make another bad, *bad* decision. Good thing she'd caught herself. Good thing she was strong. *Hear me roar.*

They headed back the way they'd come, through the dark, cedar-fragrant hallway, the pictures and equipment on the wall unnerving now instead of quaint. Halfway, Cooper stopped at the third door on the left, his body tense and still.

"What—"

He broke off her question with a finger to her lips, his eyes dark and unreadable.

She heard it then, the soft scuffle from the other side of the door.

Goose bumps rose on her body as she turned to face the door, and so did the hair on her neck. Was it the person who went with the scary face? Just the thought had her letting out an involuntary whimper, but Cooper was right behind her, a hand on her shoulder now as from the other side of the door came an unexpected sound—an extremely female moan. It didn't sound sinister, it sounded—

"Oh, Patrick . . ." floated through the door in a sexy, familiar Latin accent.

Lariana.

"You like that, darlin'?" came an answering Scottish voice.

"Oh, my God, yes," Lariana gasped.

"Then how about this?"

"Yes! Yes, that, too. There. *There!*"

Breanne stared at the wood as a banging came next. "That's . . ."

"The headboard hitting the wall," Cooper said in her ear.

"Oh." She felt her face heat. "Right."

This was followed by some indescribable, embarrassingly earthy moans and more cries, and then the sound of wet flesh slapping on wet flesh.

Patrick and Lariana were getting lucky.

On *her* honeymoon.

If that wasn't just perfect, she didn't know what was, and she took a step backwards, right into the hard wall of Cooper's chest.

Just like that, the night changed. Or the darkness did, anyway, somehow becoming richer, deeper, encircling the two of them with an air of intimacy she hadn't counted on as the heavy panting on the other side of the door continued.

"Sounds like fun," Cooper whispered, stroking a finger over the back of her neck.

Now her goose bumps weren't from fear, but something else entirely. She began to heat up, and apparently so did things behind the door.

"Come," Patrick demanded of Lariana in a rough Scottish voice. "Come for me."

Breanne liked sex—sometimes she even loved sex—but she'd never had a guy tell her what to do in bed, or demand an orgasm from her. It sounded pretentious, rough, and . . . embarrassingly arousing. Her nipples hardened, her belly quivered, and her thighs tightened. Annoyed at herself for the reaction, not to mention desperate to hide it from the man behind her, she tightened her grip on the sheet wrapped around her. She was done with men, damn it, done, done,

done. She did not want one in her life, she did not want one in her bed, telling her what to do or otherwise.

"*Come for me right now.*"

Oh, jeez.

"Yes!" Lariana screamed the word into the night, the rhythmic banging turning even more frantic; along with it came Patrick's low, serrated groan, and then . . . complete and utter silence.

Breanne whipped around to face Cooper.

His eyes burned as they held hers, and in a rare anomaly, she found herself speechless. Pushing past him, she fumbled her way down the hall and into the honeymoon suite. Stopping short, she stared at the large, lush bed and swallowed hard. Her body felt hot from the inside out, sort of achy and pulsing, and she didn't get it.

What had happened to her fear?

"It got to you," Cooper said softly, almost silkily, from right behind her.

She stepped away from him because she couldn't think when he was that close. "That ridiculous exhibition? *Please*. I've heard better on any number of porn flicks."

"It got to you," he repeated, then smiled. "But let's hear more about these porn flicks."

"This isn't funny." She hugged the sheet tighter to her body.

Again he came up behind her, not touching her in any way, but she couldn't miss that delicious body heat if she tried. Dipping his head low, he leaned in and inhaled her. "You smell so good," he murmured.

She'd powdered and lotioned and primped good before the wedding, but if any of it had held to her skin through all the fear and panic and humiliation of her day, she'd be shocked. "I do not."

"You're not supposed to argue when someone gives you a compliment."

"I'm not good with compliments." She turned to face him. "Do you think she was okay? He sounded a little rough. And a lot demanding."

Cooper's eyes lit with humor. "I think she's going to be just fine, yes."

Still hugging herself, she nodded. "Right."

"You know . . . you're all tough and cynical on the outside . . ." He still hadn't touched her, though she could feel his wanting. Or maybe that was her own. All she knew was that the anticipation was going to kill her.

Leaning in, he exhaled softly over her neck, making her shiver. "But so soft and sweet on the inside."

"I'm just as tough on the inside," she assured him.

"I don't think so."

She really, really wished he didn't smell so orgasmically good, or that he didn't radiate such confidence, such intensity. Or that he didn't look like he did, which was too amazing for her fragile state of mind.

For something to do, she grabbed her bag from him and strode toward a chair. There she pulled out her Palm Pilot.

"What are you doing?"

"I have to write something down." She brought up her journal and entered: *Either learn self-defense or start carrying a baseball bat. Do not—repeat, do not—ever ask a man to protect you again.*

There. She felt better already. Sort of. She flipped through the files and reread her earlier words:

No more failures.

No more men.

She underscored both two times and then repeated them in her head like a mantra until they blurred.

"What are you doing?"

"Nothing, I'm—Hey!"

He'd snatched the Palm Pilot from her hand. "No more failures," he read. "No more men." He eyed her over the digital unit. "Interesting."

"I always make myself notes," she said defensively, reaching for the Palm Pilot, but he lifted it over his head, and by the full-on, knock-'em-out smile he flashed, he was enjoying her efforts to grab it from him.

"What else do you have in here, I wonder." Turning his back to her, he began to poke at her files.

"Stop that." She shoved at him, but he was immovable, the ape. "Those entries are *private*."

"Whoa," he said with interest. "This one's good. 'Don't expect a man with a hard-on to be able to think. He doesn't have enough blood to run both heads.' Hmmm." He shot her a wicked grin over his shoulder. "I do. Want to see?"

"You are *impossible!* Give me the damn thing!"

But he was still busy having fun reading her private thoughts. "'Never agree to marry a man because he has potential,'" he read. "'Men are not like houses, they do not make good fixer-uppers.'" His gaze met hers. "You know I'm finding this insight into your psyche absolutely fascinating."

She was still struggling to nab her journal, her fingers touching his warm, hard chest and those yummy abs. She refused to let them do anything for her. "This is serious for me, okay? Someone was leaning over me while I slept tonight." Just remembering had a shiver running up her spine, and she hugged herself again. "It gave me the creeps. I know it's silly, but writing things in my journal calms me."

He went still, then sighed, the grin vanishing from his face as he handed her back the Palm Pilot.

"I know," she said, embarrassed. "I'm being such a wuss—"

"No." He looked disgusted with himself. "Fuck, no. Anyone would have been spooked, given what you saw, and I'm an ass for trying to tease you right now. Come here."

In the act of putting away the Palm Pilot, Breanne lifted her head. His eyes were dark, opaque, and filled with things that made her swallow hard. He was half-naked, she in nearly the same condition. Moving any closer to him would be like lighting the fuse and begging to get burned.

He simply took the matter into his own hands and stepped into her personal space again, stroking a finger over her cheek before settling his hand on her arm. "Could it have been Patrick?"

"I don't think so." She shook her head. "I don't know. What do you suppose he was looking for?"

Their eyes held, and all the possibilities floated through her mind, none of which was exactly comforting. His other hand came up to cup her jaw. "You're safe now," he said. "With me. You know that, right?"

She thought of sleeping in here tonight and knew that *safe* was relative. "Sure."

"We could sit around and talk if you'd like."

"Okay." She crossed her arms and tried to look casual. "So what's up?"

"Considering what you're wearing beneath that sheet, and what we just heard in the hallway, you might want to rephrase that particular statement."

Right. Feeling a blush creep over her face, she looked away.

He sighed. "Okay, so no talking. It's been a long day, anyway. You need some sleep."

They both turned to the bed.

"At least it's huge," she heard herself say.

He didn't say a word.

And Breanne did her best impersonation of a woman hiding her panic, because sharing a bed with him would be like sky diving. Exciting, thrilling, and dangerous as hell. "I'll roll something up between us," she decided shakily.

To show him, she unwrapped herself from the sheet and began to fold it in a long strip. When she was done, she crawled up on the high mountain of a bed and situated it right down the middle, moving around on her knees to place it fairly.

A rough sound escaped Cooper.

Blowing a strand of hair out of her face, she leaned back

on her heels and craned her neck to look at him. At the expression on his face—an electrifying, sizzling expression—her stomach leapt as if she'd just taken off on the roller-coaster ride of her life. "Um . . . ready?"

He didn't answer right away, and when he did, his voice was husky. "Oh, yeah, I'm ready."

Ten

My life would be much more amusing if it was just happening to someone else.
—Breanne Mooreland's journal entry

Cooper looked at the incredibly hot woman kneeling on the massive bed wearing nothing more than a barely there silky camisole and shorts that were only called such because both legs went through them. He knew the outfit was one of her honeymoon sets that had been designed to drive her husband crazy.

The design worked.

She had one spaghetti strap slipping off her creamy shoulder, the other barely in place, the bodice of the silk dipping low enough between her full breasts to make his mouth water.

And she was cold.

Or excited.

He wouldn't have been able to tear his gaze off the hardened peaks of her nipples—perfect mouthfuls, both of them, poking against the silk as if begging for his touch—if it hadn't been for the shorts.

The shorts . . . those he could have stared at forever. Low on her hips, exposing the diamond twinkling in her belly in the front and the twin dimples at the base of her spine in the back, they clung to her like a second skin. The hem—God bless that hem—was so short it rode right up her ass, cover-ing only a tiny strip right up the middle. That strip in turn outlined her to perfection, not to mention revealed a good portion of each cheek in a way that made him want to get down on his knees and explore every inch of her.

Ah, hell, with or without those shorts he wanted to get down on his knees and explore every inch of her, and that was just unsettling enough to have him standing there, star-ing at her like a horny teen. "Breanne?"

She swallowed hard. "Yeah?"

"I know you're trying not to freak out here, and that you want me to be the good guy, but with you in that position, I'm not thinking good-guy thoughts."

She sank to her butt.

Not much better. "You really think that sheet is going to work?"

She stared at it, then bit her lip and looked back up at him, her entire heart in her eyes—along with the fear of the evening, the stress of the day, all the hell she'd undoubtedly been through to get here.

Feeling like a pervert, he swore softly, shoved his fingers through his hair, and moved to the opposite side of the bed. "Forget it. It's going to work fine."

Looking grateful, she relaxed her shoulders. She tugged up on her loose strap and down on her wayward shorts, which might have adjusted her comfort level but then showed off more of the soft curve of her belly.

Jesus. "Get under the covers, Breanne."

She scrambled beneath them with more eye-popping moves that had his blood pounding thick and heavy, draining out of his brain, heading south for the winter.

Then suddenly she sat back up, the blankets slipping to her waist. "Wait. I forgot to—"

"Whatever it is, too damn bad." He slid beneath the cov-ers on his side of the bed. "Lie down."

"Yes, but—"

"No. No buts. I hate buts." He lay back and closed his eyes but he couldn't relax to save his life, not with a nearly naked woman in his bed, the likes of which he hadn't had this close to him in . . . far too long. It'd been months since Annie had dumped him, and he hadn't been with anyone since. His family had all tried to set him up on dates. Hell, Jack had even given him his old black book, something his brother no longer needed now that he was married.

Truth was, Cooper hadn't had the energy to attempt another relationship, and while he could have had any number of pity fucks—his brother's old girlfriends were generous—he hadn't wanted that, either.

He must be getting old, but he wanted something real.

Too bad he was too screwed up for real.

Ah, hell. Sleep wasn't going to happen, not like this. Opening his eyes, he stared straight ahead in the dark and saw they'd left the door open. *"Shit."*

"I tried to tell you."

Yes, but she'd effectively distracted him with that soft, honey voice and even softer body. Unbelievable. He got up and shut the door, then stalked back to the bed. He lay flat on his back and stared at the dark ceiling, watching the last of the candlelight flickering shadows across the wood.

On the other side of the rolled sheet, Breanne was tossing and turning, and though he didn't turn his head and look at her, he imagined those silk shorts riding up, her top slipping down, and he nearly groaned. "Can't you just pick a position and stay there?"

"Sorry."

But she kept moving, and he kept picturing her, until he couldn't stand it. *"Breanne."*

"Do you really not wear underwear?"

A laugh choked out of him. *"What?"*

"I just—Never mind."

"No, this is a conversation I'm interested in."

"I saw your clothes earlier—there was no underwear. And you sleep naked."

"Yes. But I'm not naked now." Much to his annoyance.

She tossed around some more. "Sorry. It's just that every time I close my eyes, I relive my sucky day. I think about all the things that I could be doing right now."

"With your husband?" Odd how just the thought tightened his gut. He figured if she had said "I do," then she and her ex would right this minute be screwing every which way but Sunday. At least that's what Cooper would be doing if he'd married Breanne this morning. Hell, he wouldn't have waited until now, either; he'd have found a way to have her in the limo on the way to the airport, in the airport bathroom, in the airplane bathroom, on the ride into the mountains—

"Not with my husband," Breanne said softly in the night. "Because I'd have killed him by now." Her voice was steely. "The rat fink bastard."

"But if he'd shown up for the wedding, you wouldn't have had a reason to kill him," Cooper pointed out reasonably.

"Sooner or later he'd have shown me his true colors, and if he'd done it when I already had his name on my driver's license, I'd be even more pissed."

"Because hell, that's a damn inconvenience, right?"

"You're not kidding. You ever wait in line at the DMV?"

With another laugh, he turned on his side to face her. Holding up his head with his hand, he searched out her face in the darkness. "I'm sorry."

"Yeah." Her smile was sad. "Want to know a secret?"

"Sure."

"Today was my third time being ditched by a fiancé."

"Ouch."

She laughed unhappily. "Yeah."

"What happened?"

"The first time?" She sighed. "I'd loved Barry since . . . well, since kindergarten. It seemed so natural, you know? Graduate high school, get married. But my parents thought we were too young. They offered him a chance to go to Europe to study foreign diplomacy as he'd wanted, paying him with a one-way ticket and a large stash of cash. Oh, and the edict that he not look back."

"Don't tell me he didn't look back."

"Okay, I won't tell you."

He swore softly. "You were better off without him, too."

"I did learn my lesson," she admitted.

"Which was what, not to date spineless assholes?"

"No. I decided no more engaging the heart."

"But you could still get engaged?"

She laughed a bit mirthlessly. "The second engagement, that was a favor. Franco just wanted to stay in the country, but he ended up getting deported anyway. So that one doesn't really count. Right?"

He stroked a strand of hair from her cheek. A mistake. Her hair felt like silk between his fingers, her skin just chilled enough that he wanted to leave his hand on her. "Did your dad get him deported?"

"No, overprotective dad and four brothers never found out about that one."

"Four brothers." He let out a low whistle. "You must have been quite the princess," he teased.

"You did call that one right."

"So do you get engaged to everyone you meet? Is that how that works?"

"Hey, I've resisted *you* so far."

"To my great consternation."

She smiled but looked away. "Obviously I have a terrible decision-making mechanism. I'm working on it. But believe it or not, there's a silver lining here."

"Yeah? What's that?"

"I won't be fooled again, not by another pretty face and hunky body, not by sweet words, no way, no how." She shook her head, her eyes luminous in the dark "Love does not exist."

"You really believe that?"

"Yes. You?"

He shook his head.

"You've been in love?" she asked.

He lifted a shoulder. "I guess I thought it might become love."

"Did it?"

"Nope." He shot her a smile. "Got my heart crushed like a grape about six months ago."

Her gaze softened. "Oh, Cooper." She reached out and touched his chest over his heart. "I'm sorry."

"I'm over it."

Shifting up on her elbow so she could see his face, she left her hand on him and looked at him intently. "So you got hurt, and yet you'd give it another shot?"

The vulnerability in her voice made him ache. It'd been easier, far easier, to resist her when she wore her sarcastic edge like a coat, because this softer, kinder, caring Breanne tore through his defenses in a way he hadn't anticipated. "Hell, Breanne, I'm just saying it exists."

She flopped to her back, staring up at the ceiling. "Well, it can exist all it wants, as long as it stays far, far away from me."

Cooper lay back down as well, joining her in the study of the ceiling. He'd spent much of the recent past feeling exactly the same, but for some reason he didn't like to think that this vibrant, exciting woman, who had so much to offer, was going to hold back from love the next time it came around, simply because she'd been burned.

"Cooper?"

"Yeah?"

"Are you really unemployed?"

The sixty-thousand-dollar question. "I am."

"Where do you live?"

"In San Francisco."

"So what are you doing out here in the mountains? Alone?"

"My brother thought I needed to ski my brains out for a week and get over myself." *And get laid by a pretty, warm, sexy ski bunny.*

"Why?" she asked.

"Too many reasons to get into."

"We have all night."

"Maybe I'm tired."

"I thought guys liked to talk about themselves."

"Not this guy. Tell me about you. What do you do?"

"Bookkeeping for a big CPA firm." She frowned. "At least at the moment."

"At the moment?"

"I'm going to have to find another job."

"Why?"

"Because I'll have to see Dean there—that's rat fink bastard to you and me—and I still have an uncontrollable urge to kill him. That won't look good in my review, plus it'll be hard to get another job from prison."

He tried to see her in the dark. "You're not going to let him take that job from you, are you?"

"It doesn't matter," she said with a sigh. "You should see my resumé. It'd make you dizzy." She sighed. "Truth is, I don't sit still for long anyway."

"No? What jobs have you held?"

"Receivables, payables, payroll—you name it in accounting, I've done it."

"So you like numbers," he said, nodding. "Makes sense. You like order."

"How do you know that?"

"This whole setting makes you nervous because it's not what was planned."

"You can say that again," she said with feeling.

"And I've seen your journal. Very organized. Like an accountant's brain."

"I wasn't that organized when it came to staying with one job."

"Nothing wrong with that, as long as moving around makes you happy."

Now it was her turn to come up on her elbows and peer through the dark. "You really believe that?"

"Sure," he said, leaning in closer for a better look, because for a second he'd have sworn that her eyes went suspiciously bright with a sheen of tears. But then it was gone. "Breanne?"

"I'm tired," she whispered. She turned over, curling up into a tiny ball facing away from him. "'Night."

"'Night." He was confused as hell, but when it came to women, that was really nothing new. Nothing new at all.

He was just drifting off when he heard her soft whisper. "Cooper?"

"Still here." Maybe she'd changed her mind about the sheet. The thought made his body twitch. Yeah, she was going to toss that damn thing aside and roll toward him. She'd wrap that hot little bod tight to his, and he'd—

"Thank you," Breanne said very quietly.

He blinked. *Thank you?* He slid his hand down to cup himself. Still hard. Nope, he hadn't missed anything. "What are you thanking me for?"

"For chasing my boogeyman. For making me feel safe." Her smile broke his heart. "For letting me sleep with you."

Ah, hell. "No problem." But as he lay there, aching for reasons other than physical discomfort, reasons he couldn't seem to put words to, it was a very long time before he followed her into slumber.

* * *

Cooper was having the dream of his life, and he hoped he never woke up. In a bed of the softest down, surrounded by the gentle glow of dawn, she lay in his arms, the woman of his fantasies. She was scantily clad in silk that seemed to mold to her skin in an erotic, seductive way, and he couldn't keep his hands off her.

And because this was a dream, he didn't have to.

She was his. He couldn't quite remember how or why, but in dreamland, what the hell difference did it make? Around them, the air seemed thick. Spicy. Erotic. He dragged some of it into his taxed lungs and cupped her face, trying to see her through the haze all around him, but he couldn't quite—

A sound escaped her, a sort of breathy, wordless plea, and he smoothed his fingers along the line of her jaw, sinking into the lovely disarray of her hair, letting it drape over his forearms as he leaned over her, lowering his mouth toward hers.

"Mmm," she murmured as he swallowed her sigh of acquiescence. Her body seemed to melt against his like hot wax, and her mouth—God, her mouth was soft and warm and luscious, indescribably luscious.

She opened it to him, allowing his tongue to stroke hers, stroking his right back, both greedy and generous at the same time. His fantasy girlfriend was the best kisser he'd ever dreamed up. Not too wet, not too dry, but juuuust right. Her hand came up between them, opening flat on his chest. He took it in his, along with her other, and slowly dragged them both up over her head, palming them in one hand, using his free fingers to skim the hair from her face while he made himself at home between her thighs.

Eyes closed, hands captured by his, she arched up into his body with a soft, needy whimper.

In answer, he kissed her, and then again, sending shivers

of heat and desire skittering to the base of his spine, pooling in his groin, where he was so hard for her he could hardly stand it.

"Nice," she murmured, sighing with pure, unadulterated pleasure. Her full breasts pressed to his chest. Her hips cradled his. Her shorts were so minuscule his fingertips grazed bare skin as he reached down, the sweet curve of a cheek filling each hand. When he squeezed, kneading, she moaned and arched up, spreading her legs to better accommodate his, nestling his erection perfectly into the crotch of those skimpy shorts. Skimming his hand higher, beneath the silk now, he palmed her bare ass.

Not enough. Not nearly enough.

Deepening the kiss, he wrapped a finger around a tiny strap on her shoulder. Tugged.

A breast popped free.

A glorious, pale, perfectly rounded breast with a rosy, pouting nipple. Dipping his head, he very gently rubbed his jaw over the full curve, absorbing every hungry sigh. Then again, over the very tip this time, watching as it puckered up all the more as she writhed beneath him, her breath sowing in and out of her lungs.

Then her hands were fisting in his hair, and she was tugging his mouth back to hers. They kissed as if they'd been separated for years instead of seconds; he poured everything he had into that moist, hot, brain-cell-destroying connection, his heart and soul, because this was a dream, a glorious dream.

Even so, far in the back of his mind came the niggling truth: she wasn't really his. But the longer he kissed her, losing himself in the taste and feel of her, turning his head for a deeper fit, groaning with it, the easier it was to push all that out of his head.

She made it easy to do with those breathy little pants, her hands fisted on whatever part of him they could reach, stroking down his back to his butt, squeezing, pushing as she rocked to meet him with every thrust. They kissed as if it would be the end of the world to stop, as if they'd never get another chance to do this. With a low hum that reminded him of a happy kitten purring her pleasure, she slid her hands beneath his sweats. Squeezed. Cradled him all the tighter within her thighs. He could feel both her tension and his, could feel her tremble, could hear his own loud, labored breathing.

She whispered his name.

Unbelievably, his toes curled, his body tightening as he barreled down that narrow road toward climax. Given her own wild, delirious state, she was right with him. He kissed his way to her jaw, then her throat. "I'm going to taste every inch of you, Breanne."

Beneath him she went utterly still.

Abruptly he went from a blissful dreamland to brutal wakefulness. Lifting his head, he opened his eyes in the early morning light and stared down at her.

"*You*," Breanne said.

Yeah, him.

Just as in his fantasy state, he had her tucked beneath him, legs spread to accommodate his. He had one hand plumping up her bared breast for his mouth, the other gripping her butt, the very tips of his fingers dipping into heaven, his mouth wet from hers as he stared down at her.

For her part, she'd wrapped herself around him like a pretzel. "I . . . I thought it was a dream," she whispered.

"It was a hell of a great one," he said, half hoping she'd let him continue it.

She just stared up at him, hair tousled, eyes still sleepy, cheeks pink, looking like she'd just been fucked every which way but Sunday—and had thoroughly enjoyed it.

"I guess the sheet wasn't enough of a barrier after all," he said, wondering if he needed to apologize.

"Get off."

When he didn't, she shoved him off her in a sudden flurry of movement, scooting out of the bed, running into the bathroom, but not before shooting him a scathing look that might have shriveled another man's parts right off.

Not Cooper's. Nope, his part still bounced in his pants, the eternal optimist.

The bathroom door slammed shut with a finality that suggested he should go, and was going, to hell in a handbasket. Alone. "Uh . . . Breanne?"

Nothing from the bathroom.

With a heavy sigh, he got out of bed, looking ruefully down at his tented pants. "Down, boy," he murmured, and walked to the door. "Open up."

"Go far, far away!"

As if he could. "What are you mad at? That I was kissing you, or that you were kissing me back?"

She muttered something, some smear on his heritage, and then the shower came on. He hoped the water heater was powered by the propane tank he'd seen outside, or there wouldn't be any hot water.

"And for your information," she yelled through the door. "You were doing more than just sticking your tongue down my throat!"

"Same goes, Princess."

She replied with yet another unintelligible mutter, which for some sick reason made him grin.

It made no sense. Her late-night confessional warning that she was done with men still echoed in his ears. She wasn't interested in him, or at least she didn't want to be interested.

Fine by him.

But as he stood there in the early morning, getting chilled in nothing but a pair of sweatpants, a part of him wanted to prove to her that not all men were scum.

While another part of him entirely just wanted to sink into her body.

He heard the shower door open and then shut—yep, powered by the propane, because there was no way Princess was taking a cold shower—and he sighed yet again. No sinking, at least not today.

But there was always tonight.

Eleven

Breanne stared at herself in the mirror. Hot water rose from the shower, steaming the glass, but she could still see. Too much. Her hair was wild, her cheeks flushed, her lips plumped up from all the action they'd just seen . . . and there was a wet spot over the silk covering her breast—from Cooper's mouth.

She looked as if she was indeed on her honeymoon.

This was idiotic. This was dangerous. Just the *thought* of what she'd just done with that man scrambled her brain and made her squirm. He'd nearly sent her shuddering into an orgasm with just a long, languid kiss that had surprised her with its potent heat and shocking intimacy.

She looked away from herself—she had to. Lined up on the counter were an assortment of goodies laid out for the honeymooners. The condoms came in all shapes and colors, and she pictured lying in the bed, watching her man come toward her, erect penis dressed for the party in sunshine yellow, bouncing as it came closer—

Only it wasn't *that* image that made her slam her eyes shut, but the fact that the man in the vivid image had been one hot, hard Cooper Scott.

Bad. Bad, *bad* Breanne. She picked up a neck massager—uh-huh, right, she just bet that was used only as a neck massager—and then the scented body oils. The label said *edible*. *Chocolate*.

Her favorite.

No! No chocolate body oil in her near future, no way, no how. She needed to get a grip here, a serious grip. No parts of Cooper were going to be a chocolate-flavored dessert. It was not only fattening as hell, but incredibly wrong. Her life was in ruins, and she needed to remember that. She was on a mission to get the hell out of this place and back to civilization, where she could get to a Starbucks in three minutes or less, where she could hail a cab, *where her cell phone worked*.

She headed toward the shower, but on second thought stopped to drag the day couch from the far wall, pushing it against the bathroom door, protecting herself from any interruptions or boogeymen or voyeurs—never mind that she herself had been a voyeur only yesterday.

From the long, narrow windows on either side of the shower she could see only a sea of white. No depth perception, no landmarks visible, nothing but white, white, white.

Unbelievably, the snow was still falling. She turned the shower to scalding, stripped, and stepped in, and in spite of herself let out a little whimper of pleasure. My God, the showerheads were worth their weight in gold, aimed at all the good spots, hitting her already sensitized and aching flesh. For a moment she simply stood there absorbing the sensations. The soap smelled like—*Cooper*. Just the scent had her quivering, and by the time she rubbed it over her body she was aroused all over again.

Or still.

Ignoring it the best she could, she concentrated on her mission—getting out of Dodge. *Fast*.

She turned off the shower, and for lack of another choice, grabbed the lush, thick complimentary terry cloth bathrobe hanging on the back of the bathroom door. Only when it was on did she drag the couch away and open the door a crack. She had her chin up and was ready to battle wits.

Except she was alone.

Well, not completely. Lariana was making the bed. She wore black again, a snugger-than-snug, low-scooped black blouse, a pair of tight, cropped pants with a tiny white half apron tied in a perfect bow low on her spine, topped off with spike heels that sank into the thick carpeting of the bedroom as she tugged the sheets taut.

Breanne admired the strength and stamina it must take to work in those heels, and thought longingly of the suitcases she'd lost, filled to the brim with her favorite fashions. Hugging the white robe to her still-damp body, she thought of her choices—her jeans and sweater and ruined boots, or Cooper's sweats.

Ugh.

Lariana stopped nipping and tucking and faced Breanne with a holier-than-thou expression that was amusing, given that Breanne knew exactly how the maid had spent her evening.

Panting Patrick's name and giving in to his lusty demands.

"Sleep okay?" Lariana asked innocently, with only the slightest trace of sarcasm. They both knew Breanne hadn't started out in this bedroom.

"Gee, great," she said, just as innocently. "And you?"

Lariana's own superior smile didn't so much as falter. "*Fabulosa.*"

Yeah, she just bet. "So how often do you get stuck sleeping here?"

"Whenever there's a bad storm."

"Edward, too?"

Lariana began fluffing pillows. "Except him."

"Really? Where did he go?"

"I don't know—I'm not in charge of the man. He's in charge of me."

Breanne sat on the bed, so Lariana had no choice but to

stop making it and look at her. "Someone came into my room last night."

"Yes. Apparently Cooper."

Breanne glanced at the scene of the "crime," the huge, luxurious mattress around her. She still couldn't get over what she'd allowed to happen. How stupid she'd been to think that sheet would possibly keep Cooper on his side of the bed.

But to be fair, it hadn't been him alone violating the imposed border. When she'd come all the way awake, she'd been on *his* side. Humiliating, really, that in sleep she'd been so desperate. "Not Cooper."

Lariana's perfectly waxed brow shot up. "No?"

"No. I fell asleep in that room you gave me and woke up to someone standing over the bed. After a near coronary, I came running in here."

Lariana frowned. "You sure? Very sure?"

"Sure about what?" Shelly asked, appearing in the doorway with a smile. Her petite frame was in another pair of jeans and a long pink angora sweater that fell to her thighs. She had her hair neatly pulled back in a ponytail and a flush to her cheeks as she looked back and forth between Lariana and Breanne. "What's up?"

"Breanne says she saw someone in her room last night," Lariana told her. "Standing over her."

Shelly gasped. "Really?"

"A dream," Lariana said. "On a night like last night, we probably all dreamed badly."

Shelly, eyes wide, nodded. "Yes."

"I wasn't dreaming," Breanne said.

Lariana and Shelly exchanged a wordless look that probably meant *humor the crazy guest*.

"Forget it," Breanne said with an irritated sigh.

Shelly patted her arm. "I made breakfast by getting creative with the fireplace. Cooper's already sniffing around the dining room, waiting. Are you hungry?"

She was starving, probably from burning up half a million calories just from trying to inhale Cooper's body a few minutes ago.

But could she face him? Another thing entirely. "I don't have anything to wear."

"Oh, I have plenty," Shelly offered. "I'll get you something."

Everyone looked first at Shelly's tiny frame, then at Breanne's not-so-tiny one, no one pointing out to Shelly the difference between a size one and a size eight.

Okay, a ten, damn it.

"I'll get you something of mine," Lariana said with a hint of martyrdom. "I brought a small bag with me to work yesterday because of the storm."

When she'd left, Shelly looked at Breanne. "You ended up here, huh?"

They both looked at the huge bed.

"I didn't sleep with him," Breanne said.

Shelly lifted a brow.

"Okay, I slept with him. But not *slept with him*, slept with him."

"Does he kiss as good as he smiles?"

Better. "Look, I'm not interested in him, okay?" *Trying not to be.* "I gave up on men, remember?"

"Oh, don't say that! You can't. You inspired me, you know." Shelly smiled. "Today is the day."

"The day for what?"

"That I get Dante to notice me." She twirled in a circle and laughed as she fell to the bed. "Any helpful hints?"

"You shouldn't take advice from someone who was dumped at the altar." *Three times.*

"I'm sure it wasn't your fault," Shelly said loyally. "Now, come on. Give me a pointer or two."

Oh boy. She thought of Dante's world-weary, old-before-his-time eyes, and then looked into Shelly's sweet ones. "Are you sure? Because—"

"He's the one for me."

"Well . . ." Breanne wracked her brain for any advice she'd ever read about and had thought sounded good but hadn't actually tried. "Maybe you should tell him how you feel. You know, go the honest route."

"Oh, I can't do that! He doesn't think of me as a woman!" Then she flashed that sweet smile. "Yet."

Breanne took in Shelly's lovely blond hair, her brilliant green eyes, her contagious smile. And then there was that cute, nifty little body any guy would go nuts over. "He'd have to be dead not to think of you as a woman."

Shelly blushed. "You're the sweetest guest we've ever had."

Breanne had been accused of being many things, but *sweet* hadn't been one of them. "I'm just calling it like I see it."

"You really think he'll want me?"

Breanne crossed her fingers and hoped. "I *know* it."

"Because men are complicated creatures," Shelly warned.

"Not true. They just don't think with the same head that we do."

Shelly giggled.

Lariana entered again. "No kidding, men don't think with the same head we do. You can tell a man that in order to get the best sex of his life all he has to do is pay attention to a woman and say a few nice words, and you know what he'll hear? Blah, blah, blah, sex, blah, blah, blah."

Breanne laughed. "So true."

Shelly looked like she didn't want to believe this.

Lariana held up a little black skirt and a siren-red, long-sleeved spandex top with metallic sparkles woven into the fabric. Matching high-heeled boots—twice as high as hers were—dangled from her fingers. "This is what I was going to wear on my date tonight, but I don't think I'm going anywhere."

Oh boy. But Breanne took the hoochie-momma clothes

with a combination of acceptance and good humor because there was nothing left to do but just live through this *Twilight Zone* episode.

"You change," Shelly said to Breanne. "I'll be waiting to serve you downstairs." She shoved Lariana out ahead of her while Breanne just stared at the outfit. "What the hell," she muttered, and dropping the robe, pulled on Lariana's clothes.

To torment herself, she looked in the mirror. Oh boy. For starters, the skirt barely covered her ass. The top nearly blinded her and plunged due south nearly to her navel, only an inch above the hemline, which exposed a strip of belly. She tugged at it, but only succeeded in exposing a nipple. Pulling the shirt back into place showed belly again. Settling for somewhere in between, she slipped into the boots and gained four inches in height. Now, *that* she could live with. But while Lariana would look beautifully ethnic and sensual dressed like this, Breanne felt vampy and oversexed. Not a good place to be while trapped in a house with a man who revved her engines with just a single gaze. Much as she didn't want to admit it, she needed Cooper's sweats back, damn it.

Hell, she needed a damn suit of armor, but the sweats would do.

She stuck her head out the bedroom door and checked to see if the coast was clear. It was. She ran/hobbled down the hall, tugging on the skirt as she did, all the way back to the bedroom she'd deserted.

No sweats.

In fact, the bed had been made, and any sign of her brief stay erased. Odd how such a small thing could defeat her, but she was considering crawling back into the bed when a heavenly scent wafted up the stairs and into her nose.

Bacon.

Coffee.

Her stomach rumbled.

Fine. She'd go—what did she care? She took the stairs in the muted light of the early morning, gripping onto the handrail for all she was worth in Lariana's heels, hoping she didn't make an ass of herself and fall and break her ankle.

She couldn't afford such a thing, not when she planned to use her already-loaded Visa to get on a plane today headed for—

Where?

Aruba sounded good. "Or any island where there's no snow," she muttered. "And no mysterious hotties—"

Dante appeared at the base of the stairs in his usual way—without a sound, making her heart kick up into her throat. "Do you have to do that?" she asked, a hand to her chest.

"Do what?"

"Appear out of the woodwork! Walk without a peep! Show up out of midair!"

In the light of day, he still looked very much like a thug. He had a gray sweatshirt on over loose jeans riding so low on his hips she had no idea what held them up. Once again he wore a knit cap with the hood of his sweatshirt over the top of it, both nearly covering his eyes. His jaw was lean and square and smoothly shaven except for a goatee. His eyes were as dark as his hair, with no visible pupils. And he didn't smile. "Should I wear a bell?"

She paused, having no idea if he was kidding, until she caught the slight quirk of his mouth. "So you *do* have a sense of humor. Shelly mentioned it but I didn't believe her."

"Why?"

"Well, you're not exactly a barrel of laughs."

"No—I mean, why would Shelly mention me having a sense of humor?"

Because she wants to jump your bones. "Maybe because she thinks about you."

"Thinks of me?"

Were all men so innately dense? "You know, *thinks* of you."

At that he smiled, and Breanne blinked. Well, look at that
. . . quite a transformation from scary punk to hunk, with
those dark, dark eyes, tough body, and rugged face. She supposed if she'd been into the whole urban thing, she could see
what about him might draw a woman.

If she hadn't given up men.

She really needed to remember that. Maybe she ought to
have it tattooed to the inside of her eyelids. But Shelly *hadn't*
given up men, and Breanne had decided to be a better person. Here came good deed number one. "At the risk of sounding like we're in high school, do you think about Shelly as
well?"

He didn't answer.

"Okay, let's try this," she said, determined. "She's the
sweetest, kindest thing I've ever met and she has a crush on
you, and if you're at all interested, you'd better be good to
her."

He just stood there, maybe breathing, maybe not.

"Hello, anyone home?"

"I don't answer trick questions."

"Trick questions?"

"Like when a woman asks 'does that skirt make my butt
look big?' "

She clamped a hand on her butt and tried to crane her
neck to see it. "I knew it! It's Lariana's, and—"

"It was a rhetorical question," he said, his lips twitching
as if he were biting back another smile.

"Rhetorical question?" She stopped trying to see her own
behind and looked at him, exasperated. "You know, for a
man who seems to enjoy perpetuating a ghetto image, you
sure don't talk like a thug."

He merely shrugged and began walking away.

"Right," she muttered. "Mind my own business. Got it."
She pulled her cell phone out of her bag. Time to work on
her own life. "Uh, Dante?"

He glanced back. "What, are we late for history class?"

"Ha, ha. Do you know if there's anywhere I can get reception on this thing?"

"Out the double French doors from the library. There's a deck there, facing west. It's the only place in the house where cell phones sometimes work."

Sometimes? "Point me in the right direction." She wanted to get her messages, mostly because she wanted to know if Dean had been hit by a bus—the only explanation she'd accept with grace.

"Shelly made breakfast."

"Okay."

"She's hoping everyone comes."

"Ah," she said smugly. "So you're not immune to her, after all."

His eyes narrowed. "It's my job to tell you about breakfast."

"Uh-huh." That this big, edgy, dangerous-looking man *did* care about Shelly's feelings made her take a good, long second look at him. And a third. In fact, something deep inside her niggled, something that said, *See? Maybe not all men are bad.* She squelched it. "Where's the library?"

He sighed. "That hallway there, third door on the right."

Grateful for the daylight, dull as it was, she moved along the beautiful hardwood floor past the curved staircase, past the great room, counting doors until she came to a large room with floor-to-ceiling shelves filled with books. In awe, she stepped in. There were overstuffed chairs and ottomans, bigger, cushier sofas, and beneath the huge windows, beautiful benches filled with pillows. A book-lover's delight. She was most definitely a book lover. She moved close to a shelf—all the Dickens classics. Another held Shakespeare. Yet another had five full rows of contemporary and historical romances by some of her favorite authors.

She could spend all week in this room and never regret spending her honeymoon alone. She picked up a personal favorite, an old historical classic. When she'd been thirteen she'd sneaked it home from the library, reading every dog-eared page beneath her blankets with a flashlight. The story had blistered her sheets.

"Breanne."

With a startled squeak, the book went flying out of her fingers. She turned around and faced the one man whose voice could make her quiver, make her ache.

Cooper looked at her from the bluest, sexiest eyes she'd ever seen. "Dante said you were around, talking to yourself about mysterious hotties. You did mean me, right?"

She rolled her eyes, but his had locked on her body. "Wow," he said huskily. "More honeymoon attire?"

"No. I borrowed some clothes."

"Hmmm." Wearing worn cargo jeans and a long-sleeved Henley the exact color of his eyes, he picked up the book she'd sent flying and looked at the cover—a nearly naked man, pulling a dress off a nearly naked woman. "Oh, goody," he said. "A bedtime story. You can read it out loud to me tonight."

"We are not sharing a bed tonight."

"Feel free to skip straight to the good spots." He opened the book to somewhere in the middle. "Right here, for example." He cleared his throat and read out loud: "'Elizabeth tingled at the thought of putting her mouth to his throbbing manhood.'" He lifted his head, sending her a lopsided grin. "Hey, *I* have a throbbing manhood."

Breanne crossed her arms over her chest, refusing to admit she felt his smile from her roots to her toes, and in every single erogenous zone between, of which she apparently had more than she remembered, damn him. "Get out."

"Sorry, Princess, there's nowhere to go. Come eat breakfast with me."

"Why? So you can turn that into something dirty as well?"

His grin went positively wicked. "You think sex is dirty?"

"Go. Away."

Of course, he didn't budge.

"You know what?" she asked, tossing up her hands. "Never mind. *I'll* go."

"You can run, but you can't hide."

"What does that mean?"

"Means we're still stuck, baby. Snowed in. With no cable services and nothing to do except—"

"Don't say it."

"Okay. I'll just think it."

She sent him daggers, refusing to allow him to see how much his thoughts were affecting her. "I'm going outside to make a call on my cell." Whirling away from him, she stepped to the French doors. Beyond them was a view that, under any other circumstances, would have made her sigh with pleasure. Surrounded by awe-inspiring, majestic peaks, they were nestled in a valley that lay under a glistening blanket. The snow was still falling in dinnerplate-sized flakes, coating everything in sight.

It boggled her mind.

Determined to check her messages, she bravely opened the doors and was immediately assaulted by the cold. Protected by a small covered deck, she stood a foot from where the snow came down in thick, blurry lines, falling eerily without a sound, piling into drifts. If she took a step off the deck she'd have sunk, vanishing from view.

Behind her she let the door shut so she wouldn't have to hear Cooper moving around the library. God only knew what the Neanderthal would find in there to read. She didn't care. Shivering, she kept her eyes locked on her phone display as she turned it on and waited with bated breath.

Two bars! And then the familiar beep, beep, beep, signaling that she had messages. Quickly she accessed them and laughed weakly when she heard "You have thirty-seven messages." A bunch were from her parents and siblings, and all were in a similar vein along the lines of *"Where the hell are you?"* There were more from friends, wondering if she was okay. The answer was a big, resounding *no*.

And then came Dean's voice, unusually subdued, and sounding as if he was in a vacuum. "Hi, Breanne—I realize you probably hate me by now."

"Give me a reason not to," she muttered.

"—and I know this will sound like some kind of joke to you," he said, "but believe me, it's not. I'm . . . in prison."

Breanne pulled the phone from her ear and stared at it in shock before listening to the rest.

"I was arrested for identity theft and fraud, and they say I'm looking at five to ten. Oh, and you should probably toss your Palm Pilot in the nearest ocean because I once used it for some illegal downloading." Then the sound of him hanging up. That was it, nothing more.

No good-bye, no I'm so sorry, no words of everlasting love.

There were more messages but she lost her signal. Hands shaking with the chill, she turned off her cell and tried to go back inside.

The doors wouldn't budge. She'd locked herself out.

Her mind went numb as she stood there and looked at the handle. Her vision wavered. Dean was a criminal. That meant this engagement had been nothing more than a sham. Of course it'd been. Hell, her entire life had been a sham.

Damn, she was done being a screwup, done just moving through life, going through the motions.

Things were going to change!

She tried the door again, but apparently her epiphany didn't have any impact on the fact that she'd locked herself out. Already frozen, she tipped her head upward in frustration, but there was no divine help to be had.

There was nothing but more bad luck as her eyes focused on the eave of the house, and the shockingly huge web there. And sitting in it was the largest, fattest spider she'd ever seen. "Oh, God."

She really hated spiders. She'd hated them since she'd been five, when one of her brothers had put his pet tarantula in her bed. Frantic, she reached for the handle again, imagining she felt the spider drop to her head. Her breath clogged in her throat. "Oh, no. *No.*"

The doors were still locked.

She banged on the glass, and Cooper, at home in a large easy chair, reading the historical romance, lifted his head and smiled at her.

Waved.

"I'm locked out!" she yelled, banging on the door. "Let me in."

"Sorry." He shook his head regretfully. "Can't do that."

She would have sworn she felt the spider crawling in her hair and shuddered. *"Why not?"*

"You wanted to be alone, remember?"

Twelve

Men exist because a vibrator can't change a flat tire.
On second thought, I should just buy a AAA card . . .
                    —Breanne Mooreland's journal entry

Cooper waved again at a furious-looking Breanne standing out there in the snow. She was glowering at him through the glass in that outfit which made him extremely hot. Surprised to find himself aroused at just the sight of her, he set down the book and came to a slow stand.

She banged on the glass yet again, her extremely kissable lips wide open in an O of vexation. Earlier he'd had them soft and wet and open to his, and it had been shockingly good, but now they were turning a lovely shade of blue. He felt bad about that, but playing with her had proven to be more fun than he'd had in far too long, and he couldn't seem to resist.

"Open up!" she yelled. "Can't you hear me?"

"Oh, I hear you. In fact, I think the people in China hear you." He had no idea where she'd gotten that siren-red top that glittered, or the tight, tight black skirt that hugged her hips and showed off her legs, or those fuck-me boots, but he was betting it was Lariana.

God bless Lariana.

"Open the door," she said through her chattering teeth, craning her head upward, searching the roof uneasily. "*Please*."

He moved to the glass. "What's the sudden rush?"

"There's a spider the size of my fist hanging over my head, and it's going to get me. Just let me in before I start screaming and never stop." She looked up and let out a horrified squeak. "Ohmigod, it's gone!" Frenzied, she danced around in a circle, lifting her hands to her head, running her fingers through her hair. "It's on me, I just know it! Omigod, get it! *Get it!*"

Opening the door, he brushed her hands away and patted her down himself, enjoying the process immensely.

"Don't kill it," she cried. "Just get it off me."

"Hang on. I'm looking." He shifted his fingers through her hair, over her arms, her waist, brushing her breasts before streaking down her legs and back up again, briefly cupping between. "Spider-free," he promised.

"Are you sure?"

"Well . . ." Tongue in cheek, he searched her again, taking longer this time, noticing that when he stroked over her arms and neck, her breathing changed and her nipples went hard. So did he. But when he brought his hands up her legs and then between, she stopped dancing around and shoved at him, blowing a strand of hair from her face, looking furious and quite adorable with it. "You're just using this as an excuse to feel me up."

"And down," he said agreeably.

She growled, but he lifted his hands. "You really are spider-free."

"Thank you," she said through her teeth.

He cocked his head. "That didn't sound quite sincere."

Her jaw was so tight it looked as if it could shatter. "Look, it's freezing, all right? I don't suppose you could move your big, damn, hulking frame out of the way. I want inside."

"Maybe." He waited until she looked at him. "The truth is, I want something, too, Breanne."

She crossed her hands over her chest in an attempt to warm her body up, something he'd be happy to help her with. "Let me get this straight," she said. "In order to let me into the house, you *want* something."

"That's right."

A gust of wind blew in, topping her off with a layer of white powdery snow. Not him, though, because she'd been his wind barrier.

She shook the snow off. "Damn it, *what?*"

He didn't suppose she'd let him lick the snow off her body one flake at a time, which was a shame because he knew how good she would taste. Playing it safe—for now—he went for his second choice. "You have to smile."

She stared at him as if he'd grown a second head. *If she only knew.* "Are you insane?" she asked. "Just let me in."

"Smile first."

"I have nothing to smile about."

"This morning."

"Huh?"

"This morning," he repeated. "It was pretty damn fine. You could smile about that."

"Cooper—"

"Look, if smiling is too difficult, you can kiss me."

She practically had an aneurism on the spot. *"Kiss you?"*

"As a thank-you."

"For *what?*"

"For rescuing you."

"You *are* insane," she decided, tossing up her hands. "I'm trapped inside a house with an insane man."

"Actually, you're trapped outside," he pointed out helpfully.

"Forget it! I opt to freeze to death." Turning her back on him, she hunched her shoulders against the chill.

Ah, hell. He reached for her and put his hands on her arms, rubbing them up and down her chilled skin. "All right, Custer, you win. Come on, come inside." Stepping backward over the threshold, he pulled her with him, then reached around her to shut the door. Because she had goose bumps—his fault for playing with her the way he had—he put his hands back on her arms. He didn't know what it was, but he loved having his hands on her.

Lifting her head, she looked deep into his eyes, her own filled with a sadness that tugged at him. "You ever think that life just plain sucks?"

"Yeah." He cupped her cold face in his warm hands. "But right now isn't one of those times."

A shuddery sigh escaped her, but he took it as a good sign when she let him slowly pull her against him. Tucking her frozen nose up into the crook of his neck, she sighed again as he ran his hands up and down her back. And then, because he was a very weak man, he let his hand fall lower with each stroke.

She didn't object. In fact, she let out another breath, a hum of pleasure this time, and just like that, the embrace changed. Shifted. He was still holding her, touching her, but no longer for comfort. "Breanne," he said very softly.

"I know." Her lips moved against his throat. "God, this is crazy. I'm crazy."

"No." Another stroke of his hand down her back, slowly, curving his palm over the curve of her ass. *Ah, man.*

"Cooper?"

Don't say stop. Please don't. "Yeah?"

"I'm sorry you have to keep saving the stupid chick."

"You're not stupid." He let his fingers curl over the edge of her skirt, his knuckles brushing the back of her thigh now. Christ, she had soft skin. Her hair was damp against his cheek. The scent of the shampoo she'd used made him want to bury his face in it, or better yet, have the long strands teasing his bare chest as she rode him. Yeah, *that* would work—

"I went outside to get my messages."

He wondered if she knew that her entire heart was in her voice, defeated and sad, and with a breath of regret, he hugged her tight. "You heard from the missing groom?"

Still pressing her face to his throat, she nodded.

Something about the sudden tension in her body told him that whatever she'd learned had reinforced her no-more-men thing.

"He's in jail," she said. "For identity theft and fraud, and God knows what else."

"You were going to marry a helluva guy."

She let out a laugh that might have been half sob, and buried her face closer to him. "I didn't know he was a thief." She lifted her head, her eyes full of things, with anger and humiliation leading the way. "I would never have been with him if I'd known."

He stroked her cheek. "I know."

"How?" she asked, seeming surprised. "You don't even know me."

"I know you wouldn't kill a spider, even though it terrified you. I know you rushed to help Shelly feel better last night when she couldn't cook for us. I know that despite the whole kick-ass attitude, you're afraid of the dark."

"Those things don't have anything to do with dating a thief."

"You wouldn't," he said again.

She just stared at him as if seeing him for the first time. "I don't suppose you could call everyone I know and tell them that."

"Sure."

She laughed again, with a little more true humor this time. "You would, wouldn't you?"

"Yeah."

She shook her head, dropping her forehead to his chest. "It's my greatest fantasy to wake up and find myself in my own bed at home, this whole thing just a bad dream."

"Want to hear *my* fantasy?"

"No!"

He stroked her hair. "I'm sorry your week has sucked so badly."

"Thanks." Her fists had a death grip on his shirt. Slowly she loosened her fingers, and wound her arms around his neck. "That's the sweetest thing anyone's ever said to me."

"Don't take this the wrong way, Princess, but if that's the sweetest thing anyone's ever said to you, I don't think I like the people in your life."

"No, I don't think you would," she said solemnly. "And chances are, they wouldn't like you, either." Her fingers tunneled into his hair. "Cooper?"

She was looking at him with those whiskey eyes, and they'd filled with heat and desire. It took his breath. *She* took his breath. "Yeah?"

"Hang on for this one." She tugged his head down and captured his mouth with hers. It was his dream all over again, this morning all over again, and with a low groan, he hauled her up against him and dug in. She was right. On paper they didn't know each other from Adam and Eve, but in the flesh, their bodies knew enough. They stood there, straining together, dark sounds of neediness escaping each of them, and when she tangled her tongue with his, sucking him into her mouth, he nearly lost it. Her heart was slamming against her ribs, or maybe that was his, he didn't know and it didn't matter.

As long as it never stopped.

He clamped her head between his palms, inhaling her breathy murmur of pleasure as he changed the angle of the kiss to suit him. Only when air became required did he pull back a fraction, staring down at her. "I thought you were on a no-more-men kick."

"I am."

"Then what was that for?"

"Honestly? I have no idea. I just needed to." Her voice was satisfyingly thick, her eyes glazed over.

"Well, I need more." And he came at her again, settling his mouth more firmly over hers, moaning when her soft lips clung and her fingers gripped his face as if afraid he'd pull back.

Fat chance.

He had no idea how long he lost himself in the taste of her before he backed her to a set of shelves, slid his hands from her hair, down her body to her hips, which he squeezed, before gliding them both up, cupping her breasts. Her nipples were hard, pressing against the material of that eye-popping top, begging for attention, attention he was more than willing to give.

Breanne gasped when he dragged his thumbs over them, that same sexy little gasp she'd given him this morning when he'd bared one to the morning air and his own hungry gaze. Tearing his mouth from hers, he dragged kisses along her jaw to her ear. Touching the lobe with his tongue, he sucked it into his mouth in a desperate imitation of what he wanted to do to the rest of her.

Panting raggedly against his throat, she gripped him tighter, holding onto his chest in a way that would surely tear out each hair there, one by painful one, and he didn't care. He hadn't gotten enough this morning, and logically he knew he couldn't possibly get enough here, in the light of day, in the library, where anyone could walk in on them.

But she slid her hands beneath his shirt and stroked his bare back in a restless, desperate sort of gesture, and in the coup de grace . . . sighed his name, just a tiny whisper of a sound, but it was so endlessly, outrageously erotic he fisted his fingers in the stretchy, flashy red material at her shoulders and tugged. The top slid to her elbows, and her breasts popped free, exposing her for his viewing and tasting pleasure.

She wasn't wearing a bra.

"Lariana was still washing my clothes," she whispered, resting her head back against the shelving unit. "And I didn't fit into one of her bras—"

"Breanne." He stared down at her freed, bared breasts, at the way the nipples were tightening into two little buds right before his eyes, making his mouth water. "Are you somehow trying to apologize for not wearing a bra?"

"Yes, I—"

"Don't." This came out slightly more harsh than he intended, and panting for breath, he put his forehead to hers. "God, Breanne. You take my breath."

She shot him a tremulous smile, and with a ragged moan, he dipped his head and very gently rubbed his jaw along the heavy curve of her breast.

Her head thunked back against the shelf. A few books rained down over them. Not caring, he slid his hands down to the backs of her thighs and lifted her up, supporting her between the shelf and his body as he wrapped her legs around him. Her tight skirt got in the way, and impatient, he shoved that up, giving her the freedom of movement to hug his hips with her thighs.

He looked down, at her bared breasts, at the skirt gathered around her waist, which exposed the smallest pair of black lace panties he'd ever seen.

Wet lace.

Holding a warm, rounded cheek in each hand, he rocked against her, letting her opened thighs and the hot, damp spot between them cradle his aching sex. Then he bent and kissed her nipple, kissing, sucking, before nipping lightly with his teeth, gently tugging.

A sweet sound escaped her, rough and desperate, reaching out and grabbing him by the throat as he rocked against her again, moving in a tight circle, ripping more of those erotic murmurs from her as her breasts jiggled and made him so hard he was surprised the zipper on his jeans didn't split. She'd slid her fingers into his hair, doing her best to make him bald before he hit thirty-five as she brought his face back to hers to kiss him, her hips mindlessly thrusting to his.

More. He needed more. Dragging a hand down her body, he stroked a finger over that black lace, catching the edge, hooking it. Beneath he could feel her rose-petal-soft folds, hot and creamy.

For him.

He pressed against her and she writhed against him with an unintelligible whimper. With a matching groan, he rotated his knuckle in a slow circle, ripping another sexy sound from her before dragging the lace aside and drinking in his fill. She was so pretty there, all pink and glistening, her clit pouting for him the way her nipples had. He wanted to taste her, wanted to lick and suck until she screamed his name, wanted to watch her fall over the edge for him.

Lifting his head, he looked around them to see where he could get them out of plain view— "In the closet."

She let out a shaky laugh. "I don't think—"

He merely lifted her against him and began to walk.

"*Cooper*." Her voice was grainy, her lips still wet from his, her hands shaking as she pushed his chest so that he stopped, having no choice but to let her legs slowly slide down his until her feet touched the ground.

"Sorry," she said, and touched his tight jaw.

That didn't bode well for getting behind the shelves and he knew it.

"I only meant to kiss you—I'm sorry." Without looking at him, she pulled the red shirt up over her glorious breasts, and if he wasn't mistaken, shuddered when the material stroked her nipples.

"Breanne—"

"Thanks for rescuing me over and over," she said as she shoved down her skirt.

"Thanks for rescuing you?" He stared at her. "What the hell is that?"

"You helped me last night. You unlocked the door for me just now."

"Jesus, Breanne. I don't want to be thanked for those things."

"I know," she said softly, covering her face. "God, don't you get it? Look at me, I make a living making bad decisions. I don't want you to be the next one."

"Breanne—"

"Seriously. Not going to do this." And then she walked away.

The story of his life.

"You gave up men," Breanne muttered to herself as she ran out of the library, body aching, heart skipping around like a jumping bean. God. The man could put her on the edge of an orgasm with just a single look.

Except nothing about him was simple. Nothing.

"*You gave up men*," she repeated, running blindly. In this hallway, the walls were lined with picturesque scenes of the Sierras in each of the four seasons, revealing a setting so glorious and innocuous that if one hadn't known *exactly* how isolating and dangerous winter could be out here, she'd believe she was in a fairy tale.

Turning a corner, she stopped to catch her breath. Gulping in air like she hadn't breathed in a week, she realized she'd ended up in a part of the house she hadn't seen before. She stood in the center of a wide arc that broke off in several directions.

And she had no idea where she was.

What a mess she'd made out of this. Hell, what a mess she'd made out of her life, getting dumped again, getting snowed in with no clothes and big spiders and strange characters and a gorgeous, amazing kisser she could really wrap herself around and *had*—except that *she'd given up men*.

She was an idiot.

Closing her eyes, she shook her head. When her stomach

growled, she opened her eyes and drew a deep breath. One step at a time.

First up—breakfast.

If she could find it.

She went on the move again, turning down yet another strange hallway. This one had wood-paneled walls and a carpet runner on hardwood floors. At the end of it she found two doors on the left, two on the right, and a door straight ahead. From one of the left doors came the sound of someone . . . humming?

Shelly? Relieved, Breanne knocked, thinking this must be where the cook had slept. "Shelly? It's me."

The humming stopped.

Breanne knocked again but now there was no sound at all coming from inside, nothing, just a charged silence, as if Shelly was on the other side of that door, holding her breath.

Breanne stared at the door in surprise for a moment, then turned the handle.

Locked.

She looked at the door straight ahead. Narrow, and not as glossed or pretty as any of the other doors in the house.

Not locked.

When she opened it, she faced a set of wooden stairs that led down into a cellar, dimly lit only from a high, narrow window that led outside.

A wine cellar. She could see racks and racks of bottles, and smiled grimly. If she didn't get out of here today, she'd be needing a bottle.

Or two.

There was an odd smell here, musty and closed in, but also something more. She moved down the stairs, and then down a row of labels, and because she wasn't watching her feet, tripped, landing flat on her face, her legs and feet still draped over whatever she'd caught her foot on.

Which was a crumpled body.

Thirteen

*Men have it better than women; they're never required
to wear panty hose, and they don't have PMS. On the
other hand, they die earlier.*

          —Breanne Mooreland's journal entry

Breanne pushed up on her elbows and stared at the body.
"Oh, my God! Are you okay?"

It was a man. He lay flat on his back, arms and legs
sprawled, not moving. There was a gash on his forehead, the
blood dried.

Surging up to her knees, she put her hands on his shoulder. "Can you hear me?"

When he didn't budge, a very bad feeling snaked through
her. The thick, icky air seemed to close in around her as she
stared at him, heart pounding in her throat. Who was he?
Nicely dressed, he wore dark trousers and a dark, long-sleeved
shirt. He was missing a shoe, she thought inanely. "Can you
hear me?" she repeated.

Nothing. Less than nothing. "I was really hoping you'd
blink," she whispered. "Or moan. *Anything.*"

He didn't blink or moan.

Or anything.

Oh, God. She got down low and tried to peer into his face.
Please be okay, please be okay . . . Could she see a pulse in
the base of his neck? As she leaned in, her hand slipped from
his shoulder to his chest, which felt . . . stiff.

She pulled her hand back and stared at him in horror. "Oh, my God. You're not unconscious. You're . . ."

Dead.

Her entire body went as stiff as his. Her stomach sank, everything sank, weighing her down so she couldn't seem to move.

Dead.

The knowledge sort of seeped into her brain in slow motion, and when it finally landed and was processed, she did what any sensible city girl stuck in the mountains in a snowstorm without luggage, who'd found a naked guy and a dead guy within a few hours of each other, would do.

She scrunched up her eyes and screamed.

In what might have been an eternity or only a moment later, footsteps sounded above her. Cooper appeared. "Breanne?" He took the stairs two at a time, those always-aware eyes narrowing in on the body at her feet.

While Breanne's eyes narrowed in on the object in Cooper's hand.

A gun.

A gun.

It was hard to wrap her mind around much in the condition she was in, but facts were facts. She'd screamed and he'd come running, ready to slay a dragon for her.

"What the hell happened?" Cooper demanded.

"I don't know."

He hunkered down and put his fingers to the man's neck, then looked up at her, slowly shaking his head.

Breanne slapped a hand over her mouth to hold in another scream.

Rising, Cooper stuffed his gun in the waistband of his jeans low at his back and took her arms in his hands. "You okay?"

A few moments ago, he'd had her up against a wall, skirt shoved up to her belly button, hands in her panties, his fingers driving her straight to oblivion, and now . . . now he was this intense, cool, calm, and collected man.

With a gun.

"Breanne. *Are you okay?*"

She stared at him. He had his shirt loose and draped over the bulge of his gun. He looked rough-and-tumble. Badass.

Damn it, she had a serious weakness for badass.

"Breanne?"

"P-pretty sure I'm n-not okay." Her teeth were chattering again, though she wasn't cold. Or maybe she was and she couldn't tell because she'd gone numb.

With a low sound of empathy, he pulled her close, a protective gesture that felt amazingly seductive for its sweetness, so much so that she felt herself want to cling. *Just for a moment*, she told herself, and did just that: wrapped her arms around his neck and absorbed his strength, his heat.

How was she going to resist this? Him?

Didn't matter, she'd find a way. She'd promised herself a break from bad decisions, and anything she did here, while out of her element and scared and hurt, would be bad. Very bad.

Probably she should stay out of cellars, too.

Cooper pulled back, leaving his hands on her arms, and looked into her eyes. "Tell me why you're standing over a dead body."

"I got lost. I tripped over him."

"He was here when you got here? Like this?"

"Well, I didn't put him here!"

"Okay." He stroked his hands up and down her arms. "Damn. A dead body. I hate it when that happens."

She let out a hysterical laugh. "He's dead. Omigod, when did he get that way? Last night? When I saw a face over me? What if *I* was almost the dead body? What if—"

"Shh." He waited until she'd gulped in a breath and nodded.

She was okay. She was going to hold it together. She was. "You've got a gun."

"Yeah."

Was that his voice, all tight and grim, and so unlike the sexy, low, rough one he'd used only a few moments ago to murmur naughty nothings in her ear? "Cooper, why do you have a gun?"

"How about first we figure out why you have a corpse at your feet?"

She hugged herself and carefully didn't look down. "That's easy. Because I'm in the twilight zone. Or having a dream. Any minute now, I'm going to wake up."

"Sit," he said gently, and backed her to the bottom stair and pushed her down. "Hang tight."

Hang tight. Sure. She'd just do that while Cooper squatted next to the body about fifteen feet away, his eyes scanning the layout, taking it all in as he pulled out a cell phone. He looked at the display and swore at his lack of reception.

"Please tell me why you have a gun," she said as he shoved the cell back into his pocket. "And why you were holding it like a cop."

"I *am* a cop." He glanced up at her. "Or I was until last week when I quit."

More running footsteps sounded above them, then suddenly Shelly and Dante were crowding for space in the doorway above, peering down.

Shelly gasped, Dante swore, and they both came tearing down the steps.

From some dim corner of her mind Breanne realized that if Shelly had come with Dante from somewhere in the house, she couldn't have been in that next room humming, but then Shelly let out a shocked cry and lifted her apron to cover her mouth, her eyes wide and wild. "Oh, my God!"

Dante didn't say a word, just put a hand on Shelly's shoulder.

"Who is he?" Cooper asked them.

Shelly just stared at the body, her mouth still covered.

Dante lifted his gaze, hooded and inscrutable.

"Do you know him?" Cooper asked.

"Yeah." Dante's voice was like granite. "We know him."

"Who is he?" Cooper asked again, in an indisputable cop voice, one that demanded an answer.

"It's Edward," Dante said. "Our boss."

"Not missing," Shelly said into the apron. "But . . . dead."

Another gasp from the top of the stairs, and then Lariana practically flew down to them. *Dios mio. Dead?"*

Cooper shot Breanne an inexplicable look, then gave a curt nod. "Yes."

"How? Did he fall?"

"Don't know," Cooper said.

"Hey, what's that?" Dante asked, reaching in to touch Edward's chest, but Cooper stopped him.

"It's a crime scene. Don't touch anything."

Dante gave him a long, measuring look. "There's a hole in his shirt."

Breanne hadn't seen it and though she didn't want to, she crowded closer to look. There did seem to be a hole in the material of Edward's shirt, a very small one, near his right pec.

"A bullet hole." Lariana's lips went thin as a line.

"A murder!" Shelly lost all the color in her face.

Cooper shook his head. "We know nothing without forensics, okay? Let's not jump to conclusions—"

"Oh, my God, we're stuck in the house with a murderer!" Shelly's eyes were huge, glassy with shock. "We have to get out, we have to—" She dissolved into tears.

Lariana wrapped her arms around her. "Shh." She looked up at Cooper and spoke calmly enough, though her hands were shaking. "What do we do?"

"Call it in," Cooper said.

Dante shook his head. "Phones are still down, roads still closed. No one's coming in or getting out."

Shelly sobbed against Lariana. "I can't be stuck in the house with a dead body. I can't."

More footsteps above them, and then Patrick stuck his head in the door. When he saw the crowd, he stayed at the top of the stairs. "No need to be hiding yourselves in the cellar for a snowstorm—that's for tornados."

"Patrick." Lariana's voice shook slightly. "We found Edward."

"Dead," Shelly wailed.

At that, Patrick moved down the stairs, his lean body in coveralls, his tool belt low on his hips. He inspected the body himself, then whistled low in his throat. "Well, fuck me. He *is* dead. Mean old bastard."

"What are we going to do now?" Shelly asked tearfully. "We can't all just stay here—we have to get out."

"We can't just leave him here like this—"

"Yes, we can," Cooper said. When all the faces turned in his direction, he added, "Nothing gets moved."

Everyone started talking at once but he lifted a hand. "Look, I'm a cop. Or I used to be. Either way, I'm aware I'm out of jurisdiction, but no one is moving the body or any possible evidence until the proper authorities come."

"No one's coming," Dante said. "No one *can* come."

Patrick agreed with that. "We haven't seen this much snow in all the years I've been here, and it's still coming down. I'm telling you meself it's going to be a while. Days."

"Breanne was able to get a signal on her cell outside the library a little while ago," Cooper said. "Someone needs to go there and try again."

"I will," Patrick said, rocking back on his heels. "But don't be holding your breath."

Shelly sniffed quietly.

Lariana stood still, pale.

Breanne's heart was still thumping.

"Everyone needs to get out of the cellar," Cooper said,

rising, standing in front of Edward, standing for the dead. "And stay out."

"But—"

"No one comes in here," he said firmly. "No further contamination of the scene, period."

Dante turned to Patrick. "Let's get the ladies out of here."

"Will do." Patrick slipped an arm around Lariana, and Dante did the same for Shelly. With his free hand, he reached back for Breanne.

She allowed herself to be led up the stairs. At the top, she took a last look over her shoulder at Cooper.

Once again he was crouched by the body, expression grim, his big body gripped with a tension she hadn't seen in him before as he looked Edward over with careful precision.

He was a cop. *Had* been a cop. And though she had no idea why he wasn't one right now, she would bet it hadn't had anything to do with competence, because just watching him kneel on the floor and deal with a dead body—good God, a dead body!—with cool efficiency told her everything she needed to know.

He'd done this before. A lot.

It made her ache for him, not physically as she had in the library, but deeper. Odd how it felt as if she'd known him for more than just the one night. Odd how it felt as if maybe they'd known each other forever.

In that moment, he lifted his head. For a beat in time, his eyes warmed, and he gave her a small nod. *It'll be okay*.

She only wished she believed it.

Breanne sat in the great room, trying not to think about Edward. About her life being in the toilet. About Cooper. About anything.

Dante had stoked the fire, then left without a word. Equally silent, Lariana brought a tray with bagels, cream cheese, and fresh fruit, and after setting the food down in front of Breanne, moved to the door.

"Wait." She couldn't stand the thought of being alone. "Where's Shelly?"

"In the kitchen."

"Is she all right?"

"She will be."

"What does that mean?"

Lariana let out a breath but none of her tension. "Patrick couldn't get a signal on his cell phone. Shelly's upset at having to be here with . . . the situation."

No one wanted to say it. *Dead body.* There was a dead body in the house. Breanne's heart clutched as she remembered how Shelly had sobbed in the cellar. "I didn't get the feeling that she was close to Edward."

"Oh, no. We all hated him," Lariana said forcibly. "But because of the way she is—too sweet for her own good—she hated him less than the rest of us."

"I see." But she didn't. She didn't "see" anything about these crazy past two days. "What are those rooms on either side of the wine cellar?"

"Servants' quarters."

"Do any of you actually live here?"

"Honey, we're *all* living here. At least until Mother Nature decides to give us a break. Could you excuse me? I've got a long list of stuff I have to get to."

"Oh. Sure."

"Stay by the fire. No use getting cold if you don't have to," Lariana said, and left.

Breanne kept her eyes on the flames rather than look around her at all the shadows and corners. She really hated shadows and corners. She'd been afraid of them before Edward had been discovered. Now she was terrified. It was only midmorning, but with the snow still coming down, the light in the windows and skylights was muted at best. It felt like perpetual gloom.

In contrast, the fire radiated a nice, warm glow. She had nothing but those crackling flames for company as she contemplated the fact that she was entirely alone and a possible murderer walked around unencumbered.

A murderer. Her heart started pounding, and then a sound scraped behind her and the poor organ practically stopped.

Fourteen

Sometimes I just want to stop the merry-go-round that is my life and take a nap.
      —Breanne Mooreland's journal entry

Breanne leapt to her feet and whipped around, nearly falling to the floor in a relieved pile of Jell-O when she saw Cooper standing in the doorway.

At just the sight of him, tall and big and sure of himself, she began to shake. Delayed shock, she knew.

He strode across the room toward her in his loose-legged stride, looking deceptively lazy and completely at ease. He always did, as if all motion was effortless.

Somewhere deep inside, she hoped he would haul her close. Instead he lifted her chin with a finger and peered into her eyes. "You okay?"

Since her teeth were rattling in her head, she simply nodded.

"I need you to hang in there a little bit longer."

No problem. She didn't need him. She didn't need anyone.

Especially a penis-carrying human.

"The phones are still out," he said. "No cell service at all now, which means until I can reach the police, I'm it."

She stared into his set face, so determined to do the right thing, and felt something deep within her give. She was desperately afraid it was her pride, which meant that any moment now she was going to throw herself at him. "What do you have to do?"

"For starters, I'd like to know what happened. Tell me again what you know. You left me in the library and . . ."

"And I went running down the hallway. I made a couple of turns and got lost. I ended up in the wine cellar."

"You tripped over him?"

"Yes, I had my eyes locked on the bottles. I was going to take as many as I could carry to my room for a pity party."

"You didn't move him at all?"

"No. Did he fall down the stairs?"

He looked at her for a long moment. "The body's positioned just far enough away from the stairs that I don't see how that happened."

And then there was the hole in his chest.

"Have you seen any guns here?" Cooper asked.

She shivered. "Oh, my God."

He put his hands on her arms and pushed her to the leather chair. "Have you?" he asked more gently.

Her chest tightened and she moved her head in the negative.

"Have you seen or heard anything strange?"

A harsh laugh escaped her. "Are you kidding me? *Everything* has been strange."

He was still touching her, an oddly soothing gesture, considering she didn't want to need him. "You know what I mean," he said.

She sighed. "Well, yesterday I kept hearing odd noises."

"What kind of noises?"

"Odd bumps. Humming. Then there was that face over my bed last night. And then today . . ."

"Today . . . ?"

"Just before I went into the cellar, I thought I heard more noises, but I'm losing it, so what do I know?"

"What do you think of the staff?"

"Why, do you think one of them . . . ?" Unable to finish, she trailed off.

He looked at her for a long beat. "I don't know."

She saw the tension in the lines bracketing his grim, un-smiling mouth, in the dark shadows under his eyes.

"You're not making me feel better," she whispered.

"I'm not going to lie to you, Breanne." Their gazes locked. "Ever."

And she knew. He was telling her that despite what she'd learned from the men in her life, he was telling her the truth and always would.

She could believe in him.

But she just wanted to be far, far away, where there were no dead bodies, where there were no sexy-as-hell strangers now that she'd given up men.

"Can you think of anything else I need to know?" he asked.

"No."

"Are you sure?"

"No, I'm not sure! The only thing I'm sure of is I'm scared to death."

"Okay," he said, and pulled her against him. "Stay close to the fire," he murmured. "I'll be back when I can."

It took every ounce of courage she had not to cling to him when he pulled away. "Where are you going?"

"To talk to everyone else." With a quick stroke of his finger over her hairline at her temple, he was gone, leaving her to obsess over how she'd thought she'd hit bottom yesterday, but she'd been very, very wrong.

She was hitting rock bottom now.

So much for being on vacation, Cooper thought. He had a dead body and a houseful of possible suspects, including one hauntingly beautiful, high-spirited, and happy-to-hate-all-men Breanne Mooreland.

And nothing added up.

Because it didn't, he went back to the starting board—the cellar.

Edward lay exactly as he'd been left. He looked to be a man in his late fifties, and in prime shape for his age.

Except for the hole in his chest.

Several things were niggling at Cooper, the last of which was how Shelly had assumed at first sight that Edward was dead. In the dim lighting, Edward could have just been taking a damn nap, and yet she'd taken one look at him and had cried, "Not missing, but *dead!*"

A guess?

Or prior knowledge?

Another thing was that Edward lay on his back, sprawled out. Not a likely position for a person who'd fallen down the stairs and then crawled fifteen feet away to die.

Unless, of course, it hadn't been the fall that had killed him.

And what about the hole in his chest?

Cooper pulled out a flashlight he'd lifted from the foyer closet and a pair of tweezers he'd gotten from the guest bathroom, and crouched before the body. "Sorry, buddy," he murmured, and lifted Edward's shirt, pulling it away from his chest to look at the chest wound.

A small, perfectly round hole. But not, as he'd first thought, a bullet hole. Or at least he didn't think so. The hole was too small, too inconsequential. In fact, he'd have sworn that it had come from a BB gun, given that he'd had many such wounds himself, courtesy of his brother, when they'd been kids.

Which brought up another unsettling point. A BB might hurt like hell—but it wouldn't have killed him, either.

So what *had?*

* * *

When Cooper left the cellar, he wasn't too surprised to find the house quiet as a mouse, with no sight of any of the staff. They'd scattered like wild seeds in the wind.

Funny how good they were at disappearing. He just hoped they weren't as good at being criminals.

He came to the main hallway, and heard a faint murmuring, which he followed to the dining room.

The empty dining room. "Hello?" he called out.

No answer, but he could still hear the voices, faintly but definitely there, coming from . . . the far wall? Odd, as there was no door there, no closet, nothing but drywall. Putting his ear to it, the voices became recognizable.

Dante and Shelly.

"Shelly, baby, *please*. Stop crying."

"I c-can't." Her voice was more muted than Dante's, as if maybe she had her face pressed to him.

Cooper pulled back and looked around the empty room. Where were they? Leaving the dining room, he strode down the hallway and into the kitchen, which shared the talking wall with the dining room.

The kitchen was also empty.

And yet the soft voices were still audible, coming from . . . the walk-in pantry.

"I just can't believe it . . ." came Shelly's voice.

Cooper lifted his hand to knock on the closet door, wanting to alert them to his presence, but Dante spoke again, his voice low and grim.

"He was cruel to you, Shelly. Christ, you feared him and you hated him."

Cooper's hand lowered.

"But I didn't want him dead!" she cried. "My God, Dante. I don't want anyone dead."

"Shh."

"I won't shh!" Suddenly her voice was no longer muted, as if she'd pulled away. "This is bad, so bad—"

"Shelly," Dante said again, softly, so gentle that Cooper had a hard time actually believing it was the tough-looking butler speaking that way. "Come on, come here."

The sound of clothes rustling drifted through the door, followed by a shuddering sigh.

Jesus, Cooper thought, *this house saw a lot of action.*

"I dreamed of you holding me like this," Shelly whispered. "But in my dream it was because you wanted to, not because you were trying to quiet the wigged-out chef."

"Maybe I do want to be holding you like this."

"But you haven't."

"You've only worked here a few months."

"Long enough."

"Shelly." Dante's voice was rough, gravelly. "I open the front door for a living."

"So?"

"So you came from a small town. You grew up with money. Hell, you went to that fancy cooking college—"

"What does *that* matter?"

"Goddammit, I grew up in Watts."

"I don't care."

"I was in a gang. I've done things—You know it."

"You said you left that behind you years ago, when you were still a teenager."

"I'm still ghetto."

"No, you're not."

"Shelly." Dante let out a disparaging sigh. "You have people who care about you deeply. I have no one who gives a shit, no one—"

"You have us here. All of us. We all give a . . . *shit.*"

"You said shit," Dante said, sounding both shocked and amused.

"I'll say it again with a bull in front of it if you tell me that our different social backgrounds is what's holding you back from being with me."

Dante stopped laughing. "That's what I'm telling you."

"Then you are a very stupid man, Dante. And not because you open doors for a living."

"Shelly—"

"Maybe I'm not who you think I am," she whispered. "You ever think of that? Maybe I'm less."

"Or more."

"Well you won't know unless you look deeper."

"But—"

"No. Dante, listen to me. I like you. I like you a lot, and idealistic as it sounds, that should be all that matters!"

"It *is* idealistic."

"And here I thought you were so brave—"

Her words were suddenly cut off, and if Cooper wasn't mistaken, they were cut off by Dante's mouth—that is, if the slurping, kissing noises coming through the door meant anything.

Cooper resisted thunking his head against the wall, though he knew exactly how Dante felt, as if he'd just been handed a winning lotto ticket. He knew because he'd felt that way last night when Breanne had flung herself into his bed and his arms, and had stayed there all night. He knew because he'd felt it again this morning, and in the library, so he really hated to interrupt. But there was a dead guy downstairs who hadn't died of natural causes and couldn't ask his own questions, and Cooper felt honor bound to get those answers for him.

"Oh, my God," Shelly gasped, not sounding like she was crying anymore, but breathless for another reason entirely. "Oh, Dante."

Dante murmured something back to her in his South American native tongue, and Shelly sighed dreamily. "That sounds so sexy," she whispered. "Say it again."

Dante obliged her, then let out a rough groan. "No, don't—" He swore lavishly in Spanish. "*Stop*."

"Stop?" Shelly asked incredulously.

"Not in a closet." Dante sounded tortured. "Not with you."

"Why?"

"Because you're different."

"Different good?"

Dante's laugh was low. Baffled. "Yeah, different good. Jesus, Shelly."

"So we're going to be together?" she asked with so much hope in her voice that it almost hurt.

Did hurt. Cooper wondered if he'd ever been so hopeful. If so, his job, his world, had stomped it out of him long ago.

"We're going to be together," Dante said, sounding both fierce and shaky.

"Now, then."

"No." Dante let out another laughing groan. "Soon as we can get back to my place. In town."

"That might be days!"

"Shelly—"

"Come to me tonight. Please."

"Shelly—"

"*Please.*"

They were never going to come out of there, Cooper thought. He'd lifted his hand to knock again when Dante said, "Where's the guest?"

"Which one?"

"The cop."

Again, Cooper lowered his hand.

"I don't know," Shelly answered. "But he seemed . . . intense." Her voice hitched. "Didn't he?"

"Cops get that way over dead bodies."

A long silence followed, and Cooper's unease grew. What did they know that they weren't saying?

And would they tell him now if they thought he'd been eavesdropping?

Swearing to himself, he left them to their closet and went to find Lariana or Patrick. He just hoped they weren't in another closet somewhere knocking it out, because all this lusting in the house was getting to him.

As was one tough, soft, sweet-yet-hot Breanne Mooreland. She was *really* getting to him, but that in itself had just gotten complicated, very complicated.

Fifteen

*You can't date a man and not plan on being
disappointed. It comes with the territory.*
                    —Breanne Mooreland's journal entry

The house was quiet, almost eerily so as Cooper moved
through it, looking for Lariana and/or Patrick. In the main
hallway, he stopped.

A huge, round saw blade, about three feet in diameter,
hung on the wall outside the great room. On it was a beautiful, incredibly pleasing-to-the-eye landscape of the house and
the woods around it, so clearly, amazingly painted, right down
to the ripples on the lake, that Cooper would have sworn that
it was somehow lit from within.

Curious about who would hang something now, today of
all days, he headed down the hall toward the sound of running water, and found Lariana scrubbing the already spot-
less floor of the bathroom off the foyer. She had a brush in
one hand, a bottle of cleaner in the other, and was virtually
attacking the tile just below the sink with a vengeance that
spoke volumes about pent-up emotions.

As Cooper had already noticed about her, Lariana didn't
look much like a maid. Even while scrubbing as if her life
depended on it, she maintained some inexplicable sophistication and elegance. Oddly enough, she wore a different outfit than she had earlier, black jeans so tight they looked like
barely dried, spray-on paint and a silver, long-sleeved top

with slits in the sleeves, revealing her toned arms. Bent over as she was, with her jeans sliding south, he got a good look at a tattoo low on her spine.

TROUBLE, it read in cursive.

Trouble? He could believe it. "Spill something?" he asked.

With a startled scream, the brush went flying. Whirling around, she put a hand to her chest and stared at him, chest rising and falling with hummingbird-rapid breathing.

He nodded to what she'd been doing. "Scrubbing pretty hard there."

She narrowed her eyes. "Maybe *you* have nerves of steel, Superman, but the rest of us don't."

Leaning back against the doorway, he crossed his arms over his chest. "Meaning?"

"Meaning that after this morning's little surprise, I needed to keep my hands busy." Indeed, they shook as she retrieved the brush. "That's not a crime."

"Are you frightened, Lariana?"

"Only an idiot wouldn't be. If someone killed Edward—"

"If."

She nodded once. "If. Then it's one of us. Or one of you. Either way, we're all stuck here together. Not exactly comforting." She said this while continuing to scrub with a vengeance. "It's not like we often find dead bodies."

He noticed the more upset she was, the heavier her accent. "Why are you cleaning this particular bathroom?"

Her eyes narrowed and she sat back on her heels, swiping her arm over her forehead. "Just because you're a cop somewhere else, in another life, you don't get to ask questions as if I'm guilty of something." She went back to her frenetic cleaning, but when he just stood there, she once again sat back and glared at him. "*Dios mio*. Just do it. Ask. Ask me whatever you want."

"What do you think I want?"

"To know if I have an alibi."

"Okay," he said. "What were you doing between last night and this morning?"

"Sleeping."

Not exactly the truth, he knew. She hadn't been sleeping, she'd been doing Patrick. "When was the last time you saw Edward?"

"When he was screaming his lungs out at Shelly yesterday before either you or Breanne arrived."

"Why was he doing that?"

Lariana already looked as if she was sorry she'd said it. "I do not know."

"What was Shelly doing?"

She shrugged.

Cooper sighed. "Fine."

"Really? Because you don't seem like it's fine."

"Lariana, we have a dead man in the cellar. I just want to know everything there is to know."

"I suppose you cannot help yourself."

"I suppose not," he said with a ghost of a smile. It was true, he couldn't. Questioning, investigating, was just a part of him. Always had been. As a kid he'd sought to find the hidden mysteries in things. As an adult he'd gone into criminal science with a head for ferreting out the scum of the earth. He'd ended up in vice and had stayed there, even as it had slowly sucked the soul right out of him. The last case, a drug traffic ring, had taken him six months to crack, and at the end, in a fateful shootout he'd never forget, he'd had to decide which of two perps to shoot. The one he hadn't gone for had spun around and killed another cop.

That had been when he'd walked away before going under.

And yet, even now, he had no idea how to stay out of things. "Where's Patrick?"

Lariana's expression didn't noticeably change, though

she got up and turned her back to Cooper, rinsing her brush out in the sink. Watching her, he hoped to hell she wasn't washing away evidence.

"There's too many people in this house for Patrick," Lariana said. "He's off somewhere alone."

"But it's only you and the other staff, and two guests."

"Which for Patrick, the king of the unsociables, is five too many."

"Six."

She blinked. "Excuse me?"

"It's six. You, Dante, Shelly, Breanne, myself. And Edward."

Lariana said nothing, and he eyed the way her knuckles had gone white on the brush. "You said he yelled at Shelly," he pressed. "Did he yell at you, too?"

She went back to rinsing.

"I'm trying to help," he said quietly. "Tell me about him."

She shrugged. "He hired us. He was the direct contact to the owner."

"Go on."

"He dealt with the guests and the Web site, and handled all the public relations and advertising."

"And?"

She turned off the water and shook her hands dry. "And . . . what?"

"What aren't you telling me?"

She put her hands on her hips. "That he was a horrible, crotchety old man universally hated by all of us. There. Is that what you wanted to know?"

"No. I want to know who killed him."

Cooper found Breanne right where he'd left her, in front of the fire. Curled up on the couch, she was entering something into her Palm Pilot while nibbling on her lower lip, a lip he happened to know was most excellent to nibble on.

It was insane how just seeing her made something within him leap. Definitely a physical reaction, but unsettlingly, it was more than that, a phenomenon that hadn't happened to him in a long time.

His job hadn't made it easy to meet women, much less keep one. There'd been Annie, and she'd been soft and sweet and giving—and had hated his job with a passion that had made it personal. From her, from countless others before her, he'd learned to hold a big part of himself back. He didn't want to do that anymore.

But he couldn't deny that just standing there, looking at Breanne, made him want to try again.

Hearing him enter, she lifted her head, eyes wide until she focused on him, not relaxing but no longer showing fear.

"Hey," he said.

"Hey back." She hugged her Palm Pilot to her chest. "Did you just hear that? A moment ago?"

"Hear what?"

Her shoulders sagged. "Nothing. I'm hearing things again. I wish I could say I'm also just seeing things, but I'm pretty sure there is really a dead body downstairs."

"Yeah," he said regretfully.

Behind him, the fire crackled loudly, and Breanne jumped as if she'd been shot, dropping her digital unit.

Scooping it up for her, he glanced at the screen. **Last will and testament.**

"You planning on needing a will?" he asked.

Snatching it out of his hand, she shoved it in her bag, her movements jerky.

"You're not going to die, Breanne."

"Yeah? Tell that to Edward."

She was breathing shallowly again, her pupils dilated to large black marbles. He locked his eyes on hers. "I'm not going to let anything happen to you."

Looking away, she nodded.

He pulled her back to face him. "Trust me on this one."

A slow shake of her head was his answer. "I don't do trust."

"This isn't a matter of the heart, this is a matter of life and death."

"Why aren't you a cop anymore?"

Now it was his turn to look away. "That's a long story."

"Right," she said. "And I'm so busy here that I can't possibly spare the time to hear it. Come on, Cooper. Tell me."

He sighed and sank to the couch next to her. "I was in vice. Saw a lot."

Her eyes softened as she turned to face him, sitting on a bent leg, her long, wavy hair around her shoulders. "You burned out?"

"Pretty much. But I still remember how to protect someone." He twirled a long strand of her hair around his finger. "I would tell you if I couldn't."

"So you really always tell the truth?"

"Yes."

Her eyes searched his for a long time. Then she stood up and put her hands out at her sides. "All right, then, tell me this truth. Does this skirt make my butt look big?"

He laughed.

She didn't.

Ah, he thought. A test. He stood, too, pondering her seriously. Then he lifted a finger, twirled it, gesturing her to turn around.

After a pause, she did.

He took a good, long look at her mouthwatering ass, so tightly encased in that black skirt he had no idea how she'd even gotten it on. "Hmmm."

She twisted around and tried to see her own behind. *"Does it?"*

"Can't tell. I'll have to feel out the situation." Sliding a hand down her back, he cupped her bottom.

A sound escaped her, one that he was sure did not relate to distress. Her breathing quickened, and so did his, and from behind her, he rubbed his jaw along hers as he let his second hand join the fray.

"Cooper," she gasped.

He pressed against her through the skirt, feeling the heat of her as he set his forehead to her temple. "Christ, Breanne." Sliding his other hand to her belly, he held her in place while he dipped his fingers in as far as the skirt's material gave him.

A little whimper escaped her, and she arched her back, giving him better access.

"Nope. Not fat," he managed. "Not even close."

Her eyes were closed. Her tongue darted out and moistened her lips. "Okay."

He turned her to face him. "Okay—you trust me?"

Her breathing wasn't quite even, but she seemed to blink the sexual haze away faster than he could. "Maybe partially."

"Maybe?"

"Well . . . we *are* virtual strangers."

He slowly shook his head.

"We're not supposed to mean anything to each other. We're passing through each other's lives for one brief moment in time, that's all," she said, trying to convince herself.

"Which is why we practically implode on the spot whenever we touch," he answered, sounding ticked, and . . . *hurt?* "Christ, if we ever get to the big bang, it'll kill us."

"I gave up men," she whispered.

"You ever think that you chose the wrong men on purpose?"

She laughed over the vague unease his words brought forth. "Why would I do that? You think I *want* to be dumped all the time?"

"Probably easier than to be the one doing the dumping."

She stared up at him. "Let me get this straight. You think I choose men that dump me, on purpose? Because it's the easy way out?"

"Maybe."

"You know what? I don't care what you think." He wasn't right, he couldn't be right. "And I'm sticking to my plan."

"The no-more-men plan."

"That's right."

"Being careful is good, Breanne. But holding back entirely because you're scared?" He shook his head. "That'd be a damn waste."

"I told you, we're strangers."

"See, that's the thing." Again he stepped close, his broad shoulders blocking out everything but him, the azure color of his shirt emphasizing the clarity of his eyes, intent and frustrated as they were. "We're not strangers. Not anymore." His eyes captured and held hers, forcing her to face that truth, at least. "You have a passion for life. It's an attractive trait, and a sexy one. Don't waste it just because you're running scared."

"I make bad choices," she whispered, knowing it sounded like an old refrain. "You're not going to be the next one."

"But what if this is right?"

"How do I know that?"

"I think you'd just know," he said, and ran a finger over her jaw. "You'd feel it."

She gave a desperate shake of her head.

Disappointment flickered across his face, but he didn't press her. He wouldn't, she realized, and that was . . . oddly freeing and exhilarating all in itself. In her life she'd been pushed in one direction or another by a sibling, a parent, a boyfriend. Making her own decisions had been the best gift she'd ever given to herself.

Now she just had to stay on track and make the right ones. A powerful thing, really. "If I could just get out of here."

They both looked out the window, to the heavily falling snow.

"I guess wanting and getting are two different things," she said.

"I'd agree with you there." He was no longer looking outside, but at her profile.

She turned to him and felt her heart squeeze at the look on his face. "This is crazy," she whispered. "There's a dead guy downstairs. *Dead.*"

"Yeah," he said on a sigh that spoke volumes about his experiences. To her this was a new nightmare, but he'd seen it all before, and had even walked away from it. She couldn't begin to understand how it must feel for him to go on vacation to clear his head and still face death. "Well, at least one thing's clear," she said very softly. "I have an alibi for last night and this morning." Her gaze dropped involuntarily to his mouth, her body even now remembering how good it tasted. "I was kissing the hell out of the detective working the case."

Sixteen

There are only two kinds of men: dead . . . and deadly.
— Breanne Mooreland's journal entry

By afternoon, Breanne needed a distraction. She figured food would do it. Moving toward the kitchen, she stopped short in the hallway and stared at a new painting. Or at least she thought it was new because this she would have remembered.

It was an antique, two-person saw blade, at least six feet long, maybe more, painted with the most beautiful landscape of a raging river surrounded by a thick forest, with a storm brewing on the left. Gorgeous.

But where had it come from?

She was distracted from that by the sound of Shelly talking in the kitchen. The cook had made herself scarce all day, and Breanne had been worried about her. Relieved now, she knocked on the closed door.

"Just a sec!" Shelly called out. Then, a minute later, she opened the door, looking rosy and rushed, but neat as ever. "Hey!"

"Want some company?"

"Uh . . ." Shelly took a quick glance over her shoulder, then flashed Breanne a smile. "Sure. Come on in."

Breanne looked around. "Who were you talking to?"

"What?"

"I thought I heard you talking."

"Oh." Shelly laughed breathlessly as she moved behind the island countertop. "Myself. I talk to myself. A lot. Have a seat. Are you hungry? I have hot water—I boiled it in the fireplace. Start with some tea while I fix something for you."

Breanne sat at a bar stool on the other side of the island counter, feeling the cool wood beneath her thighs thanks to the short, short skirt. She began flipping through a basket of teas to choose from.

Shelly unloaded an armful of things from the refrigerator, then began chopping carrots at the speed of light, defying gravity and all laws of relativity as her knife flew through the stack. When the carrots were gone, she moved on to celery. And then fresh broccoli.

Neither of them spoke. Breanne wanted to ask about Edward, but Shelly seemed like brittle glass, so instead she sat there shoving the chopped veggies into her mouth with the same velocity that Shelly wielded her knife.

When Breanne caught up with her, eating everything in front of her, she took her tea bag out of her mug and sipped Earl Grey.

"You know," Shelly said, breaking their silence, "women are a lot like that tea bag."

"How's that?"

"You don't know how strong they are until you put them in hot water."

Breanne laughed and it felt good. "Ain't that the truth."

"If men had to be half as strong as we are, our race would have died out." A sad smile crossed Shelly's face. "My mom said that a lot."

Jumping at the chance to think of anything other than Edward, she managed a smile also. "I have four brothers, so that statement would have started World War III in my house. Are you close to your family?"

"Oh. Yes." Shelly's smile softened. "It's just me and my

sister now. More veggies?" She shoved the rest of the chopped broccoli toward Breanne. "I'd have made dip if the sour cream wasn't questionable. Damn the lack of power." She turned on a small lantern on the counter. It didn't light much. "Damn Patrick for the lack of a generator."

"A generator would be nice," Breanne agreed, glancing out at the fading daylight. Another night in the place. Another dark night, this time with a dead body in the cellar.

No one knew the exact time of Edward's death, which meant something even more disturbing. None of them had an alibi, not even her.

Did Cooper count her as a suspect?

Did she count *him* a suspect?

After all, what did they really know about each other, except that their bodies seemed to be predestined to yearn and burn when they were within sight of each other.

"He thinks it's one of us," Shelly said quietly. "The cop thinks one of us killed Edward."

It was still odd to think of Cooper as a cop. She'd not thought of him as one yesterday when he'd stripped her out of her wet clothes. Or last night when he'd held her close. Or this morning when he'd had his hands in her panties. She hadn't thought of him as a cop until he'd been standing in the cellar holding his gun, ready to take on the world for her.

Yeah, *then* he'd been a cop, through and through. And actually, given his world-weary eyes and ready awareness, she should have known.

Probably she would have at least guessed if she'd been thinking with her brain cells instead of with every fiber of her feminine being.

"He's walking around, you know," Shelly said. "Looking for answers." *Chop, chop, chop.*

Breanne marveled that the chef hadn't lost any fingers. "Maybe he's trying to clear everyone."

Shelly set down the knife and looked close to tears again. "I don't have an alibi or anything."

Join the club. "I saw you last night. I saw you this morning."

"But you didn't see me in between, or before you got here."

"No one saw me yesterday afternoon, either. It could be any one of us." An extremely disturbing thought.

Veggies done, Shelly moved to the refrigerator and searched the dark depths for something else to chop. "Dante told me he'd cover for me," she said into the crisper drawer. "Can you believe it? No questions asked."

"Maybe he cares about you and wants to prove it." *Illegally.*

Shelly shut the fridge and turned to Breanne, her cheeks two high spots of bright red. "He kissed me today," she whispered as if departing with a state secret. "I mean really, *really* kissed me."

"So I'm taking it that he noticed you were a woman," Breanne said dryly.

Shelly flashed a small smile.

"Was it good?"

She let out a shaky breath. "It was the best thing I've ever experienced, but he wouldn't make love with me because we were in the pantry at the time—"

"The pantry?" Breanne couldn't have imagined feeling like laughing, but she choked one out now.

Shelly looked uncomfortable. "So that's . . . weird?"

"Well—"

"Where's the oddest place you've kissed?"

Every time Breanne thought about that morning in the library, and what she'd let Cooper do to her there, her face burned hot as a fire poker. And other places burned, too. "For this conversation, I need something more fattening than vegetables."

Shelly went to a cupboard and pulled out a bag of BBQ chips. She opened the bag. "Tell me."

"Can't."

"That's too bad." Shelly dug into the chips with a heart-felt moan. "Yum."

Breanne could smell the salt, could practically taste it. "Damn it. In the library. Happy?"

"Wow. A public one?"

"No." Breanne snatched the bag of chips. "Here. In this house."

Shelly blinked. "You've been here before?"

"No."

"Then . . ." Understanding dawned. "Oh, my God. With the cop!"

"*Cooper*." Breanne shoved another handful of chips down her throat. "And honestly, I don't know what's wrong with me. I was just dumped. *Again*. I swore off men. Also *again*. Can't believe I let him—Well."

They munched in companionable, stressful silence for a moment before a loud thud shook them.

"What was *that?*" Breanne whispered.

Shelly sidled closer. "Hopefully, Patrick fixing the generator."

"Or Dante digging us out of here?"

"He'd have to dig us to China to get us out of here."

Another thud.

Breanne and Shelly stared at each other.

"I'd feel a lot better if I knew what that was," Breanne said.

"Yeah." Looking around her uneasily, Shelly kept eating. "Up until this morning, I thought this house the most sooth-ing, amazing place I'd ever seen. Now it's just . . . creepy."

"Agreed."

"It'll be different when the electricity is back." Shelly hugged herself. "Probably."

Another odd thump.

"That's it," Breanne said. She hopped off the stool and opened the kitchen door. *"Hello?"*

No one answered.

"It's getting dark," Shelly noted uneasily.

"Yeah."

"Wish we could make like a fat man's pants and split," Shelly whispered.

No kidding. "Where's Lariana?"

"She said she was taking a few hours off. I assumed she was having a late lunch," Shelly said.

"Wouldn't that be in the kitchen?"

They both looked around. No Lariana.

Thump.

"Come on," Breanne said.

"W-where are we going?"

"I'm tired of being scared. We're going to find out what that noise is."

"But it's nearly dark."

Was dark. Breanne tugged down the nearly obscenely short skirt, snatched the lantern, and then, on second thought, took a large butcher knife out of its block, handing it to Shelly before grabbing another one for herself. "Don't worry, we're going to be fine."

"Then why are we carrying butcher knives?"

"Just in case." She tugged Shelly out of the kitchen. The hallway was dark except for the lantern's glow, and she went still to listen. "What's down that way?" she asked, pointing with the knife past the dining room.

"A sauna, gym, Jacuzzi, and a small, indoor pool."

More thumps.

"Oh, God," Shelly said, swallowing hard.

"Come on." They tiptoed toward the area, their knives out in front of them.

The thumps got louder.

"Could you really use that knife if you had to?" Shelly whispered.

Breanne thought about the spider she wouldn't have been able to kill. "Yes," she lied. "You?"

Shelly's knife was shaking so badly it was in danger of

falling out of her hand, so she brought up her other hand to help support it. "Sure." She gulped. "No sweat."

They turned a corner and came to an open workout area, two of the walls lined in mirrors, the room filled with first-class gym equipment. There was a full-screen TV on one wall with an opened DVD case of *Friends: Season One* on the floor, and Shelly sighed in relief when the light from the lantern fell on it. "Oh, it's just Patrick."

"You sure?"

"He loves *Friends*. It's how he learned American slang. He must be around here trying to get that TV running on battery or something. *Patrick?*" she called out.

There was no response but the odd banging, which had become . . . steady. *Rhythmic.* "Oh, God," Breanne said and stopped, sagging in relief against a mirror. She couldn't believe it.

"What?" Shelly whispered.

Someone cried out, a woman.

"*Lariana*," Shelly said, and ran for the sauna.

"Shelly, wait!" Breanne took off after her, catching her just before the door. "I don't think you want to—"

As they stood there, the door to the sauna opened and Lariana appeared in the doorway holding a flashlight, wearing only a towel and a cat-in-cream smile. At the sight of Breanne and Shelly, one carefully waxed brow shot straight up. Cool as ever, she shut the sauna door behind her.

"Ohmigod, Lariana." Shelly put her hand to her heart and nearly nicked her own chin with the knife. "You're not dead."

"Do I look dead?"

Breanne took in Lariana's dewy skin, the I've-just-been-screwed satisfaction swimming in her eyes. "Nope, you sure don't." Carefully, she relieved the still-shocked Shelly of her knife. "Sorry," she told Lariana for the both of them. "Overactive imagination."

Shelly blinked. "What were you—"

"I told you I was taking a few hours for myself." Lariana

strutted past them. "Now if you'll excuse me, I'm going to get into the shower."

"Sure." Breanne didn't open the closed sauna door and peek, but she wanted to. She'd recognized those thunks. Lariana hadn't been in there by herself—she was sure of it.

"We heard you cry out," Shelly said, baffled. "We heard . . ." She trailed off when Lariana turned back.

"You're just spooked," Lariana said as she began to rein in her long, dark hair, piling it up on her head for her shower.

"You should be spooked, too," Shelly said. "And you shouldn't be alone."

For one beat, Lariana's eyes skittered back to the sauna. Then she smiled. "Don't worry about me. I can take care of myself." She vanished into the shower room.

Breanne watched her go, not missing the new love bite on the back of her neck.

"She thinks she's invincible," Shelly said. "But—"

"She wasn't alone." Breanne gestured to the sauna door.

"Oh?" Shelly's eyes swiveled to the same door as well. "*Oh.*"

Breanne transferred both knives to one hand and opened the sauna door.

Patrick jerked to a stand, hands holding his towel—the only thing he wore. "Uh, cheers, mates." Then he caught sight of the knives in her hand. "Christ Jesus, what's happened now?"

"We heard a strong noise," Breanne said. "We came to investigate."

"Oh, that'd be us—Me. I mean *me.*" Beet red, he smiled shakily and swiped his arm over his forehead. "No worries, then."

Breanne had never seen a man blush so hard that his face looked like a tomato. But the rest of his long, lean form . . . She'd imagined him like a stick, skinny and scrawny, but the opposite proved to be true. He was thin, but tough and ropey with strength. And quite attractive. In a very naked sort of way.

Shelly was trying not to stare and not having any success with it. "Um . . . yeah. We were just . . . Oh, Patrick." Closing her eyes, she covered her equally red cheeks. "You were . . ."

"Shh!" He glanced frantically around the workout room, relaxing only when he saw no one but them. "She'd kill me if she knew you saw me, no doubt about that." The shower came on, and he relaxed a bit more, hitching up his slipping towel. "Fuck me, but the woman's got eyes in the back of her head. I'm going to be screwed."

"You already were," Breanne said, and shocked Shelly into a horrified laugh.

"I'm sorry." Shelly once again clapped her hand over her mouth. "That wasn't funny."

Patrick moved past them and toward the showers where Lariana had vanished. That door was locked. "Bloody hell," he muttered, raising his hand to knock.

He lost his towel.

Shelly gasped but kept her eyes wide open.

Breanne tipped her head upward while Patrick swore and fumbled for the fallen towel, giving Shelly more of an eyeful, if her second and more audible gasp meant anything.

Still swearing, Patrick wrapped the thing back in place and knocked frantically. "Uh, darling? Open up."

Breanne was trying to look anywhere but at the flustered fix-it man, and while she did, her gaze caught on the doorway of the workout room and the man who'd appeared there, holding a flashlight.

Cooper.

He took in both her and the situation with one sweeping glance, and though he didn't so much as blink, she knew he grasped it all: the humiliated Patrick, the shocked Shelly, the unseen Lariana . . . and herself. He eyed the knives in her hand and arched a brow, but didn't say a word. He didn't have to—his expression said it all.

"We heard a noise," she said, feeling a little like Lucille Ball.

Patrick whipped around, and with a groan at the sight of Cooper, thunked his head on the door. Unfortunately, at the same moment Lariana opened it and he went stumbling in.

Lariana looked down at the man now sprawled at her feet, then up at the crowd watching. "You idiot," she said, and they all knew she meant Patrick.

"Aye," he agreed, still prone.

Lariana sighed, hunkered down, and patted his bare ass. "But you're my idiot, I suppose."

Patrick lifted his head and stared at her. "Am I?"

"Yes."

A slow smile replaced his worried frown. "You going to shut the door, darling, and give us some privacy?"

"Oh, yes," she purred, and did just that.

"That's so romantic," Shelly said with a sigh, and grinned at Breanne. "Isn't that just the most romantic thing ever?"

"You need to get out more," Breanne said.

"Yeah. So I've heard." Shelly turned to Cooper. "Is there anything I can get for you?"

"No, I'm good," he said. He looked at Breanne.

Breanne found she couldn't tear her gaze away, much as she tried.

"Well, then," Shelly said into the awkward silence. "I'm going back to the kitchen." She took the lantern Breanne offered and vanished, leaving Breanne and Cooper alone. Unless one counted Lariana and Patrick in the shower room, which Breanne didn't because she imagined they were very, very occupied.

In the dim room—lit only by his flashlight now—Cooper just stood there, calm as can be, confident in his own skin and sexy as hell, apparently not feeling the need to speak.

Breanne looked around her at the shadows of the exercise equipment, at the smooth, clean floor, anywhere but at him, wondering how long it would be before one of them cracked. Correction—before *she* cracked.

Finally she ran out of things to look at, so she looked at Cooper again. Honestly, she could have looked at him all day long, with those jeans, faded to white in all the stress spots and worn like an old friend. His shirt was snug to his broad shoulders, untucked, and, she suspected, draped over the gun at his hip.

Which reminded her.

Dead body.

Unknown murderer.

Then, as if fate thought this whole thing funny as hell, his flashlight flickered and went out, leaving them in complete darkness.

Seventeen

Cheer up—I'm sure the worst is yet to come.
                              —Breanne Mooreland's journal entry

Breanne's heart clenched and she let out an inadvertent whimper, but before she could really get behind a healthy panic, a hand settled on her shoulder.

She nearly swallowed her tongue, and with a terrified squeak, brought up the knives.

"Whoa, there," Cooper said softly, as if talking to a spooked horse. "Just me, remember?"

Right. Just him. The only man in her entire life that had—in less than twenty-four hours—made her feel precious, sexy, smart—

"What's up with the knives?"

"Oh, these?" She forced a laugh. "I thought I'd whip up some stir-fry—"

"It's going to be okay, Bree. You know that, right?"

See, now *that* should have rankled. The way he'd shortened her name was pompous, and yet . . . nice. No one had ever called her Bree before. No one had ever thought to.

But damn it, she was independent, fiercely so; she didn't need him. "How, exactly, will it be okay? I'm in a house with a dead body, and probably also the person who made him dead." She tightened her grip on the knives. "God, I hate this. I so really, really hate this."

She heard a click, and then there was a small beam of light. Cooper held up another flashlight.

She did enjoy a prepared man, but that usually applied to having a condom in his wallet, not being a flashlight carrier. "Were you an Eagle Scout or something?"

He laughed, a sound that scraped low in her belly. "Or something."

"A MacGyver type."

"A troublemaker," he admitted, leading the way to the door. "Come on, let's get to a warm room."

"Tell me about this troublemaking."

"You don't want to hear this now," he said, towing her along.

She had to run in the teetering heels to keep up with him, and tugged on the silly short skirt with the hand still holding the knives. "Yes, I do want to hear this now." She needed the distraction. This flashlight was smaller than the other, the beam of light small and narrow. Insubstantial, in her humble opinion.

"What are you doing back there?" he asked, pulling her up beside him.

Concentrating on not freaking out.

An arm slipped around her waist, and he snugged her to his side. "You hanging in?"

That was debatable. The pictures on the walls of the hallway seemed haunted, the eyes of the people in them following her. "I'd be better if you talked to me."

He glanced down at her. After a moment he said, "I was a rotten kid. I spent more time in the principal's office than class, and at home . . . don't even ask."

"Your parents had their hands full?"

"Just my dad, and yeah, he had his hands full. His answer for me and my brother's antics was his belt."

She looked up at his profile, but in the dark she couldn't see his expression. "Did it work?"

"Only momentarily. We were seriously rotten to the core. My brother and I still laugh that we ended up capturing the bad guys instead of being them."

It'd been one thing to resist him when he was merely a hot body and an unbelievable kisser. But now, with the picture of him as a kid with no mother to soften his father, she wanted to hug him. That, coupled with the knowledge that he'd grown up with a rebel heart . . .

No! She wasn't even going to go there. "We left Lariana and Patrick in the dark."

"I think that's where they want to be."

They were now back in the main hallway, between the foyer and the great room. "You ever been in any of those rooms just outside the cellar?" she asked.

"The servants' quarters?"

"Yeah, I heard someone down there right before I found Edward."

"Who?"

"I thought it was Shelly, but then she came running from upstairs, so it couldn't have been."

He studied her for a beat. "You didn't mention that before."

"I heard humming."

"You're hearing a lot of things," he said.

"I know." She rubbed her temples. "*God*. It gets dark at four o'clock here, and I *hate* the dark! I'm losing it completely, I can feel it."

"You're not losing anything. Let's go look."

She didn't exactly want to, but he had the light and the warmth, so she followed him, trying not to hyperventilate at the thought of what lay ahead.

When they stood in front of the closed cellar door, Breanne shuddered at the thought of Edward in there. Alone.
Dead.

The two doors on the right were open. In the first bedroom was a neatly made bed, a dresser, and a pair of strappy high heels on the floor—Lariana's. The second room had the same dresser, an unmade bed, and no personal effects.

Across the hall, the first bedroom looked untouched. The second . . . locked. This was the one from which Breanne had heard humming. There was no sound behind that door now, and no one answered their knock.

Cooper looked intrigued. "Wonder why that one is locked and not the others?"

Breanne thought about every cop show she'd ever seen and imagined him kicking down the door and drawing his gun to search the place. "Should we break in?" she whispered when he didn't move.

"No."

"Then let's get out of here." She glanced at the cellar door, glad when Cooper led her back down the hall.

Back in the foyer, there was a glow from the fireplace across the way, and Breanne breathed a sigh of relief. "I know you're probably used to this tense, overwhelming stress," she said, "but I'm not."

"I never get used to the stress."

When their gazes met, she could see that was true. He'd seen a lot, done a lot, and it got to him. He wasn't invincible, wasn't immune to the fear; reaching out, she took his hand.

He squeezed hers. "I know how we're going to get out of here tomorrow. Want to see?"

"Are you kidding? *Yes.*"

He turned and shined his flashlight around the foyer. The daylight had gone completely now, and from the long windows on either side of the front door came only an inky blackness, a fact that had Breanne's stomach tumbling hard.

Another long night . . .

Then she saw it, the door behind the reception desk that she'd never noticed before. Cooper opened it, and flashed the light inside.

It was a huge garage. They stepped in and Cooper shut

the door behind them. Breanne couldn't see much beyond a cavernous, dark, drywalled room, three garage doors, and several vehicles. She could smell oil, faint gasoline, and tires. Then Cooper held up the flashlight, highlighting the clean concrete floor, on which sat a Toyota truck, an SUV, and . . .

A trailer, with two snowmobiles on it.

Cooper walked toward them, stroking his hand along the hull of one. "They don't have any gas—I already checked. My guess is that it's early enough in the season that no one's used them yet. The engines look good, though."

She smiled. "What does a vice cop from San Francisco know about snowmobiles?"

He flicked open the hood of the first snowmobile and peered inside. "I know a little about mechanics."

The man fascinated her, no getting around that. He seemed such a contradiction, and she wanted to know more. "From what?"

"It goes back to that wild kid thing. I used to take everything apart." He fiddled with something in the open compartment. "It sort of stuck with me."

"What do you take apart now?"

"Cars sometimes. I rebuild them for fun. Or I used to. Haven't had time in a while."

"Because of your cop work?"

He shrugged, but she knew that was probably true. He'd worked so long and hard, he'd burned out. He'd probably desperately needed this week, and she'd wanted him to leave. She hated the selfishness of that. "I'm sorry."

Lifting his head, he looked at her. "For what?"

"For your time here being ruined. For me, for—"

He smiled at her. "I'm not complaining."

"Are you going to go back to being a cop?"

That got her another shrug.

"You know, you really talk waaay too much," she teased lightly.

His eyes lit with humor but he didn't respond to the bait

as she would have. Instead he went back to looking in the engine compartment.

"How come you don't talk about yourself?"

"I'm just not into dwelling."

A throwaway comment, but she could read between the lines, and could well imagine how it'd been for him and his brother without a mom. With a tough-ass dad. With no softness.

And yet he'd taken any helplessness and channeled it into something worthwhile. He'd become a cop, of all things, a vice cop, where he'd seen things that she couldn't even imagine.

Maybe he was on to something. Maybe not dwelling was the secret to surviving not only this madness, but life in general. For instance, if she didn't dwell on her family and friends' reactions to what had happened to her yesterday, then she couldn't be mortified. If she didn't dwell on being left at the altar three times, she wouldn't have to have that *no-more-men* rule.

Dangerous thoughts here in the middle of nowhere, with no electricity and nothing to do but look at him.

And holy smokes, was he something to look at! He'd shoved up his sleeves now and was doing something there beneath the hood, and looking sexy as hell while he was at it.

She wondered at this insatiable attraction she had for him. Was it the sexy clothes she wore making her feel so . . . horny?

No.

Was it merely because she'd told herself she could have him?

No.

Was it because he was strong and smart and didn't seem to care what anyone thought of him? That he had no problem showing whatever he felt, whether it be frustration at their situation, hunger for her body, or a shimmering anger at the sight of a dead man?

Or how about the way he'd protected her without question, putting her safety ahead of his at all times?

Oh, yeah.

And damn if that utter selflessness of his wasn't the biggest aphrodisiac she'd ever experienced. It made her want to do things to him, things that involved a lot less clothing than they had on. She wanted to see him, lost in the throes of passion, vulnerable and open, and when she had him like that, she wanted to take care of him in a way she suspected he didn't often let anyone do. "Aren't the snowmobiles useless to us without gasoline?"

"Yep." Turning, he walked to a large wall shelving unit, randomly opening one, then going very still. "Shit," he said softly.

"What—" She broke off when she saw what he saw.

A shoe.

The matching shoe to the one Edward wore, just set innocuously on a shelf all by itself. "Oh, no."

Cooper stared at it, the muscle in his jaw twitching. "I'm not happy about this."

Neither was she. Her heart had leapt into her throat.

"Jesus," he muttered. "The whole fucking house is a crime scene."

She put a hand on his tense spine, felt the heat and strength there. "Cooper? I really, really want out of here."

"Tomorrow," he said tightly, and opened another cabinet. "Bingo," he said at the sight of the cans of gasoline. "Without power, we'll have to open the garage doors manually, and that's not going to be easy—I've tried. They're heavy from the large snowdrift that's probably up against it."

"We can shovel—"

That got a smile.

"What?"

"I'm seeing you shoveling in that shirt and skirt. With those knives tucked into your boots." His expression heated. "Nice picture, actually."

"Yeah?"

"Yeah," he said huskily, looking at her, really looking at her, as if he could see inside and hear her thoughts, which were pretty much going down a path to dangerous waters.

"This is crazy," she whispered, and backed up a step. She lifted her hand to swipe her damp forehead and nearly poked out her own eye with the knives. "This whole thing is crazy. The wedding, the storm, this house—the dead body."

His smile faded. "I know."

"I'm just so damned jumpy. And we both know I hate trusting you, but the truth is . . . I guess I do. A little, anyway."

He held out a hand. "Enough to give me those knives before you lose a body part?"

She held them out. "I can take care of myself." False bravado and they both knew it. She hadn't taken care of herself; *he* had.

He stepped toward her, searing blue eyes gleaming, invading her personal space in that way he had. Instead of annoying her, it backed the air up in her lungs and made her skin feel too tight.

Oh, and it also made her nipples go happy.

Damn nipples.

"You wouldn't kill a spider," he said softly. "So I'm guessing that if it came to using a knife on a real-life, flesh-and-blood person, you might have a hard time."

She quivered. "I'd be fine."

"That tough outer shell again." He traced her jaw with a finger, a gesture that might have been casual if he'd let his hand fall away, but he stroked that finger over her throat.

She shivered. A nice shiver. A goose bump-inducing shiver.

"I nearly had heart failure when I couldn't find you before," he said very quietly. "I thought you'd stay in the great room."

"I don't stay very well."

"I just want you safe."

She swallowed hard at that. This wasn't a game. This wasn't about her pride. This was about far more than herself, and she wanted to stay safe, too. Very much. "I thought maybe there'd be safety in numbers. But then Shelly and I heard those noises."

"And you went after it."

"Not my finest decision, granted," she admitted.

His gaze flickered to the wall, where they could very faintly hear the water running through the pipes.

Lariana and Patrick in the shower.

"I do think it's sweet that they're using their fear for the greater good," she quipped.

"As long as it isn't murder that got their adrenaline flowing."

Suddenly Breanne needed more BBQ chips.

Cooper set the confiscated knives on a wooden work-bench along the back of the garage. Then he straightened and looked at her, his eyes dark, his intent clear in that fierce, hot expression. Her knees wobbled, and she took a step back, only to come up against the wall.

His hands settled on either side of her head as he leaned in, trapping her within the confines of his body.

"Why do cops do that?" she asked, her voice steady even though her entire body reacted to his nearness—and not in fear.

"Do what?"

"Feel the need to intimidate with their superior bulk?"

He arched a brow. "You think I'm trying to intimidate you?" Bending his head, he ran the tip of his nose over her earlobe, a move that shocked her like a bolt of electricity. "Do you feel intimidated?" he murmured.

"Uh . . ."

"How about now?" he asked softly, and put his lips to the sensitive spot beneath her ear.

She'd expected a quick assault on her senses, a deep, intoxicating kiss—not this light, almost sweet, touch.

"Bree?"

"N-not intimidated," she gasped.

"Aroused, then?" He went after her other ear.

"Um . . . God. I can't think when you do that."

"I'm trying to remind you that we have a thing going on," he said in that voice, the one that melted her resolve—and far too many brain cells, while he was at it.

"Not a *thing*—"

"A thing," he went on, undeterred, "that you're afraid of—"

"I'm *not* afraid—"

"A thing that makes you soft and sweet, a thing that makes you hot for me."

"I'm not . . . hot for you."

His low laugh in her ear sent goose bumps dancing over her skin, and more than just her nipples did the happy dance this time. "Sure about that?" he murmured, and sank his teeth gently into her earlobe, lightly tugging.

She nearly slid to the floor in a boneless heap of desire. Instead she locked her knees and gritted her teeth, flattening her hands against the cold wall to remind herself to keep them off of his body. "Absolutely sure," she managed.

"I could prove you wrong." He nuzzled her some more.

Who'd have thought that little patch of skin beneath her jaw was a direct line to her erogenous zones, but she felt the tug all the way to her womb. "No need."

Another low laugh huffed out of him as he made his way down her neck now, with wet, open-mouthed kisses, and then—oh, my God—licked the spot where surely her pulse was going to burst right out of the base of her throat. "Stop."

"Say it like you mean it, and I will."

Damn it. "We're going to shovel," she said weakly.

"Not now. In the morning."

"But another night—"

"Even if we got out and I got one of these snowmobiles started, I need daylight to find my way to the road and then into town."

"Dante or Patrick—"

"Even they'll need daylight. Getting lost out here at night . . . Bad idea. It'll have to wait until morning." He scraped his jaw over her collarbone, dragging the red stretchy material off her shoulder.

"Okay, but I am *not* hot for you."

"I know, baby. I know." He kissed her shoulder and her eyes crossed with lust. "It's all me."

"Yes, it's all you—"

He nipped at her as he tugged the shirt down further, baring her breasts. Her head thunked back against the wall, her body a quivering mass of need that she didn't understand. To gather herself and some desperately needed strength, she twisted around. Facing the wall now, she put her hot cheek to the cold drywall and dragged air into her taxed lungs.

"Say the word," he murmured, undeterred by her back as he slowly glided his hands down her body. "And I'll stop."

She opened her mouth to do it but nothing came out.

"Breanne?"

When she didn't answer, he dropped to his knees and kissed the back of a thigh. The feel of his mouth on her bare skin sent heat and desire leaping through her. Oh, God. She *was* hot for him, so hot she couldn't stand it, and she rolled her forehead over the cold wall trying to cool down.

Just sex, she told herself. *Just sex. Just sex*—

"You going to stop me?"

Yep, any minute now.

He slipped his hands around to her belly, which jumped and jerked like it was full of butterflies. Then he cupped her breasts, flicking his thumbs over her nipples, ripping a moan from her that was shocking in its neediness.

Still on his knees behind her, he lightly bit the curve of

her bottom through her skirt; then, with his jaw, he pushed the material up out of his way, leaving her vulnerable in the most basic sense of the word.

"God, you take my breath."

She could have stopped him. He expected her to. Instead, she pressed her hot face to the cool wall, squeezing her eyes shut against the image she must have made with her skirt shoved high, revealing her skimpy panties, the do-me boots, knowing he was going to push her past her comfort zone.

Wanting him to push her past her comfort zone.

His hands slid down her hips, her legs, and back up again, palming her bottom. Leaning in, he kissed a cheek, then the other, and then his thumbs dipped between, ripping a gasp out of her.

"Just say the word," he murmured.

Say it, her brain commanded. *Stop him.*

But her body had taken over, and she thrust her butt out.

With a low, rough growl—the only word for the lustful sound that came from him—he skimmed the itty-bitty black panties aside.

Knowing what he could see, which was everything, she kept her eyes closed, her cheek to the chilly wall, and held her breath.

While he very slowly let out his, the warmth skimming over her exposed flesh, ripping a pathetic little whimper from her throat.

He didn't move.

She did. She squirmed, thinking if he didn't touch her soon she was going to be forced to beg.

"You're the sexiest thing," he whispered, running a finger over her. "And so wet." He dipped into that wetness. "Is this all for me, Breanne?"

Good thing the question seemed rhetorical, because she didn't have breath for an answer.

"Are you?"

"Yes," she panted when his finger stroked over her again. "I'm wet. For you."

He rewarded her with another stroke, and she nearly lost it right then and there. And then another while his mouth lightly bit the back of her thigh again, his callused finger still driving her right to the edge.

And all she could do was prop herself against the wall and let the sensations bombard her. Every time she sucked in a breath, her breasts grazed the cold wall, making her gasp in shock, adding to the sensations. "Cooper—"

"Are we stopping?" His voice was tight and strained, and though he went still, he didn't remove his hands—or mouth—from her.

She was so close to coming, her hips were still rocking, tiny little oscillations of movement she couldn't stop.

"Breanne?"

"No," she whispered.

The air left his lungs in a sigh of relief, but none of the tension left the hands that held her still and in place as he whipped her around. On his knees, he looked up at her, groaned at what he saw, then ran his hands from her breasts to her belly, to her thighs, and then between. His thumbs gently parted her, and he leaned in and kissed her.

There.

Something unintelligible left her mouth, though she had no idea what she'd meant to say because then he used his tongue. With a cry, she fell back against the wall, gone, just totally and completely gone. "I don't—"

"You had your chance to stop this," he murmured, using his fingers, his tongue, his teeth. "Shh, now."

"Ohmigod." She began to shudder. "Cooper—I'm going to—"

"Come," he said against her. "I want you to."

As if she could do anything else. Biting her lip, she let go and came hard, bucking against the hands that gripped her tight as he brought her to heaven and back, and then slowly eased her down, touching her as if he could read her like a book. When her knees gave out, he caught her. Mouth wet, eyes dark and hungry, he smiled, though his body was taut.

She put her hands on his shoulders and kissed his cheek, his jaw, his mouth. He immediately opened his and she dove in, but only for a moment before working her way down his throat, smiling when his Adam's apple bounced as he swallowed hard. "Your turn," she whispered, and licked at the hollow at the base of his throat.

Beneath her hands, his heart beat steady but fast. She kissed him again, or he kissed her. God, he was good at this, his lips brushing softly back and forth over hers, his tongue dancing to hers. When her tongue followed his, he sucked her into his mouth with a gentle, warm pressure that got her hot and bothered all over again, more so when a soft groan escaped him.

It gave her a rush such as she'd never known, rendering a man like this a trembling mass of need. On their knees, facing each other, she shoved up his shirt, kissing her way to a pec, flicking her tongue over his nipple, tracing her fingers along his amazing abs, then to the waistband of his jeans. A whole new rush of excitement at his quickened breathing. "Tell me to stop," she whispered, mirroring his earlier words as she unzipped him.

A choked laugh escaped him but he said nothing.

He wasn't wearing underwear. Just a most impressive erection right there in her face, very happy to see her. "Mmmm," she hummed, and tugged his jeans to his thighs. "Is this all for me?"

"Oh, yeah." His fingers tunneled in her hair. "Perfect way to get an in with the law."

Mouth open to take him in, she paused. Tipped her head up. "What?"

He smiled, sexy and lazy, more gorgeous than sin, and she nearly pretended she hadn't heard him because she wanted his penis inside her more than she wanted her next breath, but she found she couldn't let it go. "You think that I need an *in* with the law?"

He grimaced. "Of course not. I—"

"Oh, my God." She pushed unsteadily to her feet. "You actually think I could have—" Voice shaking, she shut her mouth and shoved down her skirt, adjusted her shirt.

"Breanne. Don't be stupid. I didn't mean—"

Oh, now she was stupid. "Back off," she warned, her body still pulsing, and stepped clear. "You have got to be kidding if you think I'm going to let you touch me now."

She started to stalk off, but at the last minute whirled back and grabbed the flashlight. Let *him* be in the dark. She needed out.

When the door slammed, Cooper pulled up his jeans, wincing as he zipped them, sagging back against the snowmobile. "Genius," he muttered. "I'm a fucking genius."

Eighteen

*Everyone makes mistakes. The trick is to make them
when nobody is looking.*
                    —Breanne Mooreland's journal entry

Cooper made his way through the dark house, his temper
heating with each step. He could hear various sounds, someone walking upstairs, someone in the great room messing
with the fireplace.

Normal house sounds. As if anything about this house
had turned out to be normal.

There were candles lit in the main hallway, the glow making it easier to navigate the huge place but not taking away
the chill or the flickering shadows.

He felt painfully alert, watching out for any little movement and sound. It was getting to him.

A dead body did that to a person.

So did all the sexual play without getting off. Damn, that
was *really* getting to him. So was little Miss Fucking Attitude.

He had no idea where she'd run off to, the woman who'd
actually thought he'd touch her the way he had and yet believe her capable of murder. Wherever she'd gone, he doubted
he'd be welcomed anywhere near her. *Too bad,* he thought
grimly, because he didn't feel comfortable with her wandering around here when they had no idea what they were up
against.

He looked into the great room. Dante was the one stirring up the fire. Breanne sat on the couch, her back to Cooper, laughing at something the butler was saying.

Laughing. His temper rose a notch.

Shelly stood off to the side, smiling dreamily at Dante.

Cooper let out a breath and entered the room, prepared to be universally hated. "Hey."

Everyone looked at him but no one said anything. Yep, universally hated. Breanne looked away first. He wanted to wring her neck. Instead he nodded to the flashlight she had on her lap. "I need that for a moment. Or your other one."

"Other one?"

"The Day-Glo pink vibrator," he said, being intentionally crude, but damn it she didn't have to look at him like he was a pervert. There'd been *two* people all over each other in that garage.

"Here," she said, shoving the flashlight at him.

He took it and walked out of the room. He decided that was the smart thing to do at the moment because he was absolutely not going to defend himself to her.

In general, people had two reactions to finding out what he did for a living. There were the "cop" groupies, the women who found his job an exciting adrenaline rush. And then there were those who clammed up and got suspicious of everything he said, as if he was getting ready to shove them against a car and cuff them like they did on *COPS*. The cop-haters.

The only person who'd ever accepted him as he stood was his brother, and that had been because they were two peas in a pod. But James was married now, and Cooper had gotten used to being alone. Good thing, since they were going to be here at least another night and he had a feeling he was definitely going to be solo for this one.

No warm, sexy Breanne, a woman he'd thought for a brief moment could maybe have gotten to know him, the real him. He'd been wrong. Again he made his way down to the cellar to make sure no one had messed with the crime scene, just for fun checking the locked bedroom door next to the cellar. Still locked.

He entered the cellar and hunkered down next to Edward, shining the light over him. Poor bastard. Then he eyed Edward's shirt and went still. Had someone adjusted the body? He leaned in closer. The smell was bad, but Cooper had smelled worse so he ignored that, especially as he realized something he'd missed before. There was a curious lack of blood around the hole in Edward's chest, as if the injury had occurred postmortem.

The body had suffered blunt trauma as well, a fact that had become more apparent with the passing of time. The body was bruised from head to toe, as if he'd been beat to hell, or . . . as if he'd fallen.

Cooper craned his neck and looked at the staircase, a good fifteen feet away. "Which came first, Edward? The fall or the shot to the chest?"

And why did Cooper have the gut feeling that neither had been what had killed him?

He scrubbed a hand over his face, frustrated and uneasy. Nothing added up—not the staff's reaction, not the lay of the body, and not the fact that he'd searched the house the best he could and hadn't come up with any sign of a gun, BB or otherwise.

He shouldn't care. He'd laid down his badge, ostensibly for good. At the time, he'd meant it. Even as late as this morning, he'd meant it. He'd worked his ass off and his soul into the ground, and he'd thought leaving the job had been the only answer.

But now, staring down at Edward, he wondered at his need to know what happened, at his need for justice.

The shadow flattened against the wall, heart pounding like a primal drum, watching Cooper.

Why did he keep coming back to look at the body?

Edward was dead already, dead, dead, dead, and no amount of looking at him could change that.

So why was there still so much fear?

Breanne sat in front of the fireplace in the spare bedroom where just last night she'd foolishly believed she could sleep. Shelly was pouring her a glass of wine.

Breanne figured she needed the whole damn bottle. But remembering what had happened when she'd oh-so-innocently gone into the cellar for a bottle, had her shuddering.

"There." Shelly pushed a tray of food toward her, a bowl of canned chili heated by the fire and some fruit. "I can't believe your bad luck. Missing out on my cooking for two of your days here."

"As if that's the worst of my problems."

Shelly let out a shuddery sigh. "Yeah. It's been a rough one around here, huh? First the break-in, then Edward—"

"What?" Breanne set down her wineglass and twisted around to look at Shelly. "You had a break-in?"

"Well, we're not sure exactly, to tell you the truth."

"What do you mean?"

"Last week Lariana went to town and cashed her check at lunch. That night after work, her wallet was missing from her purse out of the main hallway closet. Her entire paycheck, gone." Shelly lifted her hands. "Not that we get paid all that much, let me tell you, but still."

"Did she call the police?"

"No. Nothing else was taken that we could tell."

"Shouldn't the police have been notified?" *Or the future guests warned?*

"To tell you the truth, it wasn't my place to do so. And Lariana said it was her own stupid fault. We'd left the front door open that day for a big spring cleaning. Edward freaks when we leave the front door unlocked. If he'd found out—"

"But the front door was unlocked when I got here," Breanne said.

"Yeah." Shelly flashed her a guilty look. "See, the house is so big, and we all have so many chores because Edward's too cheap to hire a rotating staff. It's just easier to leave it unlocked rather than miss a delivery or a guest."

Breanne stared into the fire and remembered last night. The face hovering over her in bed. "But you make sure to lock the front door at night, right?"

"Always," Shelly promised, then winced. "Or at least I think so."

Terrific.

"It's just that I used to leave after I cooked dinner, so I don't know the late night habits."

"But last night you slept here. In the servants' quarters, right?"

"Yes."

"How about Dante?"

Shelly's smile congealed. "Him, too."

"And Patrick and Lariana?"

"Are you trying to get our alibis?"

Well, yes, but now she felt like a jerk for doing so. "I'm just trying to make sure I'm not scared out of my mind again tonight. If I know where you are, I just might be joining you in a slumber party."

Shelly laughed. "Dante slept on the floor next to me because I was scared and he's a sweetie."

"You mean before you got him in the closet today and showed him your feminine wiles."

"Hey, no wiles were shown." She moved to the door. "Sleep tight."

"Is Dante going to be on your floor again?"

Shelly turned back at the door. "Next to me would be better, but we're waiting until we get out of here."

"Good luck with that, because there's just something about this house that revs a person's energy."

"Maybe it's the altitude?"

"I meant *sexual* energy."

"Oh." Shelly grinned. "Right. I knew that. You're not the first guest to notice."

"It's not difficult when the staff goes around screwing each other at will."

"*Hey.*"

"I meant Lariana."

"I knew that, too."

"Just be careful."

"I should say the same to you. You're the one that ended up sleeping with the cop."

"Cooper. His name is Cooper."

"I know."

Oddly enough, Breanne felt a slight censure in her voice, which made no sense. Shelly didn't seem the type of woman to judge another soul on anything.

And yet Shelly didn't like Cooper, hadn't ever since she'd found out he was a cop.

The others were the same. Not only odd, but unsettling, and when Breanne was alone, she locked the door, then scooted her chair closer to the fire. Hugging her legs in close, she set her chin to her knees, staring at the flickering flames.

Did she like him? Even after what he'd said to her? Yeah, she did, because she knew she'd overreacted, just as she knew she'd done so as a self-protective gesture.

She was still pondering the why of it when a knock came at her door.

Leaping up, she whirled around and stared at it. "Hello?"

"Hey."

Just that, just *Hey*, but the unbearably familiar voice entered her system and jolted her out of her reverie and right into a high state of anticipation she didn't welcome.

Nineteen

When everything's coming your way, you're in the wrong lane.

—Breanne Mooreland's journal entry

Breanne stared at the door, her pulse drumming away madly, along with her resistance.

Cooper knocked again, just one light rap.

She could feel him on the other side of the door, his heat, his strength, and her body reacted as if it already belonged to him. Well, damn it, she didn't belong to anyone, especially a man.

"Let me in, Bree."

That'd be like opening the door to the big, bad wolf and inviting him in to blow her life down. As said life had been built fragile brick by fragile brick, she didn't dare.

"Please," he said.

Ah, hell. The magic word. Even knowing it was the mother of all bad decisions, she opened the door.

"About earlier," he said.

Turning her back to him, she moved to the fire and plopped down into the recliner, nonchalantly lifting her hands to the flames. "You mean when you asked if I was putting my hands in your pants because I wanted . . . how did you put it . . . to get an *in with the law?*"

"Yeah, that." He came close and hunkered down beside her chair. "You cannot think I was serious."

She studied the fire and didn't respond. She knew now he hadn't meant it, but just his voice alone was making her want to melt.

"Look at me, Breanne."

No. Looking at him would be like looking directly into the sun. Amazing but stupid.

But then his hands settled on the arms of the leather recliner and he whipped it around to face him. His face was grim, intense, and . . . still angry.

"I didn't mean it," he said. "You know I didn't. Now I want to hear you say it, damn it."

"Fine. I know you didn't meant it. End of conversation, please."

"Just like that?"

"Just like that."

He looked at her for a long moment, then let out a breath. "I'm a cop, Bree. Through and through, as it turns out. I thought quitting would change that, but apparently no."

Damn it, she knew that, but hearing him say it, knowing he felt as if he *had* to say it, got to her.

"I've seen and heard it all," he said. "And it's changed me, maybe even hardened me. I can't help that. But when I'm with you, I feel a little . . . clumsy." His eyes were dark and genuine. "I didn't mean to hurt your feelings. But you hurt mine."

"I'm sorry." She could admit it now. "I'm so sorry. It's all me, I'm just . . . going crazy. Edward—"

"Was dead when we got here. Or so I think, anyway." His hands were fisted on either side of her, the sleeves of his shirt rolled up past his elbows, his forearms corded with strength as he leaned over her. "You sleeping in here tonight?"

Sleeping? Probably not. More like watching the shadows on the wall all night long. But she lifted a shoulder. "The bed's comfortable enough."

"I figured you wouldn't want to be alone."

"I'm a big girl, Cooper."

"Yeah, you are." He lifted her chin. "And you're running scared."

She jerked her chin free. "If I was running scared, would I be sleeping alone?"

"You're running scared of me."

She let out what was supposed to be a disbelieving sound, but it convinced neither of them.

"You expect me to believe you'd rather face another midnight intruder than sleep next to me?" His voice was heavy with disbelief. "I don't think so."

She shook her head. "How did you ever fit through the door with that big head of yours? Look, I'm going to be fine, okay? In fact, I'm quite exhausted." She made a big show out of stretching and yawning really wide, before putting her hands to his chest and pushing so she could stand up.

Only she didn't budge him.

"Excuse me," she said.

"You're going to sleep."

"Yep."

"Right now."

"That's right."

At that he backed up, leaning against the wall, arms crossed over his chest, the picture of an irritated, frustrated, sexy-as-hell man.

She made a big deal out of climbing up onto the high bed and tugging down the white down comforter. "Shut the door on your way out."

"You're going to sleep in those fuck-me boots and Lariana's clothes?"

Her own personal armor, and yes, she was going to sleep in them if that's what it took. "I'm sorry if the boots misled you today," she said primly.

"Trust me, it wasn't the boots. Though they are something—" Saying so, he moved forward and took hold of one.

Before she could kick him, he'd flipped her to her back, but instead of flattening her down on the bed with his body as she'd figured, he began to undo the boot with a quiet calm.

"Watch out," she warned. "Have you seen the heels on these things?"

"Shh." He'd bent his head to the task, and she might have melted at the unexpected sweetness of the gesture except he drove her crazy.

"If you shh me one more time . . ." she warned.

Lifting his head, he smiled grimly as the first boot came off and he tossed it over his shoulder. "You'll what?"

Damn it, she had no idea what.

"Come on, Breanne. Finish the threat—I'm all ears."

"Shut up," she said, utterly without rancor because he was looking at her with such genuine warmth and affection that her mad drained right out of her.

People she'd known all her life didn't look at her like that, yet he did. She didn't know what to do with him. "I wish you'd go away," she whispered, confusion and exhaustion, not emotion, creating a lump in her throat. She had no emotion left.

Or so she told herself. "*Please.*"

He went very still, staring at her for a long moment before lifting his hands from her and taking his weight off the mattress. "You know where to find me if you need me."

"I won't." With only one boot off, she turned over into a little ball and closed her eyes tight, not relaxing until she heard the door shut behind him.

"It's locked," he said through it. "Keep it that way."

Sleep didn't come as easily as it had the night before. For the longest time she lay there, muscles sore from holding herself so tense. The fire crackled. The walls creaked.

So did a floorboard.

Uneasy, she sat up, her gaze frantically searching out each corner of the room.

No floating face.

No boogeyman.

Nothing.

And yet she was in this house with a dead body. And someone who'd made him dead.

She lay back down, but that lasted only until the next mysterious creak.

Why had she wanted to be alone?

Damn bad time to have given up men.

Then, from somewhere in the house, came an odd, indistinguishable sound. Not the house creaking, but she couldn't place it. Again she sat up.

She'd definitely been hasty in sending Cooper away. Truth was, she didn't have to give up men as long as she did one thing—hold on to her heart and soul for all they were worth, never letting them go.

For anyone.

Hoping she was right, she slipped out of bed and slowly cracked open her door. The hallway was pitch black—not a sound, not even a whisper of air. She couldn't see all the way to the honeymoon suite where her salvation lay in one tall, hard, gorgeous package.

Couldn't see anything.

That's when the house creaked again.

Goose bumps rose over her skin, fear bubbled in her throat, and she ducked back into her room looking for a flashlight or a candle or something.

But the candles had burned down to stubs and Lariana hadn't replaced them. She'd had the fire for light and that had been enough. Stumbling into the bathroom, she went straight to the gift basket and fumbled for the vibrator that had reappeared. *Thanks, Lariana, for your obnoxious sense of humor.* Rushing back to the fire, Breanne held the thing up in front of the flames for a moment until it began to glow pink.

At the next creak of the walls, she gasped, gripped the vibrator out in front of her like a beacon, and bolted for the honeymoon suite, limping in her one high-heeled boot.

This time she didn't jump Cooper in the bed. She didn't have to because he wasn't in it.

Shirtless, wearing only a pair of jeans low on his hips, he stood facing his own fireplace, hair rumpled, feet bare. For a moment she hung onto the doorjamb staring at him, a yearning welling up within her so strong she didn't know what to do with it.

What was it about him? Granted, he had an amazing body. His back was sinewy and sleek, broad and sculpted, tapering in at his waist and hips. And that butt . . . Lord, she just wanted to bite it.

Only it wasn't her body that tingled at the sight of him, but something deep inside. *Note to self: your heart and soul are locked up tight! Not accessible! Remember that!*

"You going to shut the door?" he asked without turning around.

With a sigh, she did, no longer surprised that he seemed to have eyes in the back of his head because she was getting used to that sense of awareness he had. She imagined he'd honed it over the years of being a cop.

Craning his neck, he finally looked at her, taking in her makeshift flashlight. "You need me to show you how to work that thing?"

"In your dreams."

"Oh yeah, in my dreams." He sighed and rubbed his forehead as if she gave him a headache by just being.

She had to admit it was entirely possible that she was a walking/talking headache inducer. "I, um, forgot to tell you something."

"Well, then." He turned toward her and slipped his hands in his pockets. The movement shifted his jeans even lower on his hips, gaping away slightly from his rippled abs that she always wanted to touch. "I'm all ears, Princess."

Actually, he was all solid, tough muscle, but she wasn't going to point that out. *Locking up the heart and soul and tossing out the key!*

He jerked a shoulder toward the fire. "Come here."

Yeah, colossally bad idea. "Don't you want to know what I forgot to tell you?"

"I want you to be warm."

His words made her realize she was hugging herself, and extremely chilled. "Getting close to you is bad for my mental health."

"And yet you're here instead of with anyone else in the house." He waggled his fingers. "Come on."

Her feet carried her, damn them, one boot on and one boot off, while he watched, calm and thoughtful. Coming to a stop next to him, she stared into the fire, ignoring his gaze, which she could feel running over her. "Better?" he asked softly as the warmth began to seep into her bones.

"Yes," she said so grudgingly he laughed as he bent down and helped her out of her single boot.

"So." When he straightened, he smiled into her eyes with that same confusing mix of heat and affection that felt infinitely terrifying to her. "What did you forget to tell me?"

"It's a deal sort of thing."

"Ah. Meaning you want something in return." Again he slipped his hands into his pockets and turned back to the fire, his smile gone, shoulders slightly hunched. "The question is, *what.*"

Too late, she realized the truth. As a cop, he probably got requests for "deals" every day. Guilt stabbed through her that she hadn't treated him any better than any of the criminals he'd dealt with, but there was no going back now. "I want to sleep with you."

That got his attention. Those eyes once again turned and locked on hers, blazing and filled with things that banished her chill. She swallowed hard. "That is, um . . ."

"Yeah," he said. "I thought you might want to clarify that."

"I want to sleep with you so I'm not the next body found dead on the cellar floor."

He let out a long breath. "Breanne, you don't have to make a bargain for that."

Her heart began to tumble but she bucked it up because, damn it, neither her heart nor her soul were involved here. They were locked up.

Tight.

"In return for letting me sleep here," she said, "I wanted to tell you what Shelly mentioned tonight. They had a break-in last week."

"A break-in?" He went from mere man to sharp cop in the blink of an eye. "What was taken?"

"From what I understand, just cash from Lariana's purse. Nothing else."

He frowned. "That makes no sense. There's a lot of valuable stuff here."

"I know."

"Only Lariana's money? Are you sure?"

"That's what she said."

"That sounds personal. What did the police say?"

"They didn't call the police."

He made a rough sound of disgust.

"They didn't want the owner to find out that they'd been leaving the front door unlocked."

"Anything else?" he asked.

"No."

He nodded. "Then there's only one thing left to do."

"What's that?"

"Go to bed," he said, and his hands went to the buttons on his Levi's.

Twenty

A conclusion is where you go when you get tired of thinking.

—Breanne Mooreland's journal entry

Cooper didn't miss the leap of emotion in Breanne's gaze. Except it wasn't *Oh, please take me to bed*, it was *Oh God, he thinks I'm going to sleep with him.*

With a harsh laugh directed entirely at himself, he ran his fingers through his hair and headed toward the mattress. "I'm taking it we need something bigger than a sheet between us this time." He snatched the folded comforter off the foot of the bed and stalked toward the overstuffed chair in the corner. The *small* chair. "'Night, Bree."

She stared at him as he sat and pulled the comforter over the top of him. It was a short comforter, and didn't cover both his chest and his feet at the same time. Perfect. Not only had he been stupid enough to give up the bed, he was going to be cold to boot.

Breanne was still staring at him. "I thought that you— that we'd—" Her gaze flickered to the bed.

"You thought what?"

"Nothing." She pulled back the big, thick down comforter that Cooper had reason to know was not only warm and toasty, but would cover him entirely, and slid beneath it, vanishing entirely except for the top of her head and her eyes. Eyes that were still locked on him.

Trying to forget her, he shifted to his side, aiming for some level of comfort. There was none to be had. His jeans were cutting off circulation to vital parts. With a sigh, he stood up and stripped them off, then wrapped himself in the blanket that came only to his shins.

Popsicles. His feet were going to be popsicles.

So were his balls. Good move, Ace. With another sigh, he stood up, put his jeans back on, and took a longing glance toward the bed. Looking considerably more comfortable, not to mention warm and toasty, Breanne lay there with only her hair and eyes showing.

Eyes which were closed.

He turned away, thinking, damn, she'd gone directly to sleep, peaceful as a baby, while he sat here chilly, frustrated, and—

"I have another deal," she whispered.

"The last one didn't work out too well for me, so no, thanks."

"This one's better."

He rolled back toward her, then was sorry. Her eyes were dark and haunted, her face strained, her fingers clutching the blanket up to her chin. Not wanting to be affected by her meant shit when his heart clenched without his permission every time he so much as looked at her. "What is it?"

"I'm . . ." She let out a breath. "I'm really scared."

He sighed. "Nothing's going to happen to you here, Bree."

"Yeah." Sitting up, she pulled her knees to her chest and wrapped her arms around her legs. "I keep telling myself that. The truth is, I'm a little shaky for a lot of reasons."

"You've been through a rough few days. Anyone would be shaky, even without finding a dead body."

"Yeah, makes that whole being dumped at the altar thing not that big a deal."

"It was a big deal for you," he said quietly.

"You know it's for the third time."

"Breanne—"

"Don't even try to tell me that's normal," she said firmly. "Face it, Cooper. There's something wrong with me. I'm not quite sure what, but there is."

"No."

"Maybe it's a sexual thing. Maybe . . ." She winced. "Maybe I'm bad in bed."

Christ, no man was strong enough for this. He pushed out of the chair and moved to the mattress.

She watched him, her eyes sad and shimmering. "About the deal. Do you think you could—I mean, would you—"

He put a knee on the mattress. "Don't say it."

"—have sex with me?" she whispered. "Make sure I'm not doing something really wrong?"

Definitely not big enough to walk away from that request, or the lingering hurt in her eyes, not to mention the offer of her sweet, hot body.

"I'll do all the work," she promised. "*Everything.*"

His knees actually wobbled.

"And afterwards, you can critique me—"

"*Breanne—*"

"And then tomorrow morning, we'll dig out and go our separate ways."

She was serious. She wanted to have him tonight, bare their bodies and souls, then walk away in the morning.

After he told her what was wrong with her.

"Think of it," she said softly. "A whole night of unattached, unemotional sex. Any guy's idea of Christmas, right?"

"Stop." Walking over here had been a massively stupid idea, because now he was inches from her, with a knee already on the bed.

She pulled her lower lip between her teeth. Stared up at him.

All he had to do was lean over her—

She tossed the covers aside.

On her back in that stretchy red top and painted-on skirt,

both of which showed off her curvy body in a mouthwatering way, she smiled up at him—shaky, but a smile nevertheless. "Do you want me, Cooper?"

Only more than his next breath. He wanted to pull her beneath him, he wanted to slowly strip her out of those sexy clothes that were hot but not *her*, wanted to run his tongue and teeth over every inch of her.

But not like this. Damn it, not like this, not with her hurting, and vulnerable. Not with her trying to set it up so that for once she could be the one to walk away before she got hurt. It took every ounce of restraint he had, but he backed up.

"I know you want me," she said softly, and they both looked down at the unmistakable bulge behind the buttons on his jeans, offering vivid proof of that wanting. "Yes," he said hoarsely. "But—"

"No. No buts."

"*But* . . . not like this, Bree. Not because you're hurting and sad."

"*Cooper*—"

"I don't want you to wake up in the morning and regret anything. Especially me."

Her eyes were as luminous as the fire's glow while she digested this. "And I thought you said you weren't a gentleman."

A sound of deep need escaped him—he couldn't help it.

She turned on her side away from him and pulled the covers back over her head.

Was she embarrassed now? He didn't want that, anything but that. "Breanne—"

"Forget it."

He didn't move, couldn't get himself to walk away.

"Every minute you stand there," she said, her voice muffled by the covers, "you risk being jumped by the pathetic chick. I'd run if I were you."

Shit. He stalked the length of the room, heading back to

the fire, even though he didn't need the heat; he was damn hot enough.

Craning his neck, he glanced back at the bed. The lump that was Breanne hadn't budged. Good. She was going to be a good girl and go to sleep.

He only wished he could, but as he was currently hard enough to pound nails, he doubted sleep would come any time soon. James would have smacked him upside the head for turning down the sexiest, hottest woman he'd ever seen. He couldn't believe he'd done it. He was truly an idiot.

Suddenly exhausted, he dropped into the chair, sprawled out his legs, and tipped his head back. Closed his eyes.

His mind did not turn off. Nope, it kept whirring and cranking out disturbing thoughts.

Wake her up.

Tell her you changed your mind—

Better yet, *show* her you've changed your mind.

"Cooper?"

He opened his eyes to find her standing right in front of him, his living fantasy in the flesh. "Thought you'd gone to sleep," he said.

Slowly she shook her head.

"You should go to sleep." He was sounding a bit desperate, even to his own ears, but damn it, he could only take so much with her standing there two inches from him, looking as if maybe she wanted to gobble him up whole.

He could really get behind that. "Breanne."

"I know. You want me to go far, far away, but I can't do that."

"Why not?"

"Because."

Her eyes held his, shadowed by insecurity. There was no use in pretending he couldn't see because he might as well try to stop breathing. Every part of him was focused on her, locked in some hypersensitive state. "You can't go back to bed because . . . ?"

"Because I want you in it with me."

"Breanne—"

"I need you, Cooper. Don't make me beg."

Ah, Christ. "Are you sure?" he whispered fiercely.

She straddled his legs and sat on his lap.

Okay, she was sure. "Breanne," he groaned. "We've taken this about as far as we can with our clothes on, and I don't want to stop again."

She shook her head. "No stopping this time."

"Good, because I've been hard since you got here. I'm going to damage myself if I keep it up." He shot her a lop-sided grin. "Have some mercy."

She laughed, but her eyes shone with emotion as well, yanking at his heart, and his smile slowly faded.

"I need somebody tonight," she whispered, her hands going to his shoulders. "And I want it to be you. You, Cooper Scott, and no one else."

The promise was far more than he could have, or would have, asked for. He sat up a little straighter, running his hands up her body to cup her face, tugging her down for a kiss.

She obliged him in the sweetest, hottest connection he'd ever known, then pulled back, her lips leaving his with a little suction noise that tugged all the way through his body.

With a little smile, she got off of him and shimmied out of her skirt. God, he loved those black satin panties, the way the small patch of material barely covered her, how the stretchy fabric rode low on her hips, and though he couldn't see her ass at the moment, he knew the material was riding up, outlining her to perfection. "Breanne," he said hoarsely.

She crossed her arms in front of her, grabbed the hem of that red shirt, and pulled it over her head.

Leaving her in nothing but those panties, and suddenly he wished he'd let her keep the boots on, because holy shit, that would have made quite the picture.

Not that he needed the boots at the moment. Hell, no. She

made his mouth water without the boots. She made his mouth water, period.

Then she climbed back into his lap, tucking a knee on either side of his thighs. His hands went to his favorite part, her sweet ass. He squeezed, then slid inside her panties, cupping her bare skin before gliding downward—

She gasped.

He groaned, his fingers delving deeper, finding her wet and creamy, making him groan again.

She said his name in a rather strangled voice, having gone utterly still in what he hoped was anticipation. "Good?" he asked.

The sound that came from her was rough, low, and the most erotic thing he'd ever heard, and he slowly pushed a finger inside her.

This elicited yet another breathy cry, and he added a second finger.

"More," she whispered, squirming. "Please, more."

He'd give her more, and it would take all night. Even knowing that wouldn't be enough, he slid his fingers free, nudging her closer, then closer still so that her satin-covered crotch slid to his denim-covered one . . . oh, yeah . . . and those full breasts were only an inch from his mouth. He kissed the pouting tip of one and pulled back to watch it pucker up and darken for him. "You're so sexy, Bree. You're the sexiest thing I've ever seen."

"You don't have to say that." Her voice sounded strained. "I'm here. I'm willing. You don't have to say anything you don't mean. Just . . . take us to the finish line. *Please*."

After all the teasing they'd done over the past two days, he wanted that more than anything, but not as badly as he wanted her to believe him, believe in this. He cupped her face, waiting until she lifted those whiskey eyes. "I never lie, Bree, remember? Never. This isn't just about the finish, spectacular as that's going to be. It's going to be about far more. Now do you still want to do this?"

She didn't take her eyes off him as she thought about that for so long he got worried.

"Yes, I still want to do this," she finally said. "But one of us is way overdressed." Saying so, she pulled back slightly, bending her head to the task of unfastening his jeans. Her hair fell forward, brushing against his bare shoulders and chest, and it was so much like his fantasy, he groaned. "There's no rush," he said huskily when she let out a frustrated cry, struggling. "We have all night."

"I like it fast."

Finally she slid her hands into his jeans, freeing him, humming with pleasure as she wrapped her fingers around the biggest erection he'd ever had. He tried to reach for her but she shook her head. "I'm doing all the work, remember?" She stroked him. Perfectly.

And then again.

At this rate, he'd last all of two seconds. Not wanting that to be the case, he captured her hands in one of his and held them at the small of her back.

Lifting her head, she looked at him from hot, hungry eyes. Flattering as hell, and he began to think maybe she didn't even have to touch him to get him off.

"Cooper." Frustrated, she rocked her hips, gliding that satin over his erection.

He saw stars.

"Mmm," she said, arms still trapped behind her, and rocked again.

And then again, her breasts jiggling so pretty and enticingly in his face, the little diamond in her belly button twinkling.

And again.

Her satin was wet now, causing the most delicious friction against him, and desperate, he squeezed her hip, trying to hold her still. "Don't," he said. Begged. "God, don't move."

"I can't help it." And she very purposely rocked again.

Abruptly he pushed her off him and stood up, shoving down his jeans.

She staggered back and stared at his body.

Staring right back, he kicked free of the denim.

And then she lost the last of the lingering doubt in her eyes and smiled at him, a real smile that he felt all the way to his heart.

Had she really believed he'd reject her? Was she really that unsure of her own appeal?

She was still looking at him. From head to toe, and back again, then zeroing in on the part of him the most happy to be having this special little sleepover.

"You're . . . big," she whispered.

Not that big, but hell, he wasn't going to argue the point. "Hold that thought," he said, and went to the little goodie basket, which amongst other things, had condoms. On the way back to the chair, he grabbed the vibrator she'd left on the bed, shooting her a grin that changed hers from anticipatory to . . . nervous.

He decided he liked that. He liked that a lot.

Twenty-one

*If everything seems to be going well, you have obviously
overlooked something.*
                              —Breanne Mooreland's journal entry

Breanne stared at the glowing vibrator in Cooper's hand, so
innocuous-looking—until he twisted the end and it buzzed
to life.

The sound of humming filled the air, making her body
hum as well. "Um . . ."

"Come here, Breanne."

Her feet stood rooted to the spot. He wasn't touching her,
nothing was, but her nipples were hard, and between her legs
she throbbed.

Then she lifted her gaze to Cooper's, and at the long,
slow, hot-eyed look he shot her, she swallowed hard.

He set the basket of condoms on the floor beside the chair
and sat, crooking his finger at her.

She went, and when she got close, he pulled her down on
his hips, his hands urging her thighs wide over his so that she
straddled him.

"Mmm," rumbled from his chest at the skin-to-skin contact. Holding her legs sprawled open, he leaned forward, put
his mouth on her throat, kissing his way over to her shoulder,
from which he took a little bite. She jumped when he brought
his other hand up, trailing the vibrator along first one inner
thigh, then the other.

And then between.

She felt the jolt clear to her toes, and put her hand over his.

He lifted his gaze. "Too unromantic?"

Unromantic was exactly what she wanted here, to keep her heart out of the mix. "No. It's just that—" She felt herself blush.

"You've never used one of these before?" he guessed.

"Only for a flashlight," she admitted, sucking in a breath when the vibrator slid even higher, rumbling lightly, tingling her flesh, making her pulse leap with both excitement and trepidation.

"Ready?" he murmured.

"Um—" She broke off with a gasp when he sucked a nipple into his warm mouth at the exact moment he hit ground zero with the vibrator.

Her body tightened, strained, and the sound that tore from her throat was not a *no, don't* but a definite *oh, please*. An on-the-edge *oh, please*, to boot.

Slowly he circled the tip around, dipping into her own wetness, spreading it, and then back to her happy spot, just skimming lightly over her sensitive flesh.

She jerked again, let out another of those shockingly needy whimpers, and arched up for more. Suddenly her skin felt too tight, her pulse beat in her ears so loudly she could hear nothing but the rush of her own blood, heading south, pooling between her legs.

Another slow, purposeful circle of the vibrator, combined with a hot, wet glide of his tongue over her other nipple, and she was actually going to come without straining for it. In less than thirty seconds. "Cooper—"

"You taste amazing." Lifting his head a fraction, he stared down at her breast and lightly blew out a breath. "Do you know that?"

Luckily he didn't seem to require an answer, leaving her free to moan again.

And at the sound, he eased back, and she had to bite her lip rather than beg for more.

He was watching her. He knew exactly what she wanted, damn him. "Hurry," she managed, knowing she sounded too desperate, too impatient. She didn't care. She arched toward him.

His answer was another maddeningly slow circle of the vibrator, and just as she nearly tossed herself over the chasm into a glorious orgasm, he pulled back again, brought it to his mouth and licked the tip. "Amazing," he repeated huskily.

Staring at him, something within her snapped. Grabbing the vibrator, she tossed it aside, wrapped her fingers around his erection, sighing her pleasure at finding him both so silky and steely, and rubbed the very tip of him against her.

In. She needed him in.

"God, Bree." His fingers dug into her hips as he held her off, his expression tight. "Wait," he ground out.

No. No waiting. He was thick, even just the head of him—all she could get at the moment—stretched her. It felt glorious. She rocked her hips, wanting more.

He caved with a softly uttered "fuck," and thrust into her, making her gasp with pleasure.

"The bed," he ground out. "I want to—"

"Here. Now." Fast and hard. Just two bodies straining toward the same thing. No minds, and especially no hearts, no souls. She rocked again, running her hands down his damp chest. His body was tense and quivering, every muscle straining. "Please, now."

"Condom, then," he grated out, sweat breaking out on his brow as he struggled to remain still. "Get it."

Reaching down into the basket, she pulled out the first one her fingers touched. "Very berry," she read on the purple-colored prophylactic. "Grape flavored." She looked at him. "Yum."

This ripped a rough, laughing groan from his throat as he took it from her fingers, tore it open, and stroked it down his length. He stroked a thumb over her throbbing flesh. "I wish you'd let me—"

"No, let *me*." And she guided him home.

"Slow," he said tightly, jaw bunched, his gaze never leaving hers.

"There's no *slow* tonight." She needed the oblivion, needed him to be the one to give it to her, and she sank down on him, almost melting at the feel of him gliding all the way home.

His quiet "Oh, yeah" mingled with hers. She would have moved on him, *had* to move on him, but his fingers dug into her hips, holding her. "Just for a second," he whispered, stroking a strand of hair from her eyes, looking at her so intensely, so sweetly, so incredibly deeply, she felt her throat tighten.

"No," she whispered, shaking her head. No *sweetly*. No *deeply*. No tenderness at all. Closing her eyes, she took his mouth in a kiss, entwining her hands with his so that she could lift up until he almost slipped out of her, then sinking back down. "Like this," she said, and as if she finally broke his reins, he swore lavishly and took over, arching up thrust for thrust, hips pistoning wildly as he took her. Hard. Fast.

She cried out, but he swallowed the sound with his mouth, one hand on her bottom, guiding her down as he arched up, his other hand in her hair, holding her head for his possessing, fierce kiss.

Hot.

Wild.

Out of control as they gasped for breath, damp flesh slapping against damp flesh, fingers digging into trembling muscles . . . and then straining toward that finish line she'd wanted, where a turbulent whirlpool of colliding sensations waited.

Breanne got there first; she felt it building, felt it sweep over her, an unstoppable freight train homeward bound. Through a kaleidoscope of lights going off in her head, she heard Cooper let out a low, guttural groan as he found his own release. Still trembling, she fell over his hot, damp chest, snuggling in when he wrapped his arms around her tight.

"Jesus," he breathed softly in her hair, his arms still trembling. After a long moment he sagged back and looked at her from beneath those sexy, heavy-lidded eyes.

Okay, no big deal, she thought. Sure, she'd broken her no-men rule, but she'd managed to keep her heart and soul safe and tucked in. But she hadn't accomplished that by meeting his see-all eyes and letting him warm her from the inside out. "Well." She smiled with forced cheer and didn't look at him. "That was fun." She tried to get up, but he held on.

He was still inside her, not hard but not soft, either. Sinking his fingers into her hair, he forced her head back so that he could look at her. Suddenly his eyes weren't so sleepy. *"Fun?"*

She swallowed hard at the indescribable expression on his face. "Yeah, you know. As in, let's do it again sometime."

"Fun is eating ice cream. *Fun* is having a day off. *Fun* is a walk in the fucking park, Breanne."

"Um—"

"What we did was pretty far beyond fun. What we did was off the fun chart." He narrowed his eyes. "You wanted to know what was wrong with you?"

"Uh . . . no. I changed my mind." The tension he'd banished with an orgasm was back.

"Did you, now?" he murmured. "Interesting."

Around them the fire crackled, the house creaked, all assuring her that this was real, not some sort of fantasy dream. It was real and she had a man, still buried inside her, staring into her eyes, seeing things she wasn't ready for him to see, trying to get to the bottom of something she didn't want to discuss.

So she cheated. She tightened her thighs, as well as her inner muscles, and hugged him.

Immediately his eyes went opaque. Almost helplessly, he thrust up with his hips. "No fair," he whispered.

Which is why she did it again.

This time he closed his eyes and groaned. "Let me guess. You want some more *fun*."

"Good guess," she murmured, and leaned in for a kiss, squeaking in surprise when instead he surged to his feet, still holding her wrapped around him. With a hand on her butt, the other still fisted in her hair at her back, he headed toward the bed. "You're not going to rush me this time," he warned her, and before she could say otherwise, he let go of her.

She fell through the air and hit the mattress, bouncing twice.

She rolled to her belly to crawl away, just as a new condom landed right in front of her nose.

Lemon yellow. In spite of herself, her entire body tightened in anticipation.

"But first," he said silkily, holding her down with a hand low on her spine. "Back to that critique of your performance."

"No, I—"

"I'm not sure what you've been told before," he went on, unconcerned with the fact that she'd gone stiff and unhappy. "So we'll start at the beginning."

No way was she going to stick around for this. Surging up to her hands and knees to crawl away, she said through her teeth, "I told you, I changed my mind—"

Snagging her ankle, he held on with a grip she couldn't shake off, though she tried with the sudden strength of a samurai warrior.

He merely caught her other ankle and slowly dragged her back across the mattress, with her fighting the whole way. Kicking didn't help; he had a hold on her that didn't allow for it, though she gave it her best.

"Oh, go ahead and play dirty," he said conversationally, not even winded, the bastard. "I'm used to fighting dirty."

Gripping onto the covers gave her no traction at all as she was hauled closer and closer to her greatest source of stress. "Damn it, Cooper. Let me go—"

He simply yanked her the last few inches, then flipped her over, switching his grip from her ankles to her thighs, effortlessly holding her down, leaning over her to see directly into her face.

If he laughed, she swore to herself, she was going to kick his balls into next week.

He wasn't laughing.

Instead, he was looking down at her with a softened expression of tenderness that froze her limbs and sucked the breath out of her lungs, making her throat so damn tight she couldn't even swallow.

"Breanne," he said very gently.

"Don't." Somehow she managed to swallow the ball of emotion lodged in her throat, though it burned like fire. "*Don't*." Though it was silly, she tossed an arm up over her eyes.

He simply reached up and pulled it away from her face, that much closer now, kissing first one cheek, then the other. Then her jaw, nuzzling the spot just beneath. "You are the sexiest, most amazing woman I've ever met," he said. "There is nothing wrong with you, nothing at all, except . . ."

She kept her eyes tightly closed. "Except . . . ?"

"Except that I missed a few spots the first time. I need to make sure I've thoroughly researched each area before giving you my full opinion."

She heard the rip of the condom packet and opened her eyes.

"Look at you," he murmured, staring down at her. "So sexy, so amazing. We're going to make love again, Bree, just so I can prove it to you. And then again, if need be. No task is too much for the cause—"

"Cooper—"

"Right here, babe." He slipped into her body, fitting like he'd been made just for her. "Feel me?"

Was he kidding? With his hands cupping her face, his body buried within hers, she could feel nothing *but* him. "I feel you." Closing her eyes, she escaped a little bit that way, a desperate attempt to bring this back to the purely physical act. And what a physical act it was.

Decimated from their lovemaking, Cooper watched Breanne sleep. A new experience. With Annie, he'd always gone home afterwards, to his own bed. With any others, he'd always run off before the condom even cooled.

Never in his life had he felt like *sleeping* with someone, as in actually closing his eyes and drifting off. Sleep was a personal thing, something one did alone.

Like jacking off.

But he didn't feel like sleeping by himself. Truthfully, he didn't feel like sleeping at all. He just wanted to hold her and look at her. Christ, he'd turned into such a sap.

Breanne hadn't gone easily into slumber. She'd tossed and turned until he'd hauled her back against him, her spine and butt snug to his chest and crotch—a very nice position because it left him a free hand to caress. Now he pressed his face into the crook of her neck to inhale her intoxicating scent, and rubbed his thumb over her nipple.

In sleep she reacted, the tip hardening.

He wanted to wake her up.

But he knew how exhausted she was, mostly from stress, so instead, he kissed her shoulder and listened to her breathe, with no idea what he was doing, because this sure didn't feel like a quick little ski bunny sort of thing.

It didn't feel like a quick little anything.

He wondered if it was still snowing, if they'd indeed be able to shovel out tomorrow and get into town. Then there was the matter of the dead body.

Even as he thought it, from far, far below, somewhere in the house, came a very soft thud.

Cooper's hackles rose. It was past midnight. Past the hour that Shelly would be making noise in the kitchen, or Dante would be doing whatever it was he did.

Maybe it was Lariana and Patrick with their habit of screwing in every room of the house. He didn't know, but there would be no relaxing now until he made sure. He slipped out of the bed.

Breanne rolled to her belly, spread-eagle, hogging all the space and the blankets, which made him grin. "Be right back," he whispered, but she didn't move.

He slipped into his Levi's, stuck his gun in the waistband, grabbed the flashlight he'd commandeered, and headed out.

The hallway was pitch black. He flicked on the flashlight, which didn't help much, but he knew his way by now. The noise had come from somewhere downstairs; he knew this, though as he searched, he found nothing in the great room, the kitchen, or the dining room.

Nothing anywhere.

He was halfway back to his bed and Breanne when he remembered.

Edward.

Swearing, he whipped around, making his way to the servants' quarters. The doors there were all shut, and silent. So was the cellar door. But the strand of his own hair he'd carefully draped across the jamb had fallen.

Someone had been in here.

Alert, he let himself in, shining the light down the stairs. "Hello?"

No one answered, but then again he hadn't expected anyone to advertise the fact that they'd gone against his command to stay out of there.

Edward was beginning to smell bad.

Bending down, Cooper tried not to inhale as he looked over the body. Because of the cellar's icy temps, decomposition had begun slowly, but it had begun. "Your bruises are surfacing," he murmured, especially the long, dark bruise now accompanying the gash on the forehead. There was another bruise just below the Adam's apple. Cooper knew if he unbuttoned Edward's shirt, he'd see another across his chest.

The lines of the stairs, where he'd hit them face-first.

"Were you pushed?" he wondered out loud. "Or was it a terrible accident?"

And who'd moved him from the bottom of the stairs to his current spot?

And how had he gotten the hole in his damn chest?

Questions he really had no right to ask, but the cop in him just wouldn't let it rest. With a sigh, he rose, looking around.

There was no clue as to who'd come in here, or why, but at least the body didn't appear to have been moved.

He thought of Breanne asleep in the honeymoon suite, trusting him to keep her safe. He wasn't exactly sure when it had happened, but he trusted her, too.

Almost as unnerving as the dead body at his feet. "Hang tight, Edward," he said, and made his way back upstairs, to the warm woman waiting there for him.

Okay, so she wasn't waiting so much as snoring lightly into his pillow.

But he'd take that.

He'd take her.

She let out a soft "Mmm" when he slipped back into the

bed, sleepily moving into his arms. "Cooper?" she whispered groggily.

Who the hell did she *think* it was? "Yeah," he said, tucking her beneath him, making himself at home between her thighs. "Me."

And then he set out to show her . . .

Twenty-two

Life is like a boner: long and hard.
> —Breanne Mooreland's journal entry

The next morning—Cooper's second in the middle of his so-called vacation—was a mixed blessing for him. He'd slept all night with an incredibly hot, sexy woman, and nothing beat that.

But unfortunately, it was still dumping snow. And by dumping, he meant huge, fat snowman-sized flakes that accumulated in a blink of an eye. Not a good day for going outside, but it was a great day for being in bed with that hot, sexy woman. They had a whole basket of condoms left, in some extremely inventive colors and flavors.

But he was alone in the bed.

Damn bad luck for him.

He rolled off the mattress and stepped on an empty, lime-green condom packet.

And then a wily watermelon one.

Yeah, he thought with a grin . . . last night had been something. To his delight, Breanne had turned out to be a sensual, earthy, passionate lover. He couldn't believe she'd doubted herself. Kissing, licking, touching every single one of those doubts away had been his pleasure.

There'd be no more nights, though. Today they'd shovel out, then ride a snowmobile for help.

And go their separate ways, just as she wished.

Telling himself he was good with that, he hit the shower, then made his way down the stairs, noting there was still no electricity.

Dante appeared out of nowhere, dressed in black, over-sized jeans and a football jersey, hat low on his head. "If you're hungry," he said, "Shelly's put together what she can for breakfast."

"Still no generator?"

Dante lifted a shoulder. "Patrick's on it."

"He's been on it a long time."

"To tell you the truth, Patrick's not all that great at his job."

Gee, Cooper thought, there's a news flash. "Then why does the owner keep him?"

"The owner doesn't know. Patrick was hired by Edward."

"And Edward never noticed that Patrick the fix-it guy isn't any good at fixing stuff?"

Dante lifted his shoulder again.

"Come on, Dante. By all accounts, Edward was a tough boss. Why would he keep Patrick on here?"

"Edward's sister made him hire Patrick," Dante admitted.

"Why?"

"Because she's Patrick's mom."

Yesterday, when a very dead Edward had been discovered, Patrick had had little reaction. *No* reaction, actually.

And yet Edward had been Patrick's *uncle?* An uncle who'd given him a livelihood? "How does Patrick feel about his uncle's death?"

"Why don't you ask him?"

"Did Edward give Patrick as hard a time as he did the women?"

"Yes."

"Sounds like the guy had some management issues."

Dante let out a hard laugh.

"And maybe some social issues."

"If you mean he was an asshole, you're dead-on." Dante's gaze never wavered. "No pun intended."

"We need to get him out of here," Cooper said. "You knew that. We need to get through to town."

"The generator—"

"Forget the generator. I saw the snowmobiles. If we all put in some effort, we can dig out. Two of us can ride until we get reception, or into town to report Edward's death."

Dante just looked at him.

"It has to be reported sooner or later," Cooper said.

"That's not what I'm hesitating over," Dante said.

"Then what?"

"The shoveling-out part."

"How hard can it be?"

Dante shook his head. "Spoken like someone who's never had to spend hours digging out his car. That snow is some heavy shit, man."

"Don't you have a snowblower?"

"Sure. But Patrick was a bonehead and left it under the eaves of the shed, which has unloaded about two tons of snow onto it since the storm began. That should take all day alone to shovel out—if it's not crushed, that is."

"You're exaggerating."

"You think so?" Dante's smile was grim. "I'll be happy to prove a cop wrong."

Cooper sighed. "I don't know what your beef is with cops, but—"

"Just go eat," Dante said. "Then we'll start."

"We'll get Patrick to help, too."

Dante nodded. "Sure. But just so you know, he's not much better at shoveling than he is at fixing stuff."

"Great." Cooper started to walk away, then turned back. "Hey, did you stay up late last night?"

Dante's expression closed. "Why?"

"I heard something, around midnight. Just wondering if you heard it, too."

Dante slowly shook his head. "Didn't hear a thing." With that, he turned and vanished.

Cooper stood there watching, thinking . . . *but I never told you what I heard*.

The lack of electricity wasn't nearly as disconcerting in the light of day—even though that light of day was so muted as to be nearly inconsequential. Cooper passed the foyer and stopped short. A huge mountain of snow stood in front of the open door.

Then the mountain began to move, turning into the outline of a man as he shook the snow off like a great big dog.

Powdery white flakes flew through the foyer, landing on every surface, including Cooper. That wasn't what sucked the air from Cooper's lungs, though; the shocking wind whipping through the open door did that.

"Bloody hell." Patrick looked around at the mess he'd just made. "Lariana will be killing me for this." Undeterred by the prospect, he stomped his feet, and more snow fell off him. He wore some sort of head-to-toe snowsuit, which still had snow stuck to every inch, his ever-present tool belt rattling as he stomped. "Sticky shit," he said conversationally in his Scottish brogue.

Cooper shivered. It had to be close to zero degrees. "Any luck with anything out there?"

Patrick shook his shaggy head regretfully as he shut the door, closing out the unbelievably bitter cold. "The generator is a no-go. The thing needs to be replaced. We actually have one on order but this storm came early. Didn't expect to be needing it so soon." With a rather absent smile, he walked past Cooper.

"Patrick?"

Lifting a hand to remove his beanie, which left his red hair standing up on end, the fix-it guy glanced back.

"Did you hear anything odd last night around midnight?"

"Not a thing, mate. But this place is haunted."

"Haunted?"

"By Edward's ghost." He said this utterly without a flicker of emotion one way or the other.

"I'm sorry about Edward, Patrick."

"Don't be."

"He was your uncle."

"He was a sorry excuse for a man." Then he turned on his heel and clinked off.

Cooper walked to the doorway and thunked his head on the wall.

"Is that like snapping your heels together three times and saying 'There's no place like home, there's no place like home?'"

Cooper lifted his head. Shelly stood there, watching him with a curious smile. Wearing whitewashed jeans rolled up to the top of her Ugg boots and a forest-green sweater with a small apron over the top of it, she looked like a melodious, euphoric little thing.

"There are whole days where I feel like bashing my head against a wall, too," she confided, and reached up to give him a little pat on the shoulder. "But not on an empty stomach."

"You look happy."

"I like it when there's guests here."

How about when there's a dead body? "I hope we're going to dig out today. You up for lending a hand?"

"Sure." She pushed up her sweater and flexed her arms. "I work out. You don't think it's easy lifting huge pots full of stew or chili, do you? I'm a snow-shoveling machine."

He felt her biceps and found rock-hard strength. "You *are* pretty solid."

Solid enough to have moved a dead body?

"Come into the dining room and get some food," she said.

Having burned every spare calorie worshipping Breanne's body all night long, his belly twitched hopefully.

"Oh! Breanne said to give you this." Shelly reached into

her apron and pulled out a small piece of paper, folded in some complicated way that took him a minute to open. *Meet me in the theater room. B.*

"A love note?" Shelly asked.

He stuck the paper in his pocket. "Not quite. Where's the theater room?"

"Down the hall, right past the library, then left." She looked up into his face, suddenly serious. "She's a real sweetheart—you know that, right? Because she's been hurt, being stood up at the altar like that, I don't want to see anything else happen to her, especially out here where she feels alone and so vulnerable."

"Nothing's going to happen to her."

"You slept with her last night." She cringed. "I know, none of my business. Just . . . just be good to her."

And with that demand, she left him alone.

Cooper sighed—good thing so many people were worried about *him*—and left to find the theater room. Turns out he couldn't miss it with the two rows of luxurious red velvet seating, the huge screen, and last but definitely not least, the elaborate system on the right that rivaled any theater he'd ever been to.

But the room, however swank and sophisticated, was empty.

"Breanne?" His tennis shoes sank into the plush carpeting as he came to a halt just in front of a large sliding door on his right. The door slid open and a hand shot out, fisting on the front of his shirt, yanking him inside.

He smelled her just as the door slid shut again, that sexy combination of shampoo and woman, and because it was Breanne, he let her accost him. "All you had to do was ask," he murmured, lowering his mouth as he slid his arms around her.

"Mmm," she said at the kiss, and then again as she touched her tongue to his.

Oh, yeah. Now *this* was the way to start a day. Pressing

her back against something—he couldn't see a damn thing—he dove into the kiss as a few things fell down over the top of them. Probably DVDs. He didn't know, didn't care, as long as he had this woman and her body against his.

After they were both breathless, she pulled back, and at a small click, light surrounded them from the small lantern she'd turned on. They were in a closet, surrounded by shelves filled with DVDs, videos, and various electronic games. On the floor littered around their feet were the movies they'd knocked down.

And in front of him, gorgeously disheveled, stood Breanne, her mouth still wet from his.

She stared at his mouth as well, looking more than a little . . . flummoxed.

He knew the feeling, as he was currently bowled over himself, with the wanting of her; a wanting he was coming slowly to realize couldn't be sated by lust or even common sense.

She wore her own jeans today, and that pink, fuzzy sweater he'd first seen her in. It crisscrossed over her breasts and had a tie just beneath them. He itched to yank on it and unravel her.

"You came to me," she said, as if surprised.

He'd have thought they'd gotten past that, but if she needed reassurance, he could give it to her. His hands went to her hips and he brought her back against him, lowering his head, nuzzling her throat. "Soon as I got the note. I was hoping we'd still be in bed, but you vanished on me."

When he touched his tongue to her skin, she shivered, but put her hands to his shoulders and pushed back to look into his eyes. "Really?"

"Yeah, really." Leaning back in, he took a little bite out of her tasty skin, loving the way she trembled. "We could be having a great time right this very minute. Naked."

Her hands tightened on his shoulders, her fingers digging into him as his mouth cruised over her. "Is that . . . right?"

"Mmm-hmm." Letting out a slow exhale in her ear, he smiled when she shivered again. "I could be tasting you from head to toe. I'd start here—" He took a little nip out of her shoulder.

"That sounds . . . nice," she said, sounding as if she was having trouble getting air into her lungs.

"Nice?" He let out a choking laugh. "Trust me, it would have been a helluva lot better than *nice*."

She looked so intrigued he wrapped a finger around the pink angora tie beneath her breasts and tugged.

But she put her finger on the bow, preventing it from slipping out of its knot. "That's the only thing holding the sweater on."

"Is it?" He tugged again.

She held onto the bow. "Want to know a secret?"

"If it involves being naked."

"I've always had this closet fantasy . . ." She whispered this softly, as if she found the suggestion almost too naughty to bear.

But nothing was too naughty for Cooper, and though he'd been hard since she first yanked him in here, his jeans got even tighter.

"But if you'd rather go back to the bedroom—"

"No, let's stay in your fantasy." Taking her hands, he brought them down to her sides, urging them to grasp onto the shelf at her hips.

Both excitement and nervousness filled her eyes, but she held the shelf and let him pull on the string of her sweater until it popped free.

The sweater sagged in front where it was crisscrossed. A little nudge with his finger and it fell open, exposing a siren-red lace number that shot him from zero to sixty in one second flat.

"It's my other honeymoon number," she said softly. "It was my only fresh underwear."

He realized it was a one-piece, and the thought of following the lace all the way down between her legs made his mouth go dry. "It's amazing," he managed to say, tracing the edging between her breasts, watching her nipples react, poking through the material.

Letting go of the shelf, she slipped her hands beneath his shirt and laid them on his belly, making him suck in a harsh breath.

"What?"

"Cold hands," he whispered, tugging her sweater to her elbows.

With a breathless huff of laughter, she danced those cold fingers up his chest, then back down. "I love your body," she said, as if imparting another state secret. Her sweater was at her elbows, one narrow strap of her red lace off a creamy shoulder. "Especially your stomach." She stroked his abs. "Do you like to be touched like this?"

"More than breathing."

Again she laughed; then, holding his shirt up, she flicked her tongue over his nipple, making him thunk his head back against a rack of VHS tapes.

Stopping the exquisite torture, she glanced at him, then slowly sank to her knees.

His heart jerked hard. So did the rest of him, one part in particular.

"I, um, was wondering," she whispered as she set her mouth to his quivering abs. She kissed his belly button, then lower, at the edge of his jeans. "If you'd like it if I kissed the rest of you."

He undid his jeans so fast his head spun. "Kiss away," he said hoarsely.

At the first feel of her lips in the opened wedge of his jeans, he jerked again.

"Shh," she murmured with a seductive, knowing smile, enjoying finally being the one to shush *him*. Her hands fisted in the waistband of the denim. Slowly she pulled.

He moaned, and she smiled against his skin; then, in a

move that made him yelp with surprise, she sank her teeth into his hip.

His reaction made her lose it. "I'm sorry," she gasped, sitting back on her heels, covering her mouth. "I don't know why, but I had to do that. I couldn't help myself." She went to lean forward again, leading with her mouth, but he stopped her.

"You got that biting thing out of your system, right?" he asked warily.

Her eyes were lit with humor and heat. An amazingly sexy combination. "Promise." Her hands brushed his away, then slid back into his jeans.

"You liked this," she murmured, stroking the length of him.

"It's pretty much a given I'm going to like anything you do to me."

"Sure?" She stroked him again, letting out a sexy little hum while doing it. Then she licked her lips.

Oh, man. He had to close his eyes. "So damn sure— *Jesus*."

She'd taken her hot, wet tongue on a happy tour. Gripping the shelves behind him for dear life, he did his best not to humiliate himself, but her mouth . . . Unable to keep standing, he sank to his knees and reached for her jeans.

In the charged air was the sound of their heavy breathing and the rasp of her zipper. They stared at each other as he pulled the denim down.

A pink condom fell out of her pocket.

"I'm resourceful," she whispered.

"I *love* resourceful women," he whispered back, tugging her legs out from beneath her so he could strip her jeans to her thighs. Reaching between them, he toyed with the snaps of her teddy while she sucked in a breath. With one pull, all three snaps came free.

"Now," she whispered.

"Yeah, now." But her jeans caught on her boots. They

spent another breathless moment fighting their clothes, laughing like idiots, and finally, finally, she was in his lap facing him, her thighs opened and draped over his.

By the time she helped him roll on the condom, he was trembling and already on the edge. "Slow," he said, hands to her hips, lifting her up, guiding himself inside her.

"Fast," she corrected, then let out a gorgeous sound of helpless desire when he thrust up.

"Yes," she said fiercely, rocking her hips.

He'd wanted to take his time with her, draw it out, lose the both of them in the moment, but she didn't let that happen—she *never* let that happen. She wanted the kick and she wanted it now.

And buried so deeply within her that he could feel her heart beating in his ears, or maybe that was his own, he was in no position to slow them down. In a last desperate move, he gripped her oscillating hips. "Keep that up, and it's going to be over before we even get started."

"We started already. God, Cooper, I love to watch you lose it."

Just the words nearly accomplished that, and he tried to adjust his slippery grip on her hips. But she kept moving them, arching, rocking. Sweat beaded on his forehead. "Bree—"

"More," she panted. "God, please. More."

Ah, hell, he was a goner. All he could do was hold on and meet her thrust for thrust, closing his eyes to savor her clutching heat, quivering as he fought the orgasm building like a bus barreling down the highway. But he couldn't keep his eyes closed; he wanted to see her. Her head had fallen back, her skin gleaming. "Breanne."

Lifting her head, she opened her eyes, too, adding an unexpected intimacy Cooper hadn't expected. It hit him like a one-two punch. Her gaze was clear and open, allowing him to see more of her than she'd ever allowed him. *Trusting*.

His throat tightened. "Bree—God. I'm going to—"

"I know—" Her voice was tight. Strangled. "Me, too—"

That was all she managed to get out as she exploded in a series of shudders that milked his own climax out of him. Vaguely he heard her cry out his name, and thought . . . *love the sound of that*, before the roaring of his own blood in his ears overtook all rational brain activity.

When it was over, they slumped together, breathing like misused racehorses. Breanne stirred, lifted her head from his shoulder. Her hair had rioted, sticking to her damp face, but her victorious smile said it all. "That was very . . . *nice*," she said mischievously, using the word he'd objected to. "Yes, *nice* just about covers it."

In answer, he lightly slapped her on the bare ass, making her laugh and hug him so tight he could hardly breathe.

But breathing was overrated, anyway, and he hugged her back. "Let's get the hell out of here and back into that suite so I can start all over again and do it right."

"No can do." She stood on wobbly legs. "We have to dig out."

Oh, yeah. They were getting out today. Going their separate ways, which she wanted.

He wanted that, too.

He just couldn't remember why.

Twenty-three

You have the right to remain silent. Anything you say
can and will be misquoted and used against you.
                    —Breanne Mooreland's journal entry

Breanne stood up in the theater closet, and, much to Cooper's consternation, began to look around for her clothes. "I really didn't write that note just so we could . . . Well." She laughed a little as she bent over at the waist to snap her teddy back into place.

Cooper's body twitched. Down, boy.

She shrugged the straps of her teddy back on her shoulders, then reached for the sweater. "You sidetracked me."

Watching her toss back her hair, he thought about sidetracking her again. And again. "Who sidetracked who?"

She smiled but it didn't quite meet her eyes, and then she turned away entirely to work on her jeans.

Uh-oh. Taking her arm, he pulled her back around to face him. "What's wrong?"

She shimmied her jeans up her hips. "You mean besides my life being a shambles? Besides being stranded here, hearing mysterious humming that no one else does, and oh, yeah . . . finding a dead body?"

"Yeah." He tucked a loose strand of hair behind her ears. "Besides all that."

She stared at him for a long moment, her eyes dark and unreadable. "Nothing."

He nodded, started to let it, and her, go, because really, what did it matter? But it *did* matter. At least to him, he was discovering, and he pulled her around again. "Did you know you wrinkle your nose when you lie?"

"Do not."

He touched the tip of her wrinkling nose. "Do so."

She clapped her hand over her nose and made a disparaging sound. "You can't know that about me—you don't know me."

Contemplating her, he pulled up his own jeans. "I might not know every little thing yet, but I'm getting a pretty good start."

"No," she said with a denying shake of her head, her eyes unhappy. "You aren't. You can't be. Don't be."

"Too late. Want to hear what I know already?"

"No—"

"You tend to jump into things heart first—"

"I'm changing that."

"You're sweet when you're tipsy—"

"I wasn't *that* tipsy that first night—"

"I know that you hate the dark and spiders, that you have a thing for incredibly sexy lingerie—"

"Circumstantial."

He curled his hand around the back of her neck, stroking his thumb over the soft, sweet spot of her nape. "I know that you're intelligent, funny, and incredibly passionate. You care about others, sometimes too much, and you care about me. None of that is circumstantial."

"It's too early to care."

"Yeah? Then why did you come to me last night?"

"I was scared."

"I didn't see you crawling into bed with Dante, Patrick, Lariana, or Shelly."

In a telltale gesture, she looked away. "So I care too early. Another fault."

"I think you also trust me, at least a little."

"*Trust* is a bad word, Cooper."

"Doesn't have to be."

"Maybe you missed some of my background," she said. "Three failed engagements, remember?"

"I can't help but remember. You wield them around like a shield."

"*Three* engagements," she repeated. "That's a helluva lot of wielding. A lot of failures."

Which was what was getting to her, he guessed. "You didn't have your heart in at least two of those engagements, Bree. I think you *wanted* to, you *meant* to, but you didn't, not really." He kept his hands on her hips when she would have turned away. "I know that first one messed with your head, but not every serious relationship ends in pain. I promise you."

She let out a soft breath. "I don't know."

"But I do. Getting engaged was a way to make a great showing. You could hide behind it, holding back all you want, especially with the particular men you picked."

"I don't follow you."

Yes, you do. "You picked men who weren't going to love you, not the way you want to be loved."

She stared up at him.

He stroked her silky hair. "Am I close?"

"No." But she swallowed hard. "*No.*"

"I'm different, Bree. What we could have is different."

"It's a chemical attraction. Period."

It was so much more than that, but she was standing there, arms tight around herself, breathing a little ragged, her poor bruised heart in her eyes, and he found he couldn't tell her. It was something she had to see herself.

Unfortunately for him, she wouldn't see it, because willing as she was to share her body, she wasn't willing to share much else. She shied away from true intimacy, and apparently that bothered him more than he would have thought possible.

"I'm still trying to wrap my mind around the fact that this

was supposed to be my honeymoon," she said, closing her eyes. "I didn't count on meeting you, Cooper."

"Yeah, well, you weren't on my calendar, either. But I'm glad it happened."

This brought a ghost of a smile to her lips. "I wanted to talk to you about Edward."

He sighed. From lovers to spies.

"They were all afraid of him."

"I know."

"I think he was rough."

"Physically?" he asked.

"I don't know, but he yelled at them. A lot."

"Even Dante and Patrick?"

"Patrick, yes," she said. "Lariana said he totally demeaned him at every turn, and he only put up with it because—"

"Because they're related."

"Yes." She sounded surprised. "How did you know?"

"Dante told me that much. What else?"

"Patrick has trouble keeping jobs. He's sweet and kind, but not all that great at what he does. Apparently he really wants to be an artist, but he needs the money from this job. He's a painter. That's how he and Lariana got together—she bought one of his paintings as a gift for her father. Shelly said that Patrick was late for work the morning before we got here because he'd been up all night painting, and he and Edward had a terrible fight about it."

"A physical fight?"

"I don't know."

"Did Shelly tell you what Edward yelled at her for that morning?" Cooper asked.

"No. That she didn't mention."

"I can picture Edward yelling at the women," Cooper said. "Possibly even Patrick. But Dante?"

"Supposedly none of them escaped the wrath."

He shook his head. "The problem is, I just can't see Dante standing for it, job or no job."

"And you know what else I can't see," Breanne said slowly, "is Dante standing idly by while Edward treated either of those women badly."

"Me, either."

She tipped her head up to his. "So what does all this mean?"

It meant that there were too many motives, and too many suspects. It meant there were going to be lots and lots of questions once the authorities got here. It meant unpleasant times ahead for all of them. Exhausted at the thought, he leaned back against the door and sighed. "We need to round everyone up and start digging."

"It's still snowing."

"I know, but we should do it now, while we have lots of daylight hours left. I don't know how long it'll take to reach town."

"You really think someone can get that far on the snow-mobile without a problem?"

"I'm counting on it," he said grimly.

"Yeah." She let her arms fall to her sides and stepped close. Reaching up, she touched his face, her fingers warm now. Her touch was so unexpected and sweet, he closed his eyes to savor it.

"I'm glad we happened, too," she whispered, making him open his eyes again in surprise.

For her, it was equal to a shouted declaration of her feelings, and he felt his chest tighten, more so when she set her head against his shoulder and let him hold her.

"There's two snowmobiles," she said. "Who's going?"

"Hopefully, Dante and me. I think he'd be more capable than Patrick if we got stuck out there."

She slowly fisted her fingers in his shirt, staring at them as she said, "I dreamed about you."

"Yeah?" His hands squeezed her hips. "Tell me."

"I was running through the dark hallways here. Something was chasing me." She frowned. "Or someone."

"You should have woken me up."

"You had me wrapped up in your arms tight and snug, and I knew I was safe."

"You are safe."

She'd been watching her fingers move in little circles on his chest, but now she lifted her gaze to his, and he could see her uncertainty, her fear. "Once you leave on that snowmobile, no one left here is safe."

"Bree." He sank his fingers into her hair, leaning in, but just as his mouth touched hers, the doors slid open.

Lariana stood there with a DVD in hand, staring at them.

"Whoops," she said, and handed them the case. "Just found this and wanted to put it back. Uh . . . carry on." With a smile, she slid the door shut again.

Breanne winced. She knew the staff was probably used to such indiscretions, but she sure wasn't. "Well, that was . . . awkward."

Cooper just lifted an *oh, well* shoulder. His shirt was wrinkled, from her. His hair stood up on end. Also from her. And he was wearing one of those after-sex expressions that there was no hiding. He looked thoroughly debauched, and so rough-and-tumble sexy that she wanted him all over again.

Oh God, she wanted him all over again.

But that had to stop. Sex was sex, and they'd just had it. The end. But wow, he was potent. And something else . . . with Cooper, it never felt like just sex.

At her nod, he slid open the door, and together they stepped out.

"I'm starving," she admitted. "I need something before digging."

He followed her down the maze of hallways to the kitchen. At least she was no longer getting lost. She figured if she didn't get lost, she couldn't find another dead body.

In the kitchen, she beelined directly to the refrigerator.

Cooper grabbed a glass from a cupboard and moved to the sink for water. Hands wet, he looked around for a towel, then finally opened the door beneath the sink. "You need to drink, too," he said. "Before you get dehydrated—"

When he broke off so suddenly, Breanne turned from the drawers to look at him.

He was hunkered before the open cupboard, mouth tight, body tense. Absolutely still.

"Cooper?"

Turning only his head, he looked at her from eyes that were no longer lit with sexual prowess or good humor, but flat with concentration.

A cop's eyes.

"What is it?" she whispered.

"Beneath the bathroom sink in the foyer there's a brand new pair of rubber gloves, still in their packaging. I saw them yesterday when Lariana was in there cleaning. Can you go get them for me?"

She was so startled by the odd request, not to mention his cool, calm but utterly badass expression, she simply nodded and turned on her heels to do just that.

She encountered no one in the hallway on the way there or back, and when she re-entered the kitchen, Cooper was no longer by the sink.

"Here," he said from behind her, startling her into a gasp as she whirled to face him, a hand to her chest as he took the gloves from her. "What—"

His finger went to her lips. Then he pulled a chair in front of the double doors, so no one could come in on them unannounced.

She could only stare into his extremely tense face. "What's going on?"

He looked at her for a long moment, and she knew she wasn't going to like it. "Cooper, you're scaring me."

"Not as much as this is going to." He put an arm around her shoulders and walked her toward the kitchen sink. "Take a deep breath, but don't scream. Promise me you're not going to scream."

"Okay." She gulped in a deep breath, then crouched down with him and looked beneath the sink. At the towel shoved behind the pile, covered in something dried a brownish color. They both stared at it for the longest moment of Breanne's life.

"Fuck," Cooper finally said on a sigh.

Yeah. Her thoughts exactly.

Twenty-four

I suppose the word "calm" would lose its meaning if it wasn't sandwiched between moments of terror.
                              —Breanne Mooreland's journal entry

"Gee, that's funny," Breanne heard herself say. "It almost looks like a bloody towel."

Cooper didn't say a word, just began to put on the rubber gloves.

"Shelly probably cut herself chopping vegetables," she said through the roaring in her ears. "You should see how fast she chops. And then she probably shoved the towel down there and forgot about it. Probably."

Cooper flicked on his flashlight and stuck his head in the cupboard, carefully not touching the towel but trying to see around it.

"Or it could be ketchup," she said inanely, her mouth running away with her thoughts. "Maybe she spilled ketchup. That could have happened, right?"

Cooper pulled his head back out of the cupboard and looked at her. "Are you breathing? Because you don't look like you're breathing."

"Oh." She gulped in a few breaths and tried a smile, which quickly wobbled. "That's not ketchup, is it?"

Cooper slowly shook his head.

"Something really bad happened here."

"Something," he agreed. He turned off the flashlight and

shut the cupboard door. Then he removed the rubber gloves and reached for her hand.

"What are we going to do?" she whispered.

"Shovel. Shovel like hell."

They'd found the towel.

That was bad. They shouldn't have found the towel.

What would happen now?

If only it would stop snowing. If only they could all get out, get away from here.

If only, if only, if only . . .

For Breanne, getting outside felt like a culture shock, not to mention an actual physical punch to the chest. Her poor lungs weren't adapted to the altitude, much less this biting cold.

At least inside the house, though sometimes equally icy, she'd been in somewhat of a cocoon. There she could see the snow, but had been distanced from it by the huge, frosted windows, buffered by the warm fires.

But standing on the front porch, the ramifications of their situation, with the storm still dumping more precipitation every passing minute, hit her hard. Twelve feet of snow had fallen, setting records, shutting down airports and businesses, closing roads, breaking electrical and phone lines.

The Sierra mountain range, spanning some two million acres of national forests and wilderness land, had come to a screeching halt.

Terrific time to almost honeymoon.

Way out on the outskirts of civilization as they were, this unbelievable storm was apparently accepted as a part of the life here. People were prepared for it with extra food, water, and gasoline for their generators and snowblowers. They'd become an independent entity.

Everything had taken on a whole new meaning these past few days, and it wouldn't have been a problem but for two things. One, the occupants of *this* particular house weren't as prepared as they should have been, and two—and this was the biggie, in Breanne's opinion—*there was a dead body*.

Dead bodies changed everything.

No longer did the house feel cute and quaint—if it ever had. And getting out of here, storm of the century or not, had become a requirement. She stood wrapped in a borrowed stadium-length down coat, a leftover from some forgotten guest. She also had on one of Dante's beanies, and wool socks courtesy of Patrick.

Ever so helpful, her staff.

Huddled in her borrowed gear, she let out a breath that crystallized in front of her face as she took in the scene.

White as far as the eye could see.

And more white.

From here, the humongous mountain peaks that surrounded them in a three-hundred-and-sixty-degree vista looked innocuous and breathtaking. The flakes fell with an odd gentleness, and utterly silently, stacking on top of the banks of snow that had already fallen, piling up against the house, against the shed, against the garage, so that the three-story log-cabin house appeared to be only a little more than one.

Thanks to the lack of electricity, the house itself was dark. No sparkling lights shining from the windows, no scent of cooking food, nothing but a rather disconcerting hollowness that made it seem lifeless. There was four feet of snow on the roofs despite the fact that they'd unloaded themselves at least twice, leaving huge drifts stacked alongside of each structure, some more than eight feet high, making it impossible to get close to the shed or the garage until they moved the snow.

There were two power lines along the driveway, coated in white and sagging nearly to the ground. The trees were completely covered, and swaying from the weight as if alive.

Four of the pines in the front yard had split or collapsed under the tremendous weight of the snow, and would undoubtedly have to be removed. The windows on the north side of the shed had shattered inward.

And still the snow came.

They all shoveled. Or rather, Dante, Patrick, and Cooper shoveled, while Breanne, Shelly, and Lariana watched. Mostly because there were only three shovels, but also because it was damn hard work, and Breanne for one wasn't very good at hard work.

"Look at that sky," Shelly breathed.

Lariana and Breanne both looked up. In San Francisco, Breanne had rarely ever noticed the horizon. In fact, the last time she'd looked up at all had been on one of her first dates with Dean, when he'd taken her to the roof of his building to show her the summer constellations.

What he'd really wanted to do was impress her, and then get into her pants. Damn it, she *had* been impressed, but she hadn't let him into her pants.

Not that night, anyway.

The point was, though, she wasn't an anal person, or rushed for time on a daily basis, and still, she'd never really spent much time sky-gazing.

Leaning back now, she staggered back a step, found her balance, and stood there in awe as the flakes fell onto her face, cool to her heated skin. It was like an explosion in a mattress factory the way the white flakes, not round, not any particular shape, really, drifted down from the sky like fluffy pieces of cotton in no particular hurry.

Cotton that sure piled up into not-so-innocent drifts that needed to be moved.

By them.

"It's making my mascara run," Lariana said. "I'm going in."

Watching the guys work, Shelly nodded. "Me, too, but wow, look at 'em. They're all . . ."

"Hot," Lariana agreed. "Very, very hot. But even the hottest of the hotties is not worth freezing to death. Let's go."

Breanne stayed behind. The cold temperature speared right through her but the guys were sweating. Dante wore a black sweatshirt nearly coated over in snow now. Patrick wore his Abominable Snowman outfit. He wasn't as effective a shoveler as Dante, taking smaller shovelfuls and half the time dumping the contents in his own way, swearing with gleeful abandon as he did.

Cooper moved with a steady, easy precision that made it look extremely easy. He wore the blue sweatshirt he'd given Breanne that first night, now also crusted over with snow, but he didn't appear to notice as he labored. Breanne felt entranced watching him, mesmerized by the way his body worked as if poetry in motion. He was like that in bed, too. She figured he was like that in everything he set his mind to, and for a moment, her mind wandered.

What would it be like to see him outside of here, in the real world? Before the answer could come to her, Shelly came back out with bottles of water for the guys.

Breanne looked at the shovel Cooper leaned against a post. Feeling extremely aware of his gaze as he drank, she lifted the shovel. Wow. All by itself, the thing was heavy. But he was watching her, so she dug in, filling the bucket, then attempting to lift it.

It didn't budge.

Okay, no problem. She tipped half of the snow off. That worked.

By the third shovelful, she was panting. By the fourth, she couldn't lift it one more time.

A big hand closed over hers. She raised her gaze to Cooper's. "I'll get it," he said.

She could see the exhaustion in his face. "I'm sorry," she murmured. "I wish you didn't have to do this."

"You feel bad?"

"Very."

That seemed to perk him up. "Enough to make it up to me?"

She had to laugh at the teasing light in his eyes, but as he turned back to work, her smile faded. Because she found she *did* want to make it up to him. She wanted to do that, and more.

A lot more.

Breanne went inside to get more bottles of water. Shelly would have gone but Breanne insisted, needing a moment alone. In the kitchen, she set the tray on the counter and loaded more water bottles onto it. As she did, her eyes strayed to the cupboard beneath the sink.

Was the towel still there?

Heart in her throat, she nudged the door open with her toe. Yep, bloody towel still in place.

Her stomach lurched sickly, and she considered staggering weakly back to a chair but heard something behind her.

She spun around fast enough to get dizzy but realized the sound had come from beneath her.

Beneath her.

Whirling back, she peeked out the kitchen window. Dante, Patrick, Cooper, and Lariana were there. Shelly, too.

Everyone was outside.

Every single person.

At least every single *alive* person.

Oh God, don't go there. This wasn't the movies. There had to be a perfectly good explanation for that noise, and she was going to find out what. Yes, she was. She grabbed a flashlight, and on second thought, another knife from the butcher block.

Just in case.

Just in case what, she had no idea.

The hallway to the servants' quarters was going to give her nightmares for the rest of her natural-born days. Halfway down it, her heart was pounding so hard and fast she couldn't have heard a tornado ripping through over the sound of her own pulse drumming in her ears. She actually had to stop and breathe for a moment to be able to hear at all.

Nothing but silence greeted her, and then . . . a faint thud.

It'd come from behind the one locked bedroom door, naturally. Forget evening out her pulse now—the best she could do was gulp in a breath. She knocked once. "Hello?"

Nothing, though she imagined she heard panicky breathing. On *both* sides of the door. "Anyone in there?" She knocked again and told herself she was fine. Nothing could happen to her; she held a butcher's knife, for God's sake.

No one answered. Of course not, because the only one down here was Edward, and his answering days were long over. Turning, she peeked into the room where Lariana had been sleeping. Neat and tidy as a pin.

The bedroom next to it—Dante's, she could tell by the beanie on the foot of the bed—wasn't nearly as neat. He hadn't made his bed, and he had yesterday's clothes on the floor.

But from under the bed peeked out a hand.

Oh God.

In some kind of trance, her feet took her inside the room, and then to the mattress, knowing if she found another body she was going to truly start screaming and never stop. Cringing, she bent down, then let out a short, rough breath as she realized the truth.

Not a hand, but a glove. A rubber kitchen glove stained with the same dark brown stuff that was on the towel upstairs beneath the sink. Desperately she wanted to believe what she'd told Cooper, that she was looking at dried ketchup, but she knew better, and had to shove a fist against her mouth.

And then she heard the one sound she hadn't wanted to hear. *Footsteps.* Wildly, she looked around her. No time to get out; oh God, no time to do anything but flatten herself to the floor and scoot beneath the bed, which she managed just as someone came into the room.

Two black boots and two white Keds. *Two* someones.

"We only have a few minutes," Dante said, sounding out of breath. "The cop is determined to get out of here."

"I know. I'm sorry." *Shelly.* "Dante, I lied to you."

Breanne, already frozen in place beneath the bed, stiffened in shock. *No, Shelly.*

"Tell me." Dante's voice was low and gruff, and yet infinitely gentle. "It's okay, just tell me."

"Oh no, it's not what you think!" Shelly rushed to say. "I meant I lied just now, upstairs, about having to talk to you. Because really what I wanted was . . ."

"You wanted what?"

The two Keds shifted until they were toe-to-toe with the black boots. Breanne didn't dare move but the gloves, the bloody gloves, were too close. *They were really beginning to get to her.*

"It's all so complicated," Shelly whispered.

Yeah, yeah, it's complicated, Breanne thought, trying not to look at the gloves right at her cheek. *Get back to shoveling!*

Then the unmistakable sound of a wet kiss floated down and Breanne scrunched up her eyes. Surely they weren't going to—*No.* Not here, not now—

"I know you said you wanted to wait until we got out of here," Shelly said breathlessly. "But everyone's outside and will be for a while. Haven't we waited long enough?"

"Shelly—" Dante broke off with a low groan. "God, Shelly, don't do that."

Helluva time for Shelly to find her sexuality, thought Breanne.

The mattress sank as the two lovebirds fell upon it, and Breanne wished for a large hole to open up and swallow her.

"Oh, Dante," Shelly whispered.

Dante whispered something back in his native tongue.

Breanne resisted thunking her head on the ground. She

made the mistake of opening her eyes then, focusing in on the bloody gloves before slamming her eyes shut again and doing the only thing she could—stick her fingers in her ears and silently sing at the top of her lungs. *Lalalalalalalala*.

"Oh!" Shelly cried out louder than Breanne's silent singing. "Oh, Dante."

Something fell to the floor. Shelly's sweater.

Her jeans came next.

Breanne shifted from singing to pretending she was on a beach. In the Bahamas. It was hot there, and cute cabana boys were bringing her drinks. Nice, big *alcoholic* drinks—

Something else hit the floor. Dante's shoes.

Then his jeans and sweatshirt. And his beanie.

Then his BVDs.

And finally, an empty condom packet.

Oh, good God.

The springs began to squeak as the mattress began moving in earnest.

"Dante—" Shelly cried. "That's—do that again. Please do that again!"

Squeak, squeak, squeak.

Breanne tried not to look at the bloody gloves. Instead she studied her fingernails. Oh, look at that. She needed a manicure.

"Yes, yes, *YES*!" cried Shelly.

Breanne decided she was going to need a vacation to recover from her vacation.

Scratch that.

She was never going to vacation again.

Finally the bed stopped moving, and there were more kissy-face noises and soft murmurs.

Breanne had long ago left the Bahamas and moved to the moon when four feet—bare now—hit the floor.

It took forever for them to dress—laughing and kissing—but finally, finally, they were gone. Breanne didn't know what she'd have done if they'd stuck around for round two. One time had been bad enough—*what was it with this house?*

She eyed the gloves. She needed Cooper to see them, needed anyone other than her to see them. Touching evidence was bad, she knew this. But . . . what if someone moved them before she could show Cooper? Not wanting to take that chance, she slipped them beneath her top, then cringed—*gross!*—before sliding out from beneath the bed. She got to her feet, carefully not looking at the mattress. Sheesh. Tossing back her hair, she turned to the door.

And came face-to-face with Dante, who barely arched a brow—his only concession to his surprise at finding her here.

"I, um . . ." She hugged herself, hopefully hiding the bulge of the gloves beneath her shirt. "This is really a very funny story."

He leaned back against the doorway, blocking her way out, waiting for her to go on.

Oh boy. He had that scary face on, the one that assured her much of the ghetto still lived within him. "I heard a noise down here, and I thought it was Shelly—"

At that, he smiled all the way to his eyes. "You just missed her. She's back upstairs."

Oh, my God, was it possible he hadn't seen her coming out from beneath his bed? "Oh. Okay, well, then I'll just—"

Go tell Cooper you had bloody gloves beneath your bed.

"Sorry," he said, still smiling. "I'm just realizing something."

"What's that?" she asked bravely. *Please don't say you're wanting to kill me, too. Please—*

"—I'm in love with her." He sighed and shook his head, rubbing the spot over his heart. "Imagine that."

Yeah, imagine that. "Well, that's . . . sweet. But I've got to—" She gestured to the doorway and, miracle of all miracles, he didn't kill her, but moved aside for her.

With a last smile that was shaky to the core, Breanne scooted past him. It took every ounce of control she had not to run, run like hell, but she controlled herself until she was out of sight. Then she couldn't hold back any longer and she burst into a full gait, looking back over her shoulder—

Only to plow directly into someone.

Before she could open her lips to scream, a hand settled over her mouth and she was yanked into a dark room and held against a hard, warm body.

Twenty-five

The right lover is like a good bra: supportive, close to the heart, and damned hard to find.
                                    —Breanne Mooreland's journal entry

Cooper held a struggling Breanne against him. "Hey. Hey, it's me," he said in her ear as she fought him like a wildcat. "Breanne, it's me."

"Oh, my God." Snaking her arms around his neck, she burrowed in close, as if she wanted to climb inside him.

He stroked his hands up and down her back, trying to soothe her. "What happened?"

When she didn't answer, he reached into his back pocket and grabbed the flashlight, running it over her to make sure she wasn't hurt.

"I'm okay." But she gulped in air like water, clearly making an effort to get hold of herself. Pale, still shaking, she looked around them, saw they were in the workout room, and said, "I'm really tired of this house."

He had a feeling that was a huge understatement.

"I want noise," she said. "Airplanes. People yelling. I want a traffic jam on the bridge, *anything* but this quiet mountain, you know? Anything but more spiders and bloody gloves, and—"

"Bloody gloves?" Cupping her face, shocked at how icy cold she was, he looked into her still-glossy eyes. "What bloody gloves?"

"These." She reached under her shirt and pulled out a pair of cotton garden gloves, light blue with white trim, and stained with what could have been blood.

She shivered wildly and thrust them at him. "I can't believe I had those against my skin. *God.* I need a shower." She pulled her shirt away from her chest. "Now."

Gingerly holding the gloves by just his thumb and forefinger so as not to further contaminate them, he snagged her arm when she moved to the door. "Where did you get these?"

"I heard a noise that I thought came from the cellar, but you guys were all outside, so I—"

"Damn it, Breanne. Don't tell me you went to investigate."

"I, um . . ." She winced. "Took a knife with me."

He groaned.

"But I left it under Dante's bed because—"

"Dante's bed?"

"Yeah, I was stuck there while he and Shelly were bouncing it so hard I thought I was going to be squished like a pancake, and—"

"Whoa. Wait." He shook his head. "Start at the beginning."

"I can't." She was pulling at her sweater. "I need to scrub first." Shoving free, she ran out of the workout room and into the hallway, moving with remarkable speed through the house, up the stairs, as if she wanted to lose him.

Not going to happen.

At the honeymoon suite, she stepped inside, then tried to close the door behind her, nearly catching his nose in it.

"Maybe I wasn't clear," she said, her breath hitching. "I'm showering. By myself."

She hadn't gotten her color back, nor her breath. Her eyes sheened with emotion and much more. If he wasn't mistaken, she was an inch from losing it completely. "Thought you might like some company," he said.

"In the shower? Gee, what a shock."

"Breanne."

"So you don't want to see me wet and naked?"

"Well, yes, but that's because you look great wet and naked. Right now, however, I just want to make sure you're okay."

She hadn't taken her gaze off the evidence in his hands so he shut the suite doors, hit the lock, then very carefully set down the gloves.

She stared at them and then shivered again.

"Go shower," he said gently. "I'll wait in here."

She nodded, then covered her mouth with a hand. "I think I'm going to throw up. I really, really don't want you to see me do that."

"You're not going to be sick." But just in case, he slid an arm around her waist and nudged her toward the bathroom. There, he leaned her against the counter. "Keep breathing."

"I'm trying."

"Good." He opened the shower, flicking on the hot water; when he turned back to her, she was still concentrating on breathing. "Okay?" he asked.

"I'm peachy. Really. Just peachy."

Steam was rising from the shower, fogging the mirror and glass. "Come on, get in."

Nodding, her hands went to her sweater. She pulled on the tassel, let the material slip off her shoulders. She unzipped her jeans and shimmied out of them, doing a little dance on first one foot, then the other as she stripped down to her birthday suit.

A personal favorite of his, but he didn't say a word, just opened the shower for her.

She stepped to the door. One of her breasts brushed the sleeve of his shirt, the nipple puckering into a hard knot. "Get in," he said again, his voice a little thicker.

Nodding, she stepped in; then, before he could shut the

door, she fisted her hand in his shirt, yanking him in with her. "I don't want to be alone," she said. "Distract me, Cooper, like only you can."

Water rained down over his head, soaking into his clothes, dropping off his nose. "Breanne, I—"

His words were cut off by her mouth. Pressing him up against the wall, she tugged his shirt up, leaning in to kiss him right over his heart. "Please?"

She wanted fast, hard, casual sex. She wanted to disengage her brain, if only for a few minutes. He got that.

But he wanted more than mindless when it came to the two of them. And yet, as always when faced with her gorgeous nude body, he couldn't hold back. He shucked out of his shirt while she tugged his jeans to his thighs. "Good enough," she said, and hopped up.

He just managed to catch her, all slippery and wet, and when she wrapped her legs around his hips, arching the hottest, slickest part of her to the hottest, neediest part of him, he staggered back against the wall and groaned. "I don't have a condom in here."

She bit his neck. "Are you safe?"

He had two handfuls of her perfect bottom, her breasts mashed against his chest. He had a hard-on that could pound nails, snugged up to her sex, which was hot and creamy. His mind was befuddled, to say the least. "Huh?"

"Because I'm safe." She attached her mouth to his neck and sucked, making his vision swim. "And I'm on the pill."

"Me, too," he managed to say as she arched up and let the very tip of him slip inside. Christ, she felt good. "I mean, I'm not on the pill," he corrected as she snorted. "But I'm safe—"

Her rough, breathless laugh was cut off with a low moan as he thrust into her.

Bare skin to glorious bare skin, Breanne thought, and for her, what happened next was as wild and unpredictable as the storm outside. She felt a blinding need, a desperate ache that had to be assuaged. There was more, too; it was as if she had a hole deep inside her that only he could fill, but she didn't want to go there, not now. Later, when she was safe and back home, she could dwell; later she could relive all that had happened, even what she'd lost, but for now she'd live in the moment.

And the moment was about this. She fisted her hands in Cooper's hair and took his mouth in greedy, hungry bites, while the hot water continued to rain down over them. "Hurry, hurry, hurry."

"Always a five alarm fire with you," he murmured.

"*Please*," she heard herself whimper.

"We can hurry," he assured her. "But I'm not going anywhere." He cupped her face until her eyes met his. "Do you hear me? I'm not going anywhere, Bree. I'm here, right here."

Her throat closed up, and she couldn't speak.

He didn't seem to mind. Instead, he held her still, buried deep within her, and gave her a kiss as gentle, as tender as any kiss she'd ever known, a kiss that brought her to a new level of desire that boggled her mind.

And still he hadn't moved within her. God, she wanted him to move. She slid her fingers into his hair, along his scalp until his head fell back. Pressing her mouth to his throat, she tried to make sense of this but then he lifted his head again, his eyes glowing with heat and need and an infinite, selfless patience she was afraid she'd never understand.

"Breanne," he said—just that, just her name through the falling water. With a strength that seemed effortless, he turned them, pressing her back to the wall, opening her thighs even further. "Hold on," he murmured hoarsely in her ear. "Hold onto me. Yeah, like that." And he began a series of bone-melting strokes—slow, lengthy withdrawals and returns that she wanted to last forever and ever. But she had her limits, and Cooper was one of them. Within a few moments she began to fall apart at the seams.

He thrust a little higher, a little harder, his hands keeping her right where he wanted her. Pinned, she could do nothing but hold on for dear life, panting, blinking away the water, the steam. Nothing about any of this with him made any sense, not the depth of her wanting of him, or how it was that she hadn't gotten enough of him.

That maybe she never would.

But she didn't want it to stop.

"Christ, I can feel you," he groaned, able to talk while she could only pant. "It's like you're milking me. You're going to come."

And with a surprised cry, she did.

While she was still shuddering, she somehow managed to keep her eyes open on his, and saw his face darken, his jaw go tight enough to tic, watched his eyes go blind, even as he struggled to keep them open on hers.

He was showing her everything, every single emotion as it hit him, as he came with a gravelly groan torn from deep in his throat. This is trust, she realized as he trembled. *Naked trust.* Just the thought triggered another orgasm within her, and through the kaleidoscope of sensations, she thought maybe he murmured her name, but she was drowning in the pleasure and couldn't be sure.

Slowly she came back to herself, blinking away the water, realizing that he'd slapped a hand on the wall behind them, quivering as he struggled to keep them upright. Still clinging to him, she suddenly felt oddly close to tears. Not wanting him to see, she tried to pull free.

With what seemed like great reluctance, he let her legs slide down his body. "You okay?"

Chest tight, she only nodded. She was so far beyond okay.

He smiled, but looked a little shaky himself. "That was . . ." Words seemed to fail him.

She turned away to get a grip on her reckless emotions. "Yeah. Good shower sex." She grimaced at her own coarse choice of words. Grabbing a towel, she tossed it to him, hitting him in the face.

He pulled it down. "So . . . do you get a lot of shower sex?"

"No," she admitted. "You?"

"Yeah, but usually I'm alone."

She laughed. Damn, he was something, always able to pull her out of a funk. "You expect me to believe that a guy who looks like you, and has a sexy job like you do, has to have sex alone in the shower?"

"I'm not exactly a chick magnet. And as for that so-called 'sexy job'? You know I nearly let it suck the soul right out of me. I think with some distance I've got it figured out, but the truth is, my love life's a barren wasteland. Or was, until I met you."

She shook her head. "I'm just trying to picture a healthy, red-blooded, innately sensual guy like yourself going for a long time without sex."

"Yeah, well. I'm hoping the dry spell is behind me."

That clammed her up because she wasn't sure how to respond. The thought of jumping into another relationship made her stomach clench. She wasn't going to let herself fall for this man, but having to remind herself felt a bit like putting the lock on the chicken hatch after the chickens had escaped.

Fact was, she'd leapt feet first into many relationships, and none of them, not a single one, had made her feel like she felt with Cooper—like she was on a roller-coaster ride going too fast, like she was going to throw up, like . . . like she was alive—really, truly, vibrantly, thrillingly alive.

Oh boy.

He hadn't done anything with the towel she'd tossed him. Completely comfortable in his own skin, he stood there naked. Actually, he wasn't just standing there, he was coming toward her, then stroking a long, wet strand of hair behind her ear. "You're looking pretty relaxed."

"Funny how an orgasm does that."

"Yeah." He didn't look nearly as relaxed. "Funny."

Don't ask, she told herself. Don't. But this was Cooper, and for some reason, she couldn't turn away. "What's the matter?"

"That rejuvenated you, having wild shower sex."

"It would have rejuvenated anyone."

"Really? So why do I feel more frustrated now than before?"

Not wanting to face the answer to that, she shrugged and began to dry off.

But he waited her out, standing in the doorway when she would have breezed on out. "Why did you cry at the end?"

Her gaze whipped up to his. "I didn't."

"You did."

Embarrassed, she looked away. "I don't know."

"Is it because you're not used to feeling as much as you did?"

Hammer on the nail. "It's just that . . ." Oh, the hell with it. "I really liked it," she admitted in a whisper.

"I know." This was accompanied by a grin. "I was there."

She stared at his chest, trying to find the right words. "I want to say something that's going to sound weird." Lifting her head, she met his gaze. "You're nice to me."

"You're easy to be nice to."

He always knew what to say.

"I came here to clear my head." Lifting a shoulder, he shot her a crooked smile. "I thought maybe I'd meet a few snow bunnies, have a great time."

"I can put on a ski hat if that would please you."

"Only if that's all you put on."

She snorted at that, and got a fleeting smile from him.

"I thought being here," he said, "that I'd feel better about walking away from my work. My life."

Her flippancy vanished in the face of his quiet pain. "Oh, Cooper."

"I thought I'd go home with the answers in my head of what I want to do with myself."

"Do you have them?" she asked. "The answers?"

"Not a one that you'd want to hear."

Her heart skipped a beat, and she went very still. "What does that mean?"

He sighed, ran his hands through his wet hair. The muscles and tendons stood out in bold relief with his arms lifted, and her belly quivered. When she was around him, everything within her quivered.

She wanted him. Still. *Again*.

"Remember when we talked about love?" he asked. "You said you didn't believe in it."

"I remember," she said tightly.

"Well, I do. I believe in it, Breanne. I want it."

Oh, God.

"All the time I thought it was my job screwing with my head. And in some ways, it was." He came close again. "But I can move out of vice and not have to go under for months at a time. I can work regular shifts patrolling, or even going the detective route, and still have a life. I want a life, Breanne. And in that life, I want—"

"Don't," she said, setting her fingers to his lips. "Don't say it."

"You."

"Oh, my God."

He just looked at her.

Her throat tightened, her eyes burned. And her heart, God, her heart. It took one big tumble. "It's only been a day."

Reaching up, he pulled her fingers from his mouth, keeping her hand in his. "It's been three, and those were pretty accelerated, intense days."

"But it takes years to get to know someone," she said, sounding desperate.

"I'm game."

She stared at him. *He was game.* "I wrote 'no more men' in my journal. You saw it. It's in stone."

"There's always *Delete*."

If only she could really erase some of her mistakes. "It's my path."

"Rewrite the path." He smiled. "That's the beauty of electronics."

She swallowed hard. "You sure seem to have a lot of answers."

"You do, too."

She rubbed her temples and wished that were true. "I'm hungry. *Starving*."

"No, you're scared and you have to think," he said. But then he stepped back and finally began to dry off that mouthwatering body. "It's okay. You go eat. You go do what you have to do."

Yeah, she would. Like a chicken, she took her out and moved to the door. There she glanced back. "Probably in the real world we'd have nothing in common."

"Date me and find out."

"Date?" After what they'd done, dating seemed so . . . tame. "Men say they want to be with me," she said softly. "But they lie."

"I don't. You know that by now."

She shook her head. "Cooper. I don't know what to do with you."

A small smile touched his lips. "Yeah, you do. You just haven't faced it yet."

Keep him. That's what her heart wanted to do. Take this thing where it might go.

But her brain was saying—*are you kidding? Run like hell.*

Since she'd decided never to trust her heart again, she went with her brain, and ran like hell.

Twenty-six

*If a man is talking in the woods, and there is no
woman there to hear him, is he still wrong?*
                                    —Breanne Mooreland's journal entry

Breanne stepped out of the suite, then turned back and stared
at the door. She let out a slow breath. Cooper turned her upside down and inside out, and when she was with him she didn't
know whether she was coming or going.

Mostly coming, she admitted.

Her legs wobbled at the thought. They'd had some damn
amazing sex. She'd never been with anyone who could take
her right out of herself and then put her back, making her
feel like a new woman, a *better* one. When she was with
him, she didn't have self-doubts. She didn't wonder what he
thought of her. She didn't do anything but be herself.

And he seemed to like that woman. A heady experience.

At the bottom of the stairs, Dante appeared right out of
the woodwork, and still dizzy with thoughts of Cooper, she
nearly fell over. "How do you do that?" she demanded.

A ghost of a smile touched his lips. "I'd tell you, but then
I'd have to kill you."

He was just kidding. Probably.

"Bad joke," he said.

"Really bad." She put a hand to her chest, wondering if the
butler had a side career going—murdering obnoxious managers and equally obnoxious guests.

Shelly came up behind Dante and smiled. "Hey. You okay?"

Breanne nodded at her new friend. And Shelly *had* become a friend. She wouldn't fall for a man who could—who would—

No. No, she wouldn't.

But how to explain the bloody gloves beneath Dante's bed? Or the bloody towel in Shelly's kitchen? "I just thought I'd try to get something to eat."

"No problem," Shelly said. "I'll bring you something to the great room? Or maybe the library? Where will you be?"

Breanne didn't feel comfortable going anywhere alone—she was afraid of what else she'd find. Before she could work up a good panic over that thought, Cooper came down the stairs and stood at her side, settling a big, warm hand on the small of her spine.

Such a small gesture, really, and yet . . . yet it meant so much.

"What's the snow situation?" Cooper asked Dante.

"We're about halfway. We could be out in a few more hours."

"Just in time for nightfall," Cooper said, sounding resigned.

Dante nodded.

"Could you find your way to town in the dark?" Cooper asked him.

"It'd be a suicide run. Frigid temps, bears . . ."

"Bears?" Breanne didn't like the sound of this. "I don't want anyone to be out there with the bears."

"And believe me, no one wants to be," Dante told her, the big, tough guy letting out a shiver.

"If we kept moving—" Cooper started.

"I'd rather walk the streets of my gang-infested childhood than snowmobile through the woods tonight."

Cooper sighed. "So we all stay another night."

"Another night," Dante agreed.

Shelly bit her lower lip, and Dante set his hand on her shoulder. "It's going to be okay," he said.

Cooper nodded.

Breanne only hoped they were right.

Everyone met in the great room and snacked on whatever Shelly was able to drum up. Stranded as they were, the lines between staff and guest and wrongly booked guest had blurred.

Or maybe that was because of the unintentional bonding that had occurred when they'd all found themselves staring at a dead body.

Breanne didn't know, but she liked having everyone in the same place, where she knew that no one was off getting . . . well, offed.

Despite the relaxation of duties, in some ways, their positions here in the house still very much defined them. Shelly rushed to serve everyone. Dante handled the fire. Lariana kept straightening things up in the already perfectly straightened room. Patrick didn't do much, but he kept his tool belt on and creaked when he walked.

"We really need a new generator," he said to no one in particular.

"Maybe it's operator error," Dante suggested.

"Bugger off."

Dante laughed. "Come on. We all know you hate being the fix-it guy. The wicked witch is dead, dude. Do something else now."

"Like . . . ?"

"Like what really gets you going," Dante said, as if this was the easiest thing in the world to decide. "How about your painting stuff?"

Patrick looked over at Lariana, who smiled. "Told ya," she said softly. "Do it, Patrick. Go for your dreams. Show your paintings."

"It was you," Cooper said to Patrick. "You painted that saw blade. The one that went up the day we found Edward."

"I hung it," Lariana said. "Patrick didn't want me to, but I think the guests that come here would love to see what he can do. Sunshine doesn't have any galleries because it's not a touristy type of place, but just a little bit south of here, closer to Lake Tahoe, there are tons of shops all around the lake where he could show his work. *Should* show it."

Patrick lifted a shoulder. "Maybe."

"You're good, Patrick," Shelly told him. "And your idea of painting on antique tools is unique. You really should go for it."

Patrick clinked his way to the fire, hunkering before it to jam the poker into the red-hot coals, stirring up the fire with a bit more strength than necessary.

"He's dead, Patrick," Lariana said to his ramrod-straight spine. "No more worrying."

"Worrying about what?" Cooper asked.

No one answered.

"Come on." Cooper looked at them. "You're going to hold back now?"

Shelly and Lariana gave each other a long look.

Patrick stabbed at the fire again, making sparks leap and jump.

Dante remained broodingly silent.

Cooper shook his head in disgust.

"You know what?" Shelly surged to her feet. "It's late. And I'm really tired." She didn't look at any of them as she moved to the door. " 'Night."

Lariana shot Dante a worried look, then started to follow, but Dante stopped her. "I'll go," he murmured.

Lariana nodded, then pulled him in for a hug. When he was gone, she said, "It *is* late, and we're all overtired. Patrick?"

Seeming surprised to be so publicly summoned, he jerked to his feet and moved to the door with her, looking for all the world like an eager puppy.

"Call if you need anything," Lariana said to Breanne and Cooper.

When it was just the two of them, Cooper looked at the empty doorway. "That was fun." He stood up and held out a hand to Breanne. "Come on. There's even more fun to be had."

Her heart stopped. Parts tingled. "What kind of fun?"

"Everyone's going to sleep. Everyone but us."

The thought of "us" made her stomach sort of tremble, but not in a bad way. Oh God, she was getting used to the word *us*.

When had *that* happened?

Everything had been so simple a week ago. Sure, she'd been in an engagement that had been just a joke, but she'd had no major losses. No big disappointment—Well, maybe a few.

But she could have lived with them, because she'd never seen a dead body, she'd never lived in a haunted house, she'd never feared for her very life.

Now she knew what all those things felt like, as well as true, gut-wrenching fear for another person she truly cared about. Maybe staying one more night wasn't the end of the world. She could use it to show him how much she cared.

"We're going searching for the BB gun," Cooper said.

"We are?"

His gaze swiveled to hers. "You sound disappointed. What did you think we were going to do?"

"Nothing."

He ran a finger over the groove in her forehead. "You are such a liar. You were thinking about getting naked and losing some brain cells."

"Losing brain cells?"

He reached for her hand, the gesture sweet and tender. "Every time I get you naked, I lose brain cells. Hell, you don't even have to be naked for that to happen." He pulled her in for a tight hug. "I want more of this, Bree. When we're out of here, I want more of you."

Now her heart, all warm and cushy—*and locked up tight*—quivered. "Cooper—"

"Don't panic." He stroked a hand down her back, then pulled free.

Thank God.

"Let's go exploring."

In the dark. Damn it, she didn't know which was worse, facing her feelings for Cooper, or exploring this dark, haunted house.

He pulled out a flashlight. "I noticed Patrick did some extra digging," he said as they entered the garage through the foyer door. The large, cavernous room was icy and eerily silent. "I want to know why." With that, he let go of her hand and moved away.

Breanne bit back her pathetic whimper, gasping when Cooper lifted the garage door manually, rolling it up a few feet. "What are you doing?"

"With no power, it's the only way to open it. Come here."

Into the dark night. Into the snow. "My boots are finally dry—"

He vanished beneath the door.

"Damn it," she muttered, and hurried to the door. Taking a deep breath, she ducked beneath it.

The darkness felt different outside; colder, deeper, all-consuming, with no walls as boundaries. Nothing but trees and mountains she couldn't even see. And bears. Let's not forget the bears.

Cooper had trudged past a buried vehicle—"Mine," he tossed back—and through the snow to another parked about fifteen feet away. A truck, she saw, when his light flickered over it.

He was peeking in the windows with the flashlight. "Bingo."

She eyed the still-falling snow and sighed, then stepped

out from beneath the protective edges of the eaves. They'd shoveled here, so she didn't sink much more than a few inches into the new stuff. Buoyed by that, she grinned at him as she came up to the car. "Made it."

He didn't smile back.

"What?" she asked, hers fading.

"Hold this." He handed her the flashlight. Then he pulled the sleeve over his hand before opening the door of the truck. "No fingerprints," he whispered. "Light the backseat for me."

She lifted the light and stepped closer, her boot heel catching on an icy patch. The next thing she knew, her feet slid out from beneath her and she was down, the flashlight bouncing twice before going out.

In the dark above her, Cooper sighed at the loss. "You okay? Anything broken?"

"Just my butt, and possibly my pride."

In the pitch darkness, a hand slipped beneath her elbow and lifted her up. Another hand slid over the butt in question. "Feels good to me. Your pride'll heal, too."

"But the flashlight won't."

"No." The disconcerting darkness reigned, and that eerie, utter silence of the woods all around them.

Except for the very distant call of a coyote.

Breanne shifted closer to Cooper, hating the weakness, but hating even more the thought of facing a wild animal out here.

"Did you see?" he asked quietly. "Before you slipped?"

"I saw," she said, and hugged herself. "I saw the BB gun in the backseat. Oh, my God, Cooper. This is insane. Bloody towels, bloody gloves. Edward's shoe . . . *What does it all mean?*"

"I don't know."

Blind as a bat and disoriented with it, she shivered. Cooper pulled her closer. "Come on," he said, and nudged her around toward the house. "Back inside."

"It's just as cold in there."

"I'll warm you up."

"It's also just as dark in there."

"I'll be your light."

She managed to find a laugh. "That was hopelessly corny."

"Yeah," he said in disgust. "I'm not that great at romance."

Breanne set her head on his capable, sturdy shoulder as he led her inside. "I think you're better at this than you think you are."

Breanne woke at the crack of dawn and opened one eye. She was sprawled facedown over most of the bed with all of the covers.

There was a big, warm hand on her butt.

Lifting her head, she turned and found Cooper on his side, head propped on his hand, watching her.

"Hey," she said.

"Hey, back." Leaning in, he kissed her. "Time to rise and shine, Princess. Today is the day we get the hell out of Dodge."

Sounded good.

And yet . . . She looked into his see-all blue eyes and pictured her life back home. Searching for a new job. A new place to live. Seeing her friends and family.

Would Cooper really be interested in that life? He'd said so.

Could she trust him enough to believe it?

"I can see the wheels spinning," he said. "Want to share?"

She looked at him, trying to find the words to express her fears, her worry, but none came. "It's nothing."

If he was disappointed, he didn't let it show. He just kissed her, then rolled out of bed and took his fantastic body into the bathroom.

Breanne stretched, rolling to her back, eyeing her Palm Pilot, which was on the nightstand. She reached for it, figuring she had a new entry to make, something along the lines of enjoying the moment because that moment was about to be over.

Only there was already an entry for today. It read: **Keep Cooper.**

Keep Cooper? "What does that mean?" she murmured out loud.

"Just that," Cooper said from the bathroom doorway, one hand propping up the jamb. "Or better yet . . ." He pushed away and came closer. Naked. "Take a chance on me."

"Cooper." Her heart lodged in her throat.

"Come on, Bree. I'm falling hard here. Fall with me."

Lodged in her throat and swelled. "It's not that simple."

"Why not?"

"Because I'm bad at it." She let out a low laugh, inviting him to laugh with her, but he didn't. He wasn't kidding. "You know my track record," she said. "I fail at these things, with a regularity you could take to a bookie and make millions."

"If you never try, you've failed before you've begun."

"I *have* tried."

"No, you went through the motions, but you've never really put yourself out there. Not like you did with me."

"Cooper." Words failed. She shook her head. "You scare me, you know that? All the way to the bone."

"You either want to see me outside of here, or you don't."

"This is about more than that, and you know it," she said. "We already know we're sexually compatible. Now you're asking me if it can be more."

"Why can't it?" he asked. "I like you. You like me. Let's take it where it goes."

"But how will we know if it's right? How will we ever know?"

With a shrug, he pulled on his jeans as if they were discussing the weather. "You just do."

"You're telling me *you* know?"

"Yeah. I do."

For some reason, that made her mad. She shoved back the covers and got out of bed. Stalked toward him. Poked a finger in his chest. "Well, maybe it's not that easy for me."

"Why not?"

His eyes were clear and full of things that took her breath. She knew he had a slow and easy smile, somehow both so sweet and sexy that she always felt like smiling back when he flashed it at her. She knew how he made her feel with just a look, which was so damn special she always felt as if she could take on the world.

"Why not?" he asked again, softly, giving her one of those looks now.

"When you look at me like that," she whispered, "I lose my place."

"So start at the beginning," he whispered back. "And tell me again why this can't work."

"Besides the fact that we're so different?"

"Yeah, besides that."

"Besides the fact that neither of us is currently employed?"

"Sounds to me like a great time for a change."

"Damn."

"Is that 'Damn, you're right'?" he asked. "Or 'Damn, he's lost his mind'?"

She just shook her head, frozen to the spot.

His smile congealed a bit but he slowly nodded. "I'll tell you what. I'm going to go start digging."

"What am I supposed to do?"

"I don't know. You could sit here and keep letting life pass you by."

"Hey, I don't let life pass me by! In fact, that's the problem. I jump at things without thinking them through."

No longer quite so calm, he shoved his arms into a T-shirt and pulled it on. Inside out. Swearing, he ripped it off and righted it. "You get a jump on ignoring this thing between us, Breanne." He grabbed a fleece sweatshirt. "Because I can't convince you that this would be a good decision, or that you're just afraid because deep down you know it's different, that what we have would be better than anything else you've ever done. That this is real and deep and yeah, scary as hell, but worth it. You go ahead and pretend you don't know any of that." His hair was sticking straight up as he jammed on his shoes. "And I'll get us out of here so you can rush back to that life you want so badly, where you can pretend you never met me, where you can pretend you didn't fall as hard and as fast as I did—"

"Cooper—"

"Don't." Whipping around, he pointed at her. "Don't even try to tell me I'm wrong."

She couldn't, she didn't have the breath, and when he'd left, quietly shutting the door behind him, she turned to the bed, looking at the rumpled sheets, remembering how much she'd shared with him right there in that spot. It'd only been a few nights, and yet she'd shared more with him than she had with any other man.

How had that happened?

And what did it mean?

Afraid she knew, she reached for her clothes. She'd just laced up her boots when she heard pounding feet. Going to the door, she opened it. Shelly was running toward the stairs. "Shelly?"

Shelly stopped. Turned back. Wearing a long, flowing, flowery skirt and a blue hoodie sweatshirt with the hood up, she smiled tentatively.

"What, you're taking fashion lessons from Dante now?" Breanne asked.

Shelly's smile went from anxious to nervous as she pulled the hood off her head. Her hair wasn't neatly pulled in its usual ponytail, but wild and uncombed. Probably from another Dante romp.

"So where's the fire?" Breanne asked her.

"Fire?" Shelly's eyes went wide. "Oh, my gosh, there's a fire? *Fire!*" she screamed, and then went running.

"No, I was just—Shelly, come back! It was just an expression, there's no—Damn it." Breanne took off after her, moving down the stairs.

Daylight streamed in all the windows. It was the first time since she'd been here that she'd seen the place in full light, and she was blown away by the difference. Everything seemed warm and cozy, gorgeously simple, not gloom and doom. Above, the sky was a squinting azure blue, so big and bright as it shined through the skylights it almost hurt to look. At the bottom of the stairs, she could see through the foyer windows. Everyone was outside. Patrick and Cooper were bent over one snowmobile, its hood up. Dante was over the other one. Beside him was Lariana and . . . Shelly. She wore dark jeans and her fluffy white sweater that went to her knees, her hair up in a perfect ponytail.

No skirt. No sweatshirt. No wild hair.

Breanne turned and stared down the hallway past the kitchen, where she could still hear footsteps running away from her. "Shelly?" Feeling almost disembodied from reality, Breanne took one more look outside, then turned and headed down the hall. "Hello?"

"No one's here!"

That was Shelly's voice. Breanne would have sworn it, but Shelly was outside, she'd just seen her there. With goose bumps raised over every inch of her body, Breanne came to the kitchen.

Empty. "Hello?" she called out, half afraid to get an answer.

"I told you, no one's here! Don't you listen?"

The voice hadn't come from the kitchen. Breanne moved out of there, past the dining room, which was also empty. "Where are you?"

"Go away!"

The voice came from the back, the hallway with the servants' rooms. It was darker here, but not as dark as it had been on previous visits. Uneasily, Breanne stared at the door to the cellar straight ahead, beyond which lay Edward's body. Then she turned and eyed the other four doors, all closed.

She could feel someone behind one of them. "Who are you?"

"I'm not telling," came the soft whisper. "I'm not supposed to tell."

Twenty-seven

Everybody wants to go to heaven, but nobody wants to die.

—Breanne Mooreland's journal entry

Breanne stood there in the middle of the servants' quarters, both confused and terrified. "Shelly?"

"You like Shelly. You're her friend."

The voice came from the left. Breanne took a step toward the two doors there. "Yes, I'm Shelly's friend. Who are you?"

"You're nice. You'll understand."

Door closest to the cellar door. The one that had been locked all this time. "Understand what?"

"What happened."

Breanne froze with her hand outstretched for the handle. "With Edward?"

Silence.

"Who are you?" Breanne asked.

More silence.

"Can't you tell me who you are?"

"I'm not supposed to."

Heart pounding, Breanne wrapped her fingers around the handle. "Why not?"

"Because I'm a secret," she whispered, sounding just like Shelly.

But it wasn't, Breanne knew that now. "A secret?" Damn, the door was still locked.

"I'm supposed to stay quiet and out of trouble while Shelly does her job."

Breanne stared at the wood. "You're Shelly's sister."

"Yes." A delighted giggle followed this, and then a click, and the door opened.

Shelly's face, and yet not. The eyes were slightly different, slightly slanted down. The mouth was fuller, softer. "I'm her twin." She grinned. "I'm special."

"I bet you are," Breanne said softly, her throat inexplicably tight. "What's your name?"

"Stacy."

"Stacy." Breanne smiled gently. "Shelly told me she had a sister. She said you are close. She loves you very much."

Stacy beamed. "I love her, too. That's why I'm real quiet. I was real quiet, wasn't I? You didn't even know it was me your first night here!"

The face she'd seen hovering over her, of course. "Yes, you were real quiet."

"I can't let Edward see me. He says I'm retarded, but I'm not. I'm not!"

Breanne's heart twisted. "That wasn't nice of him."

"He's not nice. He's mean. I used to help Shelly, until I broke a plate. He—" She frowned, then hugged herself, turning away.

A surge of hatred for the unknown Edward welled up. "Did he hurt you, Stacy?"

"I'm not supposed to talk about him." She hunched tighter into herself. "He doesn't like it. He told Shelly I couldn't come here with her anymore."

"So you hid."

Stacy didn't answer. Instead she began to hum very softly beneath her breath.

"Edward's gone now," Breanne said softly. "He can't yell at you. He can't hurt you."

"He's not gone!" Stacy tossed a fearful look over her

shoulder at the closed cellar door. "He's right in there. I've seen him!"

"Stacy, he's dead."

She blinked huge, hurt eyes at Breanne. "Are you sure?" she whispered.

At this moment, Breanne was sure of exactly nothing, except she had a fierce surge of protectiveness for this beautiful, sweet woman.

"See, you're not sure, either." Stacy covered her face. "That's why I did it. So he couldn't hit Shelly—"

Breanne went cold with fear, but not for herself. "Stacy, did you have something to do with Edward's death?"

But Stacy was no longer talking. Just humming and very slightly rocking back and forth.

"Stacy?" Breanne stroked Stacy's wild hair. "Can you tell me what you did? Something to protect your sister?"

Stacy kept humming, and rocked faster.

"Oh, Stacy."

"He always yelled," she said unhappily. "He scared me. I'm glad he's dead." She covered her face again. "Bad Stacy."

"Stacy!" This shocked cry came from Shelly, standing at the end of the hallway. She looked both horrified and terrified. "Oh, honey."

Behind her was Dante.

And then Cooper. "What's going on?" he asked, locking gazes with Breanne.

"Hi," Stacy said uneasily, shifting from foot to foot, swiping her hand across her mouth. "Hi."

Shelly rushed past Breanne to pull her sister in for a hug.

"I was quiet, like you said," Stacy told her, gripping Shelly tight. "I was."

"It's okay." Shelly looked tortured as she rocked her sister. "It's going to be okay."

Lariana crowded in, took a look. "What now—" When she saw Stacy out in the open, she sighed. *"Dios mio."*

"I was telling on myself," Stacy told her.

"Oh, sweetie." Lariana pressed close and wrapped an arm around both Shelly and Stacy.

"Am I in trouble?" Stacy asked.

Shelly just hugged her tighter and closed her eyes, resting her cheek on Stacy's head. "You didn't do anything wrong." Still holding her sister, she looked into Breanne's eyes, silently begging her to believe it. "You didn't."

Cooper moved to Breanne's side. "You okay?" he murmured.

"Yeah, this is Stacy. Shelly's twin. She—"

"—Didn't do anything," Dante said, moving to join the fray, putting a hand on each twin, making a united front as he turned to face Cooper and Breanne. "I know what you're thinking, but it's not true."

"I'm not thinking anything," Cooper said.

"Like hell. You're a cop. Your mind is always spinning. But you're wrong."

"My mind might always be spinning but that doesn't make me a coldhearted bastard," Cooper said calmly. "And I'd have figured you knew that by now."

Lariana was stroking Stacy's hair, Shelly was still holding onto her, and Dante was guarding over the whole pack of them like the alpha wolf. The thought of them clinging to each other like a tight little unit, so brave and uncertain, broke Breanne's heart. "We're going to get out of here," she said. "And the proper authorities will—"

"Bullshit." Dante looked at Shelly, who was openly crying. Then he looked at Cooper. "*I* did it." He cleared his voice and said it louder. "I killed Edward."

Shelly gasped. "No. *Dante*—"

"Well, fuck me," Patrick said, joining the group. "First we play the nobody did it game, and now you're taking credit for the deed? Christ Jesus, why, when we all know it was me who done the bastard in?"

Lariana spun around and leveled furious eyes at him. "You'll not be taking the blame for this one."

"Oh, yes, I will."

"No." Lariana whirled back to Cooper. "*I* did it."

"Darling—"

"Don't *darling* me, you skinny Scottish ass!" she snapped at Patrick. "I killed Edward with my bare hands and I can prove it."

"Stop," Shelly whispered.

But Patrick looked ready to explode. "Don't do this," he said to Lariana. "Don't even think it."

Dante stepped forward. "Both of you shut up. I already said I killed him—"

"Stop," Shelly said again, louder now, but Patrick and Dante were toe-to-toe, looking ready to battle.

"Bugger off," Patrick told Dante.

"*STOP!*" Shelly yelled before Dante could respond. She was still wrapped around Stacy, who was staring at everyone, wide-eyed. She seemed confused at Shelly's tears, but solemnly lifted a finger and stroked one off her sister's cheek. "I love you, sissy."

"Oh, Stacy, honey, I love you, too. Remember that, okay? Promise me you'll remember that if I have to go away."

Dante whipped around and looked at Cooper with impotent rage and emotion shimmering brilliantly in his dark, dark eyes. "You want to prove yourself to us, cop? Fix this."

Cooper shoved a hand through his hair, leaving it standing straight up. "First up, everyone to the great room." He put a hand on Stacy, who was shivering. "By the fire. It's colder today than it's been—"

"That's because it's clear outside," Stacy said, and smiled. When no one smiled back, hers faltered. "It gets colder when there's no clouds to keep the warm air low." She looked at everyone's face. "It does."

"Yes." Dante ruffled her hair. "You're right."

Her smile wobbled. "Am I in trouble?"

"No," Dante said, looking at Cooper. "You're not in trouble."

"Goody." She danced down the hallway. "I can go anywhere now, right? No more hiding?"

"Right," Patrick said. "You go on, we'll be right there."

"Don't stoke the fire by yourself," Shelly called. "Remember what happened last time."

"Yeah." Stacy bit her lip. "But the fire trucks came really fast."

Shelly let out a half-hysterical laugh, then covered her mouth, her eyes shiny. "Yes. They came fast."

"You go with her," Lariana said to Shelly. "Go ahead."

"You go, too," Patrick insisted, pushing Lariana after Shelly.

Lariana dug in her heels. "Look, you tall, skinny beanpole, I don't need anyone watching out after me."

"Sure, you don't. But maybe I be liking to watch after you."

Lariana opened her mouth, but he set a finger to her lips. "I love you, you bossy, infuriating, huffy woman. I love you, and I plan on loving you for the rest of me life, which will not be spent watching you waste away in a jail cell. Now, for once in your life, listen to me. Go. *Please*."

For a moment Lariana just stared at him, her eyes brilliant with emotion. Then she slipped an arm around Shelly and led her after Stacy. Halfway down the hall, she paused and looked back at Patrick. *I love you, too*, she mouthed, and left.

Dante and Patrick stood united, facing Cooper, Patrick's eyes suspiciously bright.

"Does either of you want to tell me what the hell is going on?" Cooper asked.

Dante's expression went cool and distant.

Patrick's matched.

"Fuck." Cooper shoved his fingers into his hair. "Fine. It's obvious anyway."

"If it's obvious, then you don't be needing us to say it," Patrick said.

Cooper looked at Breanne in disbelief.

Breanne's heart went out to all of them, to the staff trying to protect the sweet, naive Stacy, and to the beautiful, tortured, sexy cop she'd begun to fall for. "I think Cooper means it's obvious you're covering for *someone*," she told them. "And for whom."

"Shelly didn't do anything," Dante said. "And when the police get here, she'll be gone. She was never here. She can't have been here."

"Dante, Christ." Cooper stalked the small hallway and whirled back. "Her prints are everywhere. The evidence can't lie. The truth has to come out."

"You have the truth."

"What I have," Cooper said unhappily, "is four worthless admissions of a murder and not a single truth." He stared at the two men, neither of whom backed down. Swearing again, he reached for Breanne's hand. "Okay, your choice. Don't let me help you." He looked at Breanne. "The snowmobiles are out and running. There's still no cell reception. Our goal is to at least get to a place where we can call out for help. If not, we go all the way into town."

Dante looked at his watch and raised a brow. "You plan on doing that before dark, you'd better get moving. And don't get lost."

Breanne gulped.

"Patrick is riding on one," Cooper told Breanne. "We're on the other. We'll be fine."

Dante lifted a shoulder as if to say *hope so*.

Cooper began to pull Breanne out of the hallway, then turned back to Dante. "Don't do anything stupid while we're gone. At least, nothing more stupid than admitting to a murder you didn't commit."

Dante's face was granite.

"I mean it," Cooper said. "No one goes into the cellar. *No one*. Got it?"

"I think I know the definition of *stupid*."

"Make sure that you do."

Twenty-eight

Among the great lines of all time:
1. This won't hurt a bit.
2. The check's in the mail.
3. I swear I won't come in your mouth.
And ... the granddaddy of them all (in my humble
opinion):
4. I love you (this is the most troublesome).
                    —Breanne Mooreland's journal entry

Cooper had ridden motorcycles all his life, so he figured riding a snowmobile would just come to him. Luckily, it did. It was an awesome feeling, gliding along the thick, powdery snow, beneath towering pines instead of crowded freeways. So was the sensation of Breanne snugged to the back of him, her chest pressed into his spine, her legs straddled around his.

That he could get used to. But it was cold, at somewhere around zero, far colder than he was used to. Being out here for longer than they had to be was a bad idea.

They followed Patrick, and Cooper was grateful the snow had stopped, because he had no idea where they were or which direction to go in. There were two colors; azure blue sky, and stark white landscape. The snow had thoroughly and completely wiped out any of the landmarks he might have remembered on the drive here—like roads. He figured if something happened and they were separated from Patrick, he could at least follow the tracks back to the house. Or so he hoped, because he really did not want to be a "lost in the Sierras" statistic.

Patrick led them straight for a few hundred yards, and then they veered right through a clearing, heading up over a hill. "We're still on the road," Patrick yelled back through his helmet. "Things are good so far."

"How do you know?" Cooper yelled back.

"Truthfully?" He craned his neck and lifted a shoulder. "I'm just guessing."

Great. Terrific. Perfect.

"The snow has never risen above the street poles before," Patrick yelled. "I'm estimating where they are by the slight indentations every ten yards or so. See?"

Cooper saw the indentations, and since they were at regular intervals, he could only assume Patrick was right.

Ahead, Patrick slowed, pointing to a steep incline that definitely was *not* the road.

"Should be able to get phone reception up there," he yelled, and with that, revved his snowmobile, let out a loud "Woo-hoo," and took off at a high speed, bouncing over unknown dips and curves.

Cooper's stomach sank. "Patrick—" Damn it. "He's going to get stuck—"

As soon as the words were out of Cooper's mouth, Patrick's machine took a nosedive between two dips and bogged. The engine died.

Patrick straightened, shot them an *oops* look, and tried to restart.

"He's going to have to dig out first," Cooper said with a sigh.

Sure enough, the motor wouldn't start, and as the snowmobile's entire front end was buried, there was no getting to the engine compartment without digging.

Patrick got off the snowmobile and sank up to his chest in the fresh powder. "Shit."

They dug for a few minutes and got nowhere. They were losing precious daylight.

"You go ahead," Patrick finally said. "Get to the top where you can use the cell. I'll keep digging."

Cooper didn't like the idea of separating, but it was going

to take a good, long time to get Patrick's snowmobile running again. He'd feel better about spending that time if they could just get the police notified and on their way here.

He took it slower and smarter than Patrick, or so he hoped. They made it through the trees and ended up along a ridge, looking down onto a breathtaking landscape of crystal-clear lakes, pristine forests, and abundant wildlife.

"Wow," Breanne breathed in his ear when a wild rabbit dashed right across their trail.

Cooper turned off the snowmobile and pulled out his cell phone, pausing first to enjoy the feel of her up against him, her arms around his waist, her cheek resting on his shoulder.

"What's the matter?" she asked. "No reception?"

"There's reception." He closed his eyes and tried to soak up the moment so he'd remember, so he'd *always* remember this.

Breanne ran a gloved hand up his chest, settling it right over his heart. "I was wrong before, Cooper."

He twisted around to see her. "Wrong about what?"

"To let you think I wanted this to be over when we get out of here." She pulled off her helmet, waiting while he did the same. Then she pressed her mouth to his neck, his ear, and when he turned his body, she kissed him, long and sweet. "I was scared," she said when they pulled apart. "Still am," she admitted softly. "I know it sounds silly, but thinking about what I could grow to feel for you churns me up more than finding Edward. More than being in the dark for the past two days. More than—"

"I get it," he said dryly, stroking a finger over her temple along her hairline as a gust of wind hit, sprinkling a dusting of sparkling snow over them. "I scare you."

"Yes." She looked deeply into his eyes. "But you also make me feel. I mean *really* feel, and it's just so good, it might be worth the pain."

"I'm not going to hurt you," he said through an aching throat. "No pain, Breanne."

"You say that now, but you don't really know all my faults."

"They can't be that bad."

She laughed, then pressed her forehead to his. "I can't even tell you."

"I could tell you mine first, if that would help."

"You could?"

He shifted more fully around, facing her now, putting his hands on her thighs. "I let work fuck with my head."

"I know." Everything within Breanne softened as he let her see the things he usually kept hidden: frustration, anger, even shame, and if she'd managed to hold back her heart at all, it tumbled hard in that moment. "Anyone would have after what you went through." She rubbed her cheek to his, feeling her soul follow suit and tangle with his. "That you do what you do, day in and day out—"

"I walked away, remember?"

"But you're going back."

He looked down into her face. Slowly shook his head in amazement. "You seem so sure."

"I believe in you, Cooper."

"Even when I don't." He seemed unbearably touched at that. "You should know, being a cop in a relationship hasn't worked out for me in the past."

"Then maybe I'm not the only one who's made poor choices."

He laughed softly. "Yeah." He took a deep breath. "I guess I am going back. Is that going to affect your seeing me in the real world?"

"Why would it, if being a cop is who you are?"

His eyes were misty, his voice a little hoarse. "I have other faults, too," he warned.

"Please don't say that you like to hum Elvis tunes."

"I don't hum Elvis tunes."

"Thank God. Give me your worst, then. I know you put the seat down, and you don't snore."

"No." He was smiling. "But I don't fold my clothes. Hell, I don't even own an iron."

"But you like me in sweats. You get bonus points for that." She kissed him then, gliding her tongue to his until she lost her train of thought. "I bet you never have problems deciding what to wear. Maybe you'll rub off on me."

"Tell you what." He stroked his thumbs along her jaw. "I'll rub you and you can rub me. Any time."

She laughed. "Stop it. You don't know how bad my faults are yet."

"Name one."

"My Visa is always hovering at the maxed-out limit, even though my closet is overflowing with more shoes than all of San Francisco could wear."

"I don't care what your closet looks like, but I'm rather fond of those lace-up boots. You have any more like those?"

"Stop it. I'm being sincere here. I'm a bed hog—"

"Now *that* I already know," he said, wiping snowflakes from her cheek. "And I'm here to tell you, you can hog my bed any day of the week."

"I also like to get my way," she warned.

"Well, Princess, so do I. Maybe we could take turns."

She stared at him, her throat burning. "You're not taking me seriously."

"Baby, I'm serious as a heart attack. I don't give a shit if you steal all the blankets and can't afford anything but macaroni and cheese. Just so happens I have a closet full of blankets, and a savings account. Not a big one, but it could probably handle anything that comes up, Nordstrom sales notwithstanding."

"The good stuff rarely goes on sale."

"Give me a *real* reason we can't see each other."

She swallowed hard, and a single tear slipped down her cheek. "Because I like you."

He looked as if maybe he didn't see the problem.

"I *really* like you," she said. "And that has never worked out for me before."

"Does this feel like any of those other times?"

She blinked, and thought about that. "No. No, it doesn't. Actually . . . this feels much different."

"How *does* it feel?"

"Real," she admitted.

He let out a rough sound of pleasure and hauled her across him, cradling her over his lap, pulling her close for a long, deep, and decidedly not sweet kiss. "You know," he murmured when they came up for air, "I really thought life sucked. But then I saw you in that dark foyer, lighting the night with that pink vibrator." He grinned when she smacked his chest, but then he took her hand and held it over his heart, his smile fading. "I'm falling for you, too, Breanne, and to walk away now, before we give it a shot, just doesn't seem fair."

"So what do you suggest?" she asked shakily.

"That we get the police here. Do what we can for the others—"

"Oh, Cooper. You do care about them as much as I do." Her eyes filled, and so did her heart. "Do you have any idea how lucky you're going to get?" She kissed his throat, his jaw. "How very, very lucky?"

He slid his hands down to her butt and snugged her closer. "Keep talking."

Leaning in, she bit his ear. "I'm thinking this seat is pretty cushy . . ."

On his lap as she was, she felt his very satisfying reaction as he cleared his throat and pounded out 9-1-1 with shaking hands.

She laughed. "And here I thought maybe you'd want to . . . you know. Right here."

"Princess, I love you, but I'm not risking frostbite to my favorite part of my anatomy. I have plans for that part, and plans for you—Hello," he said when he got a dispatcher.

Breanne just stared at him, stunned at what he'd just said to her, only half hearing as he gave the information, listened to the response, then disconnected.

"They're prioritizing their emergencies," he said when he was done. "They're overwhelmed, but thanks to Edward, we're moving to the top of the list. I guess we can go help Patrick dig out and then get back to the house and prepare everyone. It's not going to be easy straightening this whole mess out."

Breanne was still speechless by his declaration, her gaze locked on his face, her throat burning with emotions too big to hide. "You . . . love me?"

"I do." He put her helmet back on, smoothed back her hair and smiled into her face. "Hold on tight, 'kay?" He nudged her behind him again and pulled her arms around him. "Ready?"

When she still didn't—couldn't—answer, he craned his neck and looked into her eyes. "Breanne?"

"Yeah," she said in a steady voice but with a very wobbly smile. "I guess the truth is, when it comes to you, I really am ready."

And God help her, but she was.

By the time they dug Patrick out and got back to the house, two hours had passed.

Everyone crowded into the foyer to greet them, looking anxious. *Had they made the call?*

Patrick nodded the answer.

"It's done, then," Lariana said quietly, as everyone seemed to deflate. "Someone's going to jail."

Dante looked stoic about that, but then Shelly burst into tears into her apron and his cool façade crumpled as he pulled her close. "It's going to be okay," he murmured into her hair.

"No." She pulled free. "No, it's not." Turning away, she moved out of the foyer.

Breanne went after her, and everyone else followed them to the great room.

Stacy was in front of the fire, staring into the flames, holding her hands out. "So pretty."

"Don't touch," Shelly reminded her, trying to sound normal.

Stacy giggled and pulled back. "I know, silly. It's *hot*."

"Hot," Shelly agreed, and ruffled her sister's hair, her expression crumbling when Stacy's face turned away. Breanne hugged Shelly, wishing she could do more.

Cooper moved to the fire, squeezing Shelly's shoulder before crouching beside Stacy. "The police are coming," he told her. "Do you understand what that means?"

"They're coming for Edward."

"Yes," he said gently, and Breanne fell for him all over again. "And they're going to want to know what happened to him."

Stacy's smile dissolved.

"We told you what happened," Dante said, face stoic. "It's done."

"Yeah, you told me," Cooper said dryly. "You told me you killed him." He turned to Patrick. "And you told me you killed him." He glanced at Lariana. "You said *you* did it." He lifted a brow at Shelly. "You, too. Do I have it straight? You all killed him, then?"

Everyone looked away. Cooper shot Breanne a helpless look and shook his head.

"We're trying to help," Breanne told them. "Please help us help you. Just tell us what really happened."

Shelly looked at Dante. "It's time—"

"Shelly—"

"It started with me," Shelly said to Cooper. "It did," she said when he looked doubtful. "I swear it."

Dante stepped forward, but she put a hand on his chest, and with a pleading expression, held him back. "I'm going to tell them."

"Shelly, Christ. No."

"You know I'm all Stacy has," Shelly said to Cooper and Breanne. "It's just the two of us. We used to live in a small apartment in town over the hardware store. I was commuting out here every day and Stacy was in a day care class at the rec center. A special program so she wouldn't be by herself."

"We painted," Stacy said with a dreamy smile. "Finger painted."

Shelly smiled at her. "That was your favorite, I know."

"Edward didn't like my finger painting," Stacy said, and rubbed the top of her hand as if it'd been hit.

Dante stalked the length of the room, his expression nowhere near calm.

"Edward wasn't much fun, I take it," Cooper said lightly to Stacy, though his eyes were anything but.

She shook her head.

"A month ago the state's funds changed," Shelly said. "And the money for Stacy's rec center program dried up. I brought her here, but she got into Patrick's paints and redid the hallway. Edward blew a gasket, to say the least."

Stacy lowered her head. "I was sorry."

Shelly hugged her. "I know. He had no right to smack your hand, no right at all." Shelly looked at Cooper. "Then the rent on my apartment skyrocketed and I couldn't afford it. But the owner of this place liked my work and told Edward to let me live in one of the downstairs servants' rooms until I found another place. He said it'd be no problem."

"But it *was* a problem," Lariana said. "For Edward."

"He lived here, too," Patrick told Cooper. "And it turns out, he doesn't like to share."

Dante paced some more, muttering something in his native tongue.

Cooper raised a questioning brow.

"I said he was an asshole," Dante said. "He made the girls feel bad all the time. He said shitty things to Lariana—"

"I didn't care what he said to me," Lariana said defiantly, tossing her hair back. "I could handle him."

"*I* cared," Shelly said softly. "But there was no other job where I could have Stacy with me."

Stacy stared at her fingers, twining them together, humming softly to herself as she began to rock.

"I tried to keep her busy during the day in our room, something she could do quietly so she wouldn't bother him," Shelly said. "Like reading and coloring, but sometimes she'd get bored."

"She just wanted to help," Lariana said. "But Edward wanted her gone. He even stole money out of my purse so I'd think it was Stacy. It wasn't," she said bitterly. "But in spite of him, I'd let her help me with stuff. She's a great sweeper."

Stacy lifted her head and beamed. "I like to sweep."

"It was nice for her to be busy," Dante said. "And it made her feel good."

"I'm guessing Edward didn't agree?" Cooper asked.

Dante let out a harsh laugh. "The day before you two arrived, Stacy was helping Lariana dust."

Lariana winced. "Probably not my best idea."

Stacy went back to humming.

"She broke a few things in the dining room," Dante said. "No big deal."

"Edward went mad," Patrick remembered. "Yelling and screaming. He threw stuff, too."

"He scared her," Shelly said as Stacy hummed louder, rocking, too.

Dante's face was granite. "I wanted to kill him."

"We all did," Lariana said. "But that was just anger and frustration. None of us really would have."

"He raised a hand to Stacy," Shelly said, "and I thought,

this is it. He's going to hurt her again. And I . . . I caught his hand. I told him if he hit her, I'd kill him." She covered her face. "I told him if he did *anything* to her, even yelled at her again, I'd kill him, and I meant it. *I meant it.*"

A long silence filled the room. Breanne squeezed Shelly's hand.

"I heard him yelling from the garage," Patrick said. "But as the sight of me usually made him more mad, I didn't rush in."

"I knew I was fired," Shelly said. "And I think I was numb. I went to our room to pack, but then I heard him yelling again, at Stacy. When I ran into the dining room, Stacy was standing over Edward, who was on the floor. He was . . ." A sob choked out of her. "*Dead*. He had a gash over his forehead and there were shards of a large glass vase all around him."

"That was the sliver of glass I found that first night," Breanne remembered.

Stacy rocked so fast she became a blur.

"I panicked," Shelly admitted. "Stacy was just staring at me like I was her whole world—" She swiped at her tears. "God. I'd threatened him. Everyone had heard me. And here he was, dead. But I couldn't go to jail—what would happen to Stacy?"

Stacy stopped humming and dropped her head to her knees.

"I knew I had to make it look like an accident," Shelly said. "I tried to drag him to the cellar stairs. They're steep, and it seemed like a good idea to make it look like he'd fallen. So . . ."

"You pushed him," Cooper guessed.

"I intended to, but I had a problem. He was heavy—he got stuck around that tight corner of the dining room. He got blood on the wall. He'd lost a shoe."

"So you got help," Cooper said.

"She didn't ask," Dante told him firmly. "But yeah, she got help. I carried him to the stairs on my own. *I* pushed him."

"I cleaned up the blood," Lariana said.

"And then shoved the towel you used beneath the sink." Cooper looked at Dante. "You left the gloves you wore beneath Shelly's bed."

"We were going to dispose of both when the roads cleared," Lariana told him. "But the roads never cleared."

"How did Edward get the hole in his chest?" Cooper asked.

"That would be me," Patrick looked grim. "When I saw how terrified Stacy was—" His voice cracked. "She couldn't even talk, man."

Stacy's fingers were white as she clenched and unclenched her hands. She'd begun to shake. Breanne stroked her back, feeling utterly helpless.

"I lost it," Patrick admitted. "I just happened to be holding the gun—I'd been scaring away a few squirrels. I looked down at the son of a bitch lying there, knowing he'd ruined all of us, and I shot him."

"You know that wouldn't have killed him," Cooper said.

"Aye, I know. But he'd said those things to Lariana, he'd terrified this poor little thing—" He gestured to Stacy. "The fucker deserved to die, mate."

Cooper sighed, scrubbed his hands over his face.

"You don't think so?" Dante demanded.

"It doesn't matter what I think."

"Since when?" Dante asked.

Cooper looked at him for a long moment. "Look, the guy was an asshole, the worst kind. We all know it. But him dying wasn't for any of you to decide." Cooper dropped his hands and looked at all of them. "Why the hell didn't someone turn him in for harassment? Employee abuse? Hell, *anything*. It didn't have to get to this."

"Please don't tell the police what Stacy did," Shelly whispered. "*Please.*"

Cooper let out a long breath, filled with tension and unhappiness, while everyone waited.

Breanne ached for him, and the decision she knew he faced. For Stacy, and her sweet, helplessly contagious smile.

When the doorbell rang, it was like a collective shot in the room; every single person jumped.

Dante and Patrick stood.

Cooper did as well, and stared at both of them. "Let me do this."

Neither man budged.

"Sit down," Cooper said in his cop voice. "*Please,*" he added softly when they didn't move. "Trust me."

"You're a cop," Dante said as if *trust* and *cop* couldn't go together in the same sentence.

"Yeah, to the bone, I'm discovering," Cooper said dryly. "But at the moment, I'm not anything but a guy on vacation, Dante." He waited until the tough butler looked at him. "Trust me," he said again.

Dante stood for another long moment, then slowly sank back in his chair, arms crossed, the picture of arrogant punk.

Scared arrogant punk.

"Here's the thing," Cooper said to all of them. "The evidence never lies. You have the bloody towel, the gloves. Where's the vase that Stacy hit him with?"

Stacy turned her head. "I didn't hit him with the vase."

Everyone went still.

The doorbell rang again.

Cooper walked to Stacy and hunkered down beside her. "You didn't hit Edward with the vase?"

She shook her head, her wild hair flying about her face. "I don't hit." She leaned in with a conspirator's whisper. "I'm not allowed."

Cooper gave her a lopsided smile that Breanne felt to her toes. "Good girl. How did Edward end up on the floor?"

"He did this." Stacy stood up, clutched her chest, bugged out her eyes and stuck out her tongue, then fell sideways to the floor, gasping for breath. After three seconds of writhing, she sat up with a smile. "Like that."

Shelly clapped a hand over her mouth. "Oh, my God."

Cooper reached out and put a hand on Shelly's shoulder to keep her quiet, never taking his eyes off Stacy. "And the vase?" he asked her.

"He grabbed it on his fall. It made a pretty noise. Tinkle, tinkle, tinkle, tinkle, tinkle . . ." she sang.

The doorbell rang again. Cooper leaned in and hugged Stacy. "Thank you," he whispered. "You've been a huge help."

Stacy beamed.

Breanne raced after Cooper as he walked to the door, her heart so full she could hardly stand it. "Cooper."

"I have to get—oomph," he said when she flung herself at him. Fisting his hair in her hands, she pulled his head down for a quick kiss. "I'm not just falling for you," she whispered. "I'm falling *hard*."

Looking stunned, he stared at her.

"You." She put a finger to his chest. "Extremely lucky tonight."

That tugged a staggered-looking grin out of him. "Hold that thought."

Three hours later, the police were gone, and thankfully, finally, so was Edward's body.

Once again, everyone gathered in the great room. Cooper looked around and realized what was different—the tension was gone. He looked at Breanne and got a brilliant smile.

"Heart attack," Dante said, looking just as flummoxed as Cooper felt. "Who'd have thunk it?"

"The coroner will have to say for sure," Cooper warned. "We're only assuming heart attack, but it makes sense."

"The police thought so, too," Breanne said. "They figured

Edward was yelling at Stacy, got chest pains, gripped the vase hard. She thought he meant to throw it at her and screamed. Patrick ran in, assumed the worst, and shot in self-defense." She looked at Cooper. "Sounds like that's what's going to stick."

"It's unbelievable," Dante said. "No one's going to jail." He looked at Cooper. "You're not so bad. For a cop."

Cooper smiled at the backhanded compliment. "Thanks."

"So what now?" Lariana asked. "You two have half a week left. The weather is going to be gorgeous, and the skiing amazing. You staying?"

Breanne looked at Cooper. And with one smile, stole his heart.

"I could use a vacation," she said. "How about you?"

"A vacation sounds like just what the doctor ordered," he answered. "Starting right now." Getting to his feet, he swept her off hers and into his arms. Turning back to the staff, who were all grinning from ear to ear, he said, "I hear there's a hell of a honeymoon suite. With amenities. We'll be enjoying those tonight. Now that the road's cleared, you guys can all go home and take the rest of the week off. We'll be fine."

They whooped and hollered while Cooper kissed Breanne, then carried her out of the room and up the stairs.

She slid her arms around his neck. "Don't hurt yourself," she warned, her mouth on his ear. "I have plans for you."

"And I for you." He shouldered open the door to the honeymoon suite.

"My plans first—" she started, her words ending in a gasp as he tossed her to the bed.

With a grin, he followed her down, stripping off his shirt as he did. "Sorry. But I'm bigger—"

She rolled him. He couldn't believe it but she rolled him, held him down, and smiled wickedly before going to work ripping off his pants.

"Okay," he said, happily caving. "You first—"

This ended in a groan when she took her mouth on a

happy cruise down his chest, his flat belly, to the prize between his legs.

"Wait," he gasped.

She lifted her head.

"Earlier, when you said you were falling for me—"

"I meant it."

"So this is—"

"Yes."

"Say it."

"I love you, Cooper Scott." Her eyes stung with it, but she smiled because nothing had ever felt so right. "Now, pretty please may I ravish you?"

"For as long as you want, Princess. For as long as you want."

Look for AUSSIE RULES by Jill Shalvis!

AUSSIE RULES

It's bad enough that gutsy pilot Mel Anderson has to clean up after her lovable by completely disorganized best friend and business partner, Dimi, while her certifiable employees make more work than they do. Now, the one man she hoped she'd never see is back and looking for trouble. Scratch that, he *is* trouble. Amazing, holy-cow, more-please trouble . . .

Bo Black wants his family's airport back, and he's determined to get it. This laid-back Aussie is nobody's fool. Thing is, neither is Mel. She's intense. Uptight. Sexy. And very, very tempting. Suddenly, Bo's thinking less about revenge and more about kissing and touching and falling into a fly-by-the-seat-of-your-underpants kind of forever love . . .

The Gulfstream was a beauty, and her pilot's heart gave one vivacious kick of envy as the plane swept in for a honey of a landing, perfectly controlled by a pilot who was clearly a master of his craft.

When the engine shut off, Mel moved in, squinting against the early chill and wind, using the tie-down blocks to hold the plane steady, her mind wandering as she worked. The oven had gone out twice this month. She needed to look into the cost of a new one. The linemen clearly needed another ass chewing regarding responsibilities, specifically theirs. And then there was the little matter of fuel. She'd have to find a way to pay that bill pronto.

God, her brain hurt.

Finished with the tie-down, she straightened, patted the sleek side of the airplane just for the pleasure of touching it, and blew a stray strand of hair out of her face, wishing she had put on an extra layer of insulation beneath her coveralls because despite its being summer, the early-morning wind off the Pacific cut right through her.

From the other side of the aircraft, the door opened. A set of stairs released. A moment later, two long legs emerged, clad in dark blue trousers, clean work boots, and topped by a most excellent ass. Not averse to enjoying a good view, Mel stayed in place, watching as the rest of the man was revealed. White button-down shirt, sleeves shoved up above his elbows, tawny hair past his collar, blowing in the wind.

Yep, there were a few perks to this job, one of them catering right to Mel's soft spot.

Pilots. This one looked more like a movie star pretending to be a pilot, but you wouldn't hear her complaining. And just like that, from the inside out, she began to warm up nicely.

The man held a clipboard, which he was looking at as he turned, ducking beneath the nose of the plane to come toe to toe with her, a lock of tawny hair falling carelessly over his forehead, his eyes shaded behind aviator sunglasses.

And right then and there, every single lust-filled thought drained out of Mel's head to make room for one hollow, horror-filled one.

No.

It couldn't be. After all this time, he wouldn't *dare* show his face.

His only concession to the surprise was a raised brow as he lifted his sunglasses, his sea-green gaze taking its sweet time, touching over her own battered work boots, the dirty coveralls, the fiery, uncontrollable red hair she'd piled on top of her head without thought to her appearance. "Look at you," he murmured. "All grown up. G'day, Mel."

Yeah, he'd grown up, too. He was bigger, broader, and taller than the last time she'd seen him, she couldn't mistake the smile—of pure, devilish, wicked trouble.

Australian accent, check.

Heart-stopping green eyes and long lashes to match the long, thick tumble of light brown hair falling in said eyes, check and check.

Curved mouth that could invoke huge waves of passion or fury . . . *CHECK.* "Bo Black," she whispered, getting cold all over again.

Cocking his head, he let out a slow smile. "In the flesh, darlin'. Miss me?"

Miss him? Yeah, she'd missed him. Like one might miss a close call with a hand grenade. "Get off my property."

As if he had all the time in the damn world, he leaned back against his plane, slapping the clipboard lightly against his thigh. "No can do, mate."

"Oh, yes you can." Staggering at a strong gust of wind, she planted her feet more firmly as she pointed to his plane. "You just get your Aussie ass back inside that heap of junk and fly it the hell out of here."

"Heap of junk?" Instead of being insulted, he laughed good over that, the sound scraping at her belly because it'd been a long time since she'd heard it.

Of course, she hadn't seen him in ten years, and the last time she had, he'd been eighteen to her sixteen, all long and lanky, not yet grown into his body.

He was grown into it now, damn him, and how. Reaching back, he lovingly stroked the steel of the plane, making the entirely inappropriate thought take root in her brain: *did he stroke a woman like that?*

Clearly she needed caffeine.

And a smack upside the head.

"You know exactly what kind of plane this is," he noted easily. "And how valuable."

"Fine," she granted. "Your toy is bigger than mine, you win. *Now* you can go."

Tossing his head back, he laughed again, and she made no mistake—he was laughing *at* her.

Nothing new.

The first time she'd ever laid eyes on him, he'd been swaggering through the lobby, having arrived in town with his father, Eddie Black, an antique plane restorer and dealer. Tall and teenage rangy, Bo had smiled at Mel and said, "Hello, mate," and she'd fallen—both figuratively and literally—as hard as her tender sixteen-year-old heart could, tripping over her own two feet, landing in a potted palm, amusing everyone in the lobby but her.

The second time she'd seen him had been when she'd opened a stock closet to grab something for maintenance, and had found him in there, leaning back against a shelving unit, a pretty blonde customer wrapped around him like a pretzel, straddling his hips. Bo had had his hand beneath her short skirt, doing things Mel had only been able to imagine.

In fact, she'd done just that for many, many uncomfortably sweaty nights afterward.

He'd been so cool, so typically laid-back. When she'd only stood there at the storage door, frozen in shock, Bo had lazily lifted his head, eyes heavy and sexy-lidded as he'd smiled that killer smile. "No worries. Just lock the door for me, darlin'?"

No worries. Right. She'd just lock the door. Only everything inside her head wanted to stay, wanted to beg, *"Can I be next?"*

That had so shocked her, the unexpected longing, that she'd lost it.

Completely.

Lost.

It.

Which was her only explanation for why she'd blindly reached out, grabbed the first thing her fingers closed over— an air filter off a shelf—and . . . and beaned him on the head with it.

Not her proudest moment, but she blamed her red hair and the temperament that went with it. Dimi had always been warning her that someday the temper would catch up to the fire in her hair and that she was going to piss off the wrong person.

Only Bo hadn't gotten pissed, he'd laughed.

Laughed.

Which in turn had made her feel stupid. God, she resented that.

The last time she'd seen him had been several months later, on the day his thieving, conning father had vanished.

The day her life had changed forever.

"Get out," she said now.

That sexy little smile still in place, Bo slowly pulled out a folded piece of paper from the breast pocket of his white shirt.

She tried to read it but he held the document just out of reach, forcing her to lean in. As close as she was now, she could see his eyes weren't a solid sea green, but flecked with gold specks. This close she could draw in the scent of him— one hundred percent male. This close she could read the paper:

Quit Deed.

A quit deed to North Beach. Her stomach dropped. "How did you—"

"I recently found a box of my father's things, with a safe deposit box key." His eyes were no longer smiling. "This was in there."

"My God."

He nodded curtly. "Yeah, that's right, Mel. North Beach, and everything in it, is mine. Guess that means you, too."

Day 185

Joan, who will be starting as chief in a week, sat down and discussed the schedule with me. A mother herself, she seemed to be sympathetic to the problems I am having. I like her a lot. Her lack of anger is a relief here, but I wonder what she'll be like after three months of being chief.

Day 186

I was late for sign-out this morning because I spent too much time taking care of patients on rounds. All Jackie can do is scream at me, and then scream louder. I'm weary of six months of trying and that it is still no easier, no more manageable. Yet it is the loneliness, the isolation, that is worst.

Day 193

There is no humanity in this system, not toward patients, not toward women who both work for and care for their children. A part of me is still desperately trying to make it here, but, mostly, I begin to realize I cannot mold myself into the kind of person who could.

Day 194

Medicine is a service industry that systematically and impersonally processes sick and healthy people. Physicians are trained and conditioned to see their patients as objects to be assembled and reassembled once they enter the system. If you are sick, or even if you are having a baby, you are presumed to be incapable of intelligent judgment, and therefore under the control of experts.

A WOMAN
IN
RESIDENCE

Michelle Harrison, M.D.

FAWCETT CREST • NEW YORK

A Fawcett Crest Book
Published by Ballantine Books
Introduction Copyright © 1993 by Michelle Harrison
Copyright © 1982 by Michelle Harrison

Library of Congress Catalog Card Number: 81-19160

ISBN 0-449-22238-1

This edition published by arrangement with Random House, Inc.

Manufactured in the United States of America

First Ballantine Books Edition: October 1993

To the women
who entrusted me with their care
at Doctors Hospital—whose forgiveness I ask
for the times I did as I was ordered

The setting of this book is Everytown, so named because the stories I tell are repeated in virtually every hospital throughout the country. The particular hospital in which I worked, and the doctors who taught me, were no worse than elsewhere. In fact, they may have been better. The problems I describe are not specific to any one medical community, but are endemic to the field of medicine.

Acknowledgments

To the following friends and relatives who during the living and writing of this book provided me with encouragement, support and criticism while adding to the fullness of my life: Aaron, Abigail, Agnes, Alice, Ann, Annie, Barbara, Becky, Bobbie, Bonnie, Carrie, Charlie, Cynthia, David, Denise, Diana, Dorothy, Eli, Elaine, Ellie, Emily, Enya, Eric, Ethel, Eva, Eve, Francie, Gabriel, Gena, Gene, George, Helen, Heather, Isa, Jane, Jenny, Jerry, Jessica, Jesse, Jon, Judy, Karen, Katie, Lalitha, Lenny, Lilian, Linda, Lise, Lonnie, Maggie, Mary, Mary Beth, Mary Kate, Matthew, Missy, Mitch, Nadesha, Nick, Nicola, Noni, Norma, Pam, Pat, Peter, Phoebe, Phyllis, Rebecca, Ruth, Sam, Sara Jane, Sarah, Shirley, Sol, Trudy, Valery and W.C.

To Susan Griffin, whose book, *Woman and Nature*, helped to validate for me that I spoke a language different from the others at Doctors Hospital.

To my editor, Charlotte Mayerson, for her commitment to this book and to women's health. She often helped me to articulate my thoughts without ever trying to change them. Working together has been productive as well as pleasurable.

Introduction

I walk toward the double doors at the end of the hospital corridor, pausing first to press the large, square steel plate that opens the doors. They open, and I am once again on Labor and Delivery. Labor rooms line the hall, each door marked with a yellow index card signifying the occupant's name, her doctor, whether she is a private or a clinic patient to be cared for by residents and staff. It is still a two-tiered system, private and clinic. In that respect, little has changed.

The hall is quiet, too quiet and too calm. I look over to the nurses' station where nurses and doctors are talking softly. I am a stranger to them, sent by the university to teach ethics to medical students assigned to obstetrics. Unnoticed, I walk further along the hall, listening for the old familiar sounds of Labor and Delivery. I remain in awe of the process by which one human being emerges out of the body of another.

I listen for the sounds and movements of urgency, the moaning women, and even the angry doctors, but it is quiet. The yellow cards on the doors each have names, signifying that the rooms are occupied, but there is no sound. I check the bottoms of the doors, wondering if the labor rooms have finally been soundproofed, so women can be free to moan, cry, growl, relinquish composure, and allow themselves to be consumed by the process of giving birth. But from beneath each door, a fan of light sprays out and the marbleized floor glitters. There is no soundproofing, and there is no sound.

Through another set of double doors, I enter the small teaching conference room. As the class begins, I ask, ''Is it always so quiet on the labor floor?'' These young men and women are new to Labor and Delivery, as they are to medicine. One student tells me, ''Yes, when a patient begins to make a lot of sound, the nurses talk her into an epidural anesthetic. Then, once the anesthesia is in, they put a 'smiley face' on the blackboard next to the patient's name. The goal is to get 'smiley faces' next to every name on the board.''

The silence haunts me. It has been fifteen years since I wrote *A Woman in Residence*. The laboring women have been quieted. This isn't what I wanted. I wanted them to be freer. I wanted my experience and my book to be outdated, to be a part of a shameful past in American childbirth.

We live, as a society, with a constant tension between technology and touch. We embrace a technology that symbolizes progress, while mourning the loss of human connection. Our models of future care are hospitals run entirely by computers using imaging machines that diagnose and robots that treat, while we crave health centers staffed by physicians, nurses, educators, who know us as whole persons, who listen and talk to us, who understand our physical beings in the context of our social, emotional, and spiritual beings. And for women, the tension is particularly acute, as we become increasingly aware that women's health has been neglected, women's complaints dismissed, and women increasingly perceived as wombs, not women.

I left Doctors Hospital fifteen years ago—shattered—truly believing that I had failed everyone, including myself, and that I would never find a place for myself within medicine. I had lived out the tension between technology and caring. I had come to the hospital believing that technology and caring could coexist. I left a system that was contemptuous of women, and where quality of care was measured on a complex hierarchy of technological interventions. I left, and went about just surviving.

I finished writing *A Woman in Residence* as a way of coming to terms with what I had just been through. My savings were running out. I worried about whether I would ever be able to get a job in medicine once my book was published. One day I looked at the paper and saw an ad for a quiet night job covering a hospital. I needed work, and that was about as visible as I wanted to be. I called the agency about the job. As I told him my background, the recruiter became more and more excited. "Have you ever heard of premenstrual syndrome?" I asked what he meant. I'd heard of premenstrual tension; I knew about chocolate cravings; but I wasn't sure what he meant. "I have a different job I want to discuss with you," he said. "I represent a company that is about to open the first premenstrual-syndrome clinic in the country. They are looking for a family physician, psychiatrically-oriented, with OB-GYN training." I had called on a Thursday. I was interviewed on Friday. I began work on Monday.

In leaving Doctors Hospital, I opened a path to work that I do not believe I would have found had I stayed and been "successful." In defeat, we are sometimes left more open to the pain of others, more open to the possibility that the patient may be right, the doctor wrong. I listened to woman after woman, and I listened patiently. I had no other place I had to be. The OR wasn't calling, babies weren't about to be born, monitors didn't beep real and false warnings. In what seemed at first to be my failure in the system, I now provided care to women whose complaints had long been ignored by the same system.

For years, I listened to hundreds and hundreds of women. I was looking for a way of understanding the medical aspect better. I wanted to understand that broad area of hormones and emotions, the body and mind. It was time for more training.

I was ready to move on for another reason. I had one child, Heather, who was an ever-present figure in *A Woman in Residence*, but I had always wanted at least one more. I didn't think it would be easy. I wasn't sure I'd be happy, but then many women are unhappy as mothers, and they all seem to survive.

Cecilia Devyani Harrison was born in Calcutta, India, on

June 21, 1984, and came home to Heather and me in September of that year. I had once again arranged my work life to include child care. I had my own practice in my own office. I hired a woman to be both secretary and child-care worker, and brought my baby to work with me. I relactated and nursed her between patients. What started as a job for Shirley, my secretary, became love for my child, and she and "Cici" remain close today. With my two children in place, one for each hand, I was ready once again to make plans for my career.

I began a two-year fellowship in psychopharmacology while continuing with my practice. I was busy, but also excited by what I was learning. I was looking forward to a relatively quiet and orderly two years.

It wasn't as quiet as I had anticipated because of my radar for matters pertaining to mothers and babies. I became interested in the Baby M case because of issues of class and exploitation of women that had not been previously raised. Although Baby M was not about technology, since simple artificial insemination had been used, it heralded the beginnings of commerce in eggs, sperm, embryos, children, and women's reproductive function. I began to research, write, and publish about the changes I saw ahead. I was invited to join a hospital ethics committee, and had the opportunity to develop new ways of addressing these issues. I said to someone at the hospital once, "If we are indeed to join the stampede of technological progress, let us at least take our place with dignity." The technology of conception, like the technology of birth, has preceded our ability to make ethical and social policy decisions as to how, when, and by whom it is to be used, and to whose advantage.

The fellowship went smoothly, more smoothly than any other position I've been in. I learned much of what I wanted to learn, and I finished.

I continued my work on premenstrual syndrome. I also continued the work that began with Baby M. Margaret Atwood's novel about women used as breeders, *The Handmaid's Tale*, became a movie at the same time as I testified in a California court that a pregnant woman could love a child she was carrying, even if it were not genetically hers. I was not arguing for custody, only that the woman who bore him was a parent, one of his parents. I watched the court and the media reduce this woman to a womb, a rented vehicle of reproduction, declaring that she did not exist as a party to his creation and birth. I watched science fiction become law.

That's how I felt when I experienced the silence on Labor and Delivery. I felt I was in a scene from a science-fiction movie, not reality. And yet when I look back on the technology of childbirth, the technology I came to learn about in *A Woman in Residence* and came to be disillusioned with, I see science as fiction. For ten years now, I have collected press stories and medical literature in a file I called "Refutations." They are about the failure to live up to expectations of each of the procedures, interventions, and machines that were imposed upon women. Pregnant women who questioned their use were accused of not caring about their babies.

Electronic fetal monitoring was found to be of no use in improving outcome of either premature or full-term infants.[1] However, a story in *Ob. Gyn. News* in the June 1–14, 1990, issue read, "Obs. Still Using EFM [electronic fetal monitor] Despite Lack of Efficacy Data."

Further headlines in *Ob. Gyn. News* read, "Says Fetal Scalp Sampling Rarely Justified, Poses Significant Risks" (January 1, 1992); and "Routine Median Episiotomy Use 'Isn't Justified'" (August 15, 1991). A study published in the *American Journal of Obstetrics and Gynecology* looked at whether the use of stirrups in birth and episiotomy led to more tears and found that only 0.9% of those delivered without episiotomy and stirrups had deep tears, while 27.9% of

[1]Shy, K. K.; Luthy, D. A.; Bennett, F. C.; Whitfield, M.; Larson, E. B.; et al; "Effects of electronic fetal-heart-rate monitoring, as compared with periodic auscultation, on the neurologic development of premature infants," *New England Journal of Medicine*, 1990; 322:588–593.

Freeman, R.; "Intrapartum fetal monitoring—a disappointing story," *New England Journal of Medicine*, 1990;322:624–26.

the group with stirrups and episiotomy had deep tears.[2] Another study showed the advantages of squatting in labor.[3]

The Caesarean-section rate rose in the 1970s and 1980s from 5.5%[4] to 24.7%,[5] without any evidence that this increase represented an improved neonatal outcome. In one study, the variability in Caesarean-section rate was entirely dependent on the individual physician, with rates ranging from 19.1% to 42.3%[6] In other words, the woman's condition was of less importance in determining her Caesarean than was the practice pattern of the individual physician treating her.

Repeatedly we have embraced the promise of painless and easy birth, but also repeatedly the treatment has failed to live up to its promises. One intervention invariably leads to another. The epidural anesthesia that led to the smiley faces on the blackboard increased the chance that the woman would need a Caesarean section.[7] Interventions in labor set in motion a series of further interventions, more often leading to a Caesarean section. But for the woman, each subsequent intervention comes as a surprise, and the Caesarean section to rescue a baby who may or may not ever have been in trouble

[2]Borgatta, L.; Piening, S. L.; Cohen, W. R.; "Association of episiotomy and delivery position with deep perineal laceration during spontaneous delivery in nulliparous women," *American Journal of Obstetrics and Gynecology*, 1989;160:294-7.

[3]Gardosi, J.; Hutson; Lynch, C.B.; "Randomised controlled trial of squatting in the second stage of labour," *Lancet*, 1989;8654:74-77.

[4]Taffel, S.M.; Placek, P. J.; Liss, T.; "Trends in the United States Caesarean section rate and reasons for the 1980-85 rise," *American Journal of Public Health*, 1987;77:955-9.

[5]Taffel, S. M.; Placek, P. J.; Moien, M.; "1988 U.S. Caesarean section rate at 24.7 per 100 births—a plateau?" *New England Journal of Medicine*, 1990; 323:199-200.

[6]Goyert, G. L.; Bottoms, S. F.; Treadwell, M. C.; Nehra, P. C.; "The physician factor in Caesarean birth rates," *New England Journal of Medicine*, 1989;320:706-9.

[7]Thorp, J. A.; Parisi, V. M.; Boylan, P. C.; Johnston, D. A.; "The effect of continuous epidural analgesia on Caesarean section for dystocia in nulliparous women," *American Journal of Obstetrics and Gynecology*, 1989; 161:670-75.

leaves the woman believing she has failed, that her body has failed her and her baby.

But it is not really the technology that failed. It is the medical profession that failed to consider the woman. Medicine reflects a society that has increasingly placed the value of the fetus over that of the woman, that presumes that women are by nature a danger to their fetuses, and believes that the medical profession, and the courts, are here to protect fetuses from their mothers.

I began to apply the principles of medical ethics to my writing and research on pregnancy, reproductive technology, and motherhood. I addressed the social policy and science of drug addiction and pregnancy, finding that social policy represented institutionalized punitive attitudes toward women more than valid scientific information about drugs.

I have begun to work on new models of care for women. My training at Doctors Hospital was in obstetrics and gynecology, which is often interpreted as "women's health." But obstetrics and gynecology is really about reproductive health, and leaves unaddressed all the other aspects of a woman's body. A male can go to a doctor for a yearly checkup and have his entire body examined. Yet a healthy female often has to go to two doctors to have her entire body examined.

The splitting of a woman's body between two specialties is most clearly absurd when we consider examination of the female with abdominal or pelvic pain. There is no anatomic boundary between the abdomen and pelvis. It is one continuous cavity about 8" × 10" in size. The ovaries, when inflamed, may become attached to intestines. An inflamed appendix may become attached to the ovary and fallopian tube. In endometriosis the tissue from the uterus may spread up to the diaphragm at the top of the abdomen, or may attach itself to the colon. And yet the woman often has to go to two doctors who examine different parts of this one small space, and then discuss by phone or report or through the woman what they think is wrong. Had medicine developed with the female body as the norm, one doctor would be expected to examine this one cavity.

Research has also been modeled on a male body. Pharmaceutical companies, in researching medications, have in the past used only males as subjects. An official at one company once told me, "We can't use women. The menstrual cycle confuses our results." And so, instead of researching the effect of the menstrual cycle on drug effects and side effects, women were ignored and left out of the scientific sample. When women didn't respond to drugs in the same way as men, they were accused of being "super-sensitive" or hypochondriacs. It was easier to blame the women than to research the drugs.

Some of this is changing. More still has to be changed. I am often asked, "How would you fix it if you could?" And so, I offer my vision. Some of this change is what we want for men as well as women. Some is specific to women, due to the history of splitting women's care and the institutionalized disregard for women's concerns that have been endemic in medicine.

• Universal access to care is the first principle in the foundation of health care. There is no health care if people cannot afford it. And there is no health care if humiliation of the poor and of women is a requirement of obtaining that care.

• Models based upon primary care are the second principle of health care. Basically this means that each person should be able to go to someone—physician, nurse practitioner, etc., and have basic health screening, education, and preventive care, with attention to the role of violence and sexual abuse prevalent in women's lives. In other words, provide physical health care in the context of the more complex and destructive aspects of women's lives.

• The medical specialties must be restructured so that internal medicine incorporates gynecologic care into its body of knowledge and practice. All internists learn some gynecology, but many then drop it from their practices, preferring to have women patients go to a gynecologist for that aspect of care. Some of this is changing. There is a move afoot within internal medicine to retain gynecology as part of this discipline. Training programs are developing in internal medicine to provide models of women's care in the training of all internists.

Family medicine now addresses the whole body of the woman, and is increasingly committed to understanding and meeting the needs of its women patients.

• All specialties should become user friendly to women. This does not require major changes in the content of training, but rather in the attitudes toward women. The body of knowledge we already have about the menstrual cycle, for instance, should not be restricted to obstetrics and gynecology, or even to the primary care specialties. We have learned that women asthmatics die more often premenstrually. We don't know why. The asthma specialist treating a woman should take this into consideration. We have learned that women's symptoms of heart disease vary somewhat from those of men. The cardiologist treating a woman should be aware of this. Women with seizures may have more frequent seizures premenstrually. Neurologists need to know and consider this in their treatment. Women with panic attacks may have more attacks premenstrually. The cardiologist needs to know this, as does the psychiatrist, since the symptoms may be so confusing. In other words, every medical specialty must consider the spectrum of women's presentations of illness and responses to treatment. The differences are matters of degree, but physicians need to know the spectrum and recognize those differences. All specialties need to reframe their views of women so that a woman who doesn't respond as expected is not "blamed" but rather is heard and understood, with treatment tailored to how her body responds, not how the healthy males in drug studies responded.

• Training programs in medical specialties must also be user friendly to women. Women's biological and psychological roles as mothers must be protected, not simply tolerated. As with the human body, if medical training were based upon a model of the female student, resident, and physician, the time and energy necessary for childbearing would be part of the structure of education. There is a terrible underlying fear that a woman resident who also needs time to bear and raise her children is ''getting away'' with something, doing less work for the same money or rank or credit. Young women who are in various stages of training in medicine are still forced to choose which price they will pay.

The antagonism and resentment toward women interferes with creative solutions. Medical education must also become user friendly to women.

• A final proposal I put forth is the development of an applied academic discipline in women's health, as a way of creating structure for improving the health and health care of women. Women's Health would be interdisciplinary, bringing together medicine, public health, nursing, psychology, epidemiology, medical anthropology and sociology, women's studies, economics, and other areas which impact on the health care of woman. This discipline would create models of care, design research across disciplines, develop curriculum for Medical Schools and doctors in practice, and integrate the diverse segments of women's health that are now fragmented into their respective disciplines and specialties.

These are my visions. They are visions of change, but none is beyond our current resources. They are changes of attitude and of intent. They require a version of woman that is whole and equal. As women we should accept nothing less. As physicians we should provide nothing less.

—Michelle Harrison, M.D.
March 1993

I dreamed I was back at the hospital standing in a large white room. Steel shelves lining the walls held drums of a liquid which I understood was going to be given to everyone there to consume. Somehow I discovered that the drums were filled with the poison curare. I knew that we were all going to be killed. I was trying to figure out whether anyone else knew about the poison and whether there was anyone who would join me in fighting what was about to happen. Frightened but calm, I decided that I could take the poison, spit it out and pretend that I had swallowed it. Heather, my six-year-old daughter, was somewhere in the hospital. I figured out that I could also protect her by instructing her to spit out the curare surreptitiously. But there were many other children in the hospital. I had to save them, too, and I was trying to reach their mothers to warn them of the poison so they could protect their children. I kept trying to dial numbers but nothing was happening. Appearing before me and then dissolving were the faces of prominent obstetrician-gynecologists I had known. Each would come slowly toward me, enlarging, smiling menacingly, and then fade . . . to be followed by the next. I knew in the dream that they had planned it all and were going to kill us all.

I am a thirty-nine-year-old physician. I graduated from medical school in 1967. As a feminist, family physician and medical-school faculty member, I was one of many people in the late seventies who were challenging the way in which women were being treated by the health-care system. At-

1

tending home births, writing and lecturing, presenting testimony in Washington for HEW, the FDA and consumer groups, I still felt limited by my lack of specific expertise and training in obstetrics and gynecology—even though I had my board certification in family practice.

At the age of thirty-five, when my daughter was five years old, I left teaching and practice to become a resident in obstetrics and gynecology at Doctors Hospital, a prestigious teaching institution in Everytown, USA. I had sought and found a part-time position, which required my working up to seventy hours a week for half salary, or $8,000 a year. Part-time residencies had been developed to help physicians who were mothers obtain further training and still take care of their children.

In the end I was not to spend the four years in the hospital I had planned. I left because I had discovered there the poison of my dream, the poison inherent in obstetrics and gynecology as it is practiced in this country and abroad.

This book is the record of the time I was a resident. It exists because I am a diary keeper and have been since I was a young girl. In recent years, instead of writing in small thick journals, I switched to a tape recorder, both to save time and to use more creatively the time I spent driving to and from work. In Everytown, my tape recorder on the car seat beside me became at times an almost human companion, to whom I unburdened myself at the end of the day, and to whom I bid goodbye as I entered Doctors Hospital each morning.

Chapter One

MY PAST

I had wanted to be a doctor for as long as I could remember. I also wanted to be a mother. It seemed to me that doctoring was a form of mothering, that nurturing and healing came from the same energies, from the same center of my self that wanted to mother.

I applied to medical school knowing from advisers and other students that "I want to help people" was an unacceptable answer to the question "Why do you want to go into medicine?" I learned to say at interviews, "I find it interesting," or "I would like to combine research with practice."

In medical school I quickly found out that caring was not part of the curriculum; indeed it was discouraged. Patients, primarily black and Puerto Rican, were bodies on whom we, white and privileged, practiced. Racism among the doctors contributed to the treatment of patients as objects. My medical school memories are of patient after patient for whom I cared, but whom I felt helplessly unable to defend from the impersonal nature of hospital care.

Nancy, a seven-year-old child I admitted to the hospital one night in my final year, was one such patient. She was quite sick and was diagnosed to have a tumor of the pancreas, which is extremely rare and with which none of the doctors in our hospital were familiar. There was a surgeon at another hospital, three blocks away, who had published a paper on his experience with eight of these tumors, but because Nancy

3

was a good "teaching case," our physicians were determined to do the surgery on their own. I had an ominous feeling about her fate, not just because of the inexperience of the surgeons, but because Nancy was being used for teaching purposes by several different departments, with the result that many unnecessary tests were being performed on her.

Two days before her scheduled surgery Nancy's parents asked me, "She's going to be all right, isn't she?"

"I don't know," I answered, trying to find ways to let them be aware of my concerns. So I told them, "What she has is very serious," wishing instead I could say, "Take her out of here and get her to people who know what they are doing!"

"The doctors seem to be good . . ." In the father's voice were both statement and question.

"Yes, but this tumor is so rare that no one in this hospital has ever seen it before. In fact, it is so rare that there have been only a few reported cases, and those were described by a doctor at City Hospital." That was as obvious as I dared be.

"Well, we have to trust the doctors. They must know best." The discussion was over.

Nancy went to surgery two days later with at least twenty people in the room. The surgery seemed to go well, but as the child was being taken from the operating room, her blood pressure fell dangerously low. At first the drop in pressure was ignored because it was assumed to be related to the removal of the tumor, but suddenly there was panic as the doctors realized Nancy's belly was swelling. The surgeons quickly reopened her abdomen, and as blood poured out, they tried to locate the knot that had loosened, the blood vessel that had not been tied securely. When Nancy's heart stopped, the surgeons slashed open her chest and tried to force her heart to pump. There was blood all over, Nancy's blood all over, and after a while they gave up and said she was dead.

I wanted to leave school that day, to leave medicine forever, to take myself as far as I could from the people around me. It wasn't only that the child had died—her illness in itself was life-threatening; it was that she died because someone wasn't careful enough. In fact, no one had been careful with her since she arrived at the hospital. I blamed myself for not having tried harder. Nancy's family invited me to the funeral and stayed in touch with me for years afterward.

Staying sane in school meant saying to myself, "I'm not like them. I do care. I am different. Someday I'll be out of here and able to do some good." But those thoughts also left me very isolated. I walked a thin line between what I believed I should be doing as a human being and what my role as a medical student required.

I was one of ten women in a class of 100 at a respected medical college, all of whom shared the same concerns about how we could combine medicine with home and family. We met to give one another support, at a time when few women were involved in feminism. In those days it was not unusual to hear women in medicine and other male-dominated fields say things like "I actually never liked being with other women," or "None of my friends are women." Hungry for role models, we tried to meet with other women in our profession, always asking the same questions: "How can one combine medicine with raising a family?"; "How did you do it?"; "Why did you not do it?"; "What were your conflicts and resolutions?"; "Are you glad or sorry?"

A pediatrician, mother of three, said, "It's easy. Anyone can do those 'animal things' the first few years. Your children don't need you until they are older and can talk."

A gynecologist advised me, "Have your children early and get it over with. That way by the time you are practicing, you don't have to bother with little children."

Other women, when asked questions like these, answered in hushed tones with an air of secrecy. Women doctors weren't supposed to talk about children. In a male world, where children were not a fit topic of conversation, I referred to these women as "closet mothers."

I worried about how I would fit it all in. I didn't think

raising children was doing those "animal things," or if it was, I still wanted to do them. I wanted to mother my children and I expected to use mothering in my work.

Psychiatry had become a passionate interest for me because it seemed to promise that I would find effective ways of using myself to help alleviate pain and illness. I did my internship in a community hospital on the New Jersey shore where I rotated through all the medical services, but I also spent time in a child-guidance clinic. Delivering babies at night on OB, walking along the beach with a troubled teen-ager during the day, I developed a sense of what I might achieve as a physician.

Two years of residency training, however, left me much less certain that I wanted to be a psychiatrist. Still being taught not to care, I was told by a supervisor, "Psychiatry is a science. If, in talking, the patient gets better, fine, but that is not your goal. Your goal is to understand how the mind works." No one was ever accused of "not caring."

Although I was considered talented in my work, I myself had many doubts about what I was being taught and what I was doing. Because I felt that in our close scrutiny we were missing some of the meaning of mental illness, I wanted to step outside to look at it. As foster mother to a teen-ager for a year, I had discovered that in the isolation of the mental hospital, we often failed to understand the complexities of real life, real emotions, real relationships. Humbled by the experience of living with a troubled and misbehaving adolescent, I was aghast at the advice I had so easily given to parents who had sought help with their children. I learned the obvious—that real life experience does teach us and change us.

"Maybe I'll return when I'm sixty, when I might have some answers" was what I jokingly said when I decided to leave.

My teachers were upset that I was "leaving" and expressed hope that I would return to the program. They did, however, share with me their two major criticisms of my work: I had difficulties with authority and I could not be counted upon to carry out orders with which I disagreed.

I left with the sense that I was parting from a disturbed community—and that was not only because of the patients. Staff and patients seemed to me to share in the mental illness, much as prison guards and inmates share a jail mentality.

I didn't find a place where I could practice medicine as a caring physician until I moved to South Carolina, where I was to work in a comprehensive health program that primarily served a rural black population. I opened a clinic on St. Helena, one of the coastal islands between Charleston and Savannah. There caring was acceptable, and I thought I had found a permanent place for myself.

I made house calls to comfort the dying and the families of the dying. I delivered babies and took care of them and their mothers. Sometimes I worked around the clock, but there seemed to be a purpose in what I was doing. Thirty to fifty patients came into the clinic each day, many of whom had never seen a doctor before.

When I first moved to South Carolina I looked forward to being more casual at work, perhaps dressing in jeans and sandals. The day I opened the clinic many patients came to see me, some just to say hello and welcome me to the island. They came dressed up, though, the old ladies in hats with tiny veils and in dresses that were obviously their best. The old men came in suits. The children were immaculate. I knew I couldn't wear jeans, that it would be disrespectful. I never went without a bra in South Carolina, and I wore a dress to work every day.

Within months of our arrival in South Carolina, my brief marriage fell apart and my husband left. I found myself alone, pregnant and scared. Friends and family wanted me to return home to New Jersey, but I felt incredibly vulnerable and terrified that if I left now, I wouldn't be able to get a job because of my pregnancy. In addition, I had committed myself to my work in South Carolina, and I didn't want to abandon it. I stayed on at the clinic, working until the hours before my daughter's birth. When I was in my eighth month Heather's father had heard of my pregnancy and had called. During a long and painful phone conversation it became clear that reconciliation was not possible. We were officially divorced shortly thereafter and I've not heard from him again.

I had been trying to conceive for a year and had begun to despair of ever being pregnant. The week my husband and I separated, my menses was delayed, and when on a Friday evening it came still another time, I cried. But the next day it stopped, and the next day it started again, and continued this way for ten days.

"Doc, I've been spotting for ten days. What could it be?" I was at work and getting a corridor consultation from a colleague, the only obstetrician in town.

"Maybe you're pregnant, Michelle."

I shrugged, hiding the hope even from myself.

"Why don't you give a urine to the lab? You've nothing to lose."

The possibility that I was pregnant was thrilling but it also gave me a sense of panic because, two days before, I had admitted a baby to the hospital with a rare viral disease known to be dangerous to women in their first trimester of pregnancy. Although I asked another doctor to take care of the baby I'd admitted, I still worried throughout my pregnancy that I had infected myself and my child.

The bleeding continued on and off, and when I questioned my doctor he'd say, "Oh, don't worry, it probably means that you've already miscarried." No one was willing to believe that I wanted this pregnancy.

"But how did *you*, a *doctor*, get pregnant?" the program director asked.

"The usual way," I told him. His attitude was not as unusual as it sounds. A woman in medical school with me was once asked by a nurse, "Do women doctors have periods?"

Heather arrived in the early morning hours of December 3, 1972, propelled out of my body with a push I felt I had practiced for years. In the first moments after her birth, I knew that I wanted to be with her. I had saved enough money to hold me for a while and I would not go back to work until I wanted to or had to.

In the months ahead, sitting at the window of the small house I rented, looking out at the Beaufort River, nursing my baby from the rocking chair I'd bought years before for "when I have a baby," I felt total peace. I loved the lack of anyone else's demands. I liked knowing what to expect. Jokingly I described the difference between myself and my married friends thus: "I don't have to live with the illusion that someone is going to come home at five o'clock and make my life easier."

It was lonely, though, and at times frightening. Often Heather and I were alone for days at a time. The phone didn't ring, nor did anyone come by. My worst fantasy was that something would happen to me and it would be days before anyone would come by and find my baby. If I died, she could starve before anyone found her.

A year later the woman who was my secretary told me, "Don't get too close to that child! You'll only get hurt." It seemed that everyone was telling me that. There is something threatening to outsiders about a mother and child close to each other. Women are supposed to stay home, but they aren't supposed to be *too* tied to their babies. I was tied to Heather; I was free to be tied to her because there was no one else in my life who could lay claim to my time or attention. My life felt suspended but complete for the moment; this was the time to saturate myself with my baby, partly because I knew it wouldn't always be this way.

"Don't spend so much time with her," I was told. "You're spoiling her," I was warned. Why did anyone care so much? Why did my closeness with my baby produce such fury in others?

I said, "I want to be with her until she is bored with me and seeks others because she wants other company."

"You're making her too dependent," they warned me. "She won't be able to leave you."

I wanted Heather to be strong when she faced the world,

and although I wouldn't always be able to protect her, I could start helping her learn to feel strong.

At first it was as though Heather was a person only I had created. Then there were differences: words she didn't learn from me, ideas that came from within her. I wondered at this person who had come to be with me. She looked different, too. Her blue eyes and fine blond hair contrasted with my dark eyes and coarse black hair now streaked with gray.

"What pretty blue eyes you have, Heather," a friend said to her when she was two.

"No, I have brown eyes like my mama," she replied and burst into tears.

Since my eyes are dark, and since most of our friends were Black, their eyes and those of their children were dark. Heather, wanting to be like me and like everyone else she knew, would cry whenever her blue eyes were mentioned.

"You know, you really do have beautiful blue eyes, Heather," I told her one day, "but I have an idea. Let's trade eyes."

"How can we do that?"

"Here," I said, pointing first to my eyes. "I'm giving them to you, and now I'll take yours." It was like the game of stealing noses we'd played so often, and she laughed. After that, when someone spoke of her blue eyes, she'd say, "No. I have brown eyes. I traded with my mama."

We traded dads when she was almost three.

"Who's my dad?" she asked one day when I picked her up at the day-care center shortly after we moved up North.

"Who's been asking, Heather?"

"My teacher asked me and I said I didn't know. Do I have a dad?"

"You had a dad a long time ago but he went away. Remember I told you about him once?"

She was silent. I had told her once before, about a month before while we were out on the bike, but she hadn't been ready to hear me.

"I have an idea, Heather. Remember we once traded eyes? How about if we trade dads?"

We were in New Jersey staying temporarily with my parents, and Heather was close to them both.

"You mean I could have Poppy?"

"Sure, I'm grown up now so I don't really need a dad anymore, and Poppy's a real good dad. He could be yours."

Poppy became Heather's dad, fulfilling the role of father. He even picked her up at the day-care center so she could show him off to her friends, and he still stands in at official functions requiring the presence of a dad. He calls her, writes to her, and is able to express love in a less conflicted way than he could when his own children were younger. One Father's Day Heather teased me, saying, "You don't have a dad to give a present to."

Heather had a dad and I have had the ongoing pleasure of raising her alone.

Life was different for me at home with an infant. People who had, when I was a practicing physician, valued and sought my opinion now asked me to make sandwiches for their meetings. I was asked to act as hostess to out-of-town visitors and to "drop them off" at the health center. Treated as though my brain had atrophied with the onset of motherhood, I thought, If this is how it is for me, with all that I have already done, what must it be like for other women?

Feminism clicked for me in a South Carolina grocery store one day. I was there shopping, with Heather perched on my hip, when the store manager came over and made a pass at me. I was very angry: grocery store managers don't make passes at lady doctors. When I placed an ad in the local paper to try to form a consciousness-raising group, the newspaper's owner-editor called because he thought I was trying to place an ad for some sort of orgy. When he realized what I meant he said, "Oh, you mean as in women's lib." The ad was printed in his paper with "women's lib" in parenthesis. A group of us went on meeting and came to support one another. Eventually we formed a NOW chapter and became involved in local politics.

Eventually I wanted and needed to work, to prove I could

do it. So, with my baby in a backpack, I volunteered to do free school physicals in the local school system. Having convinced the people in the comprehensive health program that it was possible for me to work that way, I was rehired into the program to work, at first part-time, then full-time. I hired Mae, a woman who had raised eight children, and in a van, which served as a daytime sleeping and eating place for the baby, the three of us—Heather, Mae and I—went off to work each morning.

It was a wonderful way to be both mother and working woman. It's not that I was with my child all the time, but I was accessible to her, and she to me. If I worked late, she was with me in the van. She and Mae played, took walks, visited people down the road, gathered pecans, and made friends with patients in the clinics.

There's a story of someone asking, "Who's Dr. Harrison?" and their being told, "You'll know her by the trail of raisins." Though it looked very casual, in fact all my resources seemed to go into keeping the system working.

My memories reappear in vignettes. I was walking along a street in our small South Carolina town. Heather was in a backpack, a rare sight in those days when most babies were carried in plastic recliner seats with metal handles like shopping baskets. Walking in the streets was rare too. As we went by that day, people opened their doors and stared. I remembered my childhood and the times I had looked at someone who was eccentric, and wondered what it felt like to be like that. I thought to myself that day in South Carolina, I have become eccentric, certainly for where I live. It felt okay for me, but it didn't feel okay to raise Heather there. I didn't want her to be the child of the town eccentric.

We stayed in South Carolina until Heather was two and a half years old. I had risen in the administration of the program to become the director of Health Care Services, heading a department with 150 employees and a $2 million budget. I also continued to see some patients in the clinics. Then problems developed in the program which made it difficult for me to stay on. Tension around both sexism and racism was mounting, and my sense of belonging was shaken. I was basically a single white woman living in a small Southern town working for a Black poverty program. I had become involved in most of the community projects there, chairing the day-care-center board, raising money, serving on advisory committees, but I remained an outsider.

When I left South Carolina I wanted a quiet, inconspicuous life, where others were doing most of the work and there weren't such shortages of the energy needed to effect change. I wanted to be someplace for a while where I wasn't so needed.

I moved to New Jersey primarily because it seemed important that Heather be close to her grandparents. Hoping to recreate the work and child-care arrangement I had had in South Carolina, I placed an ad in the New York *Times*, in which I advertised for a job anywhere in the New York–New Jersey area with on-site child care. The ad resulted only in a few obscene phone calls. A hospital I located which had just given up its on-site child care had decided, "There was too much demand for it." Then, giving up on finding such a situation, I enrolled Heather in a nearby day-care center. She loved it immediately, and I was able to get several part-time emergency-room jobs. Heather was proud to have a "school" to attend. At eight in the morning when I stopped at my parents' house between jobs to take Heather to the day-care center, I'd discover her clothed in a long dress, bracelets, a hat, sunglasses, a couple of scarfs, and clogs, which were a passion of hers, ready to go to school for the day.

I worked at three hospitals simultaneously, trying to accumulate the money for a down payment on a house, since I yearned now to put down roots. Our household consisted of Heather and me, and of Missie, a black-and-white long-haired terrier-type dog I'd gotten from the SPCA twelve years before, along with Toodles, a mini-schnauzer left over from my marriage, and Cari, a tiger cat whom I'd paid $10 for when I was a resident in psychiatry.

I found a large old house I could afford, and Heather and I, with our animals, moved in and invited a few friends to live with us. The house needed a lot of work just to make it habitable, but we all rebuilt, plastered and painted rooms. It turned out to be very colorful inside, for anyone willing to help out got to choose the colors used.

Finding a job was no problem because I was willing to work in emergency rooms and clinics. Since I enjoyed most the part of practice that involved taking care of people, it was fine with me. As long as I wasn't trying to climb a ladder, I could find gratifying work.

"Family medicine" was a new specialty, which under its "grandfather clause" allowed physicians in practice who took the requisite continuing medical-education courses to pass an examination for board certification without having to take a family medicine residency. Determined to obtain this specialty certification, I took courses, studied and passed the examination. I began teaching at a local medical school and at a residency program where I both supervised residents and saw patients myself. Because my salary came out of teaching money, I was able to enjoy spending enough time with patients (i.e., I was not compelled to be cost-effective through the practice). The teaching scared me at first and I was unsure of myself, but I came to enjoy my work both with the students and with the patients.

Life was fairly peaceful. Heather's day-care-center hours were similar to those of my work. Often we had mornings at home together; I would take her on my bike to the center, and then I worked for the afternoon. I became more involved in the women's health movement and there found a group of women who were responsive to my feminism, my feelings about motherhood, and even my medical knowledge. Being a physician has often isolated me from the people to whom I have felt closest. For the first time, both my feminism and my work became a unified part of my life.

* * *

Years before, when I was still a resident in psychiatry, I had attended home births, but when I tried to tell my friends at work about what I was doing, I was usually warned that I could lose my license. It upset me that women were having babies in a field unattended, so I did it anyway. My first home birth, in a trailer in Maryland, was also the first time I had ever been alone with a woman throughout her labor. It took hours. There were no nurses, no shifts, no system to shield me from how long having a baby really takes. I remember opening my obstetrics book, examining the curve of labor charted on the page and feeling reassured, for the hours of the woman's labor were no longer than the hours of the curve. It only seemed longer because I wasn't used to being with the woman all that time.

When I moved to South Carolina, I didn't think about home births. There, I was taking care of a population which had just turned away from the granny midwives. Women wanted to give birth in the hospital. They wanted anesthesia, not natural childbirth. They did not breast-feed, even if that meant taking the baby home to an inadequate diet.

Our society was teaching them that almost anything was better than "old-fashioned" breast-feeding, and these mothers were committed to providing "the best" for their babies. Breast-feeding didn't regain acceptance in that community until after I had my child and was seen nursing her.

In the midst of New Jersey affluence, though, women were having babies at home without anyone in attendance, so I was again forced to confront my fears of becoming involved. After sitting on the fence for a few months, I knew that if I really believed a woman had the right to choose, I should be helping her do it safely. Little of my life remained unaffected by my decision to attend births, although there were not many actual hours involved. For example, it was necessary to give up emergency-room work, when someone's life might be endangered by my inability to be present. A woman delivering at home must have her doctor or midwife there or she is without trained help. There aren't other nurses or doctors passing in the hall who can step in and help. Always on call, I carried a beeper wherever I went. At night my sleep took on a vigilance that was a part of my work, including dreams that warned me when there was a difficult birth ahead.

Heather came with me to some of the births; her official job was to kiss the baby after it was born. Sometimes she waited in another room; at other times she was actually present for the birth. Within the growing home-birth movement, enough children have attended home births that at a national childbirth conference I once did a workshop for children who had been present either in their role as siblings or as the children of those of us who attended women at home. Children see birth differently from adults. They say, "You see, as the baby starts to come out, it turns its head and then it twists the rest of its body so there is room," and while the children talk they demonstrate to one another how the baby makes its way out. They describe the baby as an active participant both in the timing of birth and in the process of being born. "Babies like to come out when it's dark because it's more like inside the mother."

The births were a source of great pleasure for me, but also of fear. With each one that went well, I wondered how I could have been so worried. When things didn't go well, I agonized over what I should have done differently.

Although my official duties at the medical school were to teach family medicine, I also lectured on women's health care, and especially the rights of women to give birth as they choose. Appointed to the New Jersey State Medical Society Committee on Maternal and Infant Welfare, I sat with heads of OB departments throughout the state discussing such issues as midwife privileges. I accepted my function as a bridge between orthodox medicine and a community which trusted little of what medicine had to offer.

In spite of my good intentions, though, I was still suspect in the lay community because I was a physician. Originally I had planned to attend home births to support the midwives, but as it turned out, I found myself much more alone than I had anticipated. The fear surrounding home birth had affected midwives as well as physicians.

"Home birth is child abuse," was the statement coming from the American College of Obstetrics and Gynecology (ACOG). Throughout the country, doctors attending home births were being threatened with loss of both hospital privileges and malpractice insurance. Residents attending home births either had been expelled from their training programs or were being threatened with expulsion. Legislation to limit midwife privileges was being introduced in many states. Midwives were being charged with murder if a baby died after a home birth.

Eventually, however, some competent and dedicated midwives and I began to work together and to give one another support in the face of increasing pressure to refuse our services to women. At about this time it became clear that I, especially because of the growing publicity about my work, would not be able to go on attending home births and still work within teaching institutions.

I was a family physician, not an obstetrician. If a woman I was taking care of developed any complications, I had to turn her over to others who, although more trained in the technological aspects of medical care, rarely shared my political or moral views or those of the women I treated. I wanted to do more obstetrics in the hospital as well as at home. Sometimes at the medical school, counseling students about their future, I found myself wishing I were younger and had the chance to get more training.

The development of part-time residency positions around the country began to render my hopes more attainable. Up to now I'd been stopped from going on with my training because I knew that a full-time program was more than I could manage as a single parent. Another reason I was reluctant to take more training was that I didn't believe it was possible to give the kind of care I wanted to give in a hospital. Every time I walked into a hospital, I changed, without wanting to. I became cooler, more removed, less human, more antiseptic. Patients changed too, in ways that made them turn over their destinies to professionals like me.

The birthing of a young woman named Anna gave me the

sense that I *could* work in a hospital and still be myself. Anna was only eighteen when I attended her birth, and her husband seemed about the same age. When Adrienne, a nurse who worked with me, and I first arrived at the house, Kurt confessed that they hadn't practiced the childbirth exercises and he seemed frightened because he didn't know what to do. Relieved that he was not expected to "coach" his wife, he was able to be there solely as support. There is something absurd about expecting a young male, who will never experience childbirth, to be able, after six lessons, to "coach" a woman through labor and childbirth.

The young couple were living with Kurt's parents, who, along with other relatives, hovered outside the bedroom, anxiously awaiting all news. Anna labored for many hours, but then for some time she made no progress. She was a small woman with what seemed to be a large baby. A decision was made to move her to the hospital, with everyone in agreement and seemingly quite relieved.

We went to a nearby hospital where, although I did not have privileges, I did have an informal agreement that I would stay with Anna. I took her in and remained with her while she labored many more hours. The obstetrician, Anna and I agreed to postpone x-rays, since within the safety of the hospital we could just watch to see what happened. Our nurse Adrienne worked in this hospital at night on obstetrics, so she was able to assist in relations between the nursing staff and me. We didn't have privacy, because there were several nurses curious about what we were doing, but Anna didn't mind their presence.

Most important, though, was my decision not to leave the room for any reason at all. I did not take calls and there was no communication between the obstetrician and myself that did not include Anna. No conversation outside the room aligned me with the staff separate from the patient. I stayed locked in her room as if we had been at her home.

Anna was pushing and having a hard time. She tried several positions—on her knees, then standing and pushing. She stood at the side of the bed, with Kurt beside her applying pressure to her back when she wanted him to, while I stood in front of her so she could lean on me. She was leaning and breathing. We were all breathing with her. As she leaned forward, I placed my hands under her thighs to give her more support so she could bend her knees and put some of her weight on my hands. And then suddenly I realized that her feet were no longer touching the floor and that the full weight of her body was resting on my hands, in my arms. I held her that way while she pushed her baby.

The rest of the birth was as beautiful. She delivered her baby up on the bed finally, with Kurt sitting cross-legged behind her and holding her, with Adrienne listening intermittently to the unborn baby's heart beat, with me doing perineal massage to ease the passage out, with the obstetrician and the nurses watching and learning.

Reassured by this experience that I could sustain myself against institutional intimidation, I felt able to seek more training within a hospital. Strengthened by Anna's birthing, I felt I could become an obstetrician and that my hands and arms could still hold women in labor.

Chapter Two

When I started to investigate potential programs, I found that few hospitals offered part-time residency positions, and none I could find actually had a part-time resident in obstetrics and gynecology (OB-GYN). To a letter of inquiry I wrote to a hospital which must have been mistakenly listed in the part-time registry, this reply came back: "We do not offer part-time residencies ever. Please note that full time is twenty-four hours a day."

An interview at another hospital—where I didn't go—went as follows:

CHAIRMAN OF THE DEPT. OF OB-GYN: Why don't you send your child away to live?

ME: I can't do that.

HE: If you aren't willing to give up your child, you don't deserve to be an obstetrician-gynecologist. Dr. Harrison, your problem is that you lack motivation.

Doctors Hospital, in Everytown, was well known in the Midwest for its intent to provide humanitarian care to patients.

At an interview at Doctors Hospital:

DR. WALTER PIERCE: I'd be willing to offer you a position right now, pending receipt of your credentials.

ME: There's a hooker.

HE: What's that?

ME: I have a child.

HE: That's no hooker.

ME: And I want to do it part-time.

HE: That's a hooker.

Dr. Pierce, a world renowned obstetrician-gynecologist and head of the Dept. of OB-GYN at Doctors Hospital, was known for his liberal attitude toward women in training. This resulted in a higher than usual percentage of women residents in his department, but even so, he was uncertain he wanted to take anyone part-time. A full-time program at his hospital ranged from ninety to one hundred and forty hours a week. It was a schedule I didn't think I could manage as a single parent. We negotiated for a long time and Dr. Pierce finally offered me a position that was two-thirds time for half salary. I would have to work out the specific hours with the chief residents, who would be directly responsible for my daily activities.

Although I had met with Dr. Pierce to talk about the possibility of starting training the following year, eleven months hence, Pierce now said I could have the job if I could be in Everytown to start work in four weeks. He had just fired a resident that week, so he needed someone at once. With no certainty that the offer would be good the following year, I felt I had to take advantage of this opportunity.

I left Pierce's office astounded because I had the offer I had wanted in a city where I had friends, in a program with a chairperson who was supportive of women, in a residency program with other women. And because I was going to one of the finest and most humanitarian of hospitals, the difficulties would at least be fewer than elsewhere. All I needed to do was gather letters and credentials from all the places I'd been, negotiate with the chief residents about the schedule, and move halfway across the country. Each piece seemed manageable.

There would be three chief residents—all women—each for a period of four months during the year. They had started together three years before, and now, in their final year of residency, they would take turns being chief residents. Carol, a woman I knew from work in the women's health movement, was currently the chief. She had almost four months to go.

Carol was the person who had urged me to call Dr. Pierce to talk about a position, telling me, "He likes strong women."

"He offered me the job!" I reported to her ecstatically later in the day.

"I know. I've already talked with him. We have to talk about the hours."

When she found that the other residents were opposed to my coming into the program part-time, Carol had had to do her own negotiating about me. I knew I would need the support of at least the chief residents if I were to succeed at all. Jackie, who would be chief in the spring, wanted to talk with me before any final agreements were made since, as she told me that evening, "I have to live with the decisions that are made now. I'll be your chief in the spring."

Jackie and I talked on the phone. She was worried and doubtful the arrangement would work. "You know, politically I'm in favor of what you are trying to do, but I don't want to be left to do your work." However, she was surprised that the schedule tentatively worked out by Carol and me called for me to work many more hours than she had expected. "My husband once knew a part-time resident in opthalmology who was never there and never did her work," she said.

Jackie went on, thinking out loud as she tried to create a schedule that would best help the hospital but would not be full-time. Interspersed with her listing possible duties, shifts, days of greater surgery, were her doubts about my plans. "I don't think you can really do this if you have kids," she said. "I decided a long time ago that I'd have an abortion if I got pregnant while in training.

"A lot of the others will resent you," she added.

"I know that."

"They can make it tough for you."

"I know that too: that's why I wanted to be sure that at

least you and Carol felt all right about my coming here. I don't expect it to be easy.''

''Everyone here is overworked, so there will always be excess demands on your time. You're going to have to be able to protect yourself. No one will ever be satisfied with what you do because there is always more work to be done.''

Jackie finally presented a plan. I would come in five mornings at six o'clock and see patients until eight. On Monday and Tuesday I would then be free to leave for the day. If I was to be on call for the night, I would return to the hospital at five and stay either until morning or through the next day. On Wednesday, Thursday and Friday I would work from six in the morning until six o'clock at night. I would take night and weekend call every sixth night, as Carol and I had already agreed.

''But can you take orders?'' Jackie asked as though needing to satisfy one more doubt of hers; Dr. Pierce had already asked me the same question.

''Jackie, I know the rules of the game. I think I can take it. I've told myself I'll take whatever I have to in order to make it through. I'm giving up a lot to be here.''

We were both worn out by the end of the phone call. Jackie had to be at work at six, and soon I would be there too. The following morning I was on the phone sending telegrams to schools, training programs and jobs where I had been, authorizing them to send letters to Dr. Pierce.

Fran and Laurie are the friends I was visiting in Everytown when I met with Dr. Pierce. Both are women's health activists I knew from conferences around the country. I had first met them in New Jersey when they spoke there, and then I turned to them for support as pressure mounted for me to stop attending home births. Although I didn't know them well, we shared a sense that we would be close friends if we ever lived in the same city. We had planned this visit so we could finish some of the conversations that were forever being interrupted by plane schedules, conference schedules and work.

Fran's response the previous May when I first told her

what I wanted to do had been, "But you can't do that! They'll destroy you. You'll either come out thinking like they do or you won't make it through." We were in a car going to dinner from a board meeting of the National Women's Health Network in Philadelphia. Fran was navigating while I drove. With only four blocks to go and others waiting for us at the restaurant we got lost, circling numerous streets neither of us knew while Fran tried to talk me out of what I wanted to do. She didn't think I could survive, and she didn't want me to do that to myself. Failing to dissuade me, she added, "Well, if you're going to do it, Everytown is the place for you to be. At least you have support there."

Laurie, a slight young woman in her mid-twenties with a singular passion to improve the health care of women, was excited at the prospect of having someone whom she trusted trained in obstetrics and gynecology. The night I was offered the position we celebrated at Laurie's house. My mood was dampened somewhat by a call from New Jersey that Missie, my dog of fifteen years, had died that morning. Her death, though not unexpected, was tremendously painful. She had been a constant companion for most of my adult life.

By the first of August, Dr. Pierce had received my records, and he had notified me that he expected me in Everytown in three weeks. I was still obligated to work another two weeks in New Jersey, which gave me one week between jobs. School would be starting for Heather in the first week of September, by which time I needed a place to live, a school and after-school care. Critical to the entire plan was that I sell the New Jersey house, since I was counting on that profit to support me at least through part of the residency.

I made a list:

sell house	finish job
buy house	notify patients
child care	move

Heather was to have entered kindergarten in New Jersey, but was old enough for first grade in the Everytown area. I was uncertain about which grade to place her in and was unable to get help in that decision because it was August. Some of the local schools had after-school programs, but because it was summer and these programs were all parent-run, no one could give me information about them. I was told that some of the after-school groups had long waiting lists, but no one knew at which schools. Finding a house depended on the after-school care available.

When I first planned to do this training, I had expected to have six months to a year in which to make the move. Ideally I would have found a living situation with other adults and children so there would be sharing of child care and so Heather would not be so alone while I was working. But when it all happened so fast, there wasn't time to find or create such a household that could be expected to be stable. Living with others is difficult, and those arrangements always take enormous amounts of emotional energy and time if they are to be successful. Finding a place to live was again complicated by our having a dog. Toodles, the mini-schnauzer, had gone to a friend, but we still had Maggie, a sheltie who shadowed Heather and was an integral part of our family, and Corny, a brown, black and white guinea pig. Rental ads all read: "No pets."

I finally found an independent after-school program that picked up children at four schools and kept them until six-thirty. I told the real estate people that I needed a house in one of those four school districts. The major asset of the house I found was that Heather could walk out of the kitchen door and be in the school yard. If all went well we could be in the house by Labor Day. A mortgage was approved after I demonstrated that the anticipated profit from the New Jersey house would support me during the residency.

While I traveled back and forth to the Midwest looking for a place to live, arranging child care, etc., friends began preparing the New Jersey house for sale and for the move. The bright sky-blue ceilings and green banisters enthusiastically painted in the early days of making the house livable were now being covered with plain white.

Heather would stay with her grandparents for the two weeks before we closed on the house. Once we moved in, Fran and Laurie would take turns getting Heather off to school in the morning until I found someone to live with us. When I had to work all night, Heather would stay at Laurie's house.

I worried about what this would be like for Heather. She didn't want to move. She didn't want to leave her grandparents, her aunt, her baby cousin, her friends. She didn't want to leave Susan, a woman who had been living in the house in exchange for some child care, and who I had hoped might move with us. I worried about the disruption, and about what the next years would be like for her. This was the time that I had anticipated, that I had told her about when she was a baby, that time when I could no longer be with her so much. I hoped she felt loved enough and that her sense of herself was strong enough, that she would be all right.

Doctors Hospital is a university-affiliated teaching hospital with both private and "service" patients. The private patients have their own physicians, referred to as "attendings," with residents having varying degrees of control over their care. The service patients, those who in years past would have been referred to as "ward" or "charity" patients, come through the clinic or emergency room and do not have their own doctors. Most of these are black or Hispanic. The residents have control of their care. Both private and service patients are studied in the teaching program.

Residents assigned to gynecology take care of emergencies and perform time-consuming examinations and procedures for the attendings. In return for performing those tasks, the attendings allow the residents to learn surgery on their patients. This is possible because the teaching of surgical skills occurs when the patient is under anesthesia—and thus unaware of who is doing the surgery.

Residents on obstetrics follow women in labor, see both private and service patients on daily rounds, and take care of prenatal and postpartum patients who have complications. In return, the residents are allowed to do deliveries, sew episiotomies, and to assist or even perform Caesarean sections, tubal ligations, and other procedures on these patients.

Doctors Hospital also employs midwives to take care of pregnant and birthing women. Midwife literally means "with woman." The last years have seen a resurgence of midwives attending childbirth, which had become the province of physicians in this century. Certified nurse midwives are registered nurses who are also graduates of midwifery training programs and are certified by the American College of Nurse Midwives. Lay midwives, however, have come to their work through a variety of paths, usually including a period of apprenticeship with another practicing midwife. Many lay midwives become skilled at attending the large numbers of women who are choosing not to go into the hospital but, rather, to give birth at home—with or without anyone there to help them. In most states, lay midwives are practicing illegally but meeting the demand of a population alienated from the medical system.

Although certified nurse midwives have been trained to manage labor and delivery on their own—and are doing so in many areas of this country and others—at Doctors Hospital they are directly supervised by attending physicians. Other than a delivery atmosphere modified by their presence as supportive women, it was often difficult to distinguish a midwife-attended birth from any other.

The relationship between residents and midwives was not clearly defined. The residents took part in the labor management of the midwives' patients, but then usually stepped out at the time of delivery. Ultimate responsibility for the patient, however, rested with the attending physician.

Within the residency program there was a complex hierarchy. All residents are MDs who have already served a year of internship either in this or another hospital, and are now taking this four-year training to become specialists in OB-GYN. There are junior residents, senior residents and chief residents, and on each level there are varying degrees of autonomy, authority and deference given or demanded. At each level there is also fear of the person above: the chief resident is responsible for what all the others do, and subject to the anger or praise of Dr. Pierce, a tall muscular man with thick black hair and penetrating eyes.

Dr. Pierce's department is accredited for sixteen residents, four at each level, but there are rarely sixteen at any time, since residents are prone to transferring, breaking down and being fired. Fewer residents means more work for each resident, but it also means less competition for surgical cases and deliveries.

I was accepted into the program at the second-year level, having been given credit for my board certification in Family Practice.

THE GYN SERVICE—GOING TO THE OPERATING ROOM

I, as a second-year resident, was to be on gynecology for the next ten weeks. Carol was chief resident, Richard in the third year, and Barbara the first-year resident. Together, the four of us took care of all the gynecological patients in the hospital.

Richard, tall, fair, a loner, was quiet and reserved, rarely speaking unless directly addressed. Barbara was slightly more friendly. Having only begun the residency in the past month, she was already unhappy and thinking about quitting. She felt lonely and out of place in this Midwestern city, and complained that she wasn't getting enough surgical experience. Barbara had beautiful long dark hair, which was never out of place, even after a night on call. She was furthest from the stereotype of a woman doctor, and on most days could have been chosen for a beauty pageant.

We met each morning on the GYN floor at six o'clock. From six to seven-thirty we made "work rounds." Before we saw the patients we reviewed vital-signs sheets, on which were recorded the temperature, pulse, breathing rate and blood pressure of each patient on the unit. We checked each woman's intake and output sheet to see how much fluid had been consumed and excreted, and then we went to see each one.

On the first morning I followed Carol, who was warm and friendly, managing to give each woman the sense that there was all the time in the world in which to answer her questions. She hid the urgency she felt about time until she was outside the room and out of the woman's hearing. Often Carol, short and slender, her thick blond hair in a single braid, white jacket over slacks and blouse, looked and sounded incredibly young and girlish. Sometimes, though, there were dark lines and a look of deep worry on her face.

Most patients were either preoperative or postoperative. We changed dressings, took out sutures or the metal staples that were sometimes used instead of sewn stitches. We listened to lungs. We put stethoscopes to bellies, listening for the intestinal rumblings that heralded the return of proper functioning after surgery. We asked patients whether they had passed gas or moved their bowels, which helped us decide when to stop intravenous feedings and begin liquid or solid foods. If there had been a fever in the past twenty-four hours, we began searching for the source of infection, culturing urine, sputum, skin, wounds, throat, cervix . . .

We immersed ourselves in information about each patient and returned to the nurses' station to make notes on charts and write orders for tests we wanted. Orders had to be on the chart by seven every morning, or the lab technicians wouldn't draw the blood samples, and one of us would have to do it. We had to know who each patient's attending physician was and how that attending wanted his or her patients to be managed. Did the attending allow resumption of feeding with the return of bowel sounds or the passing of flatus? Did we need to consult with the attending before we made such decisions? What role did we play in the care of that doctor's patients?

The day's plan for the patient had to be established and all the work done during those rounds because we would be tied up in the operating room (OR) for most of the day.

Seven-thirty found us in the cafeteria, giving patient reports to the chief resident over breakfast. An extra muffin or doughnut became a reward for a bad night or an anticipated difficult case in the OR. We had thirty minutes in which to review all our patients and to show what we knew or didn't know. Carol began with the report from the person who had been on duty the previous night. New admissions were described to the rest of us, and then we discussed the complications of the night. Hurriedly we went through the card file of the approximately forty patients and discussed each woman's condition, progress, lack of progress, and plans.

By eight o'clock we were in the operating room. Once in the OR, how did I feel? I felt important. This was not the first OR I'd been in, but this one carried all the atmosphere of the major university of which it was a part. There is something about a uniform, too, that makes one feel important. My whole being reeked of my station. I was an insider. I looked just like the others. I had a place, a job, and I was being taught the secrets of medicine. If we had expressed our feelings of elitism, we might have said, "How terrible never to see the inside of the OR, never to have a role in the drama there." I was ashamed of the power I felt in that room, ashamed of what I was becoming, and yet I was also enjoying it.

The operating suite covered two floors. Upstairs were the changing and locker rooms, separate for men and women. There were two lounges, a smoking lounge with a coffee urn and microwave oven, and a nonsmoking room with more chairs and dictating machines and a telephone to the outside. Beyond the lounges and dressing rooms was a central hall with stairs leading down to the actual operating rooms. A large stainless-steel rack in the hallway held masks, hats and booties.

Carol took me to the women's changing room, where there were two large racks of clothing stacked by style, color and approximate size. Blues—for men and women—were for surgery, either in dress style or as pants and top. Grays were for taking temporary trips out of the OR without having to put on regular clothes. Carol and I changed into blues, shedding white coats, clothes, watches, rings, and went outside to the stainless-steel rack. Booties came in two sizes: too big and too small. They fit over our shoes and helped keep the floor of the operating room from being contaminated. The booties had little black straps hanging out the back which were supposed to be tucked in against our skin to ground us and prevent electrostatic explosion in the presence of inflammable anesthetics, but no one ever tucked them in. They either trailed behind us or were ripped off. I assumed our operating room had special flooring that made the straps unnecessary. The hats came in various shapes to cover our hair. Some for men with short hair were merely tallish skull caps. Others looked like a loose, full kind of shower cap. For men with beards there were hoods that covered both their heads and chins. The masks were put on as we headed down the stairs to the OR, and they had to be in place by the time we went through the OR door. Once inside the OR we could not be paged and all messages had to come through the OR secretary. I was suddenly conscious of being cut off from the rest of the world, and especially from my child. I had to hope that she was all right and that if she wasn't, someone would persevere in getting a message to me.

The staircase down to the OR seemed magical. It was common practice, and one in which I joined, to grab the handrails and jump the last three or four steps into the OR area.

Through the door at the bottom of the stairs was a large central nurses' area with desks, supplies, phones. Twelve individual operating rooms opened into this area. On one wall hung a huge glossy white laminated board on which each case was listed by room number. A cardboard box beside the board held magnetic name plates. We'd go first to the board, find our case, and then slap our magnetic name plates onto the board where they hung suspended, defying gravity.

I was in the OR with my name now hung on the board, officially announcing that I belonged. Everyone in the operating area was fully clothed in blues, hat, booties and mask. It was unsettling to meet people there for the first time. It took me months to put together the slits of eyes and skin with whole faces and bodies.

After Carol and I found the room where our case would be, we went to the sinks to scrub. The sinks were large shiny basins with foot pedals to control the water spouts and disinfectant dispensers. Over the sinks were instruction sheets on the various methods of scrubbing. The sheets looked old and showed the effects of years of soap and water splashed on them.

Scrubbing is a ritual that begins with a short rinse with plain water: hands are wet first, and then the arms, which are always held so that the water goes down toward the elbows, not toward the hands. Then a new, disposable brush, presoaked with pHiso-Hex or iodine, is taken from a dispenser at the side of the sink. The cover is ripped off, while taking care not to drop the brush, which becomes slippery from the wet hands. The scrubbing begins in a pattern from fingers to hands, then arms, always with the water running down toward the bent elbows, so that hands are always held up toward the ceiling, toward God.

To get from the sinks into the rooms meant going through a door, using one's rear to open the door and one's legs to close it. The task was to stay clean, to go into the OR without touching anything, without helping anyone. It was hardest not to help, not to reach as an instrument was falling, not to pick up a towel left on the floor. Hands must stay as they are, reaching upward, arms bent at the elbow, water dripping to the floor.

Next the gowning begins. The nurse tosses you a sterile towel for one hand, and then a second towel for the other hand, each one being dropped to the floor as it is used. Then the gown is put on carefully so that no part of the outside touches one's body or anything else. Finally the gloves are put on, with scrubbed hands making a dramatic dive into the gloves being held open by a nurse. To touch anything is to "break scrub"—which means you have to repeat the entire procedure.

Only the territory above the waist is considered sterile, so one's hands always have to be held above the waist. The most common position is with arms crossed over the gown, sterile gloves to sterile gown, as in a bilateral pledge of allegiance. There we stood, covered by hats, masks, gowns, gloves, booties, with arms crossed, waiting to begin.

Every precaution was taken to keep the room and ourselves as sterile as possible, but sick surgeons don't stay home. (As doctors we are not allowed to be sick. We just cough and sneeze through our sterile masks.)

THE D&C

A D&C is the "bread and butter" of gynecologic surgery. That's how it was described to me over the sinks one day as the attending surgeon and I were scrubbing to do the operation. The procedure is a dilation (D) of the cervix, and then a curettage (C) or scraping of the uterus.

The D&C patient is usually a middle-aged woman with irregular vaginal bleeding, for which she gets her womb scraped out both for diagnosis and for cure. Many women simply stop having this bleeding problem after a D&C, but no one is sure why. It reminds me of exorcism. It may be that the ritualistic and mysterious aspects of the procedure add to the success of the exorcism.

Whatever my theories, I was there at my first D&C to learn how to do the procedure. I paid careful attention to the details of how I would be expected to conduct myself within the few weeks it would take me to master this operation.

The patient awaited surgery in the "holding area," a large room with space for four stretchers against each of the walls, and curtains which could be drawn between each stretcher for some minimal privacy, if necessary. It was here that patients usually had their intravenous fluids (IVs) started, and where they waited to be called into the operating rooms, having given up their clothes, eyeglasses, jewelry and teeth before they left their rooms upstairs.

Patients left the holding area on their stretchers and were wheeled along a wide corridor that surrounded all the operating rooms and that opened into each room separately. At the door of the room where she would have her surgery, the woman was transferred to the operating table, which had been brought out into the hall. As part of the effort to keep the room as clean as possible, the stretcher from the holding area was not allowed into the room. I wondered for a moment what it must be like for the woman on her table, being wheeled into this alien atmosphere: a large room with chrome-encircled spotlights suspended from the ceiling on long arms; racks of supplies along the walls; hanging bottles on IV poles with long tubing as yet unconnected; tanks of gas with colored round dials and indicator needles; monitors with blank flat lines traveling across their screens, waiting to be given signals to measure and count. The woman, naked under the sheets, often cold in a room heated for the comfort of those of us dressed in many layers, hears of herself in the third person. She catches bits and pieces of our language which may or may not be important or related to her.

"Do you have my favorite dilators ready?" a surgeon asks a nurse.

"No, they're still in the autoclave being sterilized. Do you want us to hold up the procedure until they're out?"

"No, I'll use what you have," he tells her.

The woman on the table worries. Why are some his favorite? Are the others as good? Will he operate as well with the substitutes? Her fate in the hands of us in the room, she tries to sort out the importance of the random remarks she hears.

The summer I was nine years old I broke my arm at camp swinging off the cabin rafters. Not wanting to get into trouble for my activity, I stoically told no one about my fall until late at night when the pain was enough for me to ask for aspirin. I was then rushed to a hospital, where my arm was set and I was admitted for the night. The nurse who put me in a bed showed me a buzzer clipped to the pillow and said, "Push this little button if you need anything." Then she added, "Don't worry, we won't pump out your stomach if you call." She was referring to another child in the ER who had been screaming as his stomach was pumped, but all I could remember were the words "pump out your stomach," so I avoided touching the buzzer. I couldn't be sure if it would or wouldn't happen to me. It must be that way for a patient on an operating table.

"Bad"—a word the woman on the table catches in a conversation. Was a nurse saying her case was bad, or wasn't bad? All that remains is the word without the context. The sounds of the operating room are a fusion of medical terminology, commands, deference, interspersed with words of everyday life. The patient is an anonymous body on a table, a living cadaver about to be put to sleep.

The same summer I broke my arm, I saw a rabbit "put to sleep." For years I was terrified of being "put to sleep." I wasn't sure where death took over and when reawakening was no longer possible.

Nurses place electrodes on the patient's chest so her heart can be monitored. A grounding plate, covered with green gel, is placed under the woman's back. Almost invariably, she winces because it is cold.

Carol and I come into the room while all this is happening. Carol takes the patient's hand and tells her she will be fine, and as she introduces me, I wonder what this woman will ever remember of what she can see between my mask and hat.

The anesthesiologist, seated at the head of the table, is in charge of the preoperative procedures around the patient. Carol and I are told, "You may scrub now," and we leave the room. The patient is given a drug through her IV that puts her to sleep and then one that paralyzes her muscles, including those of respiration. A tube is put in her trachea so that a machine can breathe for her. The monitor counts the rhythmic contractions of her heart.

The anesthesiologist signals that the woman's legs may now be put up in stirrups. The nurses make sure the woman is correctly on the table, not too far toward the head or foot. Two nurses, in unison, one on each side, lift the woman's now heavy legs so that her feet can be put in the stirrups which are at the bottom of the table, about twenty-four inches apart. Once in this position, because the woman is paralyzed, her legs fall out to the side.

As Carol and I watch from the sinks, she instructs me on what we will be doing. I keep thinking about anatomy class when I was in medical school. When we got to the pelvis on our cadaver we made a joke of the body and hung the legs from the ceiling. We made a joke of death and a joke of private parts. In the OR we hang legs on stirrups. We put the woman to sleep so she is loose and we hang her. A woman with her legs in the air cannot fight. She cannot protest the remarks about her fatness, her hair, her scars, the shape of her labia, the size of her clitoris. She cannot pull her legs together to protect herself. I stop my thoughts in order to learn what I have to know and to go along with what I have to do.

Carol and I watch the nurses scrub the patient first. A disposable tray with sterile sponges and bottles of disinfectant is opened. The nurse takes the first sponge, and starting at the labia, wipes the brown staining liquid out along the thighs. Once a sponge is used on the outer portion of the body it cannot be returned to the center of the operative site. Before the sponge is thrown away, it is used to scrub the anus. The nurse's scrub ends with her patting the entire area dry with a sterile towel.

Carol now takes the smaller tray with three more sterile sponges on sticks and soaked with disinfectant. Her first sponge goes into the vagina, and remains there with the yellow plastic stick protruding out. The second sponge is used on the labia and then wiped outward about five inches along the thigh. The first sponge is then taken out of the vagina and passed down along the anus. The third sponge is used to repeat the scrub of the inside of the vagina.

Draping begins: the first drape, a large gray-green sheet, goes under the woman's buttocks, the second and third along the thighs, not quite meeting at the labia. The last sheet is on top of the woman, meets the two leg sheets at the pubis, and completes a ring of sterile sheets around the vaginal opening. There is now a complete sterile field consisting of her drapes and our gloves and gowns.

The anesthesiologist had signaled when we could begin the second scrub, and now we await the signal to begin the operation. Although the woman is asleep, if she is not at a deep enough level, she will straighten her legs and fight us when we put an instrument in her vagina.

We empty a patient's bladder as a routine, using a thin catheter which is passed through her urethra, since a full bladder could interfere with the vaginal exam.

The exam under anesthesia (EUA) is performed because we can more easily examine the pelvic organs, since the woman's abdominal muscles now offer us no resistance. The patient is examined by Carol, by me, and by a medical student who is watching us. We note the results of the exam on the chart. The anesthesiologist tells us we may begin the procedure.

The D&C is simple but it still scares me, since there is always the possibility of harming a woman. A speculum, an instrument used to stretch open the vaginal walls, with a heavy-weighted handle is placed in the vagina, thus pulling the lower portion (floor) of the vagina downward without anyone having to hold it. Carol takes a long flat L-shaped instrument that looks like a bent ruler and places it in the vagina, her left hand pulling upward with it and stretching the vagina open so that the woman's round cervix can easily be seen. A tenaculum, a thin instrument about sixteen inches long, with tiny teeth on the end, is used to grasp the upper lip of the cervix, allowing us to place traction—a pulling force—on both the cervix and uterus. Carol has me hold the tenaculum so I can feel how much traction is exerted. Then she removes the L-shaped instrument, leaving the weighted speculum in place.

The os, or opening of the cervix, is dilated by using a series of increasingly wide metal probes. Carol shows me the different ones on the instrument table, put out so surgeons can use their favorites. Some dilators are more or less traumatic to the cervix, some are easier to use, safer, look more elegant. She shows me which are her favorites and I know I will start with those when I am on my own.

We insert into the uterus a sound, a thin flexible metal rod about fourteen inches long, to see how deep it is and at what angle to insert the dilators. Then we take the smallest of the tapered dilators and begin to stretch the os. Carol puts in a dilator while I take it out and hand her the next larger size. As I remove each dilator I can feel how the uterus slopes. We dilate until we think the os is open enough to admit the curette, a long thin instrument with a curved cup at the end with tiny teeth as on the edge of a saw. If the os is not yet wide enough to admit the curette, we dilate it more. The curette is then passed through the os into the body of the uterus, and its sharp edge is used to scrape the lining as it is withdrawn. Then it is inserted again at a slightly different angle and is withdrawn again. The bits of tissue are deposited on a piece of gauze that is resting on the weighted speculum. The fragments of uterine lining will all go into a specimen bottle to be examined in the lab within the next few days.

Tissue is taken from all corners and then randomly from the cavity of the uterus, the curette making a to-and-fro motion. The scraping continues until there is a gritty feeling to the entire lining of the uterus. It is the gritty feeling which is sought and which Carol makes sure I feel. It is called the "cry of the uterus."

This time it is we who signal the anesthesiologist that we are almost finished so the level of anesthesia can slowly be decreased. We take fragments of tissue from the gauze and place them in a bottle with preservative. Then we remove the tenaculum and examine the cervix to be sure it is not bleeding excessively either from our curetting or from the teeth of the tenaculum, which sometimes pierce a vessel in the cervix or tear the os. As the weighted speculum is removed from the vagina, the woman's labia come together. We signal that we have finished by sweeping the drapes up off the patient and depositing them either in a large bin or on the floor, leaving the rest of the cleanup for the nurses.

One of us must stay with the patient until she is in the

recovery room, but now time is spent filling out pathology forms for the specimen, writing operative notes, recovery-room orders, and notes to ourselves about what care this woman may need later. The nurses will call us to help transfer the patient to a stretcher to go to the recovery room, but our attention is no longer with this woman. We are getting ready for the next case.

LAPAROSCOPY

On the third day I learned laparoscopy. "Lap" is for loins, loosely including the abdomen; "scope" is an instrument for viewing. Thus, laparoscopy is the use of an instrument for viewing the inside of the abdominal cavity including the uterus, Fallopian tubes and ovaries. During laparoscopy the tubes can be "tied" for sterilization, either by burning them with an electrode or by putting rings on them which block sperm from traveling through them. Laparoscopy is often referred to as bellybutton surgery because the laparoscope is put through a hole made in the perimeter of the navel. It is also called Band-Aid surgery because usually only a Band-Aid is needed to put on the incision. This makes the surgery seem insignificant.

Laparoscopy is simple surgery if you know what you are doing, if nothing goes wrong, if the equipment is working, if the nurses know how to run the equipment, and if the patient's insides look and behave as they are supposed to. I was assisting a private attending, Dr. Owen, on my first laparoscopy, keenly aware of the loss of Carol as my teacher. Dr. Owen's large frame and pedantic manner contrasted with Carol's slight build and gentle manner of teaching.

Much of the surgical procedure is repetitive. The patient is brought to the OR, given anesthesia, scrubbed and draped. The nurse does the initial scrub of the abdomen and perineum, and then the surgeon takes over, repeating what has just been done, but also scrubbing out the vagina. Two sets of drapes are put over the woman, thus establishing the vaginal and abdominal operative sites.

After the woman's bladder is emptied with a catheter, she is examined under anesthesia. If she is to have a D&C as well as laparoscopy, the D&C is done first. Dr. Owen did the D&C, explaining to me, "I do it to be sure the patient isn't already pregnant, since we are going to tie the tubes." He added, "I like to do whatever I can while I'm in there, anyway. You never know what you might find."

The D&C finished, Dr. Owen leaves the tenaculum attached to the cervix and then attaches it to a canula, a long thin nippled instrument, which is placed into the os. The handles of the two instruments are now hooked together, and with a sterile towel draped over them are used to manipulate the uterus during the laparoscopy. The weighted speculum at the base of the vagina is removed, allowing a 360-degree rotation of the instruments, which are now protruding out of the woman's vagina.

"In gynecologic surgery, the vagina is defined as dirty," Dr. Owen tells me as he takes off the pair of gloves he is wearing over his first pair. I, too, take off my gloves; I did not do the D&C, but I examined the woman under anesthesia and thus contaminated my gloves. Some surgeons also change their gown after touching the vagina.

We move to the woman's abdomen, I on her right, he on her left side, allowing him greater use of his right hand in manipulating the laparoscope. Taking a small pointed knife from the nurse, Dr. Owen makes a stab wound into the outer ring of the woman's bellybutton and hands the knife back. He takes a long thin needle, and as he grasps the patient's abdominal skin with his left hand, he instructs me, "Lift up now as hard as you can," and I can hear the strain of his lifting in his voice. Struggling to keep the woman's skin from sliding out from my gloved fingers, I grasp it more tightly and pull upward. While we both pull, he pushes the needle through two layers of abdominal tissue and into the abdominal cavity. He tests his success by putting a drop of water on the open end of the needle and watches to see if the water disappears as he opens the needle valve. "We're in!" he tells me triumphantly.

I maintain some traction on the woman's abdominal skin while he hooks up the needle to a machine which will pump carbon dioxide into the woman's belly.

We relax and watch the gauges on the machine. "I like to put about three liters into the abdomen before I go further," he tells me, noting that the machine already read one liter when we turned it on. The woman's abdomen begins to inflate.

Periodically Dr. Owen reaches over her abdomen to tap it and hear how it sounds, then motions for me to do the same. Her abdomen begins to sound hollow as I tap and then I move my fingers to her upper abdomen where her liver is, and where for years I have percussed the sound of liver dullness marking out the boundaries of that organ. The usual dullness now becomes tympanitic as the carbon dioxide separates her liver from the abdominal wall, against which it usually lies. When the gauge reads four liters and there is hollowness throughout her abdomen, Dr. Owen swiftly removes the needle, sealing the woman's abdomen closed in its inflated state.

"Trochar," he calls, and the nurse hands him a spikelike instrument, about eight inches long, with a pyramidal-shaped end. Surrounding the shaft of the trochar is a fiberglass sleeve with a piston valve at its end. Now that the woman's belly is taut, it is much harder to grasp her skin. As we both try, I feel that I am trying to pull her into my chest. The table is too high for me, so I don't have good leverage for what I am trying to do. "Harder," he tells me, and I try harder while he begins pushing the spiked end of the trochar through the incision we made previously at the navel. Then, with a twisting motion that seems to include his arm and his shoulder for strength, he forces the instrument through her abdominal wall. Suddenly there is no resistance and he relaxes. "Listen," he says, and as he releases the piston valve, I hear the sound of escaping air. He closes the valve, sure that we are in.

"Hose," he calls, and I hand him the hose, which he attaches to the valve of the sleeve. Then he turns to watch the machine. The nurse turns the dial to "Automatic," so the machine will slowly pump air into the abdomen to replace what leaks out during the procedure. As the trochar is removed from the sleeve, there is a momentary *whish* of air before the valve closes.

Dr. Owen now guides the shaft of the laparoscope through the sleeve of the trochar into the woman's abdominal cavity. The laparoscope is a tube about eighteen inches long and about a centimeter in diameter. It contains a magnifying lens and a connection for a light source. Its function is similar to that of a periscope, except in this case we are looking in from outside instead of looking up from under water.

"Lights out," he says to the nurse. "Tilt, please," he requests of the anesthesiologist. The room becomes darkened except for the light coming from the windows to the next room. The anesthesiologist begins turning the crank at the head of the table and the woman's body is slowly tilted backward so her head points toward the floor and her buttocks toward the ceiling, making her intestines fall downward against her diaphragm instead of into her pelvis. Because of the woman's position, the surgeon looking into the pelvis from the bellybutton is actually looking upward. The room is dark, the woman is tilted, and only Dr. Owen can see what is there.

"It looks fine in here. I have good visualization of the uterus. I can see one tube but I can't see the ovaries clearly." He reaches with his left hand through the woman's legs to the instruments protruding from her vagina and pushes them downward toward her abdomen as though trying to make both sets of instruments meet inside her. He mumbles that now he can see the left ovary, and then, with a scooping motion, he moves the instruments down and as far to the left as he can, saying, "Ah, there's the other one."

"You may look now," he tells me. I lean over the table to the laparoscope, and being careful not to touch the lens and not to contaminate any of the sterile field with my mask, I take my first look in. I see wonderful red and orange and yellow, all without form. He asks if I see the uterus, tubes, and ovaries, which he tells me are all right there. "Well, I see something," I tell him, wishing Carol were there with me. Dr. Owen takes the shaft of the scope, and looking through the lens, says, "You were angled too high." He readjusts the scope, looks through and tells me to look now, but in the passing of the instrument from his hand to mine, the angle is again changed. I catch a glimpse of something.

"Knife!" and a knife is in his hand. He angles the scope upward against the abdominal wall, so in this darkened room we can all see the light shining from inside the woman's belly, as he searches for an area where there is no large blood vessel so he can make a second incision. Finding a clear spot of light along the woman's pubic hairline, he quickly stabs at the place where the light shines through. She bleeds slightly.

"Grab the skin the way you did before," he instructs me. As we lift he forces a second trochar through the woman's abdomen at the site of the stab wound until there is no resistance, and he says again, "We're in." He removes the trochar, instructing me to hold my finger over the sleeve to prevent air from escaping, since this sleeve has no valve.

"Is the ring loaded?" he asks of the nurse, referring to the ring applicator that will be used to tie the woman's tubes. He goes on to tell me he prefers the rings to using cautery, which burns the tubes. "These rings are cleaner, and it's easier to reverse the procedure if she changes her mind in the future. It's almost impossible to reopen the tubes after they've been burned." I look at the ring, white plastic, about a quarter inch in size, which has been loaded into a long ring applicator with retractable teeth. As he inserts the ring applicator through the second sleeve I realize there are now three sets of instruments protruding from this tilted woman's body. There are the toweled instruments attached to her uterus and coming out of her vagina, there is the laparoscope coming out of the incision at the navel, and now the ring applicator coming out of the second incision near the pubic hairline.

Looking through the scope while he manipulates the toweled vaginal instruments, Dr. Owen brings the right tube into full vision. While I hold those instruments in place, he takes the ring applicator and explains what he is doing. "I'm grasping the tube and pulling it up into the applicator with the teeth at the end. Then slowly I release the ring and it slides onto the knuckle of the tube which has been drawn up into the applicator." His face becomes knotted and intense as he draws up the tube, then suddenly eases as he tells me, "I'm releasing the teeth so the tube with the ring on it drops back into the pelvis." He offers to show me. I look in and see a piece of white plastic attached to some tissue, and although the structures are still not clear, I am glad I've seen the ring. The procedure is repeated on the other side, so there is now a white ring on each tube.

The anesthesiologist asks if we are done but Dr. Owen says no, it will still be a few more minutes, and then invites me to come around to his side of the table to look inside. Taking the scope is now easier because I can use my right eye and my right hand. As I move the scope around, this time I am relieved that the colors have form and that I can begin to distinguish what I am seeing.

"You can wake her," he tells the anesthesiologist; although it will still take some time to finish, it will also take time for the woman to come out of the anesthesia. All of us wince at the sudden brightness when the nurse turns on the lights. For a few minutes it seemed as though the only world there was existed in the belly of the woman on the table.

The ring applicator is removed from the woman's abdomen, causing her belly to quickly deflate. At Dr. Owen's instruction, I remove its sleeve, which is sticky at first but with some pulling comes out, allowing the skin to close over the incision. Dr. Owen removes the laparoscope, and then, pressing on the woman's abdomen, forces out more of the air through the incision, removing the second sleeve as he continues to exert pressure on the abdomen. With the sleeves out, there are only two small wounds in the woman's belly with a few drops of clotted blood around each one.

"Staples!" he calls, and the nurse hands him a tweezer loaded with a staple which he uses to staple shut the umbilical incision. He calls for a second staple for the same incision, and then a third for the smaller incision along the pubic hairline. I am instructed to put on the Band-Aids.

Dr. Owen moves to the space between the woman's legs to remove the vaginal instruments. He detaches the canula from the tenaculum, then removes the tenaculum from the cervix. Using a speculum, he examines the cervix and vagina for any bleeding either from the D&C or the tenaculum teeth. "Done," he declares, sweeping the drapes off the woman's legs and dropping them to the floor for the nurses to pick up.

The patient is awakening. The tube is removed from her throat and she is placed on her side so that if she vomits, she won't draw the contents of her stomach into her lungs. She shivers, moans. With slurred speech thick with mucus from her throat and vomitus from her stomach, she wants to know if it is over and asks, "Am I okay?"

I am at the Formica shelf along the wall filling out the forms for her chart, but the anesthesiologist and nurses at her side answer her as they prepare her for the recovery room.

In a typical morning I would do three D&C's and a laparoscopy, or one D&C and a hysterectomy or other major operation.

THE WORK-UP

Afternoons were for work-ups—a term that includes taking a medical history and performing a physical exam (H&P), then recording them on the patient's chart, as well as writing orders for lab tests, diagnostic procedures and medications on the chart. Although we often needed to contact the private attending about any special orders or problems, it was the performance of the History and Physical that took the most time.

After leaving the OR I would stop at the bulletin board, where there would be tiny folded pieces of paper with our names on the outside, and the names of patients to be worked up on the inside, usually the ones on whom we would be operating the following day.

None of us could leave at night until all the H&Ps were done, so we had to manage whatever there was in the time available. All of us usually did a good job on the first H&P of the day, but by the second, third or fourth we were often exhausted and just wanted to go home.

The H&P seems like "busy work," since it has already been done in the private doctor's office. But it must be recorded on the chart to fulfill both legal and accreditation requirements. Since it is quite likely that no one will ever read the H&P or pay attention to what it says, it doesn't have to be thorough or legible. It just has to be there.

At two in the afternoon, when I have already put in an eight-hour day, I must gather my energy and interest to find out all about someone's life and health. Going to the room of my first patient, I tap lightly on the open door.

The woman, alert and healthy-looking, still in street clothes, is sitting on the bed, and she says into the phone as she hangs up, "The doctor is here." A second bed in the room is occupied by a woman recovering from surgery two days before, so I draw the curtain between the beds, a pretense at privacy.

Since this is my first work-up for the afternoon, I sit down, but as I get busier and more pressed for time and worried about getting out, I stand during the H&P. Sometimes when I had been awake for thirty-six hours I would hold the 5×8 card I used for taking notes in front of my eyes, and I could actually shut my eyes for brief moments while I listened to the patient. I could also take momentary naps when listening to a patient's heart. Closing my eyes, I could sink into the rhythm of the heart or of breathing, and napping between beats, would actually feel refreshed.

But this day I feel fresh when I go to see this patient, and she seems eager to see me arrive—a step closer to her surgery in the morning. She asks, "Will you be there for the surgery?"

"The schedule calls for me to be there, but it could still change," I tell her and then sit back in the chair to begin taking her history.

"What brings you to the hospital?" I ask. Of course, I already know exactly why she is here and what surgery is planned, but I must be able to write it in the chart *in her own words*.

Her chart will read: "The patient is admitted with a chief complaint of 'I have fibroids and the doctor says they have to come out.' " Continuing with my questions, I obtain the History of Present Illness. "When did the fibroids begin giving you trouble?" She says she has had two years of intermittent irregular bleeding and a D&C which took care of the problem for about a year, but now she has the bleeding again and it worries her. I ask more about the nature of the bleeding: Is it heavy, is there pain? What are her fears?

Gathering information for the chart, I move on to the rest of the OB-GYN history. Menstruation: When did it begin, how often does it occur, how long does it last? This information will appear on the chart in a formula as "Menarche [age at onset] × length of cycle × duration of menses," or "Menarche: 12 × 29 × 5." An added note will indicate whether she has cramps or any irregularities. I wonder at the relevance of these questions: by tomorrow afternoon she will not have a uterus and will have no more menses. The date of her last period, noted on the chart, will indeed be her last.

I ask about urinary problems, incontinence, infections, VD, vaginitis, birth control, sexual problems, then obstetrical questions: Has she been pregnant? How many times? Abortions? Miscarriages? Premature births? Nature of deliveries? Does she have breast pain? Lumps? I ask the most intimate questions of this woman, although I may never see her again.

Once in psychiatric training a supervisor wanted to know if I'd obtained some very personal information from a patient. "No, I didn't ask that question. I didn't think it was any of my business." We say that patients should always tell us everything, but that trust should be earned, not assumed. Charts are not really private, nor are we always discreet.

Written on the chart next will be the Review of Systems, so I ask about her general state of health, energy, weight, mood. I ask about her nervous system, tics, tremors, convulsions, dizziness, headaches. I go on to vision, eye problems, ear problems, hearing. I ask if she has had any problems with her chest. Frequent colds? Cough? Sputum? Heavy breathing? Painful breathing? If she answers yes to any problems, I ask more specific questions. I cover heart and blood vessels, then chest pain, leg cramps, leg swelling, fainting. Since this is a surgical service, we are careful to ask about bleeding disorders, whether the patient has any known bleeding problems and also whether she bleeds a lot when cut or when having a tooth extraction, for instance.

As I list possible digestive problems, which few of us are totally without, I try to sort out the serious from the inconsequential, especially from a surgical perspective. "Do you have problems with swallowing, vomiting, appetite, heartburn, constipation, diarrhea, hemorrhoids, food intolerances—especially fatty foods, abdominal pain, nausea, etc.?"

I finish with extremities and then skin. "Do you ever have pain in your joints? Have you ever broken a bone? Do you have rashes?"

"Well, I used to. Does that count?" she asks, to which I respond, "Well, no, not for this part of the history, but yes, tell me anyway," as I mark on the 5 × 8 card "Skin problem," with an arrow pointing to Past History, which comes next.

The Past History is a listing of about twenty diseases specifically asked about, including chronic illnesses, hospitalizations, surgery, and then allergies, especially to drugs and penicillin.

The Family History is the list of diseases that have occurred among her relatives. "Are your parents alive, healthy? What problems did they have, if deceased, how? Do you have siblings? What is their health?" When I ask about cancer, heart disease, diabetes, I know I have caused the woman to worry about whether she will have them because she assumes I wouldn't be asking those questions if they weren't relevant.

"Do you smoke? Drink? How much?" I ask as part of the

Social History, and then for a woman, instead of "Do you work?" I ask, "Are you employed outside the home?"

The history taking completed, my 5 × 8 card is now filled with words, cryptic abbreviations, numbers and sentences, either listed or connected by arrows. Although I have asked and she has told me "everything," there is always more remembered during the examination.

This is a routine physical exam, which aside from the internal pelvic exam is done in the patient's room, since the GYN unit has only one exam room and each of us tries to use it as little as possible.

Generally the exam is done starting at the head and working downward, covering head, eyes, ears, nose, throat, all of which will be abbreviated on the chart as "HEENT—negative." I feel the woman's neck for masses and thyroid size, then listen to her heart and lungs. I feel for masses in her breasts. Resting my hands on her abdomen, I feel for tenderness and masses. Tapping, I percuss out the size of her liver by listening for the area of liver dullness. I look briefly at the woman's legs, noting veins, looking for swellings and deformities.

We go to the exam room for the rest of the exam. There, because I am a woman, I am alone with the patient. Male physicians are accompanied by nurses when they examine women internally to protect them from accusations of sexual assault; of course, that also means they have an extra set of hands to help them in the room to get what may suddenly be needed for the exam.

The exam room is small, about ten square feet with a curtain which slides halfway across, giving some privacy from the window in the door. Cabinets, counters and sink line one wall; standing in the middle is the GYN table, short, padded, with stirrups on the end.

I direct the woman to get up on the table, where she sits while I gather my instruments. Now in a white gown and robe, she looks like a patient. Her tentative questions of me are in sharp contrast with her confident voice on the phone when I entered her room.

"Do you do breast self-exam?" I remember to ask her.

"I know I should. I just don't like to" is her response, a common one. Some women say they find it too frightening, partly because of the difficulty in distinguishing between dangerous lumps and normal breast tissue, which can at times be lumpy.

With the woman now lying on the table, her feet in stirrups, her legs covered with a drape, the light adjusted, I examine her labia, clitoris and urethra for abnormalities. Then with a speculum I examine her vagina and cervix, looking for any areas of redness, scarring, infection, abnormal glands or secretions. Following the speculum exam I palpate the woman's pelvic organs by inserting two fingers of my right hand into her vagina; at the same time, I place my left hand on her lower abdomen and try to feel her uterus and ovaries between the fingers of my hand. This woman's uterus is enlarged from the fibroids, so it is easily felt. I cannot feel her ovaries, but that is not unusual when they are normal. I finish with the rectal exam, taking a bit of stool from my gloved finger and checking it for any occult blood, which could indicate intestinal bleeding.

"You can get up now," I tell the woman, offering to help her but realizing there is no graceful way to get up from that position.

She asks what I think, and I tell her, "You seem to be in quite good health, other than your enlarged uterus. I'm sure you're worried, but fibroid tumors are benign, as you know." I speak to her unsaid fear of cancer.

As we walk back to her room I explain what will happen to her for the rest of the day and evening. An anesthesiologist will see her and take some of the same history, examine her heart and lungs, and assign a risk category for her in terms of the anesthesia. If either I or the anesthesiologist discover any problems, consultants will be called.

Every patient must be "cleared" for surgery. She must have her chart in order, lab tests done and reported, her chest x-ray done and read by the radiologist. If she is over forty, she must have had an electrocardiogram (EKG) read and cleared by the cardiologist. The resident on duty for the night will "pre-op" the patient—that is, make sure everything is done, consent forms signed, and that any consultants called have now cleared the woman for surgery in the morning. The chart must also contain an "informed consent" note written by the attending, stating that all risks of the surgery have been explained to the patient.

Leaving the woman back in her room, I return to the nurses' station, where I find a quiet corner in which to write the history, physical, summary of pertinent findings, and then recommended treatment—usually the operation, which has already been scheduled.

The order sheet is the official communication between the doctors and nursing personnel. I write "Admit to GYN," although she has already been admitted, since it can't be official until I order it. I assign a diet (she won't be fed until I order a diet), and then list lab tests, chest x-ray and EKG, all of which have already been done. I write an order, "Anesthesia to see patient," although in many instances they may be with her already or may have seen her before me. Sometimes it seems that we are doing endless perfunctory and superfluous tasks to produce a chart—which will stand up well in court.

I've promised the patient I would order sleep medication for her, so I do that. I've called her attending, who wants her to have an enema, so I order it. I order that her pubic hair and abdomen be shaved for her hysterectomy in the morning.

The chart is not written in peace. There are endless calls on my pager, questions from patients and nurses, minor or major emergencies. I write on, though, and as I write I am separating myself from this patient. It is as though I am discharging her onto paper. It is urgent that I finish and go on, because she was only my first work-up this afternoon.

Chapter Three

Last night was the annual dinner at Dr. Pierce's house and I met many of the residents in the program. They seem to be depressed, talking mostly about work and suicide. I left with a good feeling about being older than they and, I hoped, past many of the turmoils of growing up.

I'm staying at Laurie's for the next two weeks, while Heather is back in New Jersey with my parents. There is a bid on the New Jersey house and I've gotten the mortgage on the house here, so we should be able to move in ten days.

This morning feels like a new beginning, one I have worked hard to create. I feel brave and adventurous but also scared.

Later

After a day of taking care of patients, scrubbing on a hysterectomy that Carol and Dr. MacDougal were doing, and then doing work-ups, I am heading back to Laurie's for dinner and then back to the hospital, where Carol is going to give me some extra lessons on tying sutures. I feel so incredibly fortunate to be getting this training.

There has been a resident rebellion over my coming to the program as a part-time resident. Dr. Pierce met with the residents and said they had no choice but to have me here. They were somewhat appeased when he told them I was working two-thirds time for half salary and only partial credit.

52

Wednesday   Day 3

"Are you married?" Dr. Owen's questions were becoming increasingly personal as we were scrubbing at the sinks before a case.

"No," I answered, after a short hesitation, trying to indicate that I wasn't going to offer any more information than I had to.

"I hope you don't mind these questions."

"No, not at all," I answered. I knew my ability to succeed here was going to depend on how I got along with attendings as well as the other residents.

"My nephew is going out with a woman medical student and frankly I'm quite worried."

"Good choice," I said jokingly, keeping the rest of my thoughts to myself.

We went through the doors of the OR, he leading, both of us with our upward-reaching hands and bent elbows, and he asked, "What is your first name?"

"Michelle."

Nurses were handing us towels to dry our hands and listening to our exchange.

"Do you mind if I call you by your first name?"

"That's fine," I told him and after a moment I asked, "What would you like me to call you?"

There was silence; he looked uncomfortable and then responded, "In this setting I am used to being called Dr. Owen."

I went about putting on my gown, and as the nurse tied the back I said, "I'll be pleased to call you whatever makes you more comfortable."

Thursday, on the way to work   Day 4

I talked on the phone with Heather last night. I miss her and look forward to this weekend when I'll be back in New Jersey. I'm working full-time at the hospital right now, trying to build up a little equity so I can get some hours off to start Heather in school.

On the way home

My first work-up this afternoon was on a woman who is having laparoscopy for a lost IUD. An IUD, or intra-uterine device, is a plastic or metal birth control device which is inserted through the cervical os into the uterus. This woman's IUD is outside her uterus, somewhere in the right side of her pelvis. It has been located there both by x-ray and ultrasound, a technique which uses sound waves instead of x-rays to form a picture. The IUD apparently perforated through the uterus after it was put in. I asked the woman what she was planning to use for birth control after this.

"Oh, I'll have another IUD put in," she said, as though surprised by my question. Noticing my surprise, she added, "I'd just like to see what another one does."

While I was with her I could hear the woman in the next bed talking on the phone about the surgery she'd had. She is an infertility patient who, during surgery last week, "accidentally" lost an ovary. On the phone she was telling someone that "the bad ovary was removed, but the good one was left in."

Both these women had such trust in the medical system.

Friday   Day 5

At first we couldn't find the IUD. When the surgeon couldn't see it with the laparoscope, he tried to find it inside the womb. While exploring the woman's uterus he accidentally perforated it with the probe. I was looking through the laparoscope when I suddenly saw a metal probe coming through the wall. When we then did a laparotomy (opened her abdominally) we could see the two holes in her uterus, one where the IUD had presumably perforated, and a new one made while the inside of the uterine cavity was explored. We finally found the IUD in the tissue around the ovary and tube, removed it and repaired the damage.

One of the surgeons realized he knew the bank officer who had handled my mortgage, and we chatted about real estate and school systems while we hunted for the missing IUD.

I had time today to go to the laundry to try on a white coat and pants. I'll be issued four sets, which are to last my stay here. Up until now I've been wearing my street clothes under a short white jacket I found hanging in the closet of the on-call room. We all wear white coats, but some of the residents wear white skirts or pants. Residents who have been here long enough to have gained or lost weight tend to have given up on their uniforms and just wear the coats. The jackets are most necessary because of the numerous pockets in which to keep papers, pens, medical instruments, wallet, note-books, miniature textbooks and sometimes snacks.

Before leaving this evening, I took care of an eighty-two-year-old woman about to be discharged. She has a prolapsed uterus, which is falling down so badly that sometimes it pro-trudes through her vagina. Someone had prescribed a pes-sary, a rubber device to hold it up, but the pessary was too large and when I tried to insert it into the woman's vagina she screamed. I stopped, and told her I'd order a smaller one.

"My uterus has been that way for twenty years," she told me. "I don't want anything done to it. I can push it up my-self."

She was in the hospital for a medical condition when the prolapse was discovered. I'm not sure she'll come back next week for the smaller pessary. Though there are medical rea-sons to use a pessary, many older women prefer not to have a device in the vagina.

Tuesday evening   *Day 9*

I have been on duty for thirty-six hours. Most of the night was spent working in the emergency room seeing women with gynecologic emergencies as well as nonemergencies.

The work was familiar and similar to what I've done for years in family practice and emergency-room work. Richard, my chief for the night, made it difficult for me to figure out what decisions I may or may not make on my own. Each time I called to ask about a patient, I'd also ask if I was supposed to be calling him or whether I should take care of the patient myself.

"I don't mind your calling" was his perpetual answer, although it didn't address my question. Having assured Dr. Pierce I would "take orders" even from those younger or, in some cases, less experienced, I do not want to step outside the bounds of what I am supposed to do on my own.

Today I scrubbed on two D&Cs, one on a very obese woman about whom there was much joking. Anesthetized women look so vulnerable.

Sunday afternoon as I stood on the porch of my New Jersey house I realized I might not see it again. We had rented a U-Haul truck and will move next weekend. I have spent a weekend packing and there is still more to go; my friend Missy will do it for me. I have too much stuff and no time to sort out what to take or get rid of. I've loved that house, which has been a place of parties, meetings and poetry readings. It's been a resting place and refuge for me and my friends. My friends have been wonderful, though we are all sad to part from each other.

Thursday   *Day 11*

Today I scrubbed with Richard on a mini-lap, a modified abdominal tubal ligation. We began by trying to do it by laparoscopy, but when we looked inside, we saw a hydrosalpinx, a large fluid-filled sac swelling the woman's Fallopian tube. We went in abdominally, removed the hydrosalpinx and tied the tubes.

Sunday morning, on the way to work   **Day 14**

Friday afternoon we moved to Everytown. Five minutes after we began unloading the truck two girls, about eight and ten, rode by on their bikes and invited Heather to join them. Though she is only five, she learned to ride last week—just in time—and she proudly went off with them. An hour later she returned, asking if she could go swimming with them; I said that was fine if one of them could lend her a suit, since I couldn't locate anything of ours. Heather has moved in.

Friday night my friends Missy and Sandra arrived from New Jersey to help unpack and put the house together. Then last night we went to a party at the home of Catherine, a woman physician I've also met at many conferences. I finally met other members of the Midwestern Women's Health Alliance, including Diane, a woman at whose apartment Heather and I stayed when we were visiting in July. It was an evening of music, talk and food, and although I was tired, I was glad to be there.

Snuggles, a multicolored kitten, is the latest addition to our household. She joins Maggie, the sheltie, and Corny, our guinea pig. Barbara had gotten the kitten when she moved to be a resident, but she cried all the time because Barbara was never home.

Beginning this morning I will be on duty for twenty-four hours; Missy will stay at the house with Heather. I feel very taken care of by my friends.

Monday morning, on the way home   **Day 15**

Yesterday morning I arrived at the hospital to find that the woman whose hysterectomy I watched last week was going back to the operating room for the third time. Last week they took her back to remove a blood clot from the site of surgery, and yesterday they opened her and cleaned out all the clotted blood and pus, which should probably have been removed the first time they took her back.

The afternoon was spent doing work on the unit and taking

emergency-room calls. Jackie, who is covering for Carol as chief resident for the weekend, came in for a while. She is a short, slim, intense woman who rarely looks relaxed. Trying to catch her attention, I said "Hello." She turned to me and said, "I have a lot of scut work for you to do, Michelle." "Scut" is work of no educational value, like drawing bloods or taking EKGs, work usually done by a nurse or technician but also done by residents in teaching hospitals. Jackie was letting me know that she had the authority to assign scut work to me. The work wasn't bad because I had plenty of time, but I didn't like being treated that way, especially by a woman with whom I expected to be friends. Her casual dress, jeans and loafers, make her authoritarian demeanor more of a surprise.

A woman who had laparoscopy last week has been running a fever for the last two days, but no one has found the source of the infection. Yesterday Barbara wanted to put a probe into the incision to see if pus drained. "The woman is infected in the incision," Barbara insisted. "It's because of her obesity." Richard claimed the infection was intra-abdominal and wanted to take her back to the operating room and open her up.

"Don't you have anything else that would explain the fever, like a cold or something?" I asked the patient last evening, partly in jest, partly because I was so frustrated at not being able to find the source of infection.

"Well, as a matter of fact, I've had a sore throat for days but no one seems interested."

Examining her, I discovered she had a large tender and swollen neck mass. She told me she has had infections of her parotid (saliva-producing) gland before. I'm sure that is what she has now.

Richard ridiculed me at rounds this morning when I told the others what I had found, but we're still getting an Ear, Nose and Throat consult on the woman.

Late last night a woman came into the emergency room with a lot of abdominal pain and looking very sick. Richard and

I argued about whether or not to admit her because he didn't think her problem was so serious, but at three in the morning he finally agreed to admit her. The two most probable diagnoses were pelvic infection or an ectopic pregnancy, which is a pregnancy in the Fallopian tube and which is potentially fatal. Richard said they would no doubt take her to surgery in the morning, and told me to go to sleep. The nurses and I were upset about leaving the woman for that long because by then we strongly suspected it was an ectopic pregnancy that had ruptured. One nurse said she thought the woman's belly was becoming more swollen; this would happen if she was bleeding internally. Instead of going to sleep, I ordered another hematocrit, a blood test I expected to show blood loss.

An hour later I woke Richard with the results. He called Jackie, who called the attending, and we rushed the woman into the operating room. When we opened the woman's abdomen, the blood came pouring out. It continued to spill out until the bleeding tubal pregnancy was located and tied off.

As I kept trying to sponge up blood—my job as the junior member of the team—Richard would tell me to stop, that I was in his way. Then a male nurse would do exactly what I had been doing, and there would be no comment from Richard. At one point, when the field was filled with blood and it seemed impossible to see anything, I reached in with a sponge and Richard slapped my hand. The nurse went on sponging. I can't let myself respond. I've promised myself I will put up with anything.

The patient did well through surgery and is expected to have a normal recovery. Jackie congratulated Richard for his good work, and especially for having quickly gotten the hematocrit which showed the woman was bleeding.

Richard will be my chief when I am on obstetrics in another month. This worries me a lot.

Tuesday   *Day 16*

This morning at breakfast rounds, Jackie seemed to be trying to pit Barbara and me against each other, referring to my having higher rank as a second-year resident, and changing her mind several times about who would do which surgery. As we were dressing for surgery, Barbara and I agreed that we wouldn't let Jackie set us up against each other. We could go along with Jackie today because we knew that the issues would disappear when Carol returns. Carol can make the same assignments or ask that the same work be done but without polarizing issues or people. In the same way that she gives patients the sense that she cares, she makes taking orders seem right and even pleasurable.

This afternoon on my way home I stopped at the school to register Heather. The kindergarten–1st grade combination (K-1) seemed the most logical place to put her since that would give everyone a chance to see where she really belongs. The principal, however, said the K-1 was full and he wanted her in the 1-2 class. I'm worried about that because, although she is five years old and of first-grade age, she hasn't been in kindergarten yet. It's so hard as a mother to know when to insist and when to leave it up to the experts.

"I'm not going to after-school!" Heather said adamantly.

"But why? You've always loved day care and you've always loved being in child care wherever we've gone."

"I'm not going, Mama. I'm not going," and this time she was weeping.

I didn't understand. She had loved the after-school center when we went to see it and to meet the teacher. After a few minutes at the center, Heather was able to tell me why she was so upset. "The kids said when I was in first grade I would have so much homework I couldn't do anything else in the afternoon. They also said that if you didn't do your homework, the teacher would hit you over the head with a book and I'm scared because I don't want to get hit."

Heather accepted my reassurance and is now looking forward to being at the center. I suspect that after a while she will prefer to be home in the afternoon with her friends, but I have a sense of relief that the center is there if I need it.

Wednesday morning   *Day 17*

There are beautiful pinks and blues and touches of yellow coming across the sky as I drive in to work at sunrise.

Finding a live-in baby-sitter will be my next project. Some days I think I can manage Heather, the house and work, but most of the time I feel pulled in so many different directions. The hours I'm working make it more difficult than most situations, but my problem is not unlike that of any working woman—especially if she is a single parent. There's never a breather.

On the way home

The woman who had the ectopic pregnancy met me on rounds this morning with, "You know, I was awake for the surgery and I can remember it." She is eighteen years old and this morning, hair in curlers, mildly distracted by the TV cartoons, she looked like a testy teen-ager.

"What do you remember?" I asked, aware that what she was saying was possible, especially with a drug which paralyzes people even if they are not fully asleep.

"I remember thinking I was at a party, and everyone was standing over me passing joints from one person to another. Then I remembered being opened up, and having my blood spilling out all over and everyone looking frightened. That's all I remember," she said, looking triumphant, daring me to disagree.

"I guess you were there, but I don't remember any joints," I told her jokingly.

The joints must have been the instruments being passed from hand to hand. Her memory of the fear we felt when the blood spilled out of her was accurate.

Later in the day I mentioned her story to the anesthesiologist, who became angry and said she was crazy.

Dr. Neisel is a very old surgeon who still operates at the hospital, but with an unofficial rule that he must have a chief resident with him. This morning I scrubbed with Jackie and him, while Dr. Pierce came by to watch for a while. Dr. Neisel seemed to suspect that he was being watched closely, so before surgery, while we were all scrubbing, Jackie and I pretended that Dr. Pierce has been making surprise visits to look over everyone's shoulders.

Dr. Neisel became aphasic during the hysterectomy—that is, he couldn't find the words for what he wanted, for the instruments he needed. He kept saying "Kelly," which is a kind of clamp used in surgery. But when the nurse handed him the Kelly clamp, he pushed it away and repeated "Kelly." At one point the nurse had handed him every instrument on the tray but he rejected each one and then reaching onto the tray himself, took a scalpel.

Trying to lighten the situation, Jackie said to him, "I just think you've got the sweets for Kelly," referring to a nurse in the OR. Jackie also kept trying to do surgery for him, since his hands weren't very steady. She'd kid him, telling him that he wasn't giving her enough teaching experience because he was doing it himself. Several times I caught Dr. Pierce's eyes and he seemed upset about what was going on.

Thursday   *Day 18*

This morning as I walked Heather out the back door and over the small hill to her school, I was overwhelmed and tearful at the sense I had of the repetition and continuity of generations. Heather was dressed up in a new skirt and a blouse her grandparents had sent from New Jersey. She was still wearing her clogs. At first she was scared in the classroom, but she relaxed and let go of me after meeting her teacher and another child. The day-care-center bus will pick her up at school, and then I will pick her up at six. I feel bad about her going right from school to the after-school program today without my being there. I'll be concerned about her all day, hoping she is all right.

This morning at five-thirty, before taking Heather to school, I went into the hospital, made rounds, and left for home again at seven-thirty. By ten I was back in the operating room, scrubbed on a laparoscopic tubal ligation.

I remember one day last year at the day-care center when a new teacher didn't show up for the first day after vacation. Since my time at the medical school was flexible, I was able to stay, but I remember other mothers who were rushing to work and couldn't stay because a boss was due back, or a class was waiting, or they simply had to be on time. Motherhood in our society means always being on the edge between two existences which rarely allow for any overlap.

Friday   *Day 19*

Usually when a woman has fibroid tumors that are giving her discomfort or bleeding, she has her entire uterus removed. Today, however, I scrubbed on a myomectomy, or a removal of the tumors from the uterus, on a woman who wants to become pregnant. The tumors look like round red balls imbedded in the walls of the uterus and bleed profusely when they are removed. The woman had two large ones, each the size of a lemon, and then some tiny "seedlings," which were also removed. The outer capsule of the tumor is shelled off, like peeling an orange, and then the bulk of the tumor is tied off in sections. It is a more difficult procedure than a hysterectomy, and seems to have a higher complication rate.

I have been practicing tying knots on napkins and furniture at home, but it is different from tying knots in surgery, where my gloves are wet and slippery with blood, I can't see well, there's never enough room in the operative site, and I'm trying to hurry.

Laurie will pick up Heather at the after-school program and keep her for the night because I'm on duty for the next thirty-six hours. This morning when I left, I realized that no one will be home, so I left a note asking Laurie to let Maggie out once tonight and again in the morning when she drops Heather off at school. The dog is one more responsibility.

Arlene, a college student, is the only person who showed up for an interview for the job, although I had many calls over the weekend. She says she likes children and is used to them; she is the second oldest of nine. She would be able to attend her classes and still be home in time for Heather. I have to call her last reference today, but I feel almost certain I will hire her.

Dr. Neisel has been telling his patient on whom we operated last week that Jackie is the one who is taking care of her. Whenever the woman mentions my name as the one who sees her on rounds, changes her dressings, etc., he looks at her blankly. Today she called me into her room to ask when I would start my own practice, because she wanted me to be her doctor. "Dr. Neisel is getting old," she told me, as though apologetic for noticing. "One of these days I know I will need another doctor."

I have been watching a lot of D&Cs and noticing the motion used to scrape out the inside of the uterus. The curette is jabbed in and out of the vagina repeatedly, held in the surgeon's hand as if the force of the thrust is coming from his/her body. Watching the procedure, I found it difficult not to think of the word "fucking." I don't know why that style is necessary or why they aren't more gentle.

Wednesday   *Day 24*

When I am on call for so many hours, my body becomes bloated and feels out of shape. My legs are swollen and my clothes are uncomfortable against my skin.

I've hired Arlene, although I wasn't able to reach her last reference, but I need some relief. She should be at the house when I get home.

Fran called about a friend of hers and Laurie's who has just come to Everytown and needs a place to stay for a while. I offered her the spare room, so she should also be at the house when I get home.

I slept last night at the hospital between three and six in the morning, so I don't feel as terrible as I might.

Thursday   *Day 25*

Arlene has moved in and Heather is delighted to have a new baby-sitter, especially since she has been complaining about having to go to the after-school program instead of being able to come home and play with her friends. Heather is thrilled to have someone else in the house who enjoys hair fixing and dressing up. I am relieved that the constant arranging of child care is over.

Gail, Fran and Laurie's friend, was also at the house when I got home last night. She is resettling here after having been in England for the past ten years, and she may stay on at the house for a while. Fran and Laurie came and we cooked a big dinner for everyone. Home is beginning to feel the way it did in New Jersey.

On the way home

I had a busy morning in the OR with two D&Cs, a laparoscopy and a mini-lap. Dr. Catan, the surgeon with whom I was scrubbed for most of the cases, is an older, roundish, kindly man who was quite nice to me. Afterward, though, he took me aside and said, "Dear, you hold your instruments like a plumber." His criticism struck me with peculiar accuracy. Between cases I had been on the phone trying to reach a plumber about a shower leak, and had said apologetically to one, "Ordinarily I would do the work myself, but I don't have the time now."

Richard, who has excellent surgical skills, was operating this morning when one of the older attendings began yelling at him and belittling him over a case, asking in a rage, "Where did you get your training, anyway?" Richard held back the obvious "Here." Last week the same surgeon had Carol in tears when he told her, "You're retarded and you've been that way since you were two!" She is his favorite resident but he becomes verbally abusive in the operating room.

Tuesday   *Day 30*

It's been another thirty-six-hour stretch and I'm in a bad state. Carol told me at three this afternoon that she wants me to work every Sunday from six A.M. to eight P.M. when I start OB next month. Our agreement when I took the job was that I'd be able to leave at five, and although I'll be working six days a week on OB, I had been looking forward to being home for supper every night.

"But, Michelle, I'll even let you leave early every afternoon," she offered, obviously not understanding why I couldn't do that—obviously under pressure herself.

"Carol, I'd love to get out early, but I'm not needed at home in the afternoon the way I am in the evening."

"I'll even give you a whole day off in exchange for those hours." I knew she needed me and I felt torn, caring about the work, about Heather, guilty about both.

"Carol, if I work those hours, then I won't see Heather from Saturday evening until Monday evening, every week. She'll be asleep when I leave Sunday morning before six, when I get home Sunday night, and when I leave again Monday morning. Why don't you make that offer to someone else, three hours for a whole day? I'm sure the others would love it.''

''I can't do that!'' was her short reply as she left.

I have such a sense of single motherhood, because if I'm not there, my child is without a parent. My being able to be home at suppertime gives a stability to our life because whatever else happens in the day, I'll be home to take care of it.

A woman in medical school with me had four young children. She used to get up at five every morning and wake the children so she could spend time playing with them, since that was the only time she could count on.

At Heather's day-care center, the other mothers and I, whatever our jobs, shared the feeling that we had already put in a day's work by the time we got to work.

There is a woman on the GYN unit who is seriously ill from an IUD infection. She has been in the hospital for three weeks getting intravenous antibiotics, but signs of infection are still present. We have been doing everything necessary to prevent surgery, which would end her reproductive life.

''You may still have to have surgery,'' I told her last night because she has been getting worse.

She nodded. ''I know that.''

Because she seemed so resigned, I told her, ''You know, if we do operate, you won't be able to have children.''

''But I don't ever want to have children,'' she said. ''I made that decision years ago.''

No one had asked her. We had just assumed she wanted to preserve her fertility.

Last night I was upset by all the other women doctors in the hospital—I was struck by how much women have become a part of the system. Years ago when I was working in the hospital for days at a time, it didn't seem so bad because I could tell myself all the others were men and I knew women were different. Now, ten years later, there are many more women, but they are just like the men, taking part in and defending the militaristic training and the insensitive treat-

ment of the patients. Now I feel even more isolated because
both men and women comply with the system.

It's not being awake for such long hours that I mind so
much; it's the meaninglessness of much of the work. During
the day if a patient needs blood, the nursing department gets
it from the blood bank, but at night, we have been told, there
is no one responsible enough on duty to do that. So at two
or three in the morning, only a resident is considered competent enough to go to the lab, compare numbers on the
patient's slip and the bag of blood, and bring it back to
the patient's room. Half asleep at that hour, I think we are
the least capable of the task. It might be all right if we were
going home in the morning instead of into the OR for another
long day. It would also be easier if those who had been
through it weren't saying, "It's good for you. It separates the
men from the boys. If you can't take it, you shouldn't be in
medicine." I never minded being awake in South Carolina
because I was doing useful work, and I don't mind it here
when I am doing useful work. It is the senseless, institutionalized "way of doing things" I resent.

I'm so tired after these two days of work without sleep,
but tonight I have to go to a gathering of the parents of the
children in Heather's class.

Wednesday   *Day 31*

Heather broke down crying as I was leaving for the meeting
and asked, "Why are you going out tonight? Why can't you
just stay home?"

"Heather, I'm only going out so I can meet the other parents of your school and make it easier for you here," I told
her. I stayed and read stories to her until she was feeling
better, and then left. It's not like her to act that way. In fact,
this has never happened before. Because she so enjoys being
with people, a more usual response has been, "When are
you going out? I want a baby-sitter."

Among the parents in Heather's class, there are three
mothers who are doctors and one who is a medical student.

Joan, who will be my chief resident at the end of the year, has a daughter in the same class, but she and her children are away for three months, so the girls have not met each other. She had warned me when I was looking for a place to live, "Don't move as far from the hospital as I have. I don't see my children enough." I don't believe it is the five miles that kept her from them; it's working over a hundred hours a week.

Later

A woman with an infertility problem had a laparoscopy today during which we found adhesions, filmy, spiderweb-like scar tissue that ties organs and structures to each other. As I looked through the laparoscope I could see the purple dye which had been injected through the canula in the cervix and which showed that the Fallopian tubes were open. Nevertheless, the woman will have another operation to remove them because it is presumed that the adhesions are preventing the Fallopian tubes from moving freely.

This evening Barbara came for dinner, partly to meet Heather and partly to see Snuggles, the kitten she had given us. Away from work we relaxed with each other and managed not to talk about work or the people there. Once past her initial shyness, she is open and warm. When she left she said that she now understood why I needed to be home for dinner. As I drove her home she told me that she thought I was very lucky to have a child and that she was jealous. The house is great these days, with Arlene, Gail and Heather. They were all playing music in the living room when I left to take Barbara home.

Thursday   Day 32

Fran, a tall graceful woman, was busy setting her coal-black hair and getting ready for a meeting when I stopped by her house on my way home. She took the time, though, to fix me a protein drink, and we talked while she got ready. We

talked about how hard it is for women to take care of themselves. She thinks I ought to have something like that drink
every morning, and although I agree with her, I know I won't
do it. I do such a good job of taking care of Heather. Women
seem so often to deny themselves and to nurture others. We
worry about balanced meals for our children and then settle
for their leftovers as our own.

Before it's too late, I want to get bulbs to plant. I wonder
if the house already has bulbs that will come up in the spring.
I left many bulbs in the ground when I left the New Jersey
house. I especially loved to see the crocuses coming up
through the snow.

Friday　　　　　　　　　　　　　　　　　　　*Day 33*

Bob Carter is a well-known gynecologist with a reputation
for charm and a general attitude of "Don't worry about a
thing, dearie. I'll take care of you."

Dr. Carter and I were at the sinks scrubbing this morning
when he asked, "Can you do a D&C?"

"Sure," I answered.

"Then it's yours to do."

The woman was also having a mole taken off her face, so
I did the D&C while he and the plastic surgeon removed the
lesion on her face at the other end of the table.

Our next case together was an ovarian cyst and he let me
do a lot of it. The woman had been worked up yesterday by
Al, a medical student on GYN. She had refused to allow him
to do the pelvic exam.

"Okay," he said, "but how about while you are under
anesthesia tomorrow?"

"No, I don't want you to examine me then, either. I only
want Dr. Carter to examine me."

Today when we were all scrubbing, Dr. Carter told Al to
go into the room and examine the woman while she was
under anesthesia.

"No. She doesn't want me to," Al said. Dr. Carter kept
insisting that it didn't matter whether she had consented, but

Al still refused. I admired him for his refusal, but knew the trouble he would be in for what he was doing.

After surgery Carol and I were standing out at the OR desk when Dr. Carter came by to say he was leaving town. Then he leaned over and gave me a pinch on the ass as he left. Containing my rage, I smiled and said, "Have a good trip." Carol and I joked at his having no idea who I really am or how I feel. I was glad to be "in" and accepted, but furious at what that seemed to take.

Monday morning   Day 36

Yesterday Heather, her friend Megan and I went to the park and flew a new octopus kite with filmy colorful streamers. Heather said it was the "bestest" day ever.

I'm disappointed that I spend so little time reading, but after the intensity of work, I can't pick up a book. I hope to read more on OB, where I imagine there will be more time spent sitting around.

Saturday there was a meeting about women's health care which I didn't attend, but Fran and Laurie brought some of the speakers back to my house for the evening. Maintaining contact with women involved in the politics of women's health care is my antidote to Bob Carter's ass-pinching.

Later

My surgical skills are rapidly improving. This morning I scrubbed on a tubal ligation and then the removal of an ovarian cyst.

The issue of the OB schedule and Carol's wanting me to work a fourteen-hour day every Sunday has me preoccupied. Sometime this morning I told Carol we needed to talk about it, and apparently, I commented that if I had to work those hours I might not stay in the program. I don't remember saying that, but I probably did, since that's how I feel. In one week the thirty-six-hour shifts will be over for a while, and I need that time at home.

Carol and I didn't get to talk until late in the afternoon when she told me she had been in tears after my comment. She felt I didn't care about the program if I could think about leaving, that I didn't care about what it would do to be short a person. It was especially strange to hear that I'm needed on the service since mostly I feel that my presence only reminds the others that they are working even more than I.

Starting to cry, I said, "You don't understand the strain I'm under. There's no more of me to go around. All I'm saying is that I've faced the possibility that I may not be able to do all this, that's all. I don't want to leave, but I may not be able to take it."

We were both in tears by then, and I suddenly felt so sorry for her, knowing the strain she is under too. Carol had been chief resident for the past four months, and with the exception of four days in September, she was on call seven days a week, twenty-four hours a day, held responsible for what all the residents did, and subject to Dr. Pierce's rage when anything went wrong.

I didn't want to be fighting with Carol. We were both feeling pushed to our limits. I walked across the room to put my arms around her, and she suddenly stepped back. "You're little!" she said with amazement, standing in front of me.

"Of course I'm little," I told her. "I only seem big," and we both laughed.

Wednesday   *Day 38*

I kept dreaming last night that I was climbing off elephants and devising systems for climbing off elephants so other people could do it also. I knew it was too far to jump, and I remember that one of the options was to make friends with the elephant so it wouldn't destroy you as you climbed down near its mouth.

Fran and I went wallpaper hunting yesterday. I can't stand the paper in the dining room, but I haven't decided what to put up instead. I debate whether to get vinyl paper, which is easy to put up and care for, or something more formal. The vinyl paper would make it easier to put up Heather's pictures and posters, but I keep finding more formal papers I like. The issue can't be as important as it seems to be, spinning in my head as I try to decide, but I seem stuck with trying to resolve some part of my life via the paper on the dining-room walls.

Heather, Arlene and I had a quiet dinner last night, and then Heather's friends came over and we baked cookies. Now that Arlene is here I cannot imagine how I ever managed without help in the house. It's so wonderful to come home at night to find that the salad is fixed and that dinner has been planned and is on its way. Even when I cook now I enjoy the nonessential, voluntary nature of what I am doing.

As I drive to work, already a few minutes late, there is a beautiful sunrise in the distance.

Later

Grand Rounds is a weekly formal departmental conference which usually consists of lectures and case presentations. Residents are required to wear white coats and regular clothes as opposed to the grays from the OR.

At Grand Rounds this morning a patient was presented whose current difficulties began six months ago when she had her IUD removed. She had a mild infection at the time, but a week later a tubal ligation was performed in spite of the infection. She has now had three hospitalizations for severe infections and is in danger of dying from infection.

In the second hour of the conference, an anesthesiologist lectured about resuscitation of babies, saying that he found mouth-to-mouth far superior to the bag and mask because he could get a better seal over the nose and mouth with his own mouth. That had been my experience in resuscitating babies: the mask didn't fit well and I could do better without it.

Thursday   *Day 39*

Carol had told me that Dr. Enders, one of the old-timers
here, might let me do the hysterectomy today, but after we
were gowned he went right to the side of the table, which
meant he was doing it. I went to the other side, prepared to
assist.

"Knife," he called to the nurse and then cut the woman's
skin.

"Snaps," I requested proudly, asking for the little clamps
I would use to stop the bleeders as he cut.

Angrily he said, "Marcelle, don't do that. We're not tying
them," but in a few minutes, of course we did.

Throughout the surgery, whenever I tried to do something,
it was wrong, but when I didn't do anything, that was wrong
too. When I saw a bleeder and said something to him, since
I no longer spontaneously did anything, he would snap at
me, "I have eyes. I can see!" But when I was quiet, he
asked, "Why aren't you doing something to help here? Want
her to bleed to death?"

I had looked forward to the surgery this morning, practicing knots and reading last night at home. Dr. Enders insists
on calling me Marcelle too, which bugs me.

Tomorrow I'm on for twenty-four hours, then again on
Sunday for another twenty-four, and then Tuesday I begin
three months of OB. Beth, who will be on OB at night, has
agreed to come in early Sunday evening in exchange for other
time off. I'll be working six days a week, but I'll be home
for dinner every night. With only six weeks behind me, I am
sometimes overwhelmed by what I have committed myself
to doing. I wonder how long I will last.

Saturday   *Day 41*

Much of the last twenty-four hours has been enjoyable, in
spite of only two hours' sleep, because the work was challenging, and I was learning.

In the OR yesterday morning I put on my first set of Fallope rings, finding it easy to see what I was doing. Then I scrubbed on a myomectomy with Dr. Ingle, another one of the old-timers here; he is a skilled surgeon, but reticent to say much. He asked me to dictate the operative notes when we were through, so I wished he had been open to more questions about what we were doing.

Busy in the OR until late in the afternoon, I had little time on the floor before I was called back for emergency surgery on a woman with an ectopic pregnancy. We did laparoscopy first, trying to be certain what she had, but when we saw the bleeding in her pelvis we opened her up, located the ruptured ectopic pregnancy and removed the Fallopian tube. Charlie, the chief for the night, did most of the surgery, but he let me close the abdomen. He talked about what he was doing as he worked, so I learned a great deal. He's a really nice guy who cares about his patients and about those of us who work with him.

Around midnight I was called to the emergency room to see a woman with a severe pelvic infection and an IUD still in place. I removed the IUD and began giving her antibiotics. The IUD is so dangerous, causing infections and infertility, and increasing the incidence of ectopic pregnancy because of infections and subsequent damage to the Fallopian tubes.

The rest of the night was spent taking care of the woman on whom Dr. Enders and I did the hysterectomy. Her past history of severe kidney disease had caused me to worry about her having surgery, especially since it was for fibroids, relatively harmless, though they were giving her pain. She now has a life-threatening infection following the surgery. I'm bothered by the number of life-threatening infections I am seeing.

Monday   *Day 43*

It's been a long twenty-six hours, but some of the time was actually pleasurable. The hours after midnight are the painful ones.

Yesterday morning after rounds, I relaxed and took time

to think about my patients, plan for their care for the day, and leave good summarizing notes on their charts for the next group of residents.

A woman came into the emergency room with pelvic pain. It was discovered in surgery to be a ruptured ovarian cyst, which we removed. The anesthesiology resident had a lot of trouble getting the needle into the woman's spine and she gave the impression that she didn't care. Eventually her supervisor arrived and placed the needle, but then the resident spilled the medication on the floor. Finally the anesthesiologist said we could begin.

"Knife," called the surgeon, and taking the scalpel in his hand, made one long incision. The woman screamed in pain, blood appeared on her skin, and the anesthesiologist quickly put her under with general anesthesia. It had taken two hours to begin.

An abortion is the expulsion of a nonviable fetus. In lay language, abortion usually refers to removal of the fetus through medical intervention, while miscarriage is used to denote a spontaneous loss of a fetus. However, in medicine, the term abortion includes all fetal loss.

I did two D&Cs today for incomplete abortions. In these situations a woman has placental or other tissue left and is usually bleeding. Then another woman came into the emergency room with a threatened abortion, cramping and bleeding, and she passed the fetus this morning. Early this morning I admitted another woman having an incomplete abortion, and she will have her D&C this morning.

Last night at six, Heather, Arlene and Gail stopped by the hospital on their way to the movies and brought supper for me. I had prepared a CARE package for Heather in case I couldn't get out of the OR, containing a hair brush, toothbrush, Band-Aids and skin cream I had collected from the patient supplies cabinet. I was able to see them, though, and we had a short visit in the lobby before they went off to the movies.

Tomorrow morning I begin obstetrics, the part of the program I especially came here for. I worry about what it will be like to be a part of the highly technological childbirth practiced in the hospital. I want to know the technology, to understand it and be able to use it when necessary.

Nationally the Caesarean section has become epidemic, with some hospitals reporting as much as 40 to 50 percent incidence. I want to be able to do my own Caesareans, and not have to turn over women in trouble to doctors whose childbirth philosophies may be so different from mine or that of the woman. It is learning the obstetrics that brought me to Doctors Hospital.

Chapter Four

THE C-SECTION

There is a natural opening in a pregnant woman—the vagina—through which a baby can usually pass. When babies are born this way, there is not much for a physician to do except watch. However, when the physician needs to get the baby out through the woman's abdomen, s/he can take it out using knives, scissors, clamps, needles and metal clips to cut through the abdomen and through the uterus. The Caesarean section is a major surgical operation.

The woman coming into the hospital for an elective—i.e., planned, nonemergency—section is admitted early the day before so she can have a work-up, be seen by anesthesia, have lab tests, etc. She is usually healthy and well prepared for what will happen to her. Doctors seem better able to tell a woman about a forthcoming Caesarean section than a vaginal delivery. The type of anesthesia has usually been decided, as well as whether the incision, and thus the resulting scar, will be vertical, from the bellybutton to the pubic bone, or along the pubic hairline in the "bikini cut." The type of anesthesia generally determines whether the husband will be allowed to stay in the OR, since in most hospitals he cannot be present if she has general anesthesia.

The explanation usually given for this policy is that the man's presence is only justified if his wife is awake and they can share the experience. Anesthesiologists generally do not like to have visitors in the operating room. Since they have only a transient relationship with the patient, they have less investment in meeting her needs for a support person. The obstetrician, on the other hand, often has an ongoing relationship with the woman and wants her to be satisfied with her birth experience.

Examining the woman's abdomen as part of the H&P, I first feel the general position of the baby and then listen with the stethoscope. In addition to the heartbeat, the baby can be heard as well as felt as it kicks and rolls, making bulges, arranging space, seeking a slightly more comfortable position, like someone under a deep layer of covers. Handing the stethoscope to the mother, I help her listen, sometimes commenting on what the baby is doing or trying to do.

Babies must feel good when they kick. There is a freedom and then a resistance, the freedom of weightlessness, then the gentle resistance of fluid giving way before moving limbs, and then the firmer resistance of the uterine walls. They are like swimmers in a pool who, reaching the end of the lane, twist their bodies around and kick off again. The baby in utero is never untouched, never in a void. There's always the fluid passing, there are always the walls to be felt with feet, knees, fists, head.

There are sounds inside, too, of water moving, of the baby's own intestinal rumblings, of the mother's heart, the mother's intestinal rumblings, the mother's voice. There are sensations of swallowing, of urinating, of pressure changes, of tightness, of movement. In a Caesarean birth the baby has little warning that its peaceful world will change. Without the preparation of labor, birth is abrupt.

In the morning the woman is wheeled on a stretcher to the L&D (Labor and Delivery) suite, and then to the delivery room, which doubles as a section room. For epidural anesthesia, the woman is placed on the operating table on her left side. She is told to curl into a fetal-like position to allow a needle to be inserted between the vertebrae of her curved spine. When the needle is withdrawn, leaving a tube in the spine, the woman is placed flat on her back and the table temporarily tilted slightly to lower her head in order to establish a level of anesthesia that is high enough to make the woman's abdomen numb, but won't affect her ability to breathe. There is only a fine margin of both safety and comfort: if the level is too low, she will have pain during the surgery; if it is too high, she will have difficulty breathing and will require mechanical assistance.

The woman's bladder is next catheterized and the tube left in the bladder to keep urine draining. During the surgery the bladder is cut away from the surface of the uterus as there is a great risk of perforating or cutting into it if it is full.

Preparation of the surgical site consists of scrubbing and draping the abdomen, with only that portion to be cut left exposed. It is similar to any other surgical preparation except for the inhibited discussion if the woman is awake.

I had been wondering why I always got so covered with blood and amniotic fluid during a Caesarean section, while the surgeon would come out so much cleaner. I would be soaked through my gown, my greens and my underwear. It was finally explained to me: "The table is tilted slightly so the blood and fluid run onto the assistant and not onto the surgeon."

As soon as the woman is draped, the anesthesiologist tilts the table to one side and signals for the surgeon to begin. The surgeon takes a scalpel from the nurse and with one strong and definite motion creates a crescent-shaped incision along the woman's pubic hairline. As the skin is cut, the subcutaneous tissue bulges upward as though it had been straining to get through all the time. Within moments this fatty tissue, interconnected by thin transparent fibers, becomes dotted and then covered with blood that oozes out of tiny vessels. With scalpel and forceps—delicate tweezers—the surgeon cuts deeper beneath the subcutaneous tissue, to a thick layer of fibrous tissue that holds the abdominal organs and muscles of the abdominal wall in place. Once reached, this fibrous layer is incised and cut along the lines of the original surface incision while the muscles adhering to this tissue are scraped off and pushed out of the way. The uterus is now visible under the peritoneum, a layer of thin tissue, looking like Saran Wrap, which covers most of the internal organs and which, when inflamed, produces peritonitis. The peritoneum is lifted away from the uterus and an incision is made in it, leaving the uterus and bladder easily accessible. The bladder is peeled away from the uterus, for the baby will be taken out through an incision in the uterus underneath where the bladder usually lies. When a Caesarean is done as an emergency procedure and speed is essential, the bladder is not removed and instead the incision is made much higher in the uterus. This produces weaker scar tissue and greater chance of rupture during a subsequent pregnancy and labor.

The uterus of the pregnant woman is large, smooth and glistening. Shaped like a huge pear, the top and sides are thick and muscular, the lower end thin and flexible. With short careful strokes of a knife, a small incision is made through the thinner segment. Special care is taken not to cut the baby or the membranes surrounding the baby which, if still intact, now bulge through the tiny hole in the uterus. The room becomes silent: the quiet presence of the baby about to be born causes time suddenly to stop.

The obstetrician extends the initial cut either by putting two index fingers into the small incision and ripping the uterus open or by using blunt-ended scissors and cutting in two directions away from the initial incision. If the membranes are still intact, they are now punctured with toothed forceps, and the fluid spills out onto the table. In the normal position, the baby's head is down and under the incision, so the obstetrician places one hand inside the uterus, under the baby's head, and with the other hand exerts pressure on the upper end of the uterus to push the baby through the abdominal incision. The assistant also uses force now to help push the baby out. Once the baby's head is out, the throat is immediately suctioned with a small ear syringe, and then the shoulders and rest of the body are eased out. Held in the air, the baby usually begins to cry. The cord is clamped and the baby handed over to a nurse holding a warmed towel. Sometimes, en route to the nurse, the infant is momentarily held over the woman's head with its genitals facing down into the mother's face, as she is told, "Look, it's a boy/girl!" The assumption is always made that the woman wants most to know and see the sex of her child. For many women, including those delivering vaginally, this is all they see of their babies at the time of delivery.

The rest of the surgery is more difficult for the woman. There is more pain and women often vomit and complain of difficult breathing as we handle their organs and repair the damage. This period may also be more difficult because there is no longer the anticipation of waiting to see the baby born. Sometimes the woman is given sedation for the rest of the surgery.

The placenta separates from or is peeled off the inside of the uterus. Then, since the uterine attachments are all at the lower end, near the cervix, the body of the uterus can be brought out of the abdominal cavity and rested on the outside of the woman's abdomen, thus adding both visibility and room in which to work.

With large circular needles and thick thread, a combination of running and individual stitches is used to sew closed the hole in the uterus. A drug called pitocin is added to the woman's IV to help the uterus contract and to decrease the bleeding. Small sutures are used to tie and retie bleeding blood vessels. The "gutters," spaces in the abdominal cavity, are cleared of blood and fluid. The uterus is then placed back in the abdominal cavity. The bladder is sewn back onto the surface of the uterus, and then finally the peritoneum is closed. Now sponges are counted to be sure none have been left inside the abdominal cavity, and then the closure of the abdominal wall begins.

Muscles overlying the peritoneum are pushed back in place, and are sometimes sewn with loose stitches. Fascia, the thick fibrous layer, is the most important one, since it holds all the abdominal organs inside and keeps them from coming through the incision, especially if the woman coughs or sneezes. Therefore this layer is closed with heavy thread and many individual stitches so that, even if a thread breaks, the stitches won't all come out. The subcutaneous tissue, most of which is fat, is closed in loose stitches that mainly close any air spaces which might become sites for infection. Skin, the final layer, is closed with either silk or nylon thread or metal staples. The appearance of the final scar is generally considered important, since many people judge whether a surgeon is good or not by the scar's appearance.

A dry bandage is placed over the woman's incision and then taped to her skin. The drapes are removed. A baby has been born.

MODERN CHILDBIRTH

Childbirth in a hospital is both conducted and described as a technological event. As a resident of Doctors Hospital I write on a chart: "NSD [normal spontaneous delivery] from ROA [right occiput anterior] over ML Epis. [midline episiotomy] of male infant, Apgar 9/10.EBL [estimated blood loss] 50 cc., repair 3-0 chromic sutures. Mother to RR [recovery room] good condition. Infant to nursery." I sign that note illegibly, ashamed to "take credit" for that delivery.

That is the standard way of describing the more common vaginal birth. The position (ROA in this case) refers to the relationship of the baby's head to the mother's pelvis. Its importance is primarily related to the use of forceps when it is critical to know the position of the head in order to correctly apply the blades of the forceps. The episiotomy—the cutting of the perineum of the woman to increase the size of the vaginal opening through which the baby passes—is considered by most physicians to be part of a normal delivery.

The Apgar score, taught early in medical school, is a standardized set of criteria by which one rates the condition of the baby at one minute and then at five minutes. One asks a colleague, or sometimes even the mother, "How was the baby?" and is told, "The Apgar was _____." Scores are added up from the following table.

THE APGAR SCORE

	2	1	0
heart rate	over 100	below 100	absent
breathing and cry	prompt, lusty	slow, irregular	no breathing, 1–2 gasps
reflex irritability (response to slap on foot or catheter in nose or throat)	vigorous cry	grimace	no response
muscle tone	active motion	some flexion of extremities	flaccid
color	completely pink	body pink, extremities blue	blue, pale

A top score is obviously 10. Most babies have Apgar scores between 7 and 9 at one minute, and 8 and 10 at five minutes. Those in severe distress are between 0 and 3. A baby with a high Apgar looks good, one with a low one looks bad.

The Apgar is a research tool. If we study ten thousand babies with an Apgar of 3, for ten years, we have certain information that can usually be summed up as: "Babies who are ill at birth often have a hard time in life." The Apgar tells us little, however, about any particular baby's prognosis and nothing about who that person is going to be and how that new person's life will be lived.

What do we need to know about a birth? What are we

missing when we score a baby by heartbeats per minute? What are the questions we should be asking as we try to describe the emergence of one human being out of the body of another?

Was there awe?
Do those in the room feel close to each other and the baby?
Does the baby look healthy?
Does this baby feel welcomed into the world?
Does the baby make eye contact?
Is the baby curious?
Does the baby respond to touch, to voice, to being held?
What is the mother's mood? Happy? Depressed? Frightened?
What is the baby's mood? Happy? Depressed? Frightened?
Was the baby smiling in the birth canal?
Does this mother feel good about herself after this birth?
Is the mother ready to move on to the next phase of their relationship, whether that is together or apart?
Was love present?

We listen for a new baby's crying so we don't have to look at it. A baby doesn't have to be crying for us to know it is healthy. Hold a new baby. It makes eye contact. It breathes. It sighs. The baby has color. Lift it in your arms and feel whether it has good tone or poor, strong limbs or limp ones. The baby does not have to be on a cold table to have its condition measured. What do we lose by being kind to a baby who has just been born?

Babies look serene as they are being born. I do not believe they have just been through trauma. When a baby has been hurt or frightened, it cries and is difficult to console. Babies coming out of their mothers do not cry. There is a myth shared by doctors and mothers that a baby suffers during its passage through the woman's pelvis. True, we, as adults, would find it excruciating, trying to squeeze through, but the baby is soft and pliable—even its skull is soft. When it comes out of the vagina, it bears no signs of having suffered yet. A baby cries when it hits air, when it is suspended by its feet, when its cord is cut and it must gasp for air, when it is overwhelmed by loud sound and bright lights.

Jeremy is born after fourteen hours of his mother's labor at home in New Jersey. She is kneeling, pushing him out and down between her legs. As the baby's head emerges, his lips are pursed, his eyes squeezed closed. Another push brings him out past his bellybutton, when he opens his eyes and seems quietly to be waiting to see what will happen next. His body out, I suction mucus from his mouth and he protests with short cries. The cord begins to close off his blood supply, so he takes a sudden gasp for air, and finding that successful, breathes more easily. I pass him through his mother's legs to her waiting hands, but in the awkwardness of the transfer, he begins to cry. She takes him to her chest and rocking him in her arms, is able to soothe him.

He is peaceful again, eyes open, beginning to seek out form. I do not believe he has just been through a terrible ordeal.

When I was in medical school, the ward patients in labor received little or no pain relief, while the private patients were given scopolamine, a drug that wiped out the memory of the labor and birth. Many women loved it and would say, "My doctor was wonderful. He gave me a shot to put me out as soon as I came to the hospital. I never felt a thing." Those women weren't put out, but they didn't remember what had happened to them—or at least not consciously. When these women thought they were "out" they were awake and screaming. Made crazy from the drug, they fought; they growled like animals. They had to be restrained, tied by hands and feet to the corners of the bed (with straps padded with lamb's wool so there would be no injury, no telltale marks) or they would run screaming down the halls. Screaming obscenities, they bit, they wept, behaving in ways that would have produced shame and humiliation had they been aware. Doctors and nurses, looking at such behavior induced by the drug they had administered, felt justified in treating the women as crazy wild animals to be tied, ordered, slapped, yelled at, gagged.

When it is all over, the mother thanks the doctor. She sends her friends to him, saying, "It was wonderful. I never felt a thing."

The doctor in the hospital calls out to the woman strapped to the delivery table, "It's a boy." The mother must wait to be told the sex of her child. At one of my first home births, the woman was standing up, the only position she was comfortable in. Trying to be where I could best take care of the baby as it came out and down between her legs, I lay on the floor under her, facing upward between her legs. As the baby's head came out facing backward, its buttocks slid forward between the woman's legs and in front of her. She called out, "My son! My son!" telling us the sex of her child.

When I attended home births I carried no pain medications: I told the women they would have to go to the hospital if they needed such medication, because all the drugs have some depressive effects on the babies. Mothers given drugs that derange them or do them physical damage are no better off. An angry obstetrician confronted me once at a meeting in New Jersey, where, shouting across a table which separated us, he asked, "But, Dr. Harrison, what do you do when a woman is in pain?" He was shaking his fist, accusing me of cruelty and inhumanity.

"When a woman is in pain, I put my arms around her and I hold her," I said.

I understood why he was upset. Any decent person, confronted with a woman in pain, of course wants to give her relief. The problem is that in our society, one way to say "help me" is "give me a drug." That "relief" they are seeking, that drug the physician is administering, can be very harmful to the woman and to her child.

I was trying to say that there are alternative responses to the woman's cry for help. Touch, a soothing voice, eye contact, even just the physician's supportive presence in the room can bring the woman safely through her pain.

There was a vivid example of this when a nurse I knew was giving birth at home. As soon as I arrived at her house she began screaming, "Michelle, give me something. Put me out! I can't stand it!"

"I don't have anything, you know that," I said as I sat down on the bed, my arm around her shoulder.

"Can't you give me something?" she implored.

Moved by the pain in her voice and eyes, I tried to communicate my wish to help her. "If you really can't take it, let's go to the hospital. It's okay, I'll take you in."

She said she didn't want to go and went on to deliver within the hour.

Afterward she told me, "It was good to know I could beg for anything, and you *couldn't* give it to me. It was safe to scream because I knew you didn't carry drugs and wouldn't sedate me."

Sometimes a woman screams to make the pain go away, not to be drugged.

I am not opposed to drugs on principle, but there is no painless childbirth because there is no medication that does not also interfere with the mother and/or the child. Some of that damage we know, and some we don't because we do not look. In the hospital I would not deny relief to a woman who wants it, but her decision should be made on the basis of valid information, including the risks both to herself or her child. It is not a choice for anyone else to make. Our need to "do something" to "quiet her," can even result in her being pressured to accept medication. Often the drug doesn't take the pain away. It only makes the woman less able to cope with it, making her drowsy or loosening her control of herself.

Scopolamine is not used at Doctors Hospital, where childbirth is said to be modern, technological and humane. The woman doesn't need amnesia because she is told that hers is the finest childbirth experience available, and if it doesn't seem that way to her, she assumes it's her own fault. If she is among the 33 percent of women who have a Caesarean at this hospital, then she is made to feel thankful she is living in this age of technology so her baby could be "saved."

Integral to modern technological childbirth is the fetal monitor, which is applied either externally around the mother's abdomen or internally by means of a metal electrode that is screwed into the scalp of the baby still in utero. The screw on the end of the monitor is shaped like the end of a corkscrew, and as it is twisted, it pierces the baby's scalp and hooks 1 to 2 millimeters into the skin. The external monitor uses ultrasound waves to record the heartbeat, although ultrasound has never been proven safe for babies. In experimental studies, ultrasound has been found to have effects similar to x-rays. The monitor console, a machine about the size of a portable dishwasher, is on wheels so it can be brought to the bedside. Long wires then connect the machine either to the internal or external attachments to mother and/or baby. Across the top of the machine is a window through which graph paper travels while a black needle marks each beat of the baby's heart. Additional leads can be used to measure pressure in the uterus or timing of contractions.

The amplified fetal heartbeat sounds like galloping horses, so with two or three monitors going in a room, the sound is one of a galloping herd. In the hall, the sounds of different monitors in different rooms fuse into a roar of childbirth. Frequently there are also the intermittent commands to the women, "Push! Push!," reminiscent of stampedes and posse chases in the old Westerns. Both the sound of the galloping and the vision of the needle traveling across the paper, making a blip with each heartbeat, are hypnotic, often giving one the illusion that the machines are keeping the baby's heart beating.

At Doctors Hospital I learned to screw a monitor lead into the scalp of a baby not yet born. Is the baby still smiling? Was the baby smiling before I screwed the electrical lead into its head? Was the baby frightened? Is this baby curious anymore? Does this baby still want to be with us? What have we taught this new person about what life is like?

At Doctors Hospital I attached the woman to the monitor, and after that, no one looked at her anymore. Held in place by the leads around her abdomen and coming out of her vagina, the woman looked over at the TV-like screen displaying the heartbeat tracings. No one held the woman's hand. Childbirth had become a science.

Still wanting to know more about that science and those truths promised by the new technology, I had sought further training. For a long time I believed my presence in the hospital—on the ''inside''—could make a difference, that my different perspective could affect the way in which women were treated.

Doctors Hospital was known both for its humane modern childbirth practices and its technical sophistication. From this hospital, affiliated with one of the world's leading educational institutions, originated many of the country's standards for hospital obstetrics. The doctors who taught me also created the truths taught elsewhere. I had come to Mecca, but I was unprepared for the dehumanized process—birth— I found there.

LABOR AND DELIVERY (L&D)

The L&D suite was an enclosed area in which a woman spent the duration of her labor, delivery and recovery. There were three beds in each of three labor rooms, but when they were full, the recovery room and hallways were also used for laboring women. Through heavy gray doors were the four delivery rooms, two of which were also equipped for doing Caesarean sections.

Outside the L&D suite was a converted single patient room referred to as the Alternative Birth Service, or ABS. The room was decorated with curtains, a picture on the wall, a plant on the sill, and drapes which hid all the obstetrical equipment. A single stretcher-like bed dominated the room with space enough for one chair on either side. Because the room was outside L&D it was necessary to have a nurse available to stay in the room when a woman was laboring. A woman planning to use the room had to be at "low risk," meaning no complications were expected. The arrangements had to have been made in advance of labor, her doctor or midwife had to have approved her use of the room, and there had to be available nursing personnel at the time the woman was admitted in labor.

Women who moved to ABS, after being admitted to L&D until good labor was certain, often experienced a slowing or cessation of their labor. This may have been related to the "specialness" of the room, the need for constant nursing personnel, and the fear of how far they were from the full technology available on L&D.

There was also a doctors' lounge, a large sparse room with an x-ray-viewing box, a TV, some chairs, a small desk, and lockers for the attendings. The closet rarely had any hangers, so clothes were usually folded and left on the floor. A door at the far end of the lounge led to a bathroom and then to a second small room with two beds, also to be used only by attendings. I had heard that one of the attendings had occasionally let his children sleep there, so I hoped in an emergency I could do the same.

A coffee room outside the labor rooms was the main place for congregating, especially for the nurses, who had no lounge.

The only place in which to be alone in the area was a long linen and supply closet where, even with the door open, one could hide unnoticed behind the racks of supplies. Carol showed me the closet one day during my first week on OB, saying that she and Jackie and Joan had named it the "crying closet." It was at the window of that closet, looking down at the streets, that Carol told me of the prevalent talk of suicide among the women residents.

Carol, Jackie and Joan had all come to OB wanting to change the way that women were treated. For women physicians with such a perspective, the daily assault on female patients they have to watch and take part in is painful, confusing and isolating. It is often difficult for women to make the transition that is required of them: from identifying with a sister to seeing her impersonally, as a patient. Unfortunately, many women do make the transition, and the attitudes of female obstetricians and gynecologists are indistinguishable from that of their male colleagues.

Richard was my chief on obstetrics. Hoping we could make a fresh start in working together, I went to him a few days before we started OB and asked how I could best prepare. He showed me how to fill out all the data sheets for each delivery—the only time he willingly taught me anything. I kept trying to be nice to Richard, thinking he wouldn't be so awful if he knew me better.

Richard was the most competitive person I met at DH. He was a loner who was putting in his time until the following year when he would begin a special GYN surgical fellowship. Cancer was his primary interest; he could tolerate obstetrics only because, as he said, "Childbirth is a surgical procedure."

John was the first-year resident who worked the day OB shift with me. Twenty-five years old and single, he flirted with the nurses and could often be overheard asking some of the younger attendings to arrange dates for him. John would say of *his* patients, "I like *my girls* to stay on the thinner side during pregnancy."

John resented my working part-time. When I wasn't there he complained that he had too much work to do, but when I was there he said he didn't get enough deliveries. It seems terrible that we were the people who were supposed to be taking care of women having babies. We weren't in any shape to take part in a happy event. We cried, we fought about deliveries, we competed, we dumped on each other, we argued procedures.

Tuesday morning   *Day 44*

I am living in two worlds. Fran and Laurie and Gail are using my den to work on some resource booklets on women's health. Last night I went to sleep to the sound of Fran's typing. The sound of other people carrying on was comforting for me. It erases my own sense of isolation. At home I am in the world of women, self-care, consumer control; I am living and working with people who every day challenge the health-care system, especially as it treats women.

I drive the five miles to the hospital, where the doctor's word is law, the patient's proper attitude is submission. Somewhere between these two worlds I search for a truth, a balance, and a place for myself.

Fran has been very receptive to my thoughts and feelings about abortion. I believe in the right of a woman to have an abortion, but doing them is difficult for me. When I was in medical school and abortions were illegal, we would daily treat women who were critically ill from attempted illegal abortions. It was not unusual for such a woman to die as a result of infection. Even five years ago, when I was teaching at the medical school, I realized that students were graduating without ever seeing the catastrophic results of illegally induced abortions. It's like an epidemic disease that has been eradicated, but which will surely return if the legislation is changed again and abortions become illegal.

Because Fran is so involved in protecting the rights of women to have abortions, I hesitated for a while to share with her how painful it was to do them. Her sympathetic response was a surprise.

After the day

I met Richard in the parking lot when I got to work and he told me to meet him on 3W, a floor of about twenty to twenty-five postpartum patients. I waited there for fifteen minutes, uncertain about what I was supposed to do. I began looking through charts and then making rounds on the patients, which is what the nurse said the previous residents did. When Richard came to 3W at twenty to eight, I tried to ask him some questions about the wound on a patient I'd seen. He said he'd look at her. I tried to go with him but he told me to continue rounds. By the time I finished seeing the next woman he was gone and had left a note saying "She was okay," and I couldn't ask him any questions.

I was in the middle of taking out sutures from a Caesarean incision when the nurse came by and said, "It's five after eight and Richard wants you on L&D immediately." I finished taking out the stitches and went up to L&D to find Richard angry that I hadn't been there at eight. He said I must be on L&D at eight even if I have not finished rounds, but that I was really supposed to finish rounds on those twenty-odd women before eight.

I tried to find out such details as who I was to see, who was to be discharged, what kind of responsibility I had for which patients, but Richard was of no help. I asked him about service patients, those without attendings, and he said there were none. I protested that I had seen one chart, so there must be one such patient on the floor. He answered, "I forgot." The truth is that if the service patient doesn't get seen by a resident, she gets no care.

Later in the day I went back to 3W and took as much time as I needed. One woman remarked with obvious pleasure about how much time I was taking with her and I said, "I have the luxury to do that today; by tomorrow I will have been told I can't." Of course that is what happened later in the day; Richard told me I couldn't spend so much time with patients.

I spent some time talking with Kara, a teen-ager who had a baby two days ago, and Janie, the older sister with whom she lives. Kara is planning to enter the Service, and Janie, who is still nursing her own ten-month-old, is nursing her baby for her, leaving Kara feeling somewhat left out of the care of her new baby. Last night Janie was unable to come in, and Kara pumped her own breast to put milk in a bottle for her baby. I suggested to both of them that Kara might want to nurse the baby with her sister and that they might even enjoy trading nursing times with both babies. Kara had been told that she either had to nurse all the time or not nurse at all. The two sisters and I talked about ways they could share the mothering of Kara's baby, even though Kara would be leaving after six months. I enjoyed the time I spent with them, aware that I would not often have the opportunity to speak with patients so openly or so thoroughly.

Richard showed me how circumcisions are done here, since residents on OB do them. We went to the newborn nursery, where he took the baby into the treatment room, put him in a large molded plastic frame with Velcro straps for the baby's body, arms and legs. He put a steel clamp on the baby's penis, but then left the room to take a phone call and was gone for three or four minutes. Finding myself alone in the room with the baby, I began to pat him gently and sing to him. I sang the lullaby I had sung to my niece Abigail when she was just a few hours old and I was with her in the newborn nursery.

My first delivery at DH was with Dr. Hilda Cameron, an attending I hadn't met until I was taking care of her laboring patient. I told her I was new here, but I don't think she heard me. Just before the delivery I took the woman back to the delivery room and had her prepped and draped by the time Hilda got there.

"I think you should do the episiotomy on the next contraction," she told me.

I was not used to doing episiotomies, since at home births I had learned to deliver babies without cutting the perineum. I asked her, "Do you routinely do episiotomies?" She had just commented on how much room there was for the baby, since the woman had a loose perineum, so I had hoped we might leave it alone.

She responded brusquely, "Nothing is routine in obstetrics. Now do the episiotomy."

My hand was shaking as I took the scissors and tried to make a very small cut.

"Deeper! Deeper!" she said and then angrily took the scissors from my hand and made a large cut in the woman's perineum and extended the cut into the vagina. We delivered the baby on the next contraction.

"It's a girl!" Hilda called out, and then I looked and said, "No, it's a boy," and she corrected herself. Then she began to sew. The woman was having some pain, although she had been given epidural anesthesia and should have been okay. The anesthesiologist increased the dosage, and finally the woman was numb. Hilda was thinking about giving her Demerol intravenously for the pain and I kept thinking about how drowsy the woman would then be.

The child was blue for a short while, but it cried a lot and seemed healthy. The woman kept looking over at the baby and watching him cry and trying to talk to her baby across the room.

Although I came here to learn the hospital way of delivery, I am opposed to the routine performance of episiotomies on women. The usual reasons given for doing them are: to prevent excessive stretching of the muscles by the baby pushing through, which would result in weakened support for the bladder. That this results has never been proven. A second reason for episiotomies is to maintain vaginal tightness, presumably for the pleasure of a future sex partner. That may in fact be true, but I'm not sure it warrants a surgical procedure, since there are exercises that tighten the pelvic muscles again.

Think of the episiotomy this way: if you hold a piece of cloth at two corners and attempt to tear it by pulling at the two ends, it will rarely rip. However, if a small cut is made in the center, then pulling at the ends easily rips the cloth. Doing an episiotomy is analogous, and sometimes results in tears that extend into the rectum. Physicians argue that this "clean" tear is more easily repaired than the ragged one that occurs when a woman tears without the cut. My experience has been that the small tears that sometimes occur without episiotomy are easy to stitch and less bothersome to the woman.

Episiotomies, once repaired, are often debilitating and are the source of much pain in the immediate postpartum period, at a time when a woman might most want mobility in taking care of her newborn. Whether a woman will have one done is a frequent source of anxiety during pregnancy.

My final objection is that the woman is rarely given a choice in the matter.

Later in the day John put his first internal monitor lead into a baby's scalp. The patient was a woman in her late twenties who spoke some English but with a heavy accent. Each time the curtain around her bed was opened, she would signal for someone to close it. First John ruptured the membranes, and then with the woman's legs apart, he put his hand in her vagina and screwed the electrode into the baby's head. The baby's heart rate fell and everyone worried for a few minutes, but then it returned to normal.

Present in the room, besides the patient, were: her husband, two nurses, myself, John, Richard—who was instructing John—and some student nurses. There are some old pictures around of medicine in history, in which you can see leeches being applied, or bloodletting. The paintings have an aura of foreboding about them, fear of what is happening. I thought about those pictures and suddenly wondered what had changed. The technology is different, but the crowd of people standing around the bed is the same. The only difference is that now women are among those dispensing the technology. I wanted to cry for this woman, I wanted to tell her to go home and have her baby at home without wires in its head.

Later the woman began to want to push, although she was only eight centimeters dilated. The nurses called for her attending, who was not available, and I agreed to take a look at her. She was about at that stage when, during a home birth, I would have allowed her to start gently pushing. Instead she had the nurses standing there saying "Don't push! Don't push!" and scolding her. One nurse said, "If you push, you will hurt the baby." I felt helpless.

The woman continued to want to push. Richard was located and came to check her. By then she was nine centimeters, and then quickly fully dilated. By this time, though, it was strange because she no longer seemed to have the same urge to push, and she was no longer in control of herself or able to respond to what was happening in her body. When she was told to push she had difficulty. It was sad because she had been so sure before and had been responding so strongly to what her body wanted her to do. Now she was also forced to lie on her back, rather than on her side, in order to push. I kept thinking of the women who delivered at home squatting, and on their knees, or on their sides.

Chapter Five

HOME/HOSPITAL BIRTH

At the end of the first day on OB, I wondered with panic what I had done in coming there. I had expected that what I would learn would be different from what I had been doing. What I hadn't considered was how different it would feel. It was as though these two worlds of birthing that I knew could not exist at the same time: as if the atmosphere and the power of the hospital was so overwhelming, it allowed only one definition of reality, one possibility of what could happen.

Images of the women I had delivered at home came to me and were quickly replaced by the overhanging lights of the delivery rooms; the silence of a woman laboring at home was lost in the noise of the galloping monitors and the commanding voices.

What was a home birth, that other experience I had known?

ONE HOME BIRTH: ONE DAY LAST YEAR

Marie called this afternoon to say she was having irregular contractions and she thinks she may be going into labor. She's letting me know early so I can think about which appointments I may have to cancel. It is a Saturday afternoon early in summer. Heather is off with friends and I call to be sure she can stay with them for the night in case Marie is really in labor.

I think about Marie and this forthcoming birth. I begin to feel the tension of anticipation. I sense that this will be the day. There are times my own menstrual cycle seems attuned to the births ahead. At once I feel a part of the process, a witness, participant, recorder.

Marie doesn't yet need me at the house. Her husband is with her and they will call me when they need me to be there. This is her second pregnancy, but her first birth at home.

For me the hours before a birth are long: I am already absorbed in thinking about and preparing myself for this birth, so it is difficult for me to do anything that requires my full attention. I go to a pool near my home, a place where I feel most peacefully alone. It is a strain always to be on call, always to have to respond to someone else's need. When I am in the middle of the pool, swimming long laps, I know I have until I reach the end of the lane before I can be paged. It may only be another thirty seconds, but that time is mine.

I swim until my tiredness passes, and from then on I feel I can swim indefinitely. Each lap of the pool seems to give me strength to store up for what is coming. It is hard work to deliver babies, especially at home. I use everything I have—memory, skill, intuition—as well as everything I sense. I must do all that in an atmosphere where inattention can have disastrous effects on this mother, this baby, on me personally and on the general acceptance of home birth.

Swimming laps, I recall a visit I made earlier to Marie and Alex at home, as I do with each home-birth woman in the latter part of her pregnancy. Marie's house surprised me when I first got there. It was a large white Colonial, in a community of well-landscaped suburban homes. Elegantly furnished, it had a living room of champagne-colored carpeting and a white upholstered sofa. I thought, She's got one child already, she's expecting a second—and she has white furniture.

We had set the visit for early evening so Alex, a banker, could be home. We sat in the living room, talking and drinking lemonade. From time to time Liza, their three-year-old, would amble through, say hello, play and move on. The carpet remained champagne, the sofa white.

Marie and Alex told me they wanted to have their baby at

home because they wanted control over their environment—
including no drugs. If something went wrong, they wanted
to be part of any decisions that were made. Alex said, "In
the hospital as soon as something is slightly off, they take
over completely. They use all their guns."

"Last time they gave me a needle in my back and I never
felt the rest. I want to experience childbirth. I want to know
what it is like and I want to be able to get through it" was
Marie's explanation for the home birth.

I asked about Liza, whether she would be present for the
birth, and if so, who would be watching her. Marie said,
"I'm almost certain that I want to be alone for this. I think I
would be worrying too much about her if she were here. I
need to do this thing myself." Her sister would take Liza
when it was time.

We had gone into the bedroom, where the birth would take
place. I gave them a list of equipment they would need and
talked about what to expect. When Marie asked about positions in which to give birth, I demonstrated both squatting
and kneeling, and explained that the choice would be hers,
and that I would help her find the most comfortable way in
which to deliver.

I examined Marie on her bed, with Alex and Liza watching intently. I listened to the sound of the fetal heartbeat, and
then passed the stethoscope to Marie and Alex, and then to
Liza.

Now, as I prepare for the birth, I run those memories
through my mind. I leave the pool feeling calm, whole, reassured because I have not been paged. Taking my beeper
from the front desk, I go home to call them.

At six in the evening I arrive at Marie and Alex's home,
where I'm met also by Adrienne, the nurse who sometimes
works with me. As I walk into the house and then into the
bedroom, I feel the excitement of birth approaching. I feel
the passion and spirit of life. Aware that I am about to be a
part of a miracle, I feel privileged, but scared.

Marie is in the midst of a contraction when I come in. I
say hello, and then turn to Adrienne to ask what is happen-

ing. Adrienne has just gotten there and has checked Marie's blood pressure. She has listened to the fetal heart rate and has done an internal exam. Marie's cervix is five centimeters dilated. Since by convention a fully dilated cervix is ten centimeters, Marie is halfway there.

Marie's contraction ends and she greets me with, "Glad you're here. I think this is the real thing." She is leaning back against the headboard of her bed, lovely and at ease, with hair in place, make-up on, wearing a pale-blue gown, and I am momentarily envious of a woman who can look so meticulously groomed while in labor.

"Adrienne tells me we may have a baby here tonight," I kid her. "You still feel like having another baby?"

"I think it's too late to change my mind, and anyway, the crib is set up, so I may as well go through with it." Alex is stretched out on the bed next to Marie. A contraction begins again. He puts his arm around her back and a hand on her abdomen, gently, and they both close their eyes and breathe slowly. When the contraction is over they open their eyes and join us again.

I go about setting out my equipment on the dresser near the bed. I have a head lamp, which I will plug into a wall outlet and wear so I can have light to work with. I take out the instruments to sterilize, the scissors, suction bulb, mucus trap, umbilical cord ties, cord clamps, and I put them aside. I set out a pile of sterile gloves and some oil for the perineal massage I will do as the baby's head stretches Marie's tissues.

Some of my setting up is just puttering. I put things out and chat with Marie and Alex between contractions. They are quite self-sufficient and seem to need little support from us. We try to be supportive but not intrusive.

I finish taking things out of my bag and go over to the bed to check Marie. I take her blood pressure. A contraction begins and I sit next to her with my hand resting on her abdomen. I feel the contraction and get a sense of what it is like. When it is over, I lean forward and listen with the stethoscope to the fetal heart.

I listen to the baby and think, We meet each other again.

Sometimes I feel I know the baby well by the time it is born. I tell Marie and Alex, "It all seems fine," and then ask, "How are you feeling, Marie?"

A contraction is beginning and she can only nod to me as she closes her eyes and begins to breathe slowly, quietly, rhythmically. I get up gently from the bed and go to the kitchen where Adrienne joins me as I put the water on to boil. I'll use one pot to sterilize instruments. Another pot of water will be allowed to cool and then the water will be applied to Marie's perineum as the baby is being born. Marie's sister has come to take Liza. There is no one else in the house.

Adrienne and I make ourselves at home in the kitchen. We use the time to catch up on each other's lives. It can be lonely at a birth, without someone to consult, someone with whom to share worries and gain reassurances. Adrienne pours off some water to make tea. We talk about Marie and Alex and how well they are doing. We are both looking forward to the evening ahead.

We take our tea back up to the bedroom. Contractions have increased and Marie is becoming very uncomfortable. She cries out in pain. Alex holds her. I sit down on the bed next to her and take her hand. I tell her that she is okay, that she is doing beautifully, that it will soon be over. Adrienne brings a wet washcloth and wipes Marie's face. I look at Marie and I see the terror of childbirth in her eyes. I feel it. I remember it. I know it can be survived. I tell her that.

The contraction is at its peak. Marie's eyes meet mine and she is begging me to end it. I tell her again that she is okay, that I know how she feels, that she is doing magnificently.

The contraction ends and she rests. She rolls on her side to see if it will be better that way. The next contraction is on her already and she suddenly bolts back onto her back. For her it was worse on her side. She stiffens. Alex gives her their practiced signals of relaxation. She searches our faces for relief. Her body relaxes again. She rests.

Another contraction is upon her. This time she feels a sudden flood of liquid spilling out onto the bed. Her membranes have ruptured. The fluid is thin and clear and free of indicators of fetal difficulty. Three hours have passed since I arrived at the house. The birth will be soon. I replace the wet pads under her with dry ones. I listen again to the sound of the fetal heart. I am about to examine her internally to see how dilated her cervix has become, but a contraction begins and she yells out, ''I have to push! I have to push!'' and her face squeezes up and her eyes shut and a deep pushing grunt comes from somewhere deep inside of her. She is half sitting, propped up against the headboard of her bed and she is beginning to birth her baby. The contraction ends and this time she looks up and laughs. ''Ooo, I couldn't help myself. I just had to push.'' I laugh with her and say, ''I think it's getting close.''

Adrienne brings the water from the kitchen. She soaks a pad in the water and then places the warm compress between Marie's legs. Marie finds the warmth soothing and asks for a fresh compress when this one cools. I put on my head lamp and get out the oils which I will use to massage her perineum as the baby is being born.

The contractions become less frequent but more intense. Marie complains, asks if anything is wrong. ''Sometimes they just stretch out in the last few minutes,'' I tell her, ''but at least that gives you a chance to rest a little more in between.'' Her contractions are now every four minutes instead of every two. Between them she rests, she talks with us, she adjusts her position, asks for a pillow to be shifted slightly. Night is coming and she is tired. As the world outside darkens and as the moments of birth approach, we focus our energy on Marie's laboring. A contraction comes; she grits her teeth and she pushes.

At first we see nothing except the straining of her muscles, then we see a bulging of the labia. On the next contraction there is a slight spreading apart of the labia, and on the next we see the fine hair of the baby. I dip my fingers in the oil and as the labia spread and the tissues stretch, I rub gently and strengthen the places that seem to be stretched to their limits. Between the contractions Adrienne continues to replace the warm compresses. She tells Marie, and Alex, who is beside her on the bed holding her, that their baby has fine dark hair.

Birth is a slow transition, a process. A contraction comes, Marie pushes, and we see the top of the baby's head; then she relaxes and the baby's head slides back into her. The next contraction, and her pushing and groaning that come with it, shows us more head than before, and after that contraction the baby's head slides back inside again, but not so far as it was before. The dome of head we see next gets larger and then retracts. The baby plays peek-a-boo with us and each time we wonder if that will be the moment of its birth.

Marie pushes and then lets go. She struggles with the work of birthing, caught in a will not totally hers. We tell her she can see the baby's head if she looks down during the contraction, but she shakes her head no. She is too much in it to observe. She pushes again, and then, on a signal from inside her, she lets go and the baby slides back inside her. I think of the baby saying, ''No, not just yet. Give me another moment.'' I think of the mother wanting her baby, wanting to have it outside with her, also wanting still to hold it inside her body. She plays with it as it begins to be born. Are those her hugs the baby feels as it is pushed by the uterus and by the mother's pushing, hugs and squeezes along the way?

There is a moment when it happens by itself, a moment when the circle of head that comes through the vagina stretches the opening more and more. There is one moment when the mother screams, ''It's coming!'' when the head emerges, and then it is out too far to return. My hands, which have been massaging and supporting the tissues that were being stretched, now cradle the head as a wet and slippery baby slides gently out of its mother's body. We are all quiet. Marie looks down at her child lying on the bed between her legs. Alex leans over to see his son. Adrienne hands me a towel and I lift the baby who is now beginning to stir. He is beautiful. His skin is colors of pink and blue. His tiny fists are clenched. His face is serene, his eyes as yet unopened. His chest begins to move with the shallow breaths of a baby not yet unattached from the placenta and umbilical cord. I lift him in the towel and pass him to his mother, and as I do he takes his first deep breath and lets out a cry. His eyes open for a minute, his little arms extend outward and then come back against his chest. His cry, his surprise, are answered by his mother's arms, which take him, and she holds him close against her bare skin and he is soothed.

I look him over, at once a doctor looking at the physical signs of color and breathing pattern and muscle tone, and at the same time registering the wonderment of what I have just been a part of. Marie holds her baby. Alex places his pinky in his son's hand and lets the tiny fingers close over his.

The cord has stopped pulsating. I clamp and cut it, aware again that there is no turning back now. We must now commit ourselves to taking care of this child as well as his mother was able to do for the last nine months. That seems an awesome task. She has done so well.

Marie looks up at us and says, "He's so beautiful."

"Look at him looking at you," I add as the baby stares at his mother, then closes his eyes, and then searches again to meet her eyes.

Adrienne leans over and touches his fingers. "I think he looks like you, Marie."

"He's the spitting image of Liza when she was born," Marie tells us, examining the baby as she speaks.

I am sitting on the bed, soaked with the blood and amniotic fluid that came out with the baby. I warn Marie, "You are going to feel some cramps as the placenta separates from the uterus." We go on talking as she fondles the baby and we wait for the placenta to separate.

"Ow, it hurts," she tells me within minutes, and I see a trickle of blood and more of the umbilical cord being pushed out of her vagina, so I know the placenta has separated. I put my hand on her abdomen, and then use gentle traction on the cord to help the placenta come out.

"Ow, it hurts," she shrieks. "That hurts more than the baby."

Her tolerance for pain is gone. She has her baby now and

this pain seems like an anticlimactic bother. It is out now, though. I examine it to be sure that all the parts are there, that the umbilical cord is normal, and then I look again to be sure that Marie is not bleeding.

It is ten o'clock. We are all quiet and reflective. There is now a new person here with us, but he does not seem like a stranger. It is as though someone we know has just come to join us.

Adrienne and I stay another hour at their home. After we wash the baby, Alex holds him while Adrienne takes Marie into the bathroom to help her shower. I gather the wet and bloody regular and plastic sheets together and remake the bed with fresh linens. I then examine the baby more thoroughly. I enjoy having a chance to hold him and talk to him. Alex watches the exam and then leaves me with the baby to go downstairs to bring up some food for Marie, who is suddenly very hungry.

Marie gets back into the clean bed and begins those awkward first attempts at nursing. Adrienne and I pack up our things and then we all just sit around talking for a while. Marie needs to talk about her labor, her fear, her thrill at being able to get through it all. "You know, Michelle, I was so scared because last time, when I had the anesthesia, I never felt the birth. I was afraid I wouldn't be able to do it. I wanted to feel strong but I wasn't sure I could."

"You did so well," we both tell her. I add, "It hurts. It hurts, but you can make it through."

"They don't really tell you that in the classes and the movies," Marie says. "They say, 'If you breathe right, it won't hurt,' and then when it hurts I feel something must be wrong or I'm not doing it right."

"Marie, the breathing and all the childbirth training are ways to help with the pain, but the pain is there and it is real."

"You know," she says, looking at each of us and then at her baby, "I felt like my body was being turned inside out."

Her baby is nursing now, quietly sucking and looking as though he had been doing this all his life. Alex is on the bed with them, his arm around his wife's shoulder. How peaceful they are, the three of them.

Adrienne and I go downstairs and sit out on the steps for a few minutes and talk with each other. We share both the pleasure and the relief that this birth went smoothly. Neighbors will be in to help Marie in the morning. Adrienne will visit in the evening, and I will be by on Tuesday to see how they are doing. They will call us if there are any questions or problems.

Adrienne and I say good night and give each other a hug to express the closeness we have in our work. Then we get in our cars and drive away.

I am tired, needing both solitude and sleep. I am glad it is nighttime, and that I do not have to be anywhere else right now. I want to be able to slowly separate myself from the evening, to replay what I want to, to work it over until it can all be put to rest and I am clear to go on.

It was a luxury I had in those days.

Chapter Six

I overslept this morning. When I woke up, it was light out. I had a feeling of panic because I couldn't remember what day it was or where I was or where I was supposed to be, but I knew something was wrong. I guess that is my system's reaction to what I am doing. I have to get myself together.

After two days on obstetrics, I have done three Caesarean sections and one vaginal delivery. Today I did two Caesareans with Neil Anderson, who explained that he tends to be aggressive with patient care. "And I don't give away any surgical material, since I want to maintain my skills," he told me over the operating table as we did the first section. "And I don't give anything away until I find out how conscientious a resident is."

I'm not sure that the second section was necessary. Anderson commented while we were doing it that he didn't quite believe the tracing on the monitor that seemed to indicate that the fetus was in distress. "May as well do it and get it over with, though," he added. Rarely do people listen with their ears. We act on the monitor, not on the patient. A woman is moved along like a machine, with her uterus split open, and almost no control over what is going on.

With the first section, the anesthesiologist failed to get the spinal needle in, so he told the woman he'd have to put her to sleep. The woman cried because that meant that her husband couldn't be there and because she wanted to be awake for the birth of her baby.

Fran has been at my house working steadily on the new health resources guides. Having raised her child, she now devotes all of her time to women's health issues. She is always working, and though it seems such a struggle to improve health care, she maintains both a cynicism and an optimism about what we can achieve. In spite of her reservations about my doing a residency, she repeatedly bolsters me up so I can go back for more. I think I am giving her another view of OB-GYN, which she knows mostly as an outsider. In the midst of our serious political-philosophical discussions, we sometimes run out shopping and enjoy discovering scouring pads for ten cents apiece or dresses for $8. Fran is from Everytown and knows every discount and bargain store in this area.

Today I called home and talked with Fran because I needed to share with someone outside what it is like for me here. I am so depressed over what I see happening: I no longer believe women can get proper care for labor and delivery in hospitals. I'm more confused than ever about where I am going. I have much less hope than before of surviving within the system.

I talked with Carol after Grand Rounds this morning and told her that I was feeling down and also confused about what my responsibilities were. She said I'm in charge of 3W and that Richard should have told me that. Even John is having trouble with Richard: he says that Richard doesn't want to know about patient problems, won't explain anything, and is totally centered on the paperwork of the service.

I just keep thinking about how hopeless it is, and how different I feel from when I began. I'm frightened by how far out of the system I feel. I wonder if I could practice in a hospital even if I got through training. It's not just my feminist perspective, but the whole realm of intuition, sensitivity and spirituality that has been destroyed in the medicalization of childbirth.

The process of birth and the continual emergence of one person out of the belly of another continues to overwhelm me and mystify me. It's a sacred act that has been turned into an ugly ritual, not just because of the procedures—which are sometimes necessary and lifesaving—but because of the attitude with which they are performed. It's like considering the beauty of those moments when sexuality takes on a spiritual quality and comparing that with fucking, with pornography. The medical birth is pornographic. The woman is degraded. The physician intimidates her and forcefully takes from her both the act of birth and that which she herself has nurtured. All day long I watch women who have been violated and who don't even know it.

I long for my patients in New Jersey, and for my children of home birth. I wonder if we can create new institutions. I wonder if I'll be destroyed in the process.

The whole experience today was like taking part in some great sacrificial ritual in which women come forth and sacrifice themselves and their newborns.

Thursday   *Day 46*

I've gotten myself together enough to do my work. Richard's lack of supervision has its advantages because I am freer to do what I think I should. I feel comfortable doing postpartum care. I am learning a great deal about fevers and postpartum complications.

My score is now four sections and one vaginal delivery. Today I scrubbed with Larry Morris, who explained that he would be doing the procedure and that I would get to do little of it. When it was over he said, "I had not realized how proficient you are. From now on I'll let *you* do them." I don't feel that proficient, but what I do feel is a closeness with what I am doing.

Friday morning   *Day 47*

I thought I was okay yesterday, but I wasn't. I went home and thought of all the things I had to do, but I just collapsed. I was distressed that there weren't any groceries in the house, and I felt burdened by the whole household. I knew I was unreasonable, and went to bed. I got up for supper and went back to bed, and then got up about an hour later when Maggie's barking woke me. By then I was feeling better, but I was bothered because I knew I was reacting to the day, and that I had just kept everything inside.

When I tried to sleep I kept thinking about the section I had done with Larry. After the baby had been delivered, I reached in to remove the placenta and to explore the interior of the uterus. I felt a thinned-out portion at the top of the uterus. The woman had had an abortion ten years ago in Puerto Rico. They operated through her abdomen and apparently cut across the top of her uterus in order to remove the fetus. This woman might not have survived a vaginal delivery. My shock was overwhelming because I am afraid that illegal, inept abortions will become common again if women lose control over their reproductive rights and if the "right-to-lifers" win on the abortion issue. As a physician, I see their position as demanding the "right to death," which this botched-up woman almost suffered.

Later

When I saw Carol on L&D at noontime, I started to cry. She took me into the supply closet and I wept for a long time, flooded with experience and emotion.

I had two difficult deliveries with Richard. He stops me from doing what I am used to doing, and then I lose my rhythm and I feel thrown off. It's like driving a car one way for ten years, and then, as you are approaching an intersection and trying to brake the car, having someone say, "No, use the other foot to stop it." Richard is so invested in how he wants something done, he forgets there is a baby there. One of the babies needed to be suctioned and I had to remind him to do it.

"Catching a baby is like catching a football" was what we were taught in medical school. "You catch it and hold it in the crook of your arm and close to your body." The one-armed baby catch is designed for hospitals where the woman is up in the air and the doctor needs one hand free to cut the cord, suction, etc. I used to be good at it, but over the last few years, delivering babies at home, I have become accustomed to using two hands. I had become accustomed to babies coming out onto a bed or on sheets on a floor, with a rhythm more peaceful than exists in a delivery room.

It's the episiotomy, though, that bothers me so much, and since my difficulty with Hilda the first day, Richard and the others are watching to be sure that I will do them. I can't get used to them, though. The women spend three, four, five miserable days postpartum with the episiotomy pain being the most difficult part of it all. Their hemorrhoids are bad, their episiotomies are swollen, and they have difficulty walking and sitting.

Since the episode with Hilda Cameron on Tuesday when she had to take the scissors from my hand, I felt I had two choices, because everyone quickly knew what had happened: I could either let people think I was incompetent—that after ten years of delivering babies I didn't know how to do an episiotomy—or tell them what I think and have some of them write me off as crazy.

A nurse asked about "pelvic relaxation," a loosening of the musculature of the vaginal area which has been attributed to not having an episiotomy. I told her that 1) it has never been proven that the two are related; 2) I was concerned about the degree to which women were debilitated postpartum because of the episiotomy; 3) women spend a major portion of their pregnancy worried about whether they will have one and what it will feel like; 4) women are never given a choice in the matter—it is the doctor who decides. The doctor says, "I'll only do it if I have to," and the woman feels reassured—except that episiotomy is done 99 percent of the time and few doctors seem to know how to deliver a baby without doing one.

I want those obstetricians to stop cutting open women's vaginas. Childbirth is not a surgical procedure. This time in the hospital has made that far more clear to me than it ever was before.

* * *

It's been years since I've cried as much as I have in the last week. I really don't know if I can go through with it.

Sunday morning   Day 49

I recouped a little over the weekend. I talked yesterday on the phone with Martha, a lay midwife with whom I worked in New Jersey. She said, "Hang in there, Michelle, and learn what you can. We're all waiting for you." I need to keep my sense of purpose in what I am doing. I have to do episiotomies. I have to play the game better than I have been doing.

Martha herself is in need of support. She is practicing illegally and is terrified about the outcome of a case in California, where a midwife is being tried for murder. The baby she helped deliver was doing poorly at birth but was resuscitated by the midwife and then transferred by ambulance to the hospital. It died several days later. It is not clear when the baby became worse, or why. The pressure against home birth is increasing, though.

I have hit every red light on the way to work this morning, which has never happened before. I think I'm going to be late. Because it is Sunday, I'll be the only resident on OB, with Flo covering as chief for the day.

On the way home

It was an easy day at work, with only one delivery early in the morning. I was called suddenly to the delivery room while still making rounds, and I arrived in time to watch a midwife deliver a baby. The woman had been rushed back to the delivery room because the fetal monitor had shown some patterns of distress, but the baby was fine at birth. The midwife had made a large episiotomy because she wanted to get the baby out quickly, but it didn't bother me. It was needed. After the delivery the midwife turned to me and asked, "Do you want to sew up the episiotomy?" I didn't know if I was being dumped on or given an honor. I sewed it up, though, and the attending, Dr. Curry, approved of my work.

That afternoon I did an oxytocin challenge test (OCT)—performed by the nurses during the week but by the residents on weekends. It is a test of how the fetus is doing in utero. We give the woman enough of the drug pitocin intravenously to cause her uterus to contract. Then we put a monitor on her abdomen to record the fetal heart rate and to see if the pitocin is causing a pattern suggestive of fetal distress. If the test is positive—that is, if there is distress—then the woman will be delivered in the next day or so. If it is negative, she is allowed to go on with the pregnancy. Flo was an unexpectedly good teacher. She tends to do things "by the book," but that is exactly what I am here to learn. Sometimes she is like a walking textbook as she lists off protocols of how to manage obstetrical problems. Short, slight, somewhat remote and aloof, she does not seem to mix with the other residents. She was quite friendly with me, though, making the day better than many others.

I also "labor-sat" today with a patient who was getting pitocin in order to induce labor. That is a procedure usually done during the week too, when there is enough staff around. If a woman is getting pitocin, a physician has to be on the L&D suite because of the dangers of the drug. If the doctor has to go to the floors to take care of other patients, then the pitocin must be turned off. A nurse must be in the room at all times too, as long as the pitocin is being given through the IV.

At four o'clock the nurse who came on duty refused to carry out the pitocin order as it was written, which was the way the attending (who is very intervention-oriented) had told me to write it. Margaret, the nurse, said, "If that's the way you want it written, that's fine, but I'm not giving it in that dose." I told her that I respected her decision and in fact agreed it was too much, but that I had to write the order.

"Why don't you just write it as you were instructed to and

then not pay attention to what I do about it?'' was her suggestion.

"Sure," I told her, "and I won't even ask any questions about how much is already in the bottle."

The patient had been on pitocin all day and had earlier shown signs of difficulty with the drug, so it had been stopped and then restarted. "I'm going off duty now," I told her, "but you're in good hands here. You have a nurse who cares."

Pitocin, a colorless drug, is widely used to induce labor and to speed it along. It can also cause fetal distress and rupture of the uterus. A professor of obstetrics at the medical school once said, "If they were to put a dye in the pitocin, you'd see it in the IV of almost every woman in the country who is in labor."

Monday morning   Day 50

I drove home after work last night to pick up Heather to take her with me to a pot-luck supper at Carol's, but then didn't really feel like going out. Gail, Arlene and I moved bookcases and unpacked the stereo and set it up in the living room. It seemed so lovely and friendly and cozy and warm at home. Gail has fit into the household so well and Arlene is working out wonderfully as a baby-sitter.

The party was a stiff, uncomfortable event, for which few people showed up. I stayed up late talking with Carol. Heather curled up in my lap, I took out my knitting, and Carol worked on the afghan she was making. It was quiet and peaceful, almost like being at home.

I feel bad about Carol. For one thing, she is very isolated. She lives with other people, trying to carry the same domestic load as they do and keep up her end of the housework, but they do not understand the strains on her due to her work or her fatigue. She once told me about bursting into tears in the grocery store because she had been awake for two nights straight and suddenly couldn't cope with the line for weighing vegetables.

Carol is isolated at work too, not yet having found where she fits in. I think it will happen, though, especially if she can create an out-of-hospital birth center when she finishes next year. I'm envious of how far along she is.

On the way home

I had several patients in labor at the same time today. One woman, a patient of Dr. Carter's, wanted no anesthesia, no episiotomy, no IVs, etc. She was there with her husband and a woman who had come as a labor coach. We were all hoping she would deliver precipitously in bed before her doctor could get there and take her back to the delivery room, but Ian Dorsi, who was covering for Carter, arrived.

The delivery started out fine. We were all back in the delivery room, the patient up in stirrups, and Dorsi and I were both at her perineum. I was feeling on top of what I was doing and proud that I knew what I knew. This woman wanted the kind of delivery I was more accustomed to. The head was coming out and I was commenting under my breath that the woman had plenty of room and that her tissue was thinning out fine. I was hoping Dorsi wouldn't do an episiotomy, since she didn't want one. Dorsi muttered angrily to me, "This isn't my first delivery, you know!" After the head came out, he turned it to the left and then told me to do the same. When I tried to turn the head further, it wouldn't go and he got mad and said I was turning it the wrong way, which was the way he showed me to. It's really hard when someone interferes in the middle of the delivery, because I was trying to follow what he was telling me to do. The atmosphere was pretty strained after that.

There is no clarity as to who delivers the baby. I've been told that the residents deliver the babies, but the attendings are there, and rightfully so, to deliver their own patients. I am part of a huge fraud.

I had a good delivery later on with Dr. Core. I had gotten worried about the monitor pattern, which showed severe

slowing of the fetal heart rate. I tried to get Richard to look
at it and tell me what was going on, but he wouldn't answer
my questions. He just told me not to worry. I ended up going
back into the delivery room with Dr. Core, which I was
especially anxious to do, since she was thinking of putting
on forceps to get the baby out. She used local anesthesia and
did a large episiotomy and was helpful in showing me how
she does the repair. We had a nice talk about obstetrics and
men, and I told her I was doing a part-time residency. She's
an interesting woman who did her training later in life. She
spent many years in Africa doing hundreds of deliveries and
she has a different perspective on obstetrics.

Tuesday   *Day 51*

Heather lost her first tooth, and she also really lost it! Late
last night we made a picture of the tooth and left it with a
note for the tooth fairy. This morning at five when I went in
to put the money under her pillow, I was unable to find the
note. I left the money, anyway.

On the way home

I'm becoming overtly irritated with Richard's reluctance to
teach. I'm going to tell him that he's got to explain things to
me if I'm going to manage patients, otherwise I'm just doing
his scut work. Today I took a delivery back without him and
he was really pissed afterward. The woman was having her
eighth baby and I knew she was going to be okay. It was a
nice delivery and there were no problems. I was just glad to
be there.

    I did a delivery with Dr. Jackson, who, instead of scrub-
bing, just watched while I delivered. I did an episiotomy as
I was supposed to and then sewed it up.

    I think that the acute crisis is over and that I will be doing
all right with obstetrics.

    Dr. Pierce announced yesterday that there will be another
part-time resident, Karen Dole, joining the program in two

weeks. I met her last week when she came for an interview. I guess I have mixed feelings about her. I think her arrival will take some of the heat off me because with both of us working two-thirds time, there will be more help than if there were one full-time person instead of us. I also worry, though, that she is one more person "like them" who will thus make me feel even more isolated.

There is a way in which physicians are made to resemble one another. Learning to act like a doctor is a less obvious part of the long educational process, and one which seems to happen spontaneously. Although I have been deeply committed to the work of medicine, I have never been a product of that mold which makes all doctors seem the "same" rather than "other," and which would cause other physicians to think of me as the "same" rather than "other."

Karen is friendly and assertive, with an air of self-confidence. She is coming from a full-time position in another residency so she can work part-time. She has three young children and a husband, and a baby-sitter who has been part of her family for years.

I'm hoping that Karen's arrival will allow me to cut back to the two-thirds time I am supposed to be working. I would like to stay home on Sundays, at least for part of the day. I would still come in at six, but then I could leave when she arrives.

I spent time with a fourteen-year-old who was in labor. She was in the hospital with her father, having a baby which she wanted to give up for adoption but which her father wanted to keep and raise. He came out of her room and talked with me for a few minutes while the nurses were busy with her; otherwise he stayed with his daughter. She wanted to be asleep for the delivery because she didn't want to see the baby. The anesthesiologist said she could only have general anesthesia if she had nothing else for pain. This is, actually, safe medical practice, but I have seen physicians, time and time again, give pain medication to a woman who will be having general anesthesia.

Every time this frightened girl screamed out with pain, she was offered the choice of relief then or being asleep for the delivery. I think they were just punishing her. When she was almost fully dilated she finally broke down and begged for relief. They gave her an epidural, which stopped her labor. As I left for the day, they were getting ready to do a section on her. I was furious because she was so close to making it through. They will do the section with the epidural anesthesia and she will be awake and will have to see and/or hear the baby at birth.

Wednesday, on the way home   *Day 52*

I like being alone on L&D, as I was Sunday, more than when Richard is around and harassing me, as he was today. I have a patient on 3W who has an abscess, and Richard claims she does not. We got a culture back showing infectious organisms, but Richard is still refusing to accept that she has an infection.

I took care of a patient with elevated blood pressure, and two with prolonged ruptured membranes. Usually the membranes around the baby and the fluid rupture shortly before or during labor. Once they have ruptured there is a somewhat higher possibility of infection, made even higher by vaginal exams. The definition of "prolonged" has changed over the past fifteen years from 72 hours being considered "prolonged" when I was in medical school to 48 hours when I practiced in South Carolina, to 12–24 hours at present. Once doctors define the woman as having prolonged ruptured membranes, the delivery of the baby is begun, either by induction of labor with pitocin or Caesarean section.

There is a contradiction which everyone seems to ignore regarding how often one does vaginal examinations during labor. Although the exams are a source of infection for both mother and baby, residents are required to examine women frequently in order to "chart" the progression of labor. I didn't do a lot of vaginal exams today and sometimes it was only toward the end that we discovered that a woman was in late stages of labor or near delivery time.

At Doctors Hospital we use Hill's chart of labor, a curve developed by Dr. Ernest Hill which defines on a graph how a labor should progress. Each woman's chart has a blank graph of hours and of centimeters of cervical dilation which we must record approximately hourly in order to evaluate the shape of her labor curve. When a woman's labor is off the "proper" curve, she is subjected to intervention in several possible forms.

Dr. Irv Warren did an interesting delivery with me watching. We were at the perineum and he was seated. I was standing as close as I could, trying to move away some of the things he'd put between me and the patient. He suddenly turned to me and said, "Would you do an episiotomy?" I felt that as a very loaded question, but answered, "All I can do is speak from my own experience, which has been not to do episiotomies for the past few years." I felt set-up, and I didn't know what was coming.

Warren went on, "What would you do instead of an episiotomy?"

"I'd do perineal massage."

He asked what I meant and wanted me to show him. I told him it was a technique I'd learned from the midwives. He said, "Well, do it."

I felt bad for the woman and her husband. They were aware of something going on, although they couldn't quite catch what was being said. I told Dr. Warren that I didn't feel comfortable doing perineal massage in this situation. I added, "I've never done it with a woman up in stirrups."

"What position were they in? Left lateral?" He was referring to a woman being on her side when she delivers.

"No, I have done it that way, but mostly they were squatting or kneeling on their knees."

"But where were you then?"

"Underneath," I answered.

Warren did the episiotomy. He did the delivery. As the

woman was pushing he suddenly started to yell at her to push harder. I was angry and wanted to ask what made him feel he had the right to shout.

After the delivery Warren said, ''You'll have your chance another time,'' referring to my showing him perineal massage. I said, ''Maybe in the Alternative Birth Service one day.''

While Warren's patient was in labor, the monitor had been recording a slowing of the fetal heart rate from 140/min. to 60/min. Apparently as long as the rate picks up again quickly this is not considered a problem. I wish I'd known that during my time at home births when I would become alarmed at any drop. I'm learning so much more now. It's not that I would take more chances, but I would develop a better system of knowing what is going on.

I like working with this department's criteria of labor and of good and poor progress. It is a system that assists in defining what is going on and what actions should or should not be taken. This is what I wanted to be learning when I came here.

Later in the day I talked with Carol about Warren's delivery. She told me to be careful of him. ''His pattern is to be very friendly,'' she said, ''and then to start screaming, and then to feel guilty and apologize for how he acted but to say he had to act that way.'' I remember now that he once did that with Barbara in the OR and I heard her telling him that she didn't think he should be yelling at her. I wonder if he'll yell at me. Sometimes my age is an advantage.

Heather misses me a lot on school holidays like today. Christmas and Easter will be difficult for her this year, but by next year I hope to be able to get vacation time.

Thursday   *Day 53*

I realized last evening that my house in New Jersey was supposed to have been sold by now. I didn't get a call from my mother, so I don't know what's going on and I'm afraid to find out. If it's bad news, I don't feel like coping with it. I feel overwhelmed by financial pressures because I don't have the money to do this for more than one year. After that I'll probably have to moonlight.

Last evening I dropped off the fireplace damper at a welder's and then went on to say hello to Laurie. I enjoyed being out in the evening alone casually visiting without Heather. Laurie gave me some papers about the midwife trial in California. The baby was born with a true knot in the cord. As the baby was being born, the knot tightened and stopped the blood supply. The baby died in the hospital six days later.

Last week we did a Caesarean, and that baby also had a true knot in the cord, but the section was being done for other reasons. When we delivered the baby out of the woman's abdomen the attending saw the knot and said, "This baby wouldn't have made it vaginally." If that baby had died in the hospital during a vaginal delivery, no one would have been tried for murder. In fact, even negligence in hospitals is rarely questioned and is often covered up.

Heather fussed at me a lot last night and was very cranky. It seems to me that happens on days when she is home and I am working, as on school holidays. She keeps asking about my being so busy and last night in bed asked, "Are you going to be this busy next summer?" I told her I didn't know, but the truth is that I will be, and I feel terrible about it. I am going to have to provide her with as much support as I can from others, to make up for my own absence.

Later

The day began with a direct confrontation with Richard about the, for him, nonexistent abscess. When I arrived on the floor at six this morning the nurse reported that the abscess had burst and had drained a large amount of pus. Richard and I looked at the abscess site, and he claimed again that it was not an abscess. I told him, "You can call it what you like, but where I come from, when pus comes out of a pocket and it's the only positive culture we get from the lab, then it's an abscess."

I was so discouraged that I took my time making rounds on the rest of the patients, but since I had to be on L&D by eight, I had to finish seeing them later in the day.

I scrubbed this morning on a section with Dr. Joseph, and discovered after we were in the operating room that he was letting me do the surgery. The woman had spinal anesthesia and was awake so I couldn't tell Dr. Joseph this was my first time doing a section. When I told him later he was surprised and said he had seen worse from people much further along.

Later in the day I examined a patient and told Richard that her cervix was eight to nine centimeters dilated. He then examined her and said that I was wrong, that she was only six centimeters and at -1 to -2 station, meaning that the head was still high up in the pelvis. I had said she was at 0 to +1, which is much farther down. Dr. Dorsi, worried about the lack of progress of his patient if Richard was correct, went in to check her himself. "Richard," he said, "she's nine centimeters, and in fact she's almost fully dilated. Have you forgotten how to examine a woman?" He was teasing Richard, and I took the opportunity to join in. I think if I just give Richard enough room, he will do himself in. It's not that it's so hard to be wrong, but Richard is very sharp and it's his determination to prove me wrong that is so irritating.

I think I am surviving here by tuning out certain people, including my worry about the way patients are treated. I'm keeping the distance I need in order to get through. I concentrate a lot on what I want to do in the future. I have to go on learning because I want to share what I know. There is so much more I'll be able to do for women's health if I can get this training.

Friday   *Day 54*

Last night I drove out to a wallpaper store with Heather and finally picked out paper. I got a burlap-type grasscloth, which will be a wonderful soft background for pictures and posters in the dining room. I'm planning to put it up this weekend. It feels good to have resolved that conflict.

I found myself last night thinking about the day and the Caesarean I had done. Performing a Caesarean is the one time that truly gives you the feeling of delivering the baby. I remember having my hand in the uterus. Pressure was being applied by Dr. Joseph at the top of the uterus while my hand grasped the head of the baby and assisted it out through the incision. I felt a sense of excitement and of power and of personal accomplishment that is not present in a vaginal birth. This is the time the *obstetrician* truly delivers the baby; in a vaginal birth, it is the mother.

These feelings of mine help me in trying to understand current obstetrical practices, and the spiraling increase in Caesareans. I have a vivid recollection of cutting through the uterus and first seeing the membranes bulging. I was so proud of myself for the fine surgery involved in cutting so delicately so as not to rupture the membranes yet.

I watched two deliveries today. One of the babies was born with a lot of meconium, and I was surprised that no attempt was made to suction the baby before it took its first breath. The meconium is the baby's first stool, and sometimes it is passed while the baby is in utero. A baby who breathes it into its lungs can die from the pneumonia-type reaction that is produced. The delivery table didn't even have the suction trap out. Later I talked with Art, one of the other residents, who has had a lot of training in pediatrics, and he agreed that the baby should have been suctioned immediately. He recounted to me his numerous unsuccessful attempts to get the OB department to stock the suction traps. When I delivered babies at home I always had one suction set open, ready to use if I needed it. I think that in the hospital they don't worry as much because they think that if the baby gets sick, then they'll just treat it.

This morning I made rounds on twenty-five patients in two hours. It's a testimony only to the poor care we give.

Monday, on the way to work   *Day 57*

Adrienne came for the weekend. We went to the ballet Saturday evening, and yesterday Adrienne came to work with me for a few hours. Her presence made it harder for me to slide into the routine, to shut my eyes to what I am now a part of.

I can intellectually explain why I am doing this, why I have to learn to use the fetal monitors, but I don't feel right inside. Adrienne is trying to get into midwifery school, in which case she will face many of the same issues. What she and I were able to do at home births is not taught in any school and is discouraged in almost all of them.

Adrienne and I have talked of someday practicing together again. She would be a midwife; I, as an obstetrician, would take care of her high-risk patients, the ones for whom a home birth is not safe. I want to be that person in the hospital who can carry on the work and caring of midwives who deliver women at home.

I don't like being at work Sundays. I feel deprived of the rest of my life. Yet I was torn leaving the hospital yesterday because there was a woman in labor with twins, both of whom were in a breech position, and another woman having her first baby, also in a breech position. Both women will probably be sectioned. I didn't want to leave, but once I was on my way home, I was glad to be gone.

I have learned that some of the other residents do not see the twenty-five patients they are supposed to see in the morning. Art told me he could make rounds in twelve minutes just by walking down the hall and shaking hands with patients. I had thought, however, that Beth, another of the residents, was very conscientious, since her notes were always comprehensive. On one patient yesterday I read the note Beth wrote Saturday morning, which said: "Perineum fine." I turned to the patient and said, "Did the doctor check your episiotomy yesterday?" The patient looked at me and said, "Oh no, nobody's checked me since my delivery." I guess

Beth isn't checking everyone. I'm not checking every patient either. I can't in the two hours I have.

Checking twenty-five women correctly would take three to four hours. It takes a long time just for a woman to turn over or to take off her underpants or pad for me to see the episiotomy. The pain keeps her from being able to move quickly. Sometimes the babies are in bed with the mothers, either being held or nursed, and then it takes even longer to move the woman into position to be checked.

It can take half an hour to properly take care of one woman with post-Caesarean infection or other complications. In addition to locating the source of the problem, cultures must be taken, blood tests ordered or done, and questions answered.

Yesterday I had a long talk with Jessica, the fourteen-year-old who had a section last week. She talked about what it was like to have her family want to keep the baby, while she herself would rather forget it all and go back to her life in Utah. I supported the reality of her difficult position, and I used what has become my standard approach to an unwanted pregnancy. An unwanted pregnancy has no good solution. Whatever the choice, the price is high: for abortion, for having a child and giving it up, or for trying to raise a child that is not wanted.

This girl's situation is made sadder by the degree to which the family wants her to keep the baby. I happened to walk by the nursery while Jessica and her father were there. The grandfather was crying. We were all talking about how cute the baby was, and I agreed that the little girl did look like the grandfather.

Later in the day, when I talked with Jessica, I told her that it was important for the baby, at some point, to get to a home of her own. If Jessica wasn't going to keep her, she needed to make a decision. She asked me when I thought she should decide. The advice I gave her was: after three to four months. I know that social agencies usually say six months; they feel that by six months a baby has established a personal relationship with his or her caretakers. I know that the relationship happens sooner, but I was trying to measure between this young girl's needs, what I thought was best for the baby, and what the agencies would be telling her.

Tonight I'm going to a dinner of the Obstetrical Society, and I'm sorry I agreed to go. I would rather be home.

On the way home

I was summoned quickly back to L&D from 3W because the nurse couldn't hear a fetal heart with a stethoscope. I thought of the possibilities: the fetal heart might be fine, but the nurse might not be picking it up with whatever instrument she was using to listen. The other possibility was that the baby was in trouble in utero. The most likely cause of that would be a prolapsed cord, where the cord comes through the cervix before the baby, and then when the baby's head comes down it presses on the cord and shuts off the blood supply to the baby. The rule is: "Once you feel the cord, you keep your hand in the vagina and try to hold the head up, away from the cervix, and the cord from being compressed by the head." The woman's bed will be tilted so she is head downward, and then gravity helps relieve the pressure of the baby's head on the cord. The woman is then taken immediately to the OR for the Caesarean, with someone's hand in the vagina. Even while she is prepped and draped, there is a nurse or doctor under the sheets holding the baby's head up until the baby is taken out by section.

I dashed into the room and did a pelvic exam, but I didn't feel a prolapsed cord. As it turned out, the baby was all right.

I had a discussion with Harriet, one of the midwives, about positions for childbirth. When I told her I had done home births for a couple of years, she muttered under her breath that she wished she could go to one. That had been Carol's response too. I have an experience behind me which others are frightened to have but are also envious of.

Harriet would like to be able to have siblings present at births in the Alternative Birth Service. I told her about the workshop I had last year for children who had attended births.

I wanted Heather and other children like her to have the chance to talk together about a common experience they could not easily talk about elsewhere. Harriet is hoping that when they get another midwife at the hospital they can do a research project on children being present for childbirth, which is the only way she can manage having children present.

Today I was supposed to be in Los Angeles speaking on "Feminism and Childbirth" at the American Public Health Association meeting. I had made that commitment before I took this position. Fran will be there and will speak for me.

My ability to take this program has necessitated a distancing from patients. I think about them, and care about them sometimes, but not the way I used to. I rarely know the names of the women I deliver. I do not see myself as an individual, nor can I be responsible for what I am doing. I see myself filling a certain role, without a name, without being anybody. Sometimes I am ashamed of myself as I walk into a room and realize I may have delivered the baby of the woman in that room.

Often I don't like the women I've delivered. I don't like them for their submissiveness. When I make rounds in the morning I ask, "When are you going home?" They answer, "I don't know when my doctor will let me."

They have let themselves be imprisoned. For me, the submissiveness of one woman becomes my own, as though we were all one organism. Their imprisonment adds to my own sense of powerlessness in this hospital. In my childhood, I had a tough bravado. I was forever the defender of the underdog, the kid who was being picked on. My mother would say, "You'll fight the battle of anyone who'll hold your jacket for you." When I was nine and lived in the city, I belonged to a "street gang." Having been told that red ants bite people, we spent many afternoons searching pavement and bushes for red ants we could destroy before they could hurt anyone.

In this environment, though, I am often depleted and then I can help neither myself nor anyone else. I do understand these women, but I don't want them to be weak. I want them to be strong for themselves and for me.

Tuesday, on the way home   *Day 58*

Barbara took me aside this morning and said everyone was aware of how unfair Richard is being to me. I was scheduled to scrub on a section with Jackson, who lets residents do a lot. Then at the last minute Richard sent me in with Dr. Black instead, and let John go with Jackson. As it turned out, Black, who is not known for letting residents do much, let me operate a lot, including opening and closing the uterus. Richard was surprised later when I told him what a good experience I'd had with Black.

I was sent next to the teen-age pregnancy clinic, where I enjoyed having time to spend with patients. I was doing the same thing I have done for years, but this time I had a specialist to ask when I had questions.

Thursday   *Day 60*

After work yesterday I stopped at the Sears surplus store and picked up a fireplace screen and andirons. Last night we burned newspaper and a part of a log. I've never had a fireplace before. The night before last I picked up the newly welded fireplace damper, and then crawled up under the chimney and installed it myself.

Today I watched Dr. Ingle put on forceps. He called the woman ''sweetie,'' ''honey'' and ''dearie.'' She was so thankful to him and told him to do anything he had to. The baby's head was already visible and the woman was pushing well. Then Dr. Ingle called for an extra dose of the epidural anesthesia to decrease her pain and make it easier to do an episiotomy. As the drug became effective, the woman's pushing became ineffective. She still tried to push but there was no longer any motion of her muscles. Dr. Ingle said, ''Dearie, we may have to take the baby if you can't push any better.'' The woman tried but it was clear she was getting nowhere.

Dr. Ingle took the forceps, large stainless-steel instruments that, when hooked together, look like those plastic salad tongs with scissor handles. The baby's head fits between the two tongs. Then he took the handles in his hands, and using his full body weight, pulled the baby's head out. It took force, although everyone says you don't really have to pull hard. But his leg was braced on the table to give himself extra leverage as he leaned back and pulled. The muscles of his face were squeezed tight, sweat dripping from his forehead, and the baby was dragged out from the grateful mother. She had been pushing so beautifully before they gave her that extra dose.

I will have to learn to put on forceps. I can't imagine ever pulling on a baby's head that hard, but I guess I'll learn that too.

I went to a high-risk clinic and saw a sixteen-year-old with heart disease. We couldn't figure out how someone could be seven months pregnant and not have had the heart problem followed. We were about to order tests when we discovered that her heart disease is being carefully followed at another hospital, only we didn't have the records. That seems to happen all the time, as patients, especially poor patients, are sifted through the system of hospitals and clinics in the city.

I discharged a postpartum patient who had been anxious and seemingly worried about taking care of her baby. She had apparently been visited a few hours after she had delivered, by a woman in a white coat, who introduced herself as a doctor and said, "You've had four abortions. You're single. Are you sure you want to keep this baby, or do you want to give it up?" The patient had been afraid for these past three days that the baby would be taken away from her. The roommate had heard the whole exchange and finally told the nurses about it just before the patient was leaving. I talked with the roommate and with the nurses. We thought at first it was someone who didn't belong on the floor or in the hospital but had managed to see the chart. From the description of the woman, though, it was probably one of the attending doctors who has very strong beliefs about marriage and children. It seems worse that it was not an imposter.

Friday   Day 61

I arrived home last night to discover that Heather had a badly inflamed eye. I began applying antibiotic ointment, and then, last night, I heard her screaming in her sleep. I went into her room to bring her to my bed and she was screaming, "No!" . . . "Don't" . . . "Stop it!" When I woke her at five this morning to put in more medicine she began screaming in the same way, so I guess that's what was frightening her. I held her until she fell back to sleep, and then left.

Yesterday Murray Avery gave a conference on fetal monitoring where he discussed the presumed mechanisms of control of fetal heart rate. I suddenly realized that these doctors are not obstetricians—i.e., people who take care of pregnant women—but pre-birth pediatricians, or what I call "feteotricians." The doctors have set up a relationship between themselves and the unborn child that does not include the mother. If these doctors don't care whether a woman uses natural childbirth or has epidural anesthesia, it is only because she has been written off, and her experience, whether she is awake or asleep, is irrelevant. She is the maternal environment. They are frustrated only that they cannot control her more.

On the way home

I had two deliveries today. The first was a woman who came in fully dilated and delivered quickly. I did an episiotomy, as I was supposed to. It was her third child and she didn't need it.

The second was a woman who came in almost fully dilated. Dr. Jackson ruptured her membranes and then put on the internal monitor, since there was some meconium staining of the fluid. I put a suction tube on the table and he suctioned the baby as soon as its head was out. The baby's shoulders tore through the episiotomy and then extended through her rectum. Now I have been taught to sew those tears. I never had a tear like that before I came here. It never happened in South Carolina and it never happened at home births. In those situations, the woman did not tear because she delivered at a natural pace of the birth. No one was shouting at her to "push harder" before the tissue had been slowly stretched by the baby's head or supported by my massage.

Saturday   Day 62

I took Heather to see *The Sound of Music* last night. Parenthood is difficult when one suddenly has to explain wars and killing. Heather is full of questions and ready to learn about the rest of the world, and I am reluctant to tell her. She has been sheltered by our lack of TV. She is a gentle child who doesn't hit others, who will give a toy to a friend who wants it, and who seems oblivious to violence.

On the way home

I was feeling high this morning when I went to L&D at eight. I had finished rounds early on 3W and then had gone on to help out on 3E where we keep patients when we are overcrowded.

Barbara, who was going off duty after the night, called me aside to talk. "Michelle, I think you should work late next Sunday," she said. Barbara is a friendly woman with soft features, but only coldness and anger showed on her face this morning.

"I thought we settled that weeks ago. I can't work those hours. I need to be home. What's happening next week?"

"Nothing, except Beth is tired of working those hours and she is becoming very resentful of you." Barbara and Beth have been working together at night. I imagined long hours of their complaining about my hours.

"When I took this job two months ago, the agreement was that I wouldn't work evenings on OB. I come in six mornings a week at six, but I go home at five. Beth agreed to cover those hours and she'll be getting that time back when Karen starts."

The high I had felt from my early-morning accomplishment was gone. I had finished my work and had gone on to help the others, but I still wasn't doing enough. I felt defeated. I had deluded myself into believing I could be accepted by the others, even with my limitations.

"I can't do it," I started to say, and then the weight of the past few weeks came tumbling down on me and I cried in defeat. Barbara sat down beside me and I tried to tell her what it was like for me. "I feel spread so thin. Arlene, my baby-sitter, told me last night she won't work any more weekends." I told her that Arlene had been staying out at night and just barely making it back by the time I left at a quarter of six. I needed to do something about a baby-sitter.

"Barbara, do you know what it's like getting up at five and waking Heather to put medicine in her eye and listening to her cry and having to go off to work? There just isn't any more of me to go around. Of course I'd like to help Beth. Of course I don't want the others to resent me. I can't do any more, though."

"I know that. I'm sorry. It's just that I'm on with Beth at night and I see how she resents those extra three hours on Sunday, and I just thought you could offer to work for her. I've offered to work but Richard won't let me. He won't let anyone else cover and he's making Beth take the full brunt of your being part-time. He won't even let me make rounds for you when you go to Chapel Hill, and I make rounds other times."

I was to give a talk, "Childbirth: In and Out of Hospitals," at the School of Public Health in Chapel Hill, North Carolina, a commitment made before I came to Doctors Hospital, and one which Dr. Pierce had assured me I could still keep. Richard was making my day's absence an issue, although he couldn't stop me from being away.

"There's nothing I can do about Beth or Richard. I'm working as much as I can." I told Barbara how I had tried unsuccessfully to get Carol to give Beth a whole day off in exchange for those hours.

A lingering sense of defeat stayed with me the rest of the day.

I admitted a woman for evaluation of her high blood pressure and could not hear the fetal heart at all. I took her to L&D, and when I left they had still not been able to hear the heart even with the monitor. The woman knew something was wrong. She told me she had not felt the baby move for a day. We tried to hold out hope to her while we listened for the heart, but I think she knew her baby had died.

I did a section on another woman, with Charlie, my chief for the day, assisting, and Carol in the room watching. She called later to tell me how great it had been to watch me working so competently. I knew what I was doing. I was in control. I could concentrate on the surgery and shut out the rest of the day.

In the afternoon I did a delivery with Tony Curry and he said he was amazed at the improvement in my skills. I did an episiotomy, as I was supposed to, and sewed it up.

Tomorrow evening I leave for Chapel Hill.

Tuesday *Day 65*

I spoke in Chapel Hill and as usual, the speaking engagement was a chance for me to articulate my thoughts. It was wonderful and strengthening to feel connected with my former self: teacher, lecturer, home-birth attendant, women's-health activist. I spoke in the morning, and in the afternoon showed a videotape of a home birth I had done. I also met with the head of the family practice department in Chapel Hill who had just made a ruling that no physician in his department may attend a home birth. I certainly didn't change his mind, but I was at least able to discuss the issue with him.

The videotape was of a home birth in which I had spent much of the labor stretched out next to the woman, one hand resting on her abdomen, and doing the breathing with her. I haven't been that caring doctor here, the person who could be there with her patient so fully. It is as though that healing physician is still inside me, waiting to be retrieved again when I leave this training.

I arrived back in Everytown last night and called from the airport to say I'd be home soon. Heather said, "Mommy, Snuggles was hit by a car, but she's not hurt bad and they said you could pick her up from the hospital tomorrow." Snuggles had been hit a few minutes after I left Sunday afternoon and fortunately a neighbor took her to the vet. Sometimes I feel like a sieve trying to hold on to money.

Last Friday night I dreamed I was driving on a circular ramp with a metal railing. I remember bumping into it, but being bounced off the railing instead of going over. I was frightened but not terrified. I remember the relief of the railing catching the car and I remember thinking I had to slow down. This part of my life is all about climbing off elephants and about being caught and protected by metal railings.

Thursday   *Day 67*

I am trying to deal with the isolation of the hospital by bringing books to read and by trying to concentrate on learning as much as I can.

Fran returned from Los Angeles this week, and I kept pumping her for information about the American Public Health Association meeting, the National Women's Health Network Board meeting, and the panel where she replaced me as speaker on "Feminism and Childbirth." I miss that contact and most of the time I feel very isolated from the rest of the world.

Today I watched a delivery of Dr. MacDougal's. The woman hadn't had a baby in fifteen years and was overtly unhappy about this pregnancy. She started to go to pieces during labor, but then pulled herself together for the delivery. She was given epidural anesthesia and was having trouble pushing, and Dr. MacDougal kept yelling at her, "Push,

push harder! Can't you push?'' It seemed to me she had the knack of pushing but something was missing. I was reminded of the other woman who lost her power to push as the epidural became more effective. They teach that the epidural anesthesia doesn't affect pushing or the urge to push, but that's not what I am seeing. The woman kept trying but her power seemed drained out of her.

Friday *Day 68*

I went to a school meeting Wednesday night and talked with Celeste, the medical student whose child is in Heather's class. She told me that the teacher is known for pushing children. She said, ''Your child will never be pushed again as she is this year.'' Heather seems to be happy with school, but she is doing badly in her work. She should not be in first grade.

Yesterday I took Heather to buy fabric for a Halloween costume. She wanted to be a furry rabbit, but then she saw some soft white material and we picked out a pattern for a fairy-godmother costume. Heather has a passion for soft material. When she was two she always wanted to sleep in flimsy, smooth nightgowns. I'm looking forward to sewing the costume for her this weekend.

I've received a letter from a literary agent asking if I am interested in consulting on a book about women's health care. She said it would be a book, ''not as radical as *Our Bodies, Ourselves*.'' I think I am becoming even more radical than that book.

Sunday *Day 70*

Yesterday was restorative. I went with Laurie and Fran to the Midwest Feminist Health Center's meeting. I am always torn between wanting a quiet day at home and my need to be with people with whom I can speak. Heather came along and found other children to play with. It was a quiet day and I mostly sat and sewed Heather's costume while members of the health centers discussed organizational and political is-

sues. It is good to be reminded that so many people understand the care of women as I do.

My sense of peace ended this morning when I realized
that Arlene did not come back at all last night. Last weekend
she also didn't show up by Sunday morning. It is clear that
this is not going to work out. I guess the question is whether
I fire her now or wait until it happens again. I'll have to talk
with Gail, since it will put a burden on her to see Heather off
in the morning until I find someone else. Gail, a quiet, reserved woman in her forties, has been incredibly easy to have
in the house.

Monday   *Day 71*

Arlene will be leaving. She is angry and sullen, and says she
won't work weekends at all. I'm sorry, but she has been so
distant lately there doesn't seem to be a way to negotiate.
She will stay through this week, and I will advertise again.

Tonight I have to help Heather with her pumpkin for Halloween and I have to arrange for her to get a birthday present
for a party she is going to tomorrow. In distancing herself
from Heather and the house, Arlene has stopped all but the
most essential tasks.

Karen Dole, the new part-time resident, will be starting
tomorrow. Carol brought her to the floor today to meet
everybody. Seemingly strong and certain of her opinions, she
looks like someone who can take care of herself. Karen's
arrival gives me more flexibility in my schedule: I will be
able to leave at noon on the two days Heather gets out of
school at one.

Wednesday   *Day 73*

I stayed and took care of patients on L&D instead of going
to Grand Rounds this morning. While I was there alone, a
woman came in with a baby who I thought was breech with
a foot down. The woman had a section but I wasn't allowed
to scrub on the case because this was another attending who

is very old and is unofficially not allowed to operate without a chief scrubbed with him. I joked with him about Richard's having "stolen" the case from me because I didn't want him to realize why I had been taken out at the last minute. I don't think he knows that he isn't being allowed to operate alone.

Thursday   *Day 74*

Arlene left last night saying she would like to call Heather sometime. Another person is coming for an interview this afternoon, an ad will run in the paper this weekend, and I am posting a notice at the women's center. In the meantime, Gail will be getting Heather off to school in the morning. I will be home Tuesdays and Thursdays in time for Heather, and a teen-ager will be there the other afternoons.

Karen's arrival has in some ways increased my difficulties at work. Although I think we will be friends, still she is one more person like them and not like me. Richard told me, "Karen just knows how to be a resident better than you do. She knows the routines and procedures." Which means, she doesn't question them.

Sometimes I think, "If only Richard were gone, I'd be okay," but I know if it weren't Richard, there would be someone else like him. This system is designed for people like Richard to be successful.

I've convinced Larry Morris to take us on teaching rounds in the morning. He is a good teacher and I learn a lot from him. Going on his rounds, though, means that we have to be even faster on our own morning work rounds. I hate what I've become when I see myself make rounds in the morning and pass through efficiently, giving miserable care. I hate what I've become when I am anxious for Karen to hurry up and when I feel I have to tell her she can't be so careful and take so much time with each patient. It's a wicked program that destroys so much of what we are.

The support of my friends outside the program keeps me going. There's going to be a supper for the local NOW Health

Task Force at my house next month. I talked last night to the woman who is organizing it. I'm thinking of inviting Jackie and Carol but I feel there's still a gap between us because they are chiefs. It is painful that a separation exists between me and the other women, especially since I really like them.

Chapter Seven

Friday   *Day 75*

The woman who was to come for an interview yesterday did not show up.

I arrived at the hospital this morning at six as usual, to see my twenty-two patients before eight, when I have to report to L&D. This morning I spent a few extra minutes with Maria, a sixteen-year-old who had a Caesarean section four days ago and was to be discharged today. Over the past three days I have enjoyed our brief morning encounters. I enjoyed the tenderness and delicacy with which she treated her baby. Teen-agers can be wonderful and loving mothers. It is the poverty and lack of support that create the problems, not lack of affection.

Maria loved to show me her little girl, to ask questions about baby care, but more than that, to look for my appreciation of her baby and the way she took care of her. Today she wanted to know if I thought her daughter knew her yet. Did I think the baby looked like her? This morning she had out the pink outfit the baby would wear for discharge. Each baby leaves the hospital that way, dressed up in pink or blue or yellow or white, packaged from the hospital with all the dreams of its mother's life, even the life of a teen-ager.

Maria had been standing over the bassinet when I came in, and now she slowly moved back to her bed, half bent, holding her abdomen with the palms of her hands, as though to keep her insides from falling out through her incision as she moved. This is a common position among women after

141

a Caesarean and I wonder if they all worry their insides will fall out.

She had many questions for me, which I answered as I examined her and changed the dressing on her incision. Enders, her attending, had told me to remove the metal clips that held together the edges of her incision two days ago. I had unsuccessfully protested that it was too early and he had told me, "Remove them now. I want her out of here on Friday."

I gave Maria instructions on bathing, sexual intercourse, lifting, etc. I told her to make an appointment with the clinic in six weeks for both herself and her baby. Nervous about time and the difficulty I would have finishing rounds by eight, I said goodbye and wished her luck.

I checked in at L&D at eight to relieve Barbara and Beth, who were going off duty. Richard assigned me to follow a service patient, which meant he would be supervising me. I went to meet the woman, Angie Loren, thirty-two years old, mother of four, with some mild hypertension that had developed later in her pregnancy. She had been brought in at four this morning by her husband, who had gone home to take care of the others, and then would go on to work. Angie Loren was a quiet woman who seemed passive and accepting. She didn't demand much from me, and in a situation in which demands were often more than I felt I could carry, that was a relief.

Angie's blood-pressure increase posed a risk both to her and to her baby, so she was to be monitored closely. I examined her vaginally around nine o'clock and found her cervix about five centimeters dilated. She was becoming very uncomfortable and wanted anesthesia. I said we could put in the epidural catheter and wait until she was further along to give her the actual dose. I explained to her that if we gave her the medication now, we might slow or even stop her labor, but that later on, there was less risk of this happening. I went to the desk and called Anesthesia to come and see her.

The unit secretary called to me that I was wanted back on

3W, that someone was bleeding. I went downstairs to find that the edges of Maria's incision had separated and she had begun oozing blood through the opening of the wound. I called Enders and he said, "Marcelle, put on some steristrips and send her home anyway."

"But she's bleeding" was my futile protest. "She needs a packing."

I went back to Maria, who seemed remarkably calm, and I applied the small strips of adhesive tape to hold the edges together. I relayed the message that Enders said she was to go to the clinic in one week instead of six. I said goodbye to her again.

I returned to L&D to find that Angie was gone from her room. Sally, an experienced OB nurse who is going on to midwifery school, reported to me with a skeptical expression, "Richard came in and checked her and said she was only four centimeters instead of five, and therefore had made no progress."

"That's crazy," I said. "We both checked her and she was five."

"He said she needed x-ray pelvimetry so we could see if there was room for the baby to get through her pelvis."

I went out to find Richard.

"How come you sent her for x-rays?"

"She had an arrest of labor. Your exam was wrong, therefore her labor curve is off the norm. The protocol calls for x-ray pelvimetry, to see if she had CPD (cephalo-pelvic-disproportion—when the pelvis is presumed to be too small for the baby)."

"But her labor was just picking up."

Richard shrugged his shoulders and busied himself looking at a chart. I was angry. Angie hadn't been arrested to begin with. I knew I wasn't wrong in my exam, and neither was Sally. I was even more annoyed that I hadn't been part of the decision on a patient I was to be following.

Florence, another nurse with many years of OB experience, came out of the OCT room to ask for my assistance. "I've just tried and failed twice on an IV for a patient in the room, and there's another one in there with poor veins. Could you try?''

I didn't really have a choice, since I was the only junior resident around then. John was still in the back with a section. I agreed. It's not that I'm any better than she is, I'm just the next one to try. I have more authority and sometimes that helps. Maybe the veins listen to the person highest in authority.

The woman on the first stretcher had come in for the test as an outpatient. Her baby was overdue and the test was being done to determine whether to induce her labor or to go on waiting. Carolyn was friendly, and even apologetic about the nurse's difficulty in getting the needle into the vein. ''I'm sorry you had to be called,'' she told me, ''but my veins have never been good.''

''Veins have a life all their own,'' I told her, only half in jest. ''Sometimes they seem to be right there, and then you put the needle in and they seem to disappear. They're not very obedient.''

I put the tourniquet around her arm, saw what looked like a small vein, and missed it. Apologetically I told her, ''Sorry I'm not doing any better today. Let me try the other arm.'' This time I tried at the wrist. ''This one looks good. Now all I have to do is put the needle in the vein and keep it there.'' Carolyn seemed comfortable with this banter.

I looked at the vein and squinted my eyes as I felt it with my fingers and tried to ''see'' it with both my fingers and my eyes. I held it in place lightly with two fingers of my left hand while I slid the tiny needle under her skin and into the vein. Dark-red blood ran into the needle and up into the thin plastic tubing attached to it. ''Don't move. It's in.''

Florence took the tubing and attached it to the IV bottle, and taped the needle to the back of Carolyn's hand.

Mildred had been watching us intently from the other stretcher, and as I walked over to her she said, ''I hope you do a better job with me than you did with her. I sure don't want you messing with my arm like you did hers.''

I heard about Mildred when she was admitted two weeks

ago. She has had medical complications requiring her to be on bed rest and on a special diet. She was hospitalized because she was unable to manage either diet or rest with five children at home. She was now being tested every three days with an OCT to see how the baby's heartbeat responded when her uterus was stimulated to contract with pitocin.

I had been aware of Mildred's watching me as I worked on Carolyn. "I'll try to do better," I said. "Veins can be funny, though."

"You better not mess up, or I'll walk out of here. I'm so sick of people poking me and making mistakes on me."

"I'll try, that's the best I can do."

"You better do better than that."

I wanted to be able to stop the way this was going. She was getting me upset. I had put the tourniquet around her arm as we were talking, and now I saw that no veins popped up that I could see easily. I told her to squeeze her hand, and still none showed up.

"I'll try the other arm," I told her, feeling tension mounting and my own calm disappearing. As I squinted my eyes and felt her arm with the tips of my fingers, I questioned myself: Is that a vein or a tendon I'm feeling? My eyes see nothing, what of my fingers? Am I tricking myself? Why is this so hard sometimes and so easy at other times? I need to relax to do this well.

"Why are you taking so long?" Her question interrupted my thoughts. I understood her frustration, but I didn't want to be her target. I needed to finish in here and get out to see what had become of Angie Loren. I didn't want to be in this room.

I tried to get my balance, to remember who I was, why I was here, and why she was there. "I am not responsible for your being here," I told her.

She looked at me and in a flash I knew how she had heard my words. With horror I remembered all the doctors I had heard shouting at laboring women, "You didn't scream that way when it went in!" or "You should have thought of that nine months ago." The doctor examining a woman, trying to push his fingers into her vagina, yelling at her, "You had no trouble separating your legs nine months ago, did you?" The woman in labor screaming with pain, being told, "Why didn't you say no?"

I flashed on all the times women had been told that this pain and this abuse were their punishment for the crime of their pregnancy.

I had been thinking of this woman's medical condition and her domestic difficulties, not her pregnancy. I was trying to tell her and myself that I was not there to torture her, to inflict pain on her. I was trying to tell her that she was there because of her disorders, that they were the cause of her pain, not I. What she heard instead was the abuse that, for centuries, has been heaped upon women crying out in pain and vulnerability. I was now a part of that abuse.

The room was quiet. Then Mildred snapped, "You had no right to say that to me. I'm sick. I'm the patient. I can't help how I am."

"I didn't mean what you think. I wasn't even talking about your pregnancy. I meant I wasn't the reason you were here or needed an IV started." I was angry with myself, but the harm was done.

She was crying now. "I don't want you to touch me," she said angrily between sobs. "Let Florence try."

There was nothing left for me to do. I left her with Florence, a kind woman who would comfort her and soothe her.

I went back to the labor room to look for Angie, who should have been back from x-ray by now. Richard was there, hooking up the pitocin drip, which would stimulate her labor.

"She didn't have any CPD. There's plenty of room in there. I've decided to start her on pit."

He had read the x-rays while I was in the OCT room and had determined there was plenty of room for the baby to pass through Angie's pelvis. There never was any evidence that her labor had arrested. Within a half-hour her cervix was seven centimeters dilated.

I had to leave her room again to check a new patient who had come to the floor. When I returned, Richard was standing over Angie's bed with a partially opened fetal-scalp sampling kit. He said the monitor had shown questionable variations and he wanted to get a fetal blood sample from the baby's scalp to test in the pH machine. The pH of the blood is a measurement of the chemical balance of the body's metabolism. In obstetrics, the pH of fetal blood is sometimes measured during labor if the monitor strip shows patterns indicative of fetal distress. The blood sample is acquired by using a lance, similar to a finger lance, but on a long rod, to pierce the scalp of the baby in utero. The blood is then collected in long glass capillary tubes and is quickly run through the pH analyzer, a sophisticated, sensitive and sometimes erratic machine.

I told Richard I had watched the procedure several times now, and asked that he instruct me through the procedure on Angie.

"I've changed my mind. I don't think she needs it" was his response.

Angie quickly began to want to push. Richard did a vaginal exam and announced that she was fully dilated and would be allowed to push. Angie began to push, and with each contraction there were patterns on the monitor indicative of distress and I worried about whether the baby was all right. Richard told me not to worry, and left Sally and me with orders to take her back to the delivery room when she was ready.

I watched Angie and the monitor. When it was time to go to the delivery room, I decided to take the monitor back with us, since the pattern was still abnormal and she might not deliver for a while. Sally and I began wheeling her back, and sent a message to Richard that we were going back. Once there, I reattached the monitor and found that the heart rate was down to 60/min., less than half the normal rate. Richard came in and said to scrub.

We were out at the sinks scrubbing, looking through the window to the delivery room, when he said, "I want you to go back in there and turn off the monitor."

"But the rate was down to sixty when I left."

"I want that machine turned off."

I went back into the room, unhooked the machine, and returned to the sinks. I was furious. I had come to this hospital to learn the technology. It was what Richard is best at, and yet in my presence he becomes so antagonistic and oppositional, he cannot even teach me what he knows so well.

"I want the machine out of the room."

I went back again.

I returned to the sinks, scrubbed and went into the delivery room. Angie was screaming as she pushed. The baby's head was crowning. Sally and Richard were telling her to push harder.

I took the scissor in my hand to do the episiotomy, but Richard grabbed it from me and told me to do the delivery without the episiotomy. Ironically, I argued that I wanted to do one because I wanted to get the baby out as soon as possible.

We did the delivery with Richard looking over my shoulder, supervising. The baby's head came out without a tear, but there was a small tear when the shoulders came out. Richard continued to harass me throughout the sewing of the tear. He would tell me not to sponge up the blood as I was working, and to use my fingers instead of instruments, but then he wouldn't sponge for me either, so I couldn't see what I was supposed to be sewing.

The baby was okay, except for a high-pitched cry which is sometimes indicative of distress, and it had some irregular breathing at ten minutes. There was a lot of meconium as it was coming out and I would have liked to have a suction trap on the table, but I didn't dare ask Richard for one. We sent the baby to the nursery for observation.

While we were in on that delivery, I told Richard what had happened with Mildred, the hypertense patient, since I knew he would learn of it, anyway, and he told me to go back and apologize to her. I said I would go back and I would tell her I was sorry she was upset, but that I wouldn't apologize for what I hadn't said.

By two o'clock the woman I had admitted earlier was ready

to deliver. Her attending didn't get there in time, so I was alone for the delivery. When it was over, the woman asked me, "Are you a midwife?"

"No, I'm a doctor," I told her laughingly. Her question had implied, "But you're too nice to be a doctor."

"She's really a midwife at heart," the nurse added.

"I guess I really am a midwife. It depends on where I am."

The nurses continued to joke about that exchange for the rest of the day.

The steristrips I had put on Maria's incision had not stopped the bleeding, and at two o'clock I was called back to see her. I asked Richard to take a look at it with me this time. He recommended that she be taken back to the operating room, given general anesthesia and sewn up again. He called Larry Morris, since by this time Enders had left for the weekend, and Larry said to start an IV and order blood in case she needed to be transfused. None of this was necessary but it helped legitimize her stay in the hospital. Larry finally came in to see her later in the day. He agreed we should put in a packing, which is what I wanted to do this morning. We did and it stopped the bleeding. I think she will be fine.

I went back to Mildred, who was by now back in her room, a large, gloomy place with three beds and curtains between them. I pulled the curtains which enclosed her bed.

"I'm sorry I upset you earlier." I was sorry she was upset but I wasn't sure I could explain myself any better than I had already.

"You had no right to say what you did." She was quickly tearful and angry again.

"I didn't mean it the way you heard it."

"You shouldn't have said anything. You're a doctor."

"You got me rattled, and I'm sorry that happened, but it did."

"Doctors should be able to take anything. Patients are sick."

"Well, that may be true, but I'm just another human being, and sometimes I get rattled."

"You shouldn't be that way."

I told her again I was sorry I upset her, and that I didn't
think she needed to take abuse and neither did I.

It was by then four o'clock and I called home. The teen-
ager who was baby-sitting told me Heather was playing with
a friend outside.

L&D was quiet by this time. I told the nurses where I
would be and then went to the doctor's lounge, put on the
headphones and listened to a tape I had just received from
my friend Ann in California. It was wonderful to be sitting
in that room listening to the voice of a friend. Intermittently
I looked over material from a woman's group I'm helping to
write about childbirth. That work makes me feel needed and
as if I have something to contribute.

Sunday   *Day 77*

As I drive in to work, Heather is home with my parents, who
will take her to the zoo this morning. I woke at six, realizing
I was late, but I was out of the house and in the hospital by
six-twenty, and not missed.

This morning Dr. MacDougal let me do most of a postpartum tubal ligation. I hadn't been in surgery with him since
my third week here, but was able to demonstrate my competence today. When he started to do something I knew how
to do, I would tell him. He scrubbed out at the end, leaving
me to finish alone.

I talked with him about Mildred, who is his patient. Richard had called Dr. MacDougal on Friday to tell him what
had happened, but MacDougal's response this morning was
that too much had been made of it all, that Mildred was a
very difficult patient and that I shouldn't be worrying about
it.

Yesterday I spent the entire day working on the health
resource guides, which is work that feels as important a part
of my move to Everytown as what I do at the hospital. My

sense of purpose was reaffirmed as I was able to put my knowledge into words that would be read by many women. So often my being a doctor has made my thoughts suspect in the lay community, so it was exciting to find Fran and Laurie so receptive both to my opinions and my technical information.

Monday *Day 78*

Beautiful pink light is coming across the sky as dawn approaches. I won't see the sun come up because I'll already be at work, but it looks like the day will be beautiful outside.

I spent last evening interviewing women for the job of baby-sitter. Louise, a friendly young woman from Guadeloupe, impressed me most. I called a reference in New York and was told the children there still ask for Louise and wish she'd come back. She left there to be closer to an aunt here in Everytown. I've spoken with her aunt and her aunt's employer, who told me how responsible Louise is. I am reassured by her connection with this community. It is scary to take strangers into my house and have them be alone with Heather so much. The ordeal of interviewing again has involved meeting a number of restless women who are transient and have no roots. It's a strange life that causes them to go and live in other people's homes.

Heather is convinced that baby-sitters are hard to find because, as she puts it, "I think I'm a hard kid to baby-sit for."

"No, Heather, that's not true at all." I protested, suddenly surprised by her statement.

"Well," she said, crossing her arms over her chest and looking as if she had an important answer for me. "Arlene left because I was hard to baby-sit for."

"Arlene left because she didn't want to work that many hours. It had nothing to do with you."

I knew from her expression that she was not convinced. She felt responsible.

This afternoon, I met the infection control person for the hospital, and talked with her about the infection rate follow-

ing Caesarians. She said our rate was about 30 percent, and
that nationally it ran between 30 percent and 50 percent. The
major cause seems to be the frequent vaginal exams and
prolonged ruptured membranes. She added that the internal
monitor may be a contributing cause.

The insulation man came to the house today to do the attic.
He apparently started to fall through and put a big hole in
the ceiling of Heather's room. I've had arguments with him
over the phone this afternoon, because I'm insisting that the
ceiling be fixed.

I feel overwhelmed by the problem of looking for a house-
keeper/baby-sitter, dealing with ceilings falling in, and exhaustion from my job. Today I dozed off for about half an
hour while sitting straight up in a chair.

Wednesday, on the way home   *Day 80*

I've requested a meeting with Dr. Pierce about a woman
whose baby died in utero sometime last night. I admitted her
yesterday with pre-eclampsia, an increase in blood pressure
which is dangerous to both mother and baby. Because we
were overcrowded on the floor and short of monitors, the
nurse wanted to unhook this woman from the monitor. I
refused to take her off the monitor, insisting that the baby
was at great risk and we needed to find out what its condition
was.

I had to leave the labor floor for a delivery, but when I
returned, the pre-eclamptic patient had been moved off the
floor. I felt there was nothing I could do because she had
been moved to John's floor after both Richard and the attending had written orders on the chart to transfer her. After
the baby died in utero, they looked at the monitor strip and
discovered that it was evident yesterday that the baby was
in distress. Richard has now complained to Dr. Pierce that I
didn't follow the chain of command because I transferred
her. I wish I hadn't adhered to the proper chain of command
and that I had gone to check up on her. I hadn't liked the
little bit of monitor strip I'd seen before I had to leave.

Last summer when I first met with Pierce, I had told him I could take orders. While I resent Richard's accusation and I need to clarify the truth with Pierce, I also wish I hadn't taken anyone's word that this woman was all right. In this scheme of things, though, human life is secondary to maintaining the system. My own ability to function here frightens me.

I've stopped to pick up groceries and guinea-pig food and litter. I'm almost home now.

Thursday   Day 81

"Michelle, I want to talk with you for a minute."

It was seven o'clock and I was in the middle of making rounds. I knew that Jackie, who was now the chief resident, wanted to talk with me about my meeting with Dr. Pierce. We went to a stairwell for privacy and sat on the top of the landing. Jackie's tension was evident as she ran her fingers through her curly black hair.

"I know Richard is difficult to work with, in more ways than you know."

I didn't ask what she meant. "Yeah, he gives me a hard time."

"In some ways you and he are the worst possible combination to work together, but you can't complain about him to Pierce. Pierce has to back his chief." Jackie's voice was tight and almost shrill. Tired from a long night of work, having been told she had the responsibility for whatever any resident did, Jackie was obviously worried about my meeting with Pierce.

I knew Jackie didn't want me to go to Pierce. A junior person isn't supposed to do that.

"I'm not going to complain about Richard," I assured her. "I'm going to tell Pierce that I haven't broken my agreement with him about following lines of authority. That was Richard's complaint about me and I have to answer him.

"Jackie, there's only one time I disobeyed Richard. That

was the night he told me to go to sleep and instead I ordered a hematocrit and then awakened him with the results. He took credit for the test, and both of you took credit for saving the patient's life by taking her to surgery. I've never said anything about it. I know the rules.''

Jackie seemed relieved and I think surprised that I was so cooled off about the issue. I guess someone told her how angry I was yesterday.

At our meeting I told Dr. Pierce, ''It's like going to war and knowing in advance what you're going to be going through, but then finding yourself on the front line and not wanting to be shot at.''

He laughed and said he liked my analogy.

I don't think Pierce had taken Richard's complaint about me seriously, because when I told him I had not broken my agreement with him about following orders, he said he knew that. We talked in general about how I was doing. I said I was happy that I had come here and that I never doubted that decision, although sometimes it was difficult on a day-to-day basis.

Pierce gave me some feedback. He said all my positive qualities had come through but that he had initially been worried about my surgical skills. I told him of my recent good experience with MacDougal and Black. ''When they hand me the scissors in the middle of cutting the uterus, then I know I've convinced them of my capability.''

''Well, if the old diehards are letting you do surgery, then you must be doing okay,'' he said and laughed.

I mentioned to Pierce a letter I had received about funding for research on cervical caps, a strong interest of mine before coming to Everytown, and I asked if his department was interested. I had been importing caps and fitting them in New Jersey. He asked if I was interested in doing research at Doctors on cervical caps, but I said I didn't think I could get involved in anything else now. He suggested that I not bow out so easily and that I mention to Lois Scott, their birth-control director, that there is money available.

Later Richard wanted to know how my meeting had gone. I shrugged and said, "Okay."

Friday   *Day 82*

Yesterday afternoon Heather and I walked downtown, bought groceries and walked back. She is having a tough time keeping up with the other children in school. Yesterday she asked me, "How many years do you spend in first grade?"

"Usually it's one, but if you haven't been to kindergarten, then sometimes it's two years in first grade and one in each of the rest."

"Will I be in Mrs. Nickle's class next year if I'm still in first grade?"

"I don't know that yet." Her teacher and I had talked about her repeating first grade and being in a K-1 with Mrs. Nickle. This conversation with Heather is painful to me. The whole subject is painful to me. Heather should have been in kindergarten this year and not first grade. I feel as though Heather is paying a heavy price for this move.

The meeting with Pierce has left me feeling much better about the program. I am pleased that he has not been dissatisfied with my work. I feel burdened by wanting to prove that having a part-time resident is feasible in a program.

Last night I received a call from a doctor in Washington who is interested in cervical caps. He said I may be asked to moderate a meeting in Washington of people from HEW, the Population Council, and the Feminist Women's Health Centers on research on cervical caps.

The cervical cap is a birth-control device similar to the diaphragm which has recently been reintroduced as a method of woman-controlled birth control. After reading about cervical caps in Barbara Seaman's book *Women and the Crisis in Sex Hormones*, I had begun importing them from England and using them on women who wanted to try them. The precise usefulness and statistical efficacy are still unknown, but the cap has become a political issue. Several days before I left for Everytown I learned that my last order of caps had been confiscated by the Food and Drug Administration in Philadelphia and that it would take a great deal of legal help to get them.

When I protested to the FDA officer in Philadelphia that "I spoke with the person in charge of Devices at the FDA in Washington, and she said it was legal for me to use them," he said, "Well, she may tell you it is legal to use them, but she can't give you permission to import them."

Reluctantly, I agreed to having the caps returned to the manufacturer in England.

Today I spent a lot of time with Roberta, a woman who is in her ninth month and has been having some bleeding. She is a friendly person in her mid-thirties, pregnant for the second time. I examined her, and although there was nothing obviously wrong except for a small amount of bleeding, I was worried about her. The two most usual causes of bleeding in the ninth month are a placenta overlying the cervix (placenta previa) or an abruptio placenta, in which the placenta prematurely separates from the wall of the uterus. Both of those are dangerous conditions for both the mother and baby. Dr. Catan, her attending, ordered an ultrasound examination, which would locate the placenta, and I went with Roberta to the lab to watch the pictures on the screen. The radiologist decided they were okay and could find no reason for the bleeding.

I wanted Roberta to be monitored for the day, but Richard said no. I called Dr. Catan and by suggestion got him to say he wanted her on the monitor. Then I went back to Richard and said, with a shrug, "There's nothing I can do. Catan ordered the monitor."

Sunday   *Day 84*

Hilda Cameron and I had a long talk about the baby who died in utero earlier this week. Hilda told me she had never seen the monitor strip when the woman was transferred off the floor. The patient had been wheeled past her in the hall and she had asked, "But what about the strip?"

"It's fine" was the nurse's reply, and Hilda assumed someone else had read the strip. Her note on the chart that the strip was fine and that the woman could be transferred reflected what she had been told, not what she had observed herself.

Monday   *Day 85*

Last night I dreamed my mother and I were at the shopping center looking at Hush Puppies because I thought they would be more comfortable on my feet. The reality is that my feet are terribly sore from my having to stay on them hour after hour. I've been wearing my running shoes, but even they hurt. Tomorrow I'm planning to get some comfortable shoes, the shiny kind, because it will be easier to wash the blood off them.

Louise moved in yesterday, giving me hope that it will be easier at home. She is wonderful with Heather, outgoing, cheerful, offering to read to her, play with her. Heather has latched on to her and has taken on the job of showing her around, telling her about the house, me, the pets . . .

On the way home

Nurses have usually been my friends. Contrary to the general belief that women doctors can't get along with nurses, there is often a woman-to-woman bond that can result in an easy and close relationship. Nurses and I have usually been allies.

There is a tension between me and the nurses here that I have never experienced before, and I don't understand why. I think it is partly due to my low position in the power structure. Richard is the chief of OB, and the nurses defend him. He flirts with them, though behind their backs he talks about how he can't stand them.

Then, too, I think the nurses are put off by how different my ideas are. I think they feel unappreciated by me because they believe totally in the kind of obstetrics they are practicing. They believe this is one of the best places in the country in which to have a baby, and they don't understand why I question so much, why I don't act as though this hospital is the best place there is.

Today they got mad at me because I didn't call ahead about a patient I was rushing up from 3W and they took out their anger on the patient. I had ordered some medicine for her severe vomiting, but instead of getting the medicine, the nurse went to make some private calls. There were six nurses sitting out in the hall just talking, and one on the phone and no one would help the woman who was vomiting.

The worst part of the isolation is that I begin to think, Maybe they're right. Maybe I'm all wrong about childbirth. I begin to doubt myself and to think I'm simply someone who can't fit in anywhere.

Wednesday   *Day 87*

I've probably done as many sections as vaginal deliveries this month. I like sections because I enjoy being away from the floor for two or three hours. The demands on me become limited by my being in surgery, and I can't be called for three things at once. Because sections are done with attendings, and my relationship with them is better than with the residents, I am free of harassment for a while.

Today I scrubbed with Dr. Owen, with whom I haven't worked since my first week here. The surgery went well and I impressed him with my abilities. I delivered the head, sewed part of the uterus, cut and tied the tubes, and finished the skin closure. The woman had become pregnant with an IUD in place, and we found the IUD in the membranes that surrounded the baby. Dr. Owen felt her uterus was too thinned out for future pregnancies, so after the baby was out, he said, "Doreen, I really think you should have your tubes tied."

Doreen was lying on the table, paralyzed from the abdomen down. Her husband stood at her head, holding her hand.

"Why do you say that? You know I was thinking about it but had decided not to."

"Your uterus is so thinned out that I would worry about a future pregnancy. I want to tie these tubes now."

"Okay. I guess that decides it."

Then, addressing the rest of us in the operating room, he said, "We have decided to tie her tubes. I want you all to be witness that the patient has consented." She had not signed a consent for tubal ligation and I asked myself whether what we were doing was legal.

I tied both tubes, and when we reached skin closure, Dr. Owen left me to finish.

Sunday   Day 91

The blue sky is beautiful today. The days have been warmer than usual for November, so I am enjoying this bit of Indian summer.

My friend Missy is visiting from New Jersey. Yesterday we went out to Lake Animal Farm and enjoyed the animals and just being out in the country. Heather found a long rope swing to play on, and we all sat out on a blanket and talked. Louise is off for the weekend and Missy is taking care of Heather while I work today. This afternoon we'll probably go downtown to wander around and have dinner.

I am finally getting the knack of what they are trying to teach me. Ian Dorsi taught me today to have the woman stop pushing, and once I had control of the head and chin, to deliver the head myself without the woman's assistance. While this speeds up the process it is almost as though the woman is not there.

When I was delivering babies at home and even when I was practicing in South Carolina, the mother was the one who had control over what was going on. I never sought to take control, but worked instead at coordinating my hands with what the woman was doing.

Monday   *Day 92*

"Missy! I just realized why that delivery bothered me so much."

I had come home to find Missy knitting in front of the fire while Heather played with a friend. I sat and talked with her for a while but was then overwhelmed by a need to sleep. Now, two hours later, I awoke with a start, having reached an understanding in my sleep.

"The delivery of the head by the obstetrician reminds me of men who boast of being able to make a woman come on command."

Missy said, "They like to be in control. No one challenges that control."

Later

My first patient this morning was Elise, a woman who had delivered at home last night and then came in because she hemorrhaged. It is uncertain why she bled because there was such chaos here last night when she arrived. The attending who was covering was so angry she had delivered at home with a midwife that he refused to come in to see her. The resident who examined her was never sure why she was bleeding, but it stopped.

This morning at six I went in to meet Elise, who had her baby with her, since a baby born outside cannot be kept in the nursery. I told Elise I had done home births and she seemed relieved to find a sympathetic doctor. She made up a story about who had been with her in order to protect her midwife. She said, "Some friends happened to stop by and they started an IV." I didn't press her for the truth because she needed to protect them, since they are practicing illegally. I enjoyed knowing that they were there, that they had taken care of her properly, and even that she was protecting them.

I heard in the afternoon that Elise was planning to sign out "AMA"—against medical advice. She was still being transfused and I didn't think she should leave. I was too busy on L&D to leave the floor and go to 3W, but I had her call me on the phone. She wanted to leave because she has a two-year-old at home, whom she is still nursing. I arranged for the little girl to be able to come in, and she agreed to stay until tomorrow. When I stopped down to see her for two minutes on my way out, she was in tears, having just put down the phone.

"What's wrong?" I asked. "Is it your baby at home?"

She nodded and then said, sort of embarrassed, "I just talked to her and she is fine without me." She was laughing and crying at the same time. I understood the feeling.

Tuesday   *Day 93*

It's still dark out and snowing and quite beautiful. Louise is working out so well at the house. Last night I came home, relaxed while Louise gave Heather her bath and then fixed supper for Heather and me, since Louise was going out for dinner. Then we ate some of the leftover ice cream sundaes, which were cold all through and reminded me of the old Good Humor sundaes I used to eat as a kid in New York. By eight-thirty I was in bed and asleep.

I told Fran on the phone yesterday that I felt as though the truths were being revealed to me about obstetrics, and I shared with her my new insights. I realize I never knew any of this before because I never had any close obstetrical supervision. When I was a student at City Hospital, I was simply left in a room with women about to deliver and I learned how to get the babies out without tearing. I fear I will lose that skill I developed naturally as I realize that what I do is so different from standard practice. I've had lots of people with whom to consult, but until now, no one has ever put their hands on mine and supervised me in the moment-to-moment delivery of the infant.

Later

Yesterday Tony Curry said to me, "If you can get Elise, the home-birth patient, to stay this one night, that's all I want. Once she's had her transfusions, I don't care when she goes home."

I had persuaded Elise to stay that day. Then, this morning Tony went into her room and she asked him when she could go home. When he didn't answer her, she said, "Dr. Harrison said I could go home today."

He became enraged at what I had told her—despite his instructions to me. In front of one of the nurses and a midwife, he said, "You cannot tell people when they can go home. You can only say to them, 'Dr. Curry will tell you when you can go home.'"

I was suddenly angry myself. The members of his group practice seldom saw their patients—the residents did all the work. "Dr. Curry, I've been told to treat your patients like service patients, and if that's not so, then you can see your own patients for postpartum care."

"Don't threaten me, Michelle."

"Well, I find it hard to get contradictory messages. If I'm doing all their care and you never see them, then I need to be able to tell them when they can go home."

"Well, just don't threaten me. You know we can do all our own cases." That was always the threat. They could take away our surgery. My mind spun off the answers I would have liked to give him, like, "I don't care if you do all your own cases," or "You don't want to do all your own cases, anyway, since you're a lazy bunch of doctors." However, I said none of those things, only "Okay."

I was surprised later when he came to me and said it had all been a misunderstanding. The midwife who was there told me later that he had asked her, "I was right, wasn't I?" and she said, "No, Michelle was. If you aren't going to see your patients, she has to be able to take care of them." There are some patients from his group who come and leave and never see their doctors.

Today at four o'clock Jackie sat down with those of us on

OB and worked out the Christmas schedule. I will be off for three days at Christmas. I would like to go somewhere with Heather.

Wednesday   *Day 94*

This morning it is still dark and there is a fine snow falling to the ground. It is so peaceful.

Tomorrow is Thanksgiving and I miss my family, I miss a *sense* of family. I don't want to go to New Jersey, and I really wouldn't want them here. I feel too drained to deal with intense or close relationships, and superficiality is hard to achieve with close family—but I miss them, anyway.

Starting in January, I will be back on GYN and working nights again. I shall miss this freedom in my time and miss being home every night. I am already anxious about that schedule.

Sometimes I feel like an anthropologist at Doctors Hospital, where I study this strange culture of doctors and patients. Each morning I drive off to my field site, spend the time with the people there, and then dictate my notes of what I have observed as I drive home at night.

The great benefit of doing this training in Everytown is that I am not alone with the hospital culture, but rather that I am constantly provided with support and affirmation of who I am, by the community of friends I have here. Fran and Laurie, so often there for me themselves, have eagerly introduced me to their friends.

Later

Roberta, the woman who was bleeding last week, has lost her baby. Yesterday she had an ultrasound scan, which showed that the baby was dead. Today, in tears, she came into the hospital to deliver. We used prostaglandin suppositories to stimulate her labor, and then high doses of Valium and an epidural so she wouldn't feel anything. Extra Valium was used at the moment of delivery to put her to sleep so she wouldn't see the baby. I felt close to Roberta and wanted to be there for the delivery. I watched the dead baby, a little girl, come out.

Carol's patient Annette also delivered today. I had seen her once for prenatal care when Carol was sick, and she talked of wanting a homelike birth experience. I didn't tell her I had attended home births, but I was able to talk about her concerns. When I came in this morning Annette was in the Alternative Birth room, but her labor had stopped as soon as she was moved there.

Carol sent Annette for x-rays, which showed there was room for the baby to go through her pelvis. She then started her on pitocin to stimulate her labor. The use of pitocin and the fact that the labor had stopped meant that Annette was no longer of low-risk category and she was moved back to a labor room instead of the Alternative Birth room. Annette's contractions picked up and she progressed slowly throughout the day. Carol asked me to stay with Annette while she made several trips to the OR for other patients. We kept hoping that Annette would deliver while Carol was with her, but then she had to leave for an hour to give a talk across the street. When she asked me to do the delivery, for then it would be as close to a home birth as possible, I felt caught in a dilemma because without Carol there I had no protection against Richard.

"Carol, I want you to know that leaving me here to do the delivery isn't a good idea. As you know, Richard and I don't do well together and I can't guarantee I'll be able to do it the way you want."

"Well, what am I supposed to do?" was her angry response to me as she left. I had thought that maybe she could get Jackie to cover the delivery, or someone else to give the talk. Later she came back and apologized for her outburst. She had wanted reassurance from me, which I couldn't give her because I had no control over the situation.

Annette's cervix dilated fully. The internal monitor would tell us if there was any sign of distress, so I felt we could take our time in getting the baby out and that Carol might even get back in time. The nurses kept urging Annette to push harder—they sometimes act as though a baby can't get out without the nurses' pushing. I said Annette could relax, push as she needed to. Her contraction would suddenly peak, and without any instruction she would pull up her legs and push as hard as she could. Then, for a while, Annette seemed uncoordinated and was having trouble pushing, and she said, "I'm not doing it right, I can feel that."

"Annette, I want you to try something," I told her.

The baby's head was now only about an inch inside her vaginal opening. I took Annette's hand and said, "Feel with me," as my hand guided her index finger to the top of her baby's head. "That's your baby's head, right there and almost outside you."

I left her finger inside her vagina, touching the baby's hair, and went on, "Now, imagine a circle, a large circle. Flex your head, and your back, bring your bottom up, so your body is a semicircle, and now think about delivering the baby up and onto your chest." I demonstrated the circle formed by her curved neck, back and buttocks, and the path the baby would go to complete that circle and be on Annette's chest, in her arms.

Annette flexed her body, and on the next contraction the baby's head moved into sight. Annette pushed and then suddenly stopped and looked at me with terror.

"What's wrong?"

"I'm afraid the baby will tear out my insides."

After that, my main job was to tell her gently, "Don't be afraid, let your baby out."

By the time Carol was due back, the baby's head was visible even between contractions, I was doing perineal massage, and Annette was pushing well on the contractions. Carol walked in, came over to the bed, and on the next contraction Annette pushed the baby into Carol's hands. Her baby daughter gave a lusty cry and Carol placed her in Annette's arms. I think sometimes babies and mothers pick the moment for birth.

Friday   *Day 96*

Louise didn't come back from Thanksgiving at her aunt's house last night and this morning I feel like chucking the whole thing. Sometimes I think it isn't possible to do what I'm trying to do. Over the holiday Heather was weeping for the people she missed in New Jersey, and she was very upset and clinging to Louise when she left Wednesday night, crying, "You're not coming back, I know you aren't." I, too, have been missing New Jersey and the house and my friends there and feeling what Fran describes as the violence of this move. I feel strangely displaced, especially at holiday time, because my friends here are new and I miss those with whom I share a past.

Later

Louise called this morning to apologize for being late and for not calling. I am worn down by the strain of worrying.

A woman came into the hospital in very early labor and over the course of twelve hours she did not go into good labor. She was given a drug to help her sleep with the intention of stimulating her labor when she woke up. However, she was five centimeters dilated when she awoke and was quickly fully dilated. As soon as she began to push, the baby's heart rate slowed precipitously and stayed dangerously low while we prepared the woman for an emergency section. We also did a fetal scalp sample, showing a pH of 7.11, which usually means that the baby is in severe distress. Before we could do the section, though, the woman delivered vaginally and the baby seemed to be in perfect condition, breathing, crying and with excellent color. I don't understand the low heart rate or the low pH. I wonder if we know what we are doing.

Andy, my obstetrician and colleague in South Carolina, used to say, "Whenever I'm with a woman in labor and I feel like doing something, I go out in the hall and have a cigar."

Chapter Eight

I was in the middle of a section today and suddenly I just wanted to be back in New Jersey. I wondered why I was here macerating women's uteri and how I could go on with this and why I had ever decided to do this to begin with. It was hard to stay in surgery in the midst of that flood of thoughts.

The woman today had a fine uterus, but we have rules that say she can only give birth in a certain way and she did not follow our rules, so we cut open her belly. But we cut in the wrong place and now she will probably never have kids again. Now she will probably have problems with intercourse. We have really ripped apart her insides and sewn them back together again, but they are not the way they were. The woman was so close to delivering and the baby's head was so far down that we had to have someone go under the drapes to push the baby's head back up into her uterus. When the lips came up I knew that at least the baby would be able to breathe until we got it out.

I was passively watching because this surgeon was doing almost all of the operation himself. And then while he was fishing around trying to put together the parts of the uterus, he said, "Something is wrong. You must have torn apart the inside lining of her uterus when you took out the placenta." That is when I freaked out because I thought I had been very gentle when I removed the placenta. And that is when I realized I am putting my fingers in other people's bodies, and even when I am trying to be gentle I can do grave damage. I

167

knew that something was terribly wrong because it didn't look like the inside of her uterus we were working on, but rather we seemed to be seeing the whole uterus, in one piece. The woman was awake and her husband was in the room, so it was impossible to talk freely about what we saw.

In the course of the next half-hour the surgeon discovered it was not that I had destroyed that portion of the woman's uterus, but that he had cut down in the wrong place and had separated the cervix from the body of the uterus. He muttered an apology for having blamed me, but that was of no help to this woman. Richard came in and tried to get the surgeon to get more help from Dr. Pierce, but the surgeon didn't want any help and in the end he probably repaired the damage as well as it could be done.

The woman had wanted to have natural childbirth. When it was evident she would be having a section her husband asked me, ''Does this mean she'll have to have a section in the future?'' Now this woman has been so badly torn apart she is probably not safe with any pregnancy, assuming she can even conceive. Then after surgery we all got together because the couple had brought champagne, and I had a sip of champagne with them and felt torn apart.

I hate this field. I hate these people. I hate all these babies coming out through holes in the belly instead of through the vagina. I hate it because this particular baby was in no distress, but the mother was tired from laboring and we told her there was an easy way out. The easy way out is that she may not be able to have more children.

We are doing something terribly wrong. I begin to think that the full dilation of the cervix is meaningless, that we may be telling women to push long before they should and thus wearing them out. It is true that the cervix dilates and then the baby comes out, but maybe it's not the cervix that has been slowing down the process. Maybe it's an entire process about which we still know little. We study how it happens and then we try to make it happen that way, but the whole framework may be wrong. Maybe even after some people dilate, there are still hours to go before the delivery.

We set a limit of one or two hours of full cervical dilation and we say she must deliver within that time we have established after the cervix is dilated. We make women push all that time, even when their bodies do not tell them to push. We make them push until they are exhausted and then we tell them we have to take over because they are not strong enough to push out their babies. The second stage of labor is that time after the full dilation of the cervix and until delivery of the baby. It is an arbitrary distinction created by men. It is a construct. It may not mean that a woman can now push out her baby. Maybe pushing is all wrong.

Monday (my birthday)   *Day 99*

I am continually haunted by yesterday's surgery. Knowing the surgery wasn't necessary, I had such a sense of foreboding when we went in. We determine when the time has come. We respond to "maternal exhaustion" when we can't take it anymore. I'm not cruel; it's not that I want to see women suffer, but I don't know of a way to relieve maternal exhaustion without the possible loss of a woman's life, a woman's reproductive capability, a baby. We have not "cured" childbirth, nor are we on the verge, and yet for those of us who watch a laboring woman, it is a long and exhausting time and we feel called upon to offer help.

We were supposed to put this woman on an antibiotic study being conducted at this and several other hospitals, but with the help of the anesthesiologist we talked the woman out of being on the study. Even before the problems of the surgery she was a candidate for infection because of her long labor, the ruptured membranes and the many vaginal exams, all of which increase risk. If we had put her on the study, she'd have only a fifty-fifty chance of being given antibiotics, since she might get the placebo instead. Without the study, we knew her doctor would give her antibiotics, and with the subsequent difficulties in surgery, she will get large doses of antibiotics.

Several days ago I warned a woman she would have to be

strong enough to resist our need to relieve her discomfort. She, too, ended up with a section. Her labor slowed and then x-rays were taken which showed there was enough room. She was sectioned, anyway, on the assumption that the x-rays just didn't show the tightness.

It would be good and it would be easy if I could just accept what they say and learn their protocol and do what they tell me to do, but I can't.

On the way home

"Dr. Harrison wasn't as brusque today."

"She just isn't someone you would feel you could talk to," a second voice responded.

I was standing outside a room, about to move the chart rack on to the next room, when I heard myself being discussed. The words of those women were painful for me to hear although I knew they were true. I had just left that room and those two patients were two of twenty-five I had to see this morning. They both have good attendings, who will see them, so I do little for them.

It's as though my time represents a reservoir of 120 minutes which I ration to twenty-five women each morning between six and eight. After the clerical and scut work gets done, I have about three minutes left for each woman, but answering their questions takes time. "When will the stitches dissolve?" "Do you think I should have a nurse when I go home?" "Will the doctor be in today?" "What can I do about my breast soreness?" "What do you think about breast-feeding?" "Dr. Harrison, do you have children?"

The questions are important, and should be answered. It is painful not to be able to respond fully, but sometimes I guess it is easier to discourage the asking than to have to say, "I can't talk to you now. I have to go on."

I feel that what I do in the morning is so futile that I am ashamed of it, feel it is not important. I forget what it is like for these women to be waiting for the doctor to come.

Hospitals infantilize people both because of their enormous power over individuals, and because people feel very vulnerable when they are ill. Even healthy people, once admitted to the hospital and put into short white open-backed gowns, act as though they were ill. Patients, frightened by the unknown facts of their particular conditions and by their lack of expertise, become afraid to ask, "What is my temperature? What is my blood pressure?" Afraid to offend, lest their care be affected, they accept passivity and name it trust.

Most of the morning was spent doing a section and tubal ligation with Fred Brooke, who complimented me on how well I was doing. I feel so comfortable doing sections.

This afternoon I admitted a woman who was having her fourth baby. She was requesting a tubal ligation to be done right after the delivery—a common procedure—but she didn't want any anesthesia until after the delivery because she planned to have natural childbirth. Her attending and the anesthesiologist wanted to give her the epidural anesthesia for the delivery to save themselves the time that would be "wasted" between the two procedures. They said, "If we wait until after the delivery for the anesthesia, then it's considered an elective procedure and we won't do it now."

In the midst of the woman's cries of agony and insistence on natural childbirth, the nurses put her on her side and held her in place while the anesthesiologist tried to get the needle in place. When the resident failed at the epidural I had to leave the room. He had already failed on the section patient this morning.

The attending followed me, angry that I was not urging the woman to have the epidural.

"I'm not having anything to do with pushing someone to have surgery they aren't sure they want," I said, "especially a tubal ligation. She seems ambivalent about the whole thing."

"She's a patient in the Health Maintenance Program and we can't afford the extra hospital days it would cost for her to have the surgery done later," he answered angrily.

The woman became fully dilated as we were talking. I ran back and delivered her on the stretcher before we could get her onto a delivery table. The baby had a lot of fluid in her throat which I suctioned out, and then I handed her over to the anesthesiologist, who by then had arrived. He put a laryngoscope into the baby's throat in order to show another resident how to look, and each time he did, the baby's breathing and heart rate slowed down considerably.

The nurse, who had been impatient with the woman's uncertainty about surgery, said angrily to me, "She's ambivalent, that's why she isn't cooperating."

"That's precisely why we shouldn't be pushing her," I agreed.

"I think she's confused and that's why she's willing to put it off."

"All the more reason we shouldn't be doing it now." Everyone was furious at this woman because of her uncertainty. In the end she said she would have it done some other time.

A Greek woman who needed postpartum instructions met with me and an interpreter for about a half-hour to talk about care of herself and her baby. The baby is jaundiced, so he will not be going home today and the woman will be allowed to stay too. I read once that jaundice comes in waves and we seem to be in one now, or else I'm much more aware of it now.

The nurse came in and told her how to take care of the baby's circumcised penis. She whispered to me that she describes it like Carvel ice cream in telling people how much vaseline to squirt on the end of the penis. The mother seemed upset about her baby. Later I was on 3W and saw the woman and her husband standing looking through the windows of the nursery at the baby now wrapped under the bili-lights, which are used to treat the jaundice. At three days of age the baby has had the tip of his penis cut off and will spend at least twenty-four hours under purple lights with blindfolds around his eyes.

Late in the afternoon I stood and looked out the window at the snow and thought about my birthday, and wrote some notes for some poetry. I thought about how much Heather wanted it to snow on her birthday. I called her at four just to say hello, but she wasn't home.

I thought about Saturday night when I was visited by Fran, Laurie and Serena, her mother, and Catherine, who all arrived for a surprise birthday party which Gail had worked hard to put together. My worlds are so separate from each other.

Wednesday   *Day 101*

Seven of the twenty-one postpartum patients on 3W have had sections. Several of them are infected. This morning I decided to miss teaching rounds and instead to spend time taking better care of these women, which meant missing part of Grand Rounds. I can joke or laugh about patients saying I'm too brusque, but it does bother me inside, and I guess it should.

Yesterday afternoon, however, Larry Morris took me aside and said, "You're doing very well here, but talking too much with patients is a problem you have." He was being friendly and supportive as he added, "I'm sure you'll learn to correct it!"

I went on to Grand Rounds, where the last speaker was from the School of Public Health. He spoke on nutrition in pregnancy and when we talked after the meeting, we realized we knew each other from a maternity-care conference in which we had both participated. His talk today was exciting, but was met with general hostility by the attendings, who tend to disregard any aspect of pregnancy except drugs and intervention. There is also a bias among doctors against those who do not practice clinical medicine, and especially those in public health. It is as though "real doctors" are the ones who do something with a patient. Especially among surgeons, everyone else is suspect.

Thursday   *Day 102*

I'm finding it difficult to have someone in the house whose job is to help us clean—without Heather then expecting to be waited on. Louise does much more for Heather than I want her to and I think it will take a lot of talking to get a better balance.

For all that, though, I'm worried that Louise may leave because I overheard her on the phone last night talking about what sounded like a strong pull to return to Guadaloupe.

Friday   *Day 103*

There's a beautiful star in the east, not like any star I've seen before. It's morning, still dark, and I don't feel as if I've slept at all.

On the way home

I used forceps today. I was petrified as I put on the blades and pulled that baby out. The baby has a mark on its cheek, which I hope goes away. The advantage of attendings who don't care about their patients is that I get to learn more.

Yesterday on rounds I saw a baby with a cut on its face and the mother said, "My uterus was so thinned that when they cut into it for the section, the baby's face got cut." The patient is always blamed in medicine. The doctors don't make mistakes. "Your uterus is too thin," not "We cut too deeply." "We had to take the baby" (meaning forceps or Caesarean), instead of "The medicine we gave you interfered with your ability to give birth."

Sunday   *Day 105*

My mother and sister are back at the house helping get ready for Heather's birthday party this afternoon. I'm hoping to get out a little early if it isn't very busy.

Heather has been especially excited by the visit of my

sister and my ten-month-old niece. Heather has always loved babies. She is gentle with them, as she is generally with everyone. Heather was very upset about leaving her cousin Abigail when we moved, and has now had a chance to spend hours with her, talking, making her laugh, showing her toys. Heather is even better than some adults in relating to babies as real people while also recognizing the limitations of their age.

On the way home

A woman came in today twenty-seven weeks pregnant, bleeding and in premature labor. This is her third pregnancy: her first was a section, her second a vaginal delivery. Both babies were premature and tiny. She has been told she has an incompetent cervix, one that opens too early and too easily, but which in her case cannot be repaired. She has been on bed rest the past couple of weeks because the sac with the baby has been bulging through her open cervix. When I admitted her I discovered that the baby was also breech, and its tiny feet were protruding through the membranes.

We hooked the woman up to the monitor, although no one was sure why, since we hadn't yet decided if we would do a section to deliver the baby. Charlie, the chief for the day, called in Richard, who called in Jackie, who called Larry. The woman's husband said, "We want everything done that doesn't jeopardize my wife." They had never been told that a section does jeopardize a woman. Even though he didn't understand the choices, the husband's statement became the deciding factor in delivering the baby by section. The tiny baby girl, a little over one pound, is not expected to live. As in any section done for fetal distress, "saving" this baby might have been at the expense of the mother.

I didn't get out early, but I'm heading home now to my family and Heather's birthday party. The transitions are difficult. Sometimes I wish I had more time to travel between work and home, time to let the day be absorbed, and to be alone with my thoughts.

Monday   *Day 106*

I made it through the beginning of school, through Halloween, through Thanksgiving, and now through Heather's birthday. This morning when I got to work I realized I had forgotten to bake cupcakes for Heather's class party today. I was in a panic until I remembered Louise. When I called her, she agreed to pick up cupcakes at the bakery and bring them to school for me. I called home this afternoon and found that it had all gone smoothly. I think there is a part of me that is so defensive about being a single parent and working mother that I drive myself to be sure my kid gets everything the others do.

This morning, arriving on L&D, I met Neil Anderson walking out of a labor room, his brow furrowed, and muttering, "I hate patients like that! I can't stand taking care of them!"

"What's up? Who is she?" I asked.

"It's one of those couples who obtained signed agreements in advance stating exactly what they want and don't want. Her husband is hovering over her and won't let me touch her."

"I'll be okay with them," I told him rather flatly, concealing my pleasure with such patients.

I walked into the room to see the woman laboring, her husband at her side, and another woman stroking her arms and coaching her. I introduced myself quietly and the coach said, "Yes, I've heard of you. You're from New Jersey, aren't you?" I recognized her instantly as someone with whom I felt a bond, someone who spoke a language of childbirth similar to mine. She told me her name, Nancy Carr, and said she worked as a private labor coach to women giving birth in the hospital. A warm and gentle person, she provided a support reminiscent of a home birth.

Neil came back and I was able to run some interference

for the couple, especially in their not wanting an episiotomy. Nancy and I kept telling Neil how well he was doing, so he was able to get through the delivery without doing an episiotomy and without getting too angry about the obvious pressure on him.

After the delivery Neil, in an inquiring way, said, "Michelle, why don't women like episiotomies?"

"Because it feels like a violation."

"That's ridiculous," said Rennie, another attending in the hall. "It's important to do them. Don't women understand they will stretch too much if they don't have one?"

I try to stay cool and detached for these questions, especially since I don't think my answers are heard. "Well, Neil, first of all, it has never been proven that they would stretch more. Second, it's painful after the delivery, and third, you asked why women don't like them and I'm saying that many women feel they're being mutilated without having any choice in the matter."

"But if you explain why it's necessary . . ." he protested. In medicine there is the belief that if a patient doesn't do what the doctor has suggested, then the doctor just hasn't explained the matter enough.

Feeling frustrated, I tried saying it a different way. "Look, I don't think it's something men can understand, even sensitive men. It's like you can't explain what pre-menstrual tension feels like, or childbirth—or even rape. It's something that is unique for a woman."

Neil was taken aback, and he protested angrily, "You know, my car was broken into recently and I had feelings that were like those of being raped, so I do understand the feelings of women who are raped."

I regretted having gotten into this discussion. "I don't want to argue with you. You asked me how women feel about episiotomies and I'm telling you."

We talked a bit more and they wanted to know about perineal massage, the method used by midwives to keep a woman from tearing during a delivery. "Tell me about it," Rennie said.

I'd been thinking a lot about what doctors do to women and I responded, "I'm afraid to teach you guys how to do it. You'll come up with a perineal massage machine and women will be screaming while they get their vaginal openings ironed out with it."

They took my response as a joke. Rennie, intrigued by what I was saying, told me, "I have a cousin in New York who is a feminist."

I did two more deliveries with them and then a tubal ligation with Tony Curry, who let me do the case.

I stopped on the way home to look at TV sets, having decided finally to get one. I gave up television when Heather was a baby, but I agreed to get one as part of this move to Everytown, partly I think as a replacement for me. I'm caught now in a dilemma about what kind to get, whether to get black-and-white or color. Heather wants a color set because they're nicer to look at. I'm concerned about safety and radiation from color sets. I also worry about spending money to "buy" away guilt for not being home with her more. On the other hand, I don't want especially to deprive her, at least not for the sake of deprivation. I looked at several sets and I'll have to think about it more overnight.

With so difficult a year, I get upset with myself for getting embroiled in issues like which TV to get. I feel so drained from work, I seem to be missing some resources with which I usually make such decisions.

Tuesday   *Day 107*

There is a new paper out on the benefits of ambulation, or walking, during labor. I brought it to L&D and left it there for people to read, but then I realized that the problem is one of control, not method. I suddenly saw obstetricians deciding everyone should ambulate, and I saw women being forced to march up and down the halls while in labor, and doctors—men and women—standing there with whips ordering them to march on because "It's best for you." It's "them" deciding how "we" are to labor. We are left to argue with one another about how we should be forced to labor, to give birth, to raise our children.

Wednesday   Day 108

Last night at dinner, Heather and I were joking with Louise about what a wonderful person she was to have in our lives. I told her I'd never in my life been so well taken care of, and then told Heather that Louise was my baby-sitter too. Louise laughed and said she was very happy here.

Heather has been in a wonderful mood the last few days. She's eating well, likes celery, which last week she hated, and is generally easy to live with. She's also doing better in school, and is finally in a reading group.

I've decided on a color set. Heather says, "Big Bird has to be yellow, and Grover has to be green." Maybe this afternoon I'll have a chance to look up *Consumer Reports* and decide which kind to get.

This afternoon I have to get a new driver's license, since my New Jersey one has expired without my realizing it.

Thursday   Day 109

Yesterday I received a call from a doctor in California who was looking for curriculum material on women's health care. If she can get funding, she will invite me out there to do a workshop. She told me that the American College of Obstetrics and Gynecology requires only one year of OB for a family physician to have Caesarean-section privileges at a hospital. I must also do twenty-five sections during that time. Since I am in a part-time residency, I would need about a year and a half in a program. Still, that would allow me to do my own sections as part of an OB practice. I must remember to document the sections I do.

Nancy Carr, the labor attendant, was in with another patient, and supporting her through a difficult labor. Irv Warren, the attending, was also determined that the woman would get through without anesthesia because, being over thirty, she will have a "premium baby." Besides, she was infertile for some time, so he wasn't taking any chances.

With the help of a very supportive nurse today, I managed a delivery without an episiotomy, worried all the time that Richard or the attending would show up and be angry. I was actually going to do the episiotomy, but Vivien, the nurse, encouraged me not to. The baby was fine and he cried before his body was fully out. I put the baby right onto the mother's chest instead of clamping the cord first, which is how I always did it at home. The young black woman and her husband were thrilled with the delivery. I'm always excited when I can provide that kind of experience for black women, because they rarely get good treatment in the hospital. Even middle-class blacks are treated differently from white women.

After the delivery I thanked Vivien, the nurse, several times. She gave me a hug and said it was wonderful to have me here. I wouldn't have been able to do it today without her.

Friday   *Day 110*

Next Tuesday I'm going to a lecture and slide presentation on giraffes and their style of mothering. They apparently give birth in isolation, but when their young are about two weeks old, each mother finds other mother giraffes with babies and they team together and create giraffe kindergartens. The mothers take turns staying with the babies while others go off for food and water. If there is danger, the mother left behind takes all the young to safety or protects them all.

I'm looking forward both to the lecture and to the time I will have wandering by myself around the university. I miss contact with poetry and music. I keep saying I have to do more, but I don't know where that energy will come from, since it's hard after the hours of work and child care to provide anything for myself except sleep.

I've been thinking about the ACOG requirements for sections, and my need to document more. I realize I have to push for more sections and not give them away as I have done, often preferring to watch patients in labor. I have the feeling that at night the residents want more surgery and do sections under circumstances they would take the time during the day to observe longer before deciding on surgery. They often operate for arrest of descent of the baby, but one third of those arrests are the result of their own intervention, the epidural anesthesia. Often the attendings also prefer sections because they are over with sooner, and the doctors can go home to sleep or start the day.

Later

Enders mumbled throughout the section this morning and I kept saying, "Excuse me, sir, I can't hear what you are saying." He still got angry each time I couldn't do what he wanted because I couldn't hear him. He still calls me Marcelle, although by now I am sure he knows my name.

Jerry Lambert is a young attending who let me help him do a delivery this morning without an episiotomy. He even let me hold back his hand as he was trying to stretch the perineal tissue when I knew it should be supported instead. Late this afternoon we had a long talk, during which he commented that I seemed to be more interested in learning and in patients than I had been when I began the OB rotation. I knew at the time that Jerry and others thought I was uninterested when, in fact, the problem was Richard's refusal to teach. Jerry had been especially distressed last month about a patient on whom he wanted x-rays. That was the day I was unsuccessfully trying to get Richard to teach me how to read them. Jerry had interpreted my inability to read them as lack of interest. Later I was sorry I had spoken so openly with him, since I heard him repeating what I had said to Richard. I'm also sorry because talking with him stirred up my need to talk with people here.

Chapter Nine

I've put up a year-at-a-glance calendar on my bedroom wall and it makes the whole year seem shorter. Six months is only six months away, and is made up of little units, each of which I seem, in some way or another, able to survive.

I'm on my way to work in the deep snow, having dug out the car and scraped it, and congratulate myself on having snow tires. It doesn't seem like much, but it makes me feel on top of what I am doing.

Each time we have moved, Heather has missed the friends she left behind. She was only two and a half when we went from South Carolina to New Jersey, but for months she would wake up in the middle of the night crying for Harvey, a four-year-old friend. I would find her in her crib, shaking the rails, calling his name as if she could bring him back or make him appear as he must just have been in a dream. She spoke of wanting to go to South Carolina and, in fact, remembered everyone the following year when we visited.

Heather's closest friend in New Jersey was Andrea, a girl who lived across the street, but whose father lived in Everytown. Heather, who had initially "refused" to move from New Jersey because she didn't want to leave her friends, was thrilled this week when Andrea came to visit. She will be back here for Christmas, too, so the girls will be able to spend time together.

Heather has been happy coming home in the afternoon. She spends her time playing independently in the neighborhood and is pretty responsible about letting someone know where she is. Aside from bike riding, though, the girls here tend to sedentary play. I wish I could get Heather interested in some active sports. She once told her grandmother, "Girls don't run," and in a game with her grandfather she insisted that she play the nurse, he the doctor, explaining, "Boys are doctors."

On the way home

This morning I made rounds, scrubbed on a section, did a tubal ligation, and then fought with Jackie about the next GYN rotation, which starts in three weeks.

"Michelle, I'm not prepared to pick up the slack for your being part-time," she began.

"What are you talking about, Jackie?"

"I don't want to be in the position Richard is in of covering for you. He's had to take care of patients on 3E." Her beeper went off and she left before I could respond. No one had ever suggested that I take care of patients on 3E. I did some work on the floor, checked a patient, and by then Jackie had returned. She only reluctantly let me have the rest.

"Richard has been telling everyone that it is difficult to cover the service because of your being part-time and not being able to finish your work." I pointed out to her that in the past two months the bed capacity of 3W had increased by five more patients and that my being part-time had nothing to do with making rounds in the morning.

"Well," she went on, "I'm making the schedule for the next rotation when I'm going to be your chief. I don't want to resent you, Michelle, and the only way I can prevent that is if I don't have to carry any of the load."

My frustration and resignation were mounting. "Jackie, I frankly don't care if you resent me or not because there isn't any way I can do everything." I reminded her that she had two part-time people at two-thirds time instead of one person, so she had even more help than usual.

"I want to like you," she said in a both whining and pleading way, then added, "and I want you to like me."

Jackie mentioned again, as she had the first day I spoke with her, that her husband had known a part-time resident who hadn't done *her* share of work. Once again she told me she would choose to have an abortion rather than be a resident with a child. She went on to say there was a lot of resentment about my being part-time. They're all so overworked that it's natural for them to object to anyone working less than they are. I told her I understood but was prepared to live with that resentment, since my only other choice was to quit and I wasn't going to do that.

Part of Jackie's problem is that Barbara, who is assigned to the abortion service for the next three months, doesn't do abortions on principle, so the rest of us will have to cover for her. I suggested that Jackie should be angry with Barbara instead of with me.

Karen Dole called me at home late in the afternoon to say Jackie had just told her she'd had a terrible fight with me, but that something else had been on her mind unrelated to me. Karen and I talked a long time about the schedule and how we could best share the time. Heather fell asleep while I was talking with Karen and didn't wake up until evening when I was leaving for a party. She cried because I had promised I'd make popcorn with her. For the first time I explained to her that I'd had a bad day at work and that I'd been so upset that I found myself talking about it at home and that's why I'd been on the phone. I'm not sure if I should tell her, but it may give her some insight into the reasons why I'm sometimes distracted and far away.

Monday   *Day 113*

Last night's party was in celebration of the opening of the new women's health center here in town. It was wonderful, though, and I met people of whom I'd heard but never met. I met two women who are studying at the School of Public Health and wished I could join them for lectures sometime.

I miss intellectual stimulation at work. There seems to be no one grappling with anything except the uterus and its contents. Just as important, when I'm with my friends I feel a warm response and validation that I only feel at work from the patients—almost never from my colleagues.

Later

Today, as I was sewing up a woman's episiotomy, I thought about how much more I know now than three months ago. I have to keep sight of how valuable this training has been.

I am more and more bothered, though, by the "pushing" we force on the laboring woman. Today I walked out of a room in which Alice, one of the nurses, was yelling and yelling at the woman to push harder. Alice welcomed me to the floor when I first arrived, but now I find her one of the hardest to take because of the force she applies to women. I find myself hanging back and underestimating the dilation of the cervix on her patients because I don't want that intensive pushing to start. She makes the birth a hysterical event, as though the baby wouldn't come out unless she yelled.

Tuesday   Day 114

I stopped on the way home last night and bought a small color TV, which was an instant success. I sat and watched with Heather for a little while.

Heather has been in a wonderful mood lately. Last evening as we watched TV I felt she was trying to be very "grown-up" and have an earnest conversation. She has "definitely" decided she will be a teacher when she grows up. She also wants to be a "candy striper," which she interprets as someone who gives out candy to sick people, and a vet because she loves animals. I think she'd make a good actress!

She and her friends have been covering themselves with Heather's birthday make-up. Arlene, the baby-sitter, was always heavily made up and Heather at six is trying to emulate her. Heather has always loved make-up, though—and dressing up—and playing with dolls with an intensity I never experienced. At two she was already dressing herself, insisting on choosing what to wear. It was strange to realize how different she and I were. She cannot pass a shoe store without picking out several pairs of shoes she "always wanted."

I bought her the make-up hoping she'll get it out of her system during her childhood. I also bought her some skin cream, which she is enjoying. Since she was a toddler, Heather could be trusted to leave anything alone, including cookies or candy—except skin cream. She had no self-control, and if she found any, she would cover her body with it. When I was angry, she would look at me apologetically because she really couldn't help herself.

After a quiet evening at home with Heather, I find myself thinking it would be a blessing to be kicked out of the program in July.

Wednesday   *Day 115*

Those who hold babies and bathe them and feed them in their first days should be loving people. I doubt that the question is asked of nurses who apply to work in nurseries, "Do you love babies?" Mostly it is a matter of finding people who "aren't bothered" by the crying of infants.

The woman who delivered last week with Nancy Carr's support has written a letter thanking me for being "sensitive and humanistic." She especially thanked me for the way I introduced myself to her. She had been in the midst of a contraction when I walked in, introduced myself and said, "You don't have to open your eyes. I just want you to know who I am." She then felt reassured and confident that I knew how she was feeling and that everything was going well. I remember that moment because I thought at the time that as the doctor in this setting, I'm supposed to have the patient acknowledge me, pay attention to me. Yet that attitude went against my grain. It was good to hear that I had done what I ought to.

I stopped in the nursery today to look at a baby who was

being delivered just as I went home yesterday. He has huge swelling and paralysis of the face from the forceps. The doctor who delivered him went through a uterus last week and cut a baby, and in another section a baby ended up with a fractured arm that no one can understand.

Today I worked with Jackie and realized that she is being trained to see every patient as an OB-GYN history, that for her every female must represent an onset of menstruation, pregnancy or nonpregnancy, birth control or no birth control. I fear that is what I will have to do if I am to succeed in this field, but I like to look at the women first, and wonder about them. That seems more important than training yourself to see only their illnesses.

Thursday   *Day 116*

Louise said last night, "I'm going away Saturday, for Christmas."

I was surprised, since Christmas is still two weeks away. I immediately tried to figure out how much this was going to hurt. "When will you be back? I really need you here."

"I'm going to Guadeloupe for Christmas. Afterwards I'll return." She seemed uneasy. I had a feeling I wasn't hearing something, or understanding something.

"Louise, when are you sure you will be back?" She was quiet, looking away from me, and I asked, "Are you coming back?"

"No," she said in one soft word that suddenly brought dozens of thoughts flooding into my mind, like Why is she leaving? Can I persuade her not to? What will I do about Heather? Gail is away until mid-January and she is tired of doing child care. I can't ask her anymore.

I thought of my few hours alone at the university this week and knew that the first thing to go would be any time for myself. I had even thought of having Louise work part of the time when I was home at Christmas, since it would be nice to have her taking care of Heather and her friends while I relaxed. Instead I will be worrying about dishes and laundry and garbage and keeping the house a little bit straightened up, and wishing I had a few minutes to read or answer some letters.

Louise and I talked more. Between my tears and rage, I learned the full story. She has an aunt in Guadeloupe who has power over her and has told her she must return. Louise cried because she said she wanted to stay but she is afraid of her aunt. She agreed to stay until a week from Saturday instead of leaving in three days.

In my tears, I was also furious with Jackie for treating me as though I were lazy and for not understanding the real energy that goes into keeping my home afloat. The problem is that no one respects my work as a mother. If I were doing important work for NASA, the others would still resent my being part-time, but they would understand and respect what I was doing.

Later

It was impossible to talk with Jackie without crying as I told her I was having trouble keeping everything together, that my baby-sitter was leaving, and that I couldn't work past five-thirty on my next rotation, since the teen-ager has to be home by six. So, I've now traded my few free afternoon hours for the half-hour or so between five-thirty and six. My day will be only eleven and a half hours instead of twelve or twelve and a half. I'll still be working every fifth night as part of the night-call schedule.

This evening I tried to take a nap but couldn't, because I lay in bed thinking about a woman who was almost sectioned today. Dr. Owen had told her she might need a section. Visibly upset, she replied, ''No, I don't want one.''

''I'm sorry, dear,'' he said, ''but we might have to section you, anyway, if that seems the best thing to do.'' Later, after the delivery, her husband said to her, ''If we had decided you needed one, it wouldn't have mattered if you said no.''

Friday, on the way home   *Day 117*

My left foot won't stop shaking as I drive. Dr. Pierce wants to see me in his office, but I couldn't get off L&D to meet with him and now I'll have to wait until Monday. I have no idea what it is about, but I am more and more worried as I become aware of my differences with the methods of hospital childbirth.

Today another woman came in wanting natural childbirth, and then asking for pain relief and a sedative—which she was given. The anesthesiologist wanted to put in the epidural needle, but we hadn't yet gotten a monitor tracing on the baby because no machine was available. I objected to giving the medication before we have a tracing, since it gives a pattern similar to fetal distress.

"It's too early to place the epidural," I argued. I remembered Dr. Warren's patient with the "premium baby" and his refusal to give her anesthesia because he didn't want to do anything to jeopardize that baby.

Karly, the nurse, argued with me, "Well, does that mean you wouldn't ever give an epidural?"

"I'm not thrilled with them, because of the fetal distress I've seen, but I definitely wouldn't give them to a woman who's already had fetal distress."

"But we don't have a free external monitor, so we can't get a tracing unless you rupture her membranes and get an internal monitor tracing. That's what you should do." The nurses, who are used to residents coming through for a few months at a time, year after year, are also used to telling them how to take care of patients. Usually they are less direct, though.

"I don't want to rupture membranes," I explained, and at the same time clarified for myself. "Once we give her the epidural, there is a good chance we will end up with an arrest of labor of some sort, and then doing a section." I was finally getting to say out loud the sequence I often repeated to myself. "If I have to rupture membranes now, and put on the internal monitor, then by the time we do the section she will have a higher chance of infection because of her ruptured membranes.''

The anesthesiologist was standing there impatiently, so I turned to him and said, ''If you want to put in the catheter, you can call Richard and I'm sure he'll overrule me, and that's fine. I just can't do it to her.'' Then, turning to Karly, I said, ''Maybe tomorrow I'll be able to write an order like that again, but I can't today.''

Karly walked away angrily, obviously in disagreement with my position, but came back later in the day herself in tears, telling me, ''I can't stand it! I can't stand it!'' An attending had come by and ruptured the membranes of a woman in very early labor. Karly knew the woman should have been left alone. Sobbing, she told me, ''I can't stand their always messing people up. Why can't they just be careful and leave women alone to labor as they should?''

Last week there was a woman who wanted an epidural. Once we told her that she couldn't have one because we thought her baby was in danger, she coped beautifully with the pain. It's when you know there is no relief that coping becomes possible. Maybe that's the secret to how I survive.

Sunday   *Day 119*

Virginia is a twenty-seven-year-old woman having her first baby. She and her husband wrote a four-page letter to the hospital describing what they wanted by way of a birth experience: no drugs, no episiotomy, Jack's right to be with her at all times. When the letter arrived two weeks ago, staff were really angry, and one nurse even said, ''She'd better not come in when I'm on, because I'm not about to take care of her.''

Virginia came in early this morning and her labor had been following Hill's curve until she began pushing, and then her progress slowed down. When I walked into her room she was in a panic and said to me, ''I might not make it.'' Her husband was there beside her, and also her cousin, who talked later of my calming influence on them all.

"Of course you'll make it," I told her, "but that's a common feeling." Half jokingly I added, "Anyway, you don't have much alternative."

"But it hurts so," she said between gritted teeth as a contraction ended.

"I know it does, but you know, you will survive."

"But what if I can't? What if I can't push the baby out?" I could see the panic in her eyes, the tension in her face, the white knuckles of her clenched fists as she asked the question.

"The bottom line is always the Caesarean."

She nodded with apparent relief. Her husband turned to me and snapped, "She's not ready for that yet," and I found myself angry at what seemed like insensitivity to his wife's pain.

"What about forceps?" she asked, searching for relief and an ending.

"That's been discussed, but you're not far along enough yet. It's still too soon."

The labor and her pushing went on and she delivered a beautiful baby, who breathed and cried and had perfect scores on the Apgar assessment.

I felt I had helped her have a vaginal delivery, that I had added to her strength. She was much more frightened than I had expected from her letter, which may have been motivated by fear more than strength.

I keep thinking about my upcoming meeting with Dr. Pierce. It is possible that he wants to see me about a patient I saw on rounds Friday whom I helped find an excuse for staying in the hospital. I'd found her in tears, saying that her baby was jaundiced but that she was being discharged anyway because we only allowed three days' hospitalization for an uncomplicated delivery. I suggested she develop "nausea," which would be a reason to keep her for observation another day but wouldn't require any immediate tests to be done on her. Her attending was furious with me when he found out and called Dr. Ingle, a close friend of Dr. Pierce's and also

head of the Utilization Review Committee. Over the weekend Dr. Ingle wrote a letter authorizing the woman to stay.

Monday   Day 120

Heather has an amazing ability when shopping to know exactly what she wants for whom. I envy her lack of indecision.
She picked out a beautiful robe for me, and then she and I
chose a pair of pants for her. We then pretended we couldn't
remember what we had gotten for each other. The presents
are all wrapped under the tree, ready for a Christmas of just
Heather and me.

Last night she fell asleep in my bed as I was sitting and
reading the newspaper. This morning she woke up at five as
I was having my morning coffee and reading the paper before
getting dressed. She thought it was still night and that I was
still reading the paper, so she couldn't understand why I
was getting up to get dressed.

"Mommy, do you like your job?" she asked.

"Well, there's a lot about it I don't like, but I do like taking
care of people and delivering babies."

"I wish you still worked in New Jersey because there it
didn't matter what time you got there or whether you came
in."

That wasn't quite the reality of the job, but I was happy
that she perceived it that way.

Today is my meeting with Pierce.

Later

"Michelle, your charting is terrible. You haven't learned the
basic building blocks of obstetrics, the labor curve."

Feeling his anger sweeping over me, I made a weak response—"I think that's a result of my general unhappiness
with what I see"—and then I began to weep. I had been
caught and knew I couldn't tell him the truth. The truth is
that I have been procrastinating in charting, because as soon
as a woman's labor is slightly different from the official labor

curve, she is subjected to treatment that may, in fact, make her worse. I haven't been charting properly because I have been protecting women when I could. In my confrontation with Dr. Pierce, I understood that I had to play the game their way or get out. But I also know that every time I begin to plot a woman's labor curve, I feel that I am signing a death warrant. Sometimes I imagine I'm a guard at a concentration camp, admitting unsuspecting women who, if they do not behave according to the rules, will be sent to the gas chambers.

I was able to tell Pierce how unhappy I was about the amount of intervention, to which he responded, "Someday I'll tell you how hard it was when I was a resident." I found the remark irrelevant.

"It's worse at Memorial Hospital," he told me. "I don't know if you understand, Michelle, that you're training in a hospital known all over the world for its humaneness to patients as well as its effective technology."

"That's part of what's so hard to take," I replied. "If I were at Memorial, which is known to be different, known in obstetrics for its higher rate of intervention, I could think, 'At least it's better at Doctors, which is known for its policy of natural childbirth and nonintervention.' "

"Michelle, here you're studying with the best there are. We help set the standards for the rest of the country, if not the world, and they're good standards."

Pierce was by now being kindly and sympathetic as he suggested that I try harder with my charting.

Tuesday   *Day 121*

I would love to see the data on the incidence of Caesarean sections among those low-risk women approved for the Alternative Birth Service, because I suspect it is quite high. One of the attendings says that ABS really stands for "A Beautiful Section." The general rate in this hospital is one in five of those women who have not had a section before, and one in three of all women giving birth here. I do not believe this high rate is related to babies or mothers at risk.

I remember a medical student last year who told me he would have to "hustle for sections" when he was a resident in OB-GYN. Here the residents don't have to hustle for sections; we just define a broad category of women who need them. My favorite indication is "maternal exhaustion." My friend Fran says that's when the doctor can't take any more. Last week a section was done because, according to the doctor, "She just couldn't take labor." Another chart recently read: "X-rays show room in pelvis. Will section to avoid trauma to baby."

Karen Dole challenged me at work today with, "How do you know that two hours isn't too much pushing?"

I answered, "How do you know that five minutes isn't too much?" then: "How do you know that a Caesarean is safe?"

A New York *Times* article on January 4, 1977, described the high rate (60 percent) of Caesareans in Brazil among women delivering in private clinics: " 'A substantial number of physicians in Brazil believe that the surgical delivery is the best method of childbirth—it causes no harm to the figure, it is quick, and it is a lot more profitable,' said Dr. Paolo Belfort de Aguiar, the former president of the Brazilian Federation of Gynecology and Obstetrics Associations."

The article went on to describe a woman who chose a Caesarean delivery "because 'some friends warned me' that a normal childbirth would somehow 'leave me internally deformed as far as sexual activity.' "

It is common practice after an episiotomy repair for the obstetrician to check the tightness of the woman's vagina and then announce she is "good as new."

A woman who has had a Caesarean instead of a vaginal delivery has an almost "perfect" vagina by such definitions. Never stretched by a baby's head, the vagina maintains its almost virginal state. In the Caesarean section, even the hymenal remnants, which are cut and then resewn during an episiotomy, are untouched.

No one at work thinks as I do. It's as though they have defined normal childbirth as the Caesarean section, and that vaginal delivery is appropriate only when there are special indications. I have fantasies in which women stand up in the thousands and thousands and say they are going to deliver their babies without having them cut out of their bellies.

Talking this afternoon with Nat Andrews at the School of Public Health helped me clarify why I am at the hospital and how long I ought to stay. He pointed out that getting my boards in OB-GYN wouldn't help me because I wouldn't be listened to, anyway. I told him I had given up my fantasies of rising through the ranks of the American College of Obstetrics and Gynecology and then being able to speak from a stronger position. I'd have to stay here another four years, then I'd have to practice in acceptable ways and not offend anyone in order to get my board certification. I realized that what they at the hospital define as the cure—i.e., the technology and surgery for childbirth—is what I define as the disease.

There is a camaraderie among physicians out of the mainstream, which includes public health physicians. Nat has invited Heather and me to have dinner with his family on Christmas Eve.

Thursday   *Day 123*

Heather ran a fever yesterday and complained of sore throat, headache and stiff neck. Worried about meningitis, I took her to see Catherine, my physician friend, who thought it was a strep throat. When we got home I collapsed in bed with Heather and felt sure I would never again have the strength to move. I put the TV where she could reach it and dozed on and off.

When I made the decision to stay home yesterday I didn't care if I was fired, but I felt that I was once again proving the validity of "Don't hire a woman. She'll stay home if her kid is sick." It is true, though, of me and other mothers, that we bring less to our work in terms of time and resources than people who aren't primarily responsible for children. I feel that what I am trying to do may not be possible. Louise is leaving tomorrow. Starting in ten days, I have night call again.

Later

Heather is much better today. She still has a belly ache and sore throat, but her fever is down and she's just a grumpy kid who isn't feeling well. I made it through!

Thursday morning (a week later)   Day 130

The past three days have been some of the most peaceful of my life. Heather, who slept until eleven on Christmas morning, has been in a lovely mood, giving our time together the quality it had when she was very little. I read, slept, wrote letters and puttered about the house while she played by herself and with friends. I spent several hours making tapes for friends in California and New Jersey. I hung the tape recorder around my neck and talked as I went about my day, chatting into the machine, pretending friends were here with me. When the tapes were done, I felt as though I'd been visiting.

I've been reading a fascinating book, *Woman and Nature*, by Susan Griffin, in which she describes most of our society as built around male constructs and male values. We do not recognize emotionality or intuition as basic components of our language or our truth. Her book supports my sense that at work they do not speak the same language I do. I find myself talking loudly, thinking that if I speak loud enough, they will hear me. The truth is that it is a different language altogether. For sixty hours a week now I live in a world in which I do not trust or believe in what I am doing, and where I have grave doubts about what I am inflicting on other human beings. It was so nice not to be there for three days.

On the way home

A thirty-year-old Mexican woman came into the hospital four weeks ago with a placenta previa. She was admitted for bed rest until she is closer to term, when she would be sectioned. The woman, who spoke no English, had other children at home, including a one-year-old, and she signed herself out without permission several times. The psychiatrist said she was disturbed, largely because of her determination to be home with the others. She was on John's floor, so I had no direct contact with her, but from a distance, I was never sure she understood why she was here. She was a small thin woman who was sometimes seen wandering in the hall, looking depressed, confused and alone. Today they took her in for the section. Something went wrong and there was massive hemorrhaging. Additional teams of both doctors and nurses were called in, and when I left they were taking out her uterus altogether in an attempt to stop the bleeding.

Left alone to watch L&D, I admitted the eighteen-year-old who was having her first baby. She was accompanied by her sister, who, when she saw me, asked, "Who are you, anyway?" It was like the day I met Nancy Carr and we recognized something in each other. It is like the language about which Susan Griffin writes and the unspoken signals that communicate understanding.

I answered softly to her, "I'm the resident and I'll tell you the rest later." Then I checked Janet, her sister.

The girl's cervix was almost fully dilated and the baby's head almost out. Since she was a midwife service patient, I called Susan, who was going on duty shortly, and she said she would come up. Although Janet didn't want an episiotomy, I told her I might have to do one because I was afraid the midwife's attending might show up and be critical of my not doing one. When Susan arrived I was holding the episiotomy scissors. I turned to her, and knowing that she often did episiotomies, said, "I think there might not be enough room, so I'll have to do an episiotomy." She nodded in agreement.

However, I let Janet keep her legs together between contractions and I let the drapes fall over her legs so no one else knew that the baby's head was almost out. I did perineal massage with sterile ointment on my fingers, and under the drapes was able to slowly let the perineal tissue stretch, more slowly than anyone would have allowed me to do. All the time I held the scissors, pretending that I was about to do the episiotomy. The baby was born during one of the contractions and I said, "Oops, too late for the episiotomy."

After the delivery I talked with Diana, Janet's sister from New Jersey, who wants to be a midwife, and knows one of the babies I delivered at home. Diana was happy I was there, but she'd expected me to be there, or someone like me. She had dreamed about the delivery, so she expected that it would go exactly as it did.

Although Janet had no tears I could find, I kept having the feeling that maybe she was so torn that what I thought was intact perineum must have been a tear through her rectum. They have me so brainwashed that I can't even believe my own eyes when I see an intact perineum.

I had to leave because Heather was due to be dropped off at the house after being taken skating. I drove away from the hospital, already having stayed an hour late, with mixed feelings about Janet's delivery and the tear I worried I'd missed, and about the surgery I was missing.

I arrived home to find that Maggie had had diarrhea all over the dining-room floor. I cleaned it up, then washed the floor and swept the rest of the downstairs. On my knees scrubbing, feeling angry, I thought, They think all I want to do is go home and take it easy. They don't know I go home to clean up the dog shit.

Friday   *Day 131*

I went back and checked Janet this morning, and of course she has no tears at all.

Irv Warren likes to challenge me, I think. This morning

scrubbing at the sinks before a delivery, he asked, "You don't approve of what I'm doing, do you?"

He's right. I don't. He had been screaming at the woman in the delivery room, yelling "Push! Push!" then, "You lazy female, push!" When she whimpered, "I'm trying," he yelled, "You're not trying hard enough. Now push!" and his large round face became red and his belly puffed out, making him a fearsome figure.

At the sinks I responded to his question, "Well, that's not how I would do it," and shrugged, trying not to show how strongly I felt.

He stopped scrubbing for a moment and in a patronizing way said, "Michelle, when people are in a subservient position, sometimes you just have to tell them what to do."

Implicit in obstetrics is the presumption that women having babies are subservient to their doctors. My own giving birth was no different. My due date had been November 30. Passing me in the hospital corridor on that date, Andy, my obstetrician and colleague said, "Michelle, today is your due date. Why don't you let me induce you? Aren't you tired of waiting?"

"Can't let you induce me, Andy. You'll mess up the kid's sun signs."

My being a physician made Andy nervous. Taking care of colleagues is always difficult. "If anything is going to go wrong, it will happen with you," he had told me.

Two days later, on Saturday morning, I went into labor. Making rounds that morning, I had to stop every fifteen or twenty minutes to rest until the contraction passed. I felt my body about to erupt, but I needed to keep going. For most of my life, school and then work had been the stabilizing forces and I was afraid to stop.

Eventually I lay down on my bed. Then I felt a flood of warm water seeping out of my vagina, soaking me and my bed.

I called Ellen, the friend who was going to coach me through labor. She was the only woman I knew in town who had had natural childbirth and was breast-feeding. "My membranes have ruptured," I told her.

"That's wonderful. Don't you want to go in?"

"No, I'm fine here for a while."

"I need to put Susie down for a nap, but I'll stop by for a short visit first."

Soon Ellen arrived with her girl. Susie, a lively but gentle toddler, climbed up on the bed and patted my belly as she had been doing for some months. Then she stretched out on top of me and I enjoyed the presence of the two babies together, one still inside and the other draped over my pregnant abdomen.

Ellen left and I began to think about what I knew of ruptured membranes. What if the baby's head was still high? (I knew this wasn't so, because I had checked myself.) I was still filled with "What if's?" This was me, not a patient, and I couldn't remember what was serious and what I could ignore. I was a woman having contractions, caught up in my body's process, and vulnerable.

Once in the hospital, I was placed flat in bed and told not to move except onto my side. I stared at the bare pale-green walls. Ellen arrived, and dismayed by the starkness, hung on the wall a tie she was sewing for her husband. For the rest of the afternoon and evening I lay staring at the psychedelic red-and-orange tie, holding Ellen's hand through the raised siderails of the bed.

At ten o'clock at night Andy told me I had another eight hours to go. The thought of that much time left must have further stimulated my labor because by eleven he was getting ready to take me to the delivery room. Ellen, who had been so much a part of the labor, was left at the door. She said later she understood how fathers feel being left behind.

Moved onto the table, I protested, "No, I don't want my hands strapped." But my arms were strapped to the table. My legs were put into the stirrups and suddenly I was trapped, both by the forces within my body and by the people around me.

Episiotomy? In my sixth month I had told Andy I didn't

want one. "But you have to," he had insisted. "It's for your own good. You'll get loose and that won't be very pleasurable for a man in intercourse."

"It doesn't seem to have hurt anyone for all the centuries women didn't have episiotomies. They keep having babies, so they must be having intercourse."

He said, "That's only because no man ever turns anything down."

Now, three months later, strapped to the delivery table, I told him, "I'm not going to tie your hands for this delivery. You have to do it the way you know how."

There was a lot of bustle as the table was tilted back. Andy's fingers were in my vagina and then he told me, "The kid has hair and I can see it." Reaching for the scissors, he said, "I'm going to do the episiotomy on the next contraction and then I'm going to tell you to push."

I feel my flesh being cut, creating a searing pain which at that moment didn't seem to matter.

"Push," he said, and I felt released from within me a force and direction I had been practicing for as long as I could remember. My baby flew out and suddenly there was a commotion.

"I didn't tell you to push that hard!" Andy shrieked. "Look what you've done!"

I thought, Why is this man screaming at me? I've just had a baby.

"You have a healthy girl here, but dammit, why did you have to push so hard?"

My baby was put in my arms for a moment, then whisked away. I wanted her back. I wanted to see her, hold her, celebrate her, celebrate that I had pushed her out of my body.

Andy had done the episiotomy and then, breaking an important first rule, had looked away as he put the scissors back onto the table behind him. In the second he wasn't looking, my baby had come flying out and landed in his lap. Because there was no control of the birth, the episiotomy had extended down through my rectum.

"This is going to take a lot of sewing," he said, now calmed down and somewhat apologetic.

"It's okay," I told him. I wasn't afraid of anything now. My baby was alive and crying. I just wanted it to be over. The stitches hurt as Andy sewed together the parts of my anal sphincter, my rectum, and my vagina.

There was a party in my room with Ellen, her husband and some other friends. Andy had brought champagne so we could celebrate. Then, at two in the morning, they brought my baby to me. I lay there and stared and wondered about our life together. I studied what she looked like and by morning she looked like what my baby should look like.

Saturday   *Day 132*

I spent a wonderful day out in the country meeting with some women on a project that will look at the effects of culture on biology, instead of biology on culture. I think how many women are having Caesarean sections and how their children will think that is the way babies are born. The culture will have changed.

The weather was beautiful, giving me a wonderful sense of freedom as we drove south along the lake.

Murray Avery, a young obstetrician interested in both natural childbirth and monitors, spoke to me yesterday about a study he wants to do on anxiety in labor. I tried to explain that we do not have the right language for the feelings that may be affecting labor. All his study can show is the relationship of the course of labor to a defined scale of "one to ten" of levels of anxiety. This may all be irrelevant to what we are actually experiencing in labor. He wants to quantify our experience.

Sunday   *Day 133*

"My wife is having contractions and now she wants to push." A husband was on the phone to the OB unit, and I said to bring her in right away, now.

They arrived about fifteen minutes later. Vilma, black, twenty-eight, was having her second baby, her husband was with her. They were both doing breathing exercises well and obviously in control. Vilma's cervix was eight centimeters dilated, and I sensed she was going to deliver quickly. I called the midwife who was covering, and also the attending who backs up the midwives.

Rachel, the nurse watching Vilma, asked me to check her again quickly because she thought the baby was coming soon. This time Vilma was fully dilated and her bag of waters, the membranes, were still intact. As Vilma pushed, the bag of waters would bulge out and actually stretch the perineum.

"What's that?" Rachel asked with an expression of dismay.

"Those are the membranes stretching the perineum."

"I've never seen a delivery where the membranes haven't been ruptured. It looks so strange." Rachel had been there two years.

"The membranes and the water help stretch the perineum before the baby's head gets there and the fluid helps protect the baby."

Vilma delivered slowly, pushing gently, with no episiotomy. The baby cried and then quickly settled down in her mother's arms.

The attending arrived right after the baby was born, and the midwife half an hour later.

Monday   *Day 134*

This last day on OB was fourteen hours long, spent primarily with Jackie, my chief, and Hilda Cameron, the attending for the majority of women in labor throughout the day. Jackie, Hilda and I spent much of this fourteen-hour day talking.

During the day Esther, a seventeen-year-old Puerto Rican, tall and massively obese, arrived on the floor. She said, "I'm here to have my baby today. My baby was due last week and I want it now."

She'd had no recent prenatal care, and didn't plan to return after today. She was adamant that she would have her baby today and that we were to make it happen. After asking her some questions, I tried to examine her, but she was terrified and would not let me touch her. I said I had to examine her, and the nurse backed me up. When Esther let herself be uncovered, I could see huge warts covering her labia, so it was difficult even to find her vaginal opening. As I tried to insert the speculum she pulled her whole body away from me, up toward the head of the bed. When I tried to reach her, she pulled farther away, her eyes bulging. She looked like a cornered caged animal, and I stopped.

I called Jackie, who I knew would want to examine her anyway, so my exam would have been superfluous. I also expected Jackie to do better than I because people, like veins, sometimes know who has more authority and respond differently.

When Jackie tried to examine the girl, however, she had no more success. Esther, still terrified, pulled back, drew her legs together, and would not let herself be touched. Jackie was obviously getting angry, and after two tries, ripped off her gloves and left the room. Once outside, she turned to me and to the nurse and said, "Women like that prove that no woman can be raped unless she wants to."

Realizing how shocked the nurse and I were, she qualified that by saying, "Well, maybe with a gun or a knife . . ." Jackie calls herself a feminist. She is known as a feminist physician. Women will come to her because they believe she is different from men.

I wanted especially to do well with Hilda today, since she was the attending with me on my first day on OB. Today I delivered a patient of hers with an episiotomy, then did the repair as Hilda wanted it. She complimented me on my skills and then went on to tease me about my trouble doing an episiotomy the first day.

Hilda shared with me some of her life, saying she found it easier to talk with women who had children. When she has two hours free, she runs home to do things no one else will do. She straightens up her house because her sitter will quit if the house is too messy and because "I have to keep my house neat or I'll lose my husband."

Jackie joined us for a while and Hilda asked if Jackie has children.

"No, but I probably will. My husband wants them."

"Well," Hilda said in a resigned way, "most women have children for their husbands, anyway."

Pity for them came over me. I always wanted a child more than I wanted a husband. I imagine having children for someone else must be terrible, and not any fun.

I have finally mastered running the pH analyzer as well as calibrating it for accuracy, something I've been working on for a while in spite of Richard's insistence that I didn't need to know how, since he could run all the samples.

Hilda had a woman in labor today who had a questionable monitor tracing, so she tried to get a pH sample. The woman was in heavy labor and kept moving onto her side, trying to find a more comfortable position, but Hilda had to keep moving her onto her back. Using the disposable pH kit, Hilda took the long tube, shaped like a megaphone and about eight inches long, and inserted the narrower end into the woman's vagina. She tried to get it through the slightly dilated cervix, which was especially difficult because the woman moved a lot whenever she had a contraction.

Hilda was unable twice to get the tube set right on the baby's head. After her second attempt she handed the tube to me while she got ready to do it for a third time. When Jackie happened to walk into the room, Hilda turned to her and asked if she would try. As Jackie opened a new kit and got ready to try, she said to me, "Michelle, the reason you had so much trouble getting a sample . . . ," thinking because I was holding the tube, I was the one that had failed. Hilda did not set her straight.

It wasn't until the day was over that I realized it had been a day spent mostly with women doctors, and yet it had been no different from other days at the hospital.

Last year, teaching at the medical school, I was on a panel about women's health. I was asked by an angry obstetrician, "Are you trying to say that OB-GYN should only be practiced by women?"

"No, I'm not saying that," I responded, much to his surprise, "because the women in the field are not unlike the men. The problem is with some of the basic practices and basic assumptions about women that are an integral part of the profession. The same system, with women replacing the men, would not change it significantly."

Although I said those words, I had not been without some hope that it really would be different if the doctors were women.

Chapter Ten

Beep, beep. My pager calls me, catches me, ties me like a long umbilical cord to the hospital switchboard and anyone who calls. I'm free, though, of L&D, of Richard as my chief, of asking permission to leave the floor. I can even fantasize turning off my beeper and being unreachable, saying later, "There must have been something wrong with my beeper."

Returning to GYN also gives me back the on-call room, a converted patient room with two beds, a desk, some lockers, and a closet for coats. It is a room only for women, so occasionally there is even a spirit of friendliness in there. It is a room with a telephone, where I can call home, make contact with the rest of my life.

Jackie is my chief; Thomas, someone I don't know very well, is the third-year resident; Karen Dole and I share the second-year position; and John is the first-year resident. Barbara and Richard are only peripherally part of the team, as they are on the abortion and outpatient service. However, since both of them refuse to do abortions, the rest of us do the procedures on their patients, while they do the work-ups and follow-up care.

Jackie and I were in the OR from eight to noon, doing one D&C, which probably wasn't necessary, and two abortions, which could have been done elsewhere more cheaply and with less depersonalization. The OR costs $350 an hour—for the room alone. That's $1,400 for the three procedures this morning.

Back on the GYN floor at one, I began the work-ups for the afternoon. The medical history includes the question of occupation, so I asked Mrs. Ack, "Are you employed outside the home?"

"No. I have a college education—do you have any suggestions?"

Mrs. Ack was the wife of a VIP, admitted for a procedure she didn't need. We had established an instant rapport, which made this work-up pleasurable.

"I don't have any special ideas. Are you looking for something?" I said as I went about examining her.

"I've spent twenty-five years as a housewife and mother—and that counts for nothing on my résumé," she responded. Then, after some moments of silence, she added, "I've done twenty-five years of volunteer work, but it counts for nothing because I wasn't paid."

There was a knock on the door and then Richard's voice saying he needed the room. Feeling free of his power over me, I asked, "Need a pelvic, dear?"

"Just don't take too long, Michelle, I need the room."

I turned to Mrs. Ack and said, "He used to be my chief and I had to listen to him, but he isn't anymore."

We went on talking about women and work. There was the closeness between us that unites all women. In health care the abuses of women cut across all classes, with unneeded surgery for the "privileged" and neglect for the underprivileged.

Later as I passed the treatment room I could see John examining a woman. The curtain had been only partly pulled across the room, so although she was covered with a sheet, through the window I could see John's head and face, and the sheet over the woman's knees. It was a framed and eerie picture—a vain and handsome man looking into the bottom half of a woman, who had no identity.

Wednesday *Day 136*

Heather says her stomach hurts when she sits at her desk. She is far behind the others in her class, but when I speak with her about repeating first grade she cries and says she wants to go on with her friends. I know she will survive but I keep thinking about how she's had to sacrifice for my being in this program.

Fran and Laurie seem to think I made some errors in hiring baby-sitters the last few times, so they are going to advertise and screen applicants. They seem to believe there is a right person to hire. In the meantime they are once again taking turns staying at the house to see Heather off in the morning, and they are filling in for the four hours a week between sitters.

Later

Jackie seems amazed at how easily we get along. She keeps expecting me to give her trouble, but I have been totally accepting of her decisions and of her power to make them. Yesterday I saw the OR schedule and asked Jackie if I could scrub on a hysterectomy with Dr. MacDougal, who gave me a lot of surgery on OB. "But Thomas has higher rank than you do, Michelle, so I have to give him first choice." She has apparently decided to give me the case, though, leaving me wondering what price I shall have to pay for that favor.

Thursday *Day 137*

"A twelve-week-size uterus is about the size of a grapefruit," I was telling Caroline, the medical student also scrubbed in on the hysterectomy with Dr. MacDougal. He was teaching me as we did the hysterectomy, and I was passing on what I knew to the medical student. This woman had a fibroid tumor which had enlarged her uterus to the size of a twelve-week pregnancy. The three of us were busily working at tying off vessels, probing, chatting, when Dr. Mac-

Dougal, holding one ovary gently in his hand, showed us a small cyst on the surface and said, "I just might take it out. She doesn't need two."

Suddenly worried that this woman's ovary was being so easily discarded, I tried an oblique way to argue for its being left in place. "Dr. MacDougal, I've heard of women having hormonal problems after a hysterectomy even when both ovaries are left in. What causes that?"

"I don't really know, Michelle, but it happens. I personally think that even if we are careful there is still a cutting off of some of the blood supply to the ovaries when we take out the uterus. They just don't always work as well as before."

Glancing at Caroline, hoping she understood what I was trying to do, I said to MacDougal, "But if it's possible that this surgery will hurt her ovary, then if we take one out, she is more vulnerable to any damage done to the one left in."

Just then Johnson, the fertility expert, walked in and said, "Mac?"

"Yeah," Dr. MacDougal answered. "Hi there. What's up?"

"I was just wondering if you were planning to take out any ovaries this morning. I need some for culture."

"Well, I was thinking about it. Let me think about it some more," he said and turned to me. "You know they don't work as well after hysterectomy."

"Yes, but if you take the one with the cyst, she might end up with none working."

"Maybe you're right."

"She's only thirty-two, and I think she still wants them," I added.

Johnson shrugged and said, "I don't want to push you. I was just asking," and left.

Later Caroline and I overheard Johnson talking with Enders out in the hall. "I see you have a hysterectomy later today. Are you taking out the ovaries on her?"

"Well, I hadn't made up my mind yet, John. Why?"

"I'm looking for ovaries. I need some."

"Well, I guess I could." Enders paused as though to say more.

"Don't do it for my sake," Johnson interjected, but he had his arm on Enders' shoulder, their closeness making evident the danger to Enders' patient's ovaries.

As Caroline and I walked away, I said to her, "They sure don't do that with testicles."

Yesterday I admitted a woman as an infertility case, but when I discovered it was her husband who was sterile, I found myself reluctant to put on the chart a description of his infertility. I suddenly realized the sexism of my own attitude. We label women infertile all the time, yet even I find myself reluctant to so label a man for fear of what it will do to him and for fear of how others will respond to him. We protect testicles and take out ovaries.

Later

Mel Diamond, a physician who attends homebirths in Everytown, called me three weeks ago and said, "I've heard you are having trouble at the hospital. I'd like to help if I can."

We arranged to meet at my house tonight, and then I thanked him for his offer. I had called Mel last year to offer my support when I heard he was attending home births and I knew that he was now trying to work out an agreement with Pierce for backup care of home-birth patients who might need hospitalization.

Within minutes after he arrived tonight, he said with surprise, "Oh! I thought your problems were personal. What you're telling me is that things are bad at the hospital."

"Mel, you ought to know. Look what happened to the two women you brought in."

Shortly before I left OB, Mel's partner had brought in a woman with a breech baby for vaginal delivery. She was sent for x-rays to check the exact position of the baby, but by the time she came back, she had almost delivered. As she was being taken into the delivery room someone glanced at the x-ray and said that the head was at the wrong angle for a vaginal delivery, that it was deflexed, in a poor position. The films, however, were never carefully examined. Because the baby was almost out, the woman was rushed to the section table. The anesthesiologist, failing to get the spinal needle in place, tried to give the woman general anesthesia. She began to scream for them to stop because she didn't want it. She was held down and put to sleep. The baby, delivered by section, was tiny, had congenital abnormalities incompatible with life, and died shortly after birth. The abnormalities were evident on the x-rays that hadn't been examined.

The next day I argued with a nurse about the delivery. "You know, we had no right to put her under if she was refusing anesthesia."

"But she had to have the operation for the sake of the baby," the nurse argued.

"But that's her decision. It's her body being cut into."

"No! She has no right to make that decision, and even if she refused a section, we had the right to operate." The nurse glared angrily at me, giving me the sense I had just been classified among child murderers because I thought a woman had the right to decide if her belly was going to be cut open.

Mel knew the story but had never heard it from this perspective. Silent for a momemt, he said, "It's as though we only concentrate on the baby and not on the mother at all. I wonder why that is." I didn't know how to answer that question for him.

As we talked more about breech babies Mel mentioned the 20 percent chance of spinal injury if the head is deflexed.

"Mel, I think everyone is having a deflexed head these days. They are either very deflexed, a little deflexed or minimally deflexed. But, somehow, I doubt that suddenly all the heads on babies have changed."

Mel looked thoughtfully at me, so I went on, "You practiced in rural Canada for years and delivered a lot of breeches. How many spinal injuries did you see?"

He shook his head and said, "None." Then he added, "But you know, Michelle, I feel good about the OBs who've said they are willing to back me up and take care of my emergencies. It's not altogether bad there. They're trying to make progress.''

"Well, I see it from the inside. What you get from that group is not support, but a lack of concern about who does what with their patients.''

Friday   Day 138

It was beautiful to be able to take Heather to school in the morning and to meet her at three when she got out. I brought Maggie with me to meet her and to walk home with us. Heather, in her clogs, ran across the hill with Maggie barking and running. I love to see them together. Heather's hair is the color of Maggie's Sheltie coat. When they lie next to each other, their hair is almost indistinguishable. Heather teases me about the time they were both on my bed and I was saying "Nice Maggie" as I stroked what I thought was the dog's hair.

It's four o'clock now and I'm heading into work for the next seventeen hours, dreading how I will feel at the end of that time. It's like taking Ipecac to make you throw up and knowing how miserable you're going to be when it takes effect. It's like walking out in the cold without a jacket and knowing you're going to be freezing. It's doing violence to myself and I don't know how long I can do that.

Tuesday   Day 142

One of the applicants for the job of baby-sitter sounded so wonderful on the phone that Fran and Laurie wanted me to see her right away. Last night she came to the house and told us her last job was as a sex-therapy surrogate, which she finally decided was prostitution. She is applying for Social Security Disability because she is chronically ill. She cannot tolerate either heat or stress. In the hour she was with us she never said hello or anything else to Heather.

This morning I woke to a flooded basement, so I went out and chopped a trench to let the water run off from the down-

spout, which was sending it into the cellar. Last fall I tried
several times to get someone out to fix the gutters because I
knew this would happen eventually.

On the way home

Jackie and I were at the sinks scrubbing before our first case
when she said, "Oh, this is Tuesday, the day you are off in
the afternoon."

"No, don't you remember? I gave up my afternoon time
off to be able to leave at five-thirty instead of six."

"How long is this going to last?" she asked in a sulky
way.

"I don't know. Yesterday we interviewed someone terrible. I'm trying the best I can."

Jackie scrubbed the brush against her hand harder and
harder, leaving red streaks from the bristles. I could see and
feel her anger. Pausing in her scrubbing, she glared at me
and said, "You don't realize how psychologically devastating
it is when you leave at five-thirty."

"There's not much I can do about that," I said. "After
four months it seems that whatever I do is psychologically
devastating. I'm trying to respond to my own sense of fair-
ness. I've given up trying to please you."

We both noticed the anesthesiologist waving frantically
because the patient was already asleep on the table. We went
into the operating room, and with discussion restricted to
technical detail only, did an abortion. Once the case was
over, we went out and talked some more.

"I've been surprised at how little responsibility you take,
Michelle. It really surprises me."

"What are you talking about?"

"You should be doing pelvic exams in the holding area to
see if abortion patients are having the right procedure."

"Isn't that a bit late, Jackie? Isn't that why Barbara and
Richard see them and schedule them? If they can't check
them accurately, then they are the problem." I thought about
what the holding area was like, one large room full of stretch-

ers with curtains between them which often didn't even close all the way. It didn't seem the right time to be asking someone why or when or how they got pregnant and then checking to see how large the uterus is.

"I just think you should be more interested and more involved." I felt like a naughty child being scolded. "You should have more of a personal sense of responsibility."

She was touching on the core of my compromise in being here. "Being personally responsible, though, implies some influence over what will be done. I have come to accept that I will learn procedures, but I have little say in what happens to any patient."

"But you have to be responsible for what you do," she told me in a strident voice.

Anger and tears which she may not have noticed welled up, and with a trembling voice I told her, "I can't accept responsibility for anything I've done in the past three months of obstetrics. I did what I was told to do. How can I feel personally responsible when my opinion is meaningless?"

I feel terrible about what I said, for I really know that I am personally responsible and it is a denial of that truth which allows me to be here. Deep down I know I am responsible for my actions, even when under orders.

Jackie and I ended our discussion with her saying, "It must be terrible to be doing things for which you wouldn't want to feel responsible."

A terrible sore has appeared on my wrist, a long stinging straight line, as though I had been burned. It is red and oozes fluid. Its presence on my body is so strange. I've no memory of how I got it. It seems to have come from inside, where the pain of this job resides.

Wednesday   *Day 143*

The anterior-posterior (A-P) repair is basically a tightening of the upper and lower portions of the vagina. It gives more support to the bladder and urethra as well as to the rectum.

At the same time, it makes the vaginal opening smaller. Dr. Core, Thomas and I did a hysterectomy and then A-P repair on a woman who was having this procedure done partly because her husband was impotent. The husband's psychiatrist had called Dr. Core to suggest to her that the woman's loose vagina was contributing to her husband's impotence and the procedure might help him. We were standing, all three of us, squeezed between the woman's stirruped legs, measuring the opening of her vagina, wondering how tight to make it, when I said jokingly, "Maybe her husband should have been told his penis was too small, not that her vagina was too loose."

Everyone was laughing as we continued taking turns putting two fingers into the woman's vagina, trying to guess the right size, when I suggested, "I think the husband ought to have been measured, then we could get a dildo of the right size and tighten the vagina around the dildo to make it the correct size." They were all enjoying my humor, oblivious of my rage at this woman's vagina being fashioned to fit her impotent husband.

This morning at Grand Rounds, Cassie Connor gave an eloquent and moving talk on pain control and the psychological approaches to cancer patients. The trouble is that she never does any of the things she spoke of or recommended; instead she leaves us to cover for the patients from whom she withdraws when they are in pain and dying.

Thursday   Day 144

I received a call last night from the chairman of the department of family medicine at a medical school, offering me the directorship of a new residency program. I told him I was planning to stay on here and get more training.

Bill, one of the first-year residents, has left the program, although no one seems sure why.

Everyone is in an uproar and worried about how to cover the OB service with one person less. There is a possibility I might be moved to night OB. At a residents meeting today everyone was fighting with everyone else over who had more work to do. The chief residents, who used to tell us how terrible the first years were, complained that the residents now have it too easy.

Friday   Day 145

The system in which I am functioning now has so many stress points, I worry about something going wrong.

I'm not sure if I can make it here but I will be very depressed if I have to quit. Maybe I never should have tried, but now that I am here, I do not want to leave. Certainly, without help I can't go on. This evening Fran and Laurie are coming with Bea, a candidate for the job. I need someone badly.

Dr. Pierce has hired a new resident to start in two weeks, so that crisis in the program is over.

The conization of the cervix is an operation in which the inside of the cervix is cut out, similar to the way an apple is cored in the center, but with a wider amount being cut off the outside than the inside. It is a bloody, deforming procedure which I learned to do today. It is done to remove areas of cancerous tissue or other abnormal cells.

During laparoscopy today, I found myself staring at the tubes coming out of the woman's belly and vagina, wondering if the women would be so willing to have the surgery if they knew what was being done to them. No one should be asleep for surgery.

Saturday   Day 146

Bea came to dinner Friday night. She is a slight, pale woman in her late twenties, who is trying to decide what to do with her life. She was intrigued by Fran's ad, which described the job in my house in quite glorious terms. In addition we discovered that she has worked in women's health clinics and has friends in common with Fran. We all liked her. She was

friendly and spoke with Heather, who still looks so easily t
the next person and asks, "Are you going to be my nex
baby-sitter?"

I'm missing the fun of mothering, but I see this time a
temporary. I find myself thinking about having another chil
and raising my children within a community of women. Hov
relationships with men and getting pregnant fit into that pla
is unknown, but I feel a commonality with other women i
terms of child raising that doesn't exist for me in relationship
with men.

Sunday   *Day 14*

Two weeks have passed—one twenty-fifth of what is ahea
this year—since I began marking off days on my year-at-a
glance calendar.

The road is icy and treacherous as I drive in for anothe
thirty-six-hour shift. Last night, speaking to some pre-me
students at a dinner, I realized that when I walk into th
hospital, there is no one with whom I can talk.

School is closed tomorrow, leaving me in need of two ful
days of child care, so Heather is staying at Catherine's unti
tomorrow night.

Monday   *Day 14*

Yesterday morning Larry Morris let me do most of a rup
tured ovarian cyst after we did the laparoscopy and saw tha
the woman was bleeding internally. Larry encourages m
aggressiveness in doing what I can in surgery. He told me
story of when he was a resident and scrubbed with Bob Carte
on a section. Bob wasn't letting Larry do enough, so Larr
"accidentally" nicked one of Bob's gloves, which force
Bob to step out to change gloves while Larry delivered th
baby. In doing the surgery, I was especially careful not t
jeopardize the patient because of my inexperience, so I onl
did what I was certain I could manage.

Standing over the OR table with Larry, I realized that th

next day we were scheduled to be back together in the OR doing another ovarian cyst, but in the interim he would go home for the day and night, while I had to go on working during all that time.

In the night I slept short periods of about an hour each, between trips to the ER to see women with problems often weeks old that suddenly seemed urgent. I remember once waking up after I had come back to the on-call room, suddenly thinking I had to go to the ER. I jumped out of bed, then remembered I had just been there, then couldn't remember if I had. I decided to go back to sleep, and that if it had been the ER calling, they'd call again.

People who come to the emergency room often have problems which have been present for days or weeks. On Sunday nights this is especially true when we see people who are lonely after a weekend alone, or unable to face the new week, or scared because they must be better by Monday morning. Sunday night is a crisis time in many people's lives, and in crisis, one's body becomes a reason to seek help, company, reassurance.

Today I was back in the OR with Larry, operating on another ovarian cyst. He said repeatedly, ''Michelle, Dr. Pierce would be proud of how well you are doing, even if the rest of the surgery doesn't go well.'' I had been working carefully and diligently, trying to remove the cysts without their breaking. ''You have excellent hands,'' he said, making me feel quite victorious. If I got fired today, I had proven I could do surgery. This operation was especially pleasurable because it was delicate work, no one was telling me to hurry, and Larry obviously respected my work. I told Jackie at sign-out, ''I fought to keep every millimeter of her good ovarian tissue.''

Tuesday morning   *Day 149*

An incredibly wonderful back rub by Catherine put me to sleep in front of her fireplace. Catherine has magic in her hands. They seem to exist not as physical objects but as a great warmth spreading over my back and neck. I slept until Heather woke me with "Are you awake, Mama?" It was not until ten that we got home and I finally settled Heather down in my bed.

I called Fran to ask about Bea's references, and then called Bea to say I wanted to hire her. Bea said she was looking forward to being Heather's "nanny." She said that they might have difficulties along the way but that Heather wasn't an angry child. I wasn't sure what she meant, but I thought she was making reference to what she thought of the children of working mothers. I can't say I'm convinced Bea is the "right person," but she has good references and I desperately need help: Fran and Laurie will leave for the East Coast; Gail will be away at school; and in two weeks I begin a long stretch of night call.

Heather had a beautiful time at Catherine's, so she was in good shape when I brought her home last night. It's all gone so well, and although I'm still tired and short of sleep, I feel optimistic.

Later

Gail tried to reach me all morning to say Heather was home sick, but the OR secretary wasn't letting the calls through. Heather sounded tired and down when I finally talked with her at two, but it's probably nothing more than her sore throat.

Larry and I again stood facing each other across the operating table on which a woman lay with a huge ovarian cyst, and I said to him, "Larry, we can't keep meeting this way." John had been scrubbed with him, but had suddenly developed a severe stomach ache and had to step out, so I was called in to replace him. When I arrived, the cyst had been brought out of the abdominal cavity and Larry was planning to clamp it and cut it off when I suggested that he let me do it the way I had done the last two: dissecting it out instead of cutting it off because I could then preserve more of the ovarian tissue. Larry agreed, allowing me to do the surgery with little bleeding and without breaking the cyst or removing any extra tissue. "Michelle, your hands are so good, why don't you go into infertility surgery?" was his comment today.

George Guin let me do a cone biopsy today, which surprised me because I haven't done a lot with him. There is a strange ritual dance taking place as it is being decided who will do a case, involving a balance between aggressive and nonaggressive behavior. The patient today had her legs up in stirrups, with both George and me standing between them when the nurse asked, "Will you be sitting or standing?" George said, "Yes, one of us will be sitting." The nurse lowered the table and put a stool there between the woman's legs but neither of us sat on it. I wouldn't presume he would let me do the case, yet neither did I move out of the way so he could sit down. We started to do the surgery with both of us leaning over and bending, since the patient had already been lowered. Finally he said to me, "Michelle, why don't you sit down?"—letting me know the case was mine.

Wednesday   *Day 150*

Dr. MacDougal and I were scrubbed on a mini-lap when he asked, "Have you done any?"

"No," I answered, knowing I probably could have bluffed through.

"I'll do this one, and you can do the next," he told me. Part way through, however, it was clear I knew what I was doing, so he let me take over. There is a subtleness to the exchange that implies, "Let me do this now. I know what I am doing."

Standing at the table doing the tubal ligation, I could see into the next operating room where I knew Dr. Johnson was doing a tubal re-anastamosis, or retying of tubes. I thought, It's like a supermarket. In one room a woman is having her tubes tied, and in the other a woman is having them sewn back together again. It could be an auto-body shop.

Thursday *Day 151*

Today, doing abortions, scraping out the insides of women's uteri, it became clear that women and fetuses are victims in our society, pitted against one another, without options.

Doug Weston, who supervises the abortion service, is an aggressive young macho attending. As I was scrubbing the patient he told me to change the way I held the sponge stick. I asked, "What's the difference?" knowing I was being rebellious, but that there really is no difference. Then as I was taking the instruments out of the sterilizer, a job I was doing because we were short of nurses, I tried to put the instruments in the order in which I would be using them. Doug said, "Stop what you are doing. You must do it the way I tell you. Otherwise we have role reversal here."

I saw another side of Doug in the OR one day. He was doing an abortion and said, "Some people have accused me of being a baby-killer, but I'm doing what I think is right."

Tuesday *Day 156*

Heather and I spent three beautiful days on High Island resting, reading, walking, playing. We were due back Sunday but storms closed the boatline, so we had to stay another night and day until the winds died down enough for the ferry to run. I miss being close to the ocean, which makes time at the lake even more special. Being near the water was soothing, leaving me feeling at one with the world.

The break from the hospital and the pressures of home made me wonder why I was doing this to myself. Standing on the sand, Heather searching and finding pebbles to put in a bag, I found myself questioning, "Why am I working as I am?" . . . "Why am I cutting up the bodies of women?" . . . "Why am I working with people whose values I detest, whose choices I do not respect?" Heather's voice saying, "Look at this shell, Mama," diverted me periodically from those thoughts. I didn't want to think that way, yet why was I going back? What was I going to do in the end? Did I really want what I had been fighting so hard to hold on to for the past five months?

We arrived home last night to find Bea moved in and settled before the fire. Seeing her gave me a sense of peace and calm; I was rested and felt a strong hope that she would be the relief I needed. This is the stretch of time for which we all knew I would need help. As I left for work this morning I felt that the pieces were all in order.

Later

"Heather is an unmanageable and uncontrolled child!" Bea was on the phone yelling at me, having managed to get a call through to me in the OR.

My sense of well-being shattered, I wanted instantly to be home. "What happened?" I asked, trying to be calm, waiting for the story, frightened by the anger in Bea's voice.

"Heather came home at one and refused to eat the lunch I fixed her. She said she was going to her room to watch TV. I said she couldn't, so she started to cry and scream."

"Where is she now? Let me speak to her." I didn't understand.

"Heather, what happened?" I asked from a small desk in the supply area of the OR. Around me moved figures in green, masked and gowned, getting bottles off racks, hooking up tubing, searching for labels on sterilized instruments.

"Mama," Heather was crying. "I just wanted to go to my room to watch TV and Bea blocked my door and wouldn't let me in." I wasn't used to hearing Heather crying this way. "And also, Mama, Lori stepped on my eye as I was leaving school and my eye hurts too. I just wanted to go to my room. Mama, I don't want to stay with her."

Heather had never said that before. I felt suddenly helpless and pained, for Heather and for myself. I wanted to be able to go home and make it all better, put a Band-Aid on her soul, her day, her eye. In panic I told her she could come and stay with me in the hospital Thursday night.

Bea was by now calmed down. We agreed to talk about it in the evening when I got home.

Back at the OR sinks, scrubbing for the next case with Dr Warren, I felt separated from work in a way I hadn't ten minutes before. I couldn't tell him of the crisis. Child-care issues stayed at home. Even more, though—nothing in his experience would give him empathy with what I was experiencing.

I was relieved to be back in the OR, scrubbed and ready to work, but I couldn't rid myself of anxiety about Bea's call. Was it true? Is Heather unmanageable? Has all this working and all these baby-sitters hurt her? Am I a bad mother? Will she hate me for having worked when she gets older? Thoughts usually easily dispensed with were coming through; my protection against them was shattered. I needed it to be okay at home and with Heather, so I could feel okay about myself.

I watched Irv Warren scrubbing the woman about to have an abortion and about to have her tubes tied. I wondered what he knows of women's lives.

Because this woman is a private patient, Irv does the procedure. He has a system of dilating the cervix: he puts the smallest dilator into the woman's vagina; I hand him the next largest size with my left hand, and with my right hand I remove the dilator which is still in the cervix. As I become absorbed in the rhythm of what we are doing, the phone call fades.

Wednesday   *Day 157*

Bea was apologetic. "Even as I blocked the door and wouldn't let Heather into her room, I thought to myself, Why am I doing this? She looks perfectly healthy and fine." She said she couldn't stop herself from carrying on that way.

As we all sat around talking about the afternoon, Heather added, "What Bea doesn't understand is that when I get home from school in the afternoon I'm tired and I need to go to my room to watch TV." Heather's eye is red but not seriously hurt. Apparently she fell going out the door, and then another child tripped and stepped on her eye.

Bea was also upset about the "popsicles" Heather ate— seven of them—but each was two ounces of orange juice I had frozen in Tupperware containers. So Heather had about fourteen ounces of orange juice, which, if consumed as juice, would have brought praise.

Perhaps all will be well, and today was just a difficult beginning.

Later

This morning at Grand Rounds, the woman whose Caesarean turned into a hysterectomy was discussed. She is still in the hospital, with an infection she contracted after the surgery. A small woman to start, she has lost fifty pounds and remains in unstable condition. She ignores her baby in the nursery, creating concern as to what she will do at discharge, assuming she survives. I heard a rumor that when they went in, they discovered that she might not have needed the section anyway.

Thursday   Day 158

Bea was up this morning at five, saying she had been sick to her stomach all night, and now had a severe headache. She wanted to take something strong for it, but I told her I only had aspirin, since I won't give anything stronger to someone I don't know well and for whom I am not serving as a physician. As I was leaving I noticed it was pouring outside. I asked Bea if she could walk Heather around the corner to school rather than sending her out the back over the slippery hill. She agreed.

I drove to work congratulating myself: "It's so wonderful that I have this house near the school. Otherwise I'd have to be worrying about Heather's being able to get to school in this weather." When I called home at four, Bea said, "I kept Heather home because of the weather. I took the authority to make the decision myself.'' Although I said nothing to her, I was furious that she hadn't called, that she first had agreed to walk Heather and then had felt free to do what she wanted. I had been so sure I had worked out all the problems at home, and now I had lost control over my life and Heather's again. I needed someone who would listen. I needed relief, and instead I was getting bad surprises. And I was trapped in the hospital, where I still had twenty-two hours to go before I left.

The ER called me at midnight to see a woman who was bleeding. I came down and met Barbara, a black woman in her mid-twenties who was worried but still had a sense of calm about her. I liked her instantly, and felt her trust.

After taking a brief history, I examined her and found that her cervix was still closed, so her pregnancy might continue.

''Am I having a miscarriage?'' she asked.

''It's still too early to tell. You might, or it might just be first-trimester bleeding. As long as your cervix hasn't opened, and you aren't having severe cramping, you may be okay.''

''Is there anything you can do?'' she asked, leaving me to answer what is hardest to say: ''No. At this stage, if it's a miscarriage, you'll know soon. You'll have cramps and the bleeding will get worse.'' I felt so helpless, wishing I could meet her expectations and mine of what a doctor can do.

Before she left we had an exchange over her socks, which were identical to mine, the ones I'd finally found to make my feet more comfortable.

Saturday   Day 160

I'm on for another twenty-four hours. My parents will be arriving this afternoon to relieve Bea for the rest of the weekend.

The problem with Bea is complicated by her having been chosen by Fran and Laurie, leaving me worried that they will be angry with me if she doesn't work out. The thought of the loss of their support makes it even more difficult to sort out what is happening at home.

Yesterday afternoon, able to leave work early, I went home to sleep, telling Bea that Heather could wake me to say hello when she got home. Heather came in at three, but I went back to sleep immediately. Then she returned to wake me again.

"Mommy, can I make a cake for Gramma Emmy?"

"Sure, Heather, there's a mix in the kitchen cabinet."

"I know, but Bea said I had to come up and ask you if we could use it."

Bea feels free to keep Heather home for the day without consulting me, but can't use a cake mix without waking me after I've been up for two days. She seems, however, to be getting along with Heather, so I shouldn't complain. I'm not about to fire her, anyway. I can't take another change now.

Last night, instead of going back to sleep after dinner, I packed Heather up and went to Catherine's for a feminist meeting. Forever torn between my need for sleep vs. my need for contact with the outside world, I live on the edge of exhaustion.

Sunday   *Day 161*

Jackie and I went through our old routine today. She said I'm not working hard enough and that having part-timers is a drag. I told her I'm working more than I'd committed myself to, and that she has two people doing two-thirds time, which came to more than one full-timer.

Last night Barbara, the woman I saw Thursday night, returned. Her cervix had now opened, so spontaneous abortion was inevitable. When I examined her in the ER, I could see and feel the sac beginning to come through the dilated cervix.

With a sense of competence and purpose, I took Barbara to the OR for a D&C, which would now be done to prevent the hemorrhage which often is part of a miscarriage. The attending didn't even scrub in, but stayed in the room for the procedure and then left.

I painted Barbara with scrub solution in a style that was

careful, thorough and gentle. I removed what was left of the products of conception, then gently scraped the uterus, without the usual violence. It was good to care about a patient and to feel that I could actually do something to help her.

Madeline is the new resident who replaced Bill ten days ago. I had avoided meeting her at first, afraid her start would be more difficult if she seemed to have been "contaminated" by me. Shortly after Karen started in the residency several months ago, she had said, "We shouldn't be seen talking to each other," and went off alone to a meeting to which we were both going. She spoke with me a lot in private, since I taught her how to run the unit, but she didn't want to be seen with me, even though we were friends and spent hours talking about house-decorating and children.

I met Madeline this evening, and agreed to come up to L&D to talk with her. She had many questions about the program which she was anxious to ask another woman.

I got to bed about one, but at two was awakened by a call from a nurse on L&D asking me to come up and help. The woman I was to check was having her first baby and was almost fully dilated when she arrived. I stayed for a while, thinking I might even stay with her for the delivery, but once the woman was fully dilated, the nurse began screaming at her to push, push, push, creating an atmosphere of hysteria. Feeling birth had once again been destroyed, I left.

I don't believe there is a second stage of labor. Labor is continuous. The baby moves down the birth canal at various rates depending on where it is and what the forces are propelling it. I can't help Madeline be a resident, because I no longer believe in the second stage of labor, so I can't teach her how to treat the "abnormalities," as they are defined here. There is no second stage.

Monday   *Day 162*

I'm back on for another twenty-four hours.

I have wonderful fantasies. I am up on Labor and Delivery

saying to everyone, "But I don't believe in the second stage of labor."

I imagine I am in Dr. Pierce's office, saying, "But I don't believe in the second stage of labor."

"But it's real!" he tells me, showing me a chart of what it looks like.

"Yes, I used to believe in it. That's why I came here to study with you, but I don't believe it anymore."

"But it's right here," he tells me again, his finger vigorously pointing to Hill's chart, named after the man famous for establishing the standard labor curve.

"But it's not the system I believe in."

I don't tell him it isn't real, only that I no longer believe in it. His view of labor is his religious belief, but it is no longer mine.

Tuesday   *Day 163*

Last night Bea called to complain that Heather wouldn't eat her supper. Bea's hobby is gourmet cooking, but the food she prepares isn't anything Heather is used to. It is clear that none of this is going to work out unless I can get some time home, which is what I'm now trying to do.

I spoke with Jackie about shifting my hours so I can be home in the morning for a few days to work things out between Heather and Bea. Jackie expressed her disappointment in me, both in the hours I worked and in my "uninvolvement," as she described it.

I told her again about my dismay with what goes on in obstetrics.

"I don't think we do unnecessary Caesareans, though," she protested.

"That depends on what you call necessary, Jackie." I repeated what I've said before about the choosing of the baby's life over that of the mother.

"That's very heavy to think about," she said, looking thoughtful. "I'm scared to practice, Michelle. I feel locked into a certain kind of practice because I've never experienced it another way. You at least have seen other ways.''

I sensed the absence of the usual barriers between us. Someone listening might even think we were friends.

''Jackie, I worry that in five years your practice will look like everyone else's, the only difference being that you are a woman.'' In the context of how it felt between us then, I didn't expect her to be threatened by what I was saying.

She went on to tell me how worried she was. ''You know, four years ago when I came here, I thought the attendings were terrible, that what they did was terrible, but now I don't think they are so bad. I get along with them real well.'' Her statement had a question to it, but not one I could answer.

Nor could I answer for myself what I am doing here, subjecting myself at such personal cost to a system I see as bringing poor care to the patient and dehumanization to the physician. Part of me worries that in five years I will be saying the same words as Jackie.

Wednesday   Day 164

Being home for twenty-four hours has given me a chance to work things out with Bea. It was probably unrealistic to believe it could all go smoothly from the beginning when I was never home.

Heather is being difficult, cries easily and watches too much TV. I've put her on notice I will restrict it unless she cuts down on her own. I made up a new piece of cardboard with the phone numbers of Heather's friends, telling Bea that Heather needs help calling friends and arranging to play after school. This morning we decided on dinner—scrambled eggs and cooked carrots was what Heather wanted. We may do this on a daily basis.

Thursday   Day 165

Catherine called last night to say she wasn't feeling well. Heather was in bed and Bea was watching TV, so I decided to go over and take care of Catherine. I stopped at the supermarket, where I ran into Fran, who decided to join me. The three of us sat around talking and then we massaged Catherine to sleep, turned out the lights and left. The community of women here is exciting in the nurturing and being nurtured we offer and receive.

I keep thinking it will be better with Bea because she is nice to Heather and seems to be trying, but this morning she told me she would be downtown all day. I reminded her that today Heather gets out of school at one. She said, "Oh yes," but I was left wondering what would have happened if I hadn't reminded her.

Also, all week I've been telling her that the garbage cannot be left in the yard because animals get into it. This morning I found the garbage strewn all over the yard. Bea said she would clean it up as soon as she got dressed, but then she left for the day without picking it up and I had to.

Later

The women who were to have prostaglandin abortions had come in, and since no one else was there to see them, I checked with the third-year resident and then began the insertion of the suppositories which would cause them to abort in the next twenty-four hours. When time isn't short I get genuine pleasure from my work; I can become fully engaged in taking care of someone. Even the trouble at home fades.

I did a D&C and laparoscopy this afternoon, the D&C showing a closed cervix, which is probably why the woman was having her problems. The laparoscopy showed nothing, which is what I had expected. Today's D&C was indicated, but I question the D&C for irregular bleeding. I can't understand how a hormonal disorder can respond to surgical intervention.

Putting someone in the hospital to have a D&C does seem to stop the irregular bleeding, at least for a while, but I'm not sure it's the D&C that helps. Of course, when cancer is suspected, doing a D&C gives you the opportunity to examine tissue. So often, though, procedures seem to be done "routinely" and thoughtlessly. This is not an atmosphere which encourages people to ask, "Are we doing the right thing?" or "Was this procedure necessary?"

I miss Carol because besides being friendly, she had the same perspective as I on how women should be treated. She's at another hospital, meaning that now there is no one here for me to talk to.

Chapter Eleven

Sunday   **Day 168**

Strict standards for doctors help to maintain good care, but they also exclude those people who challenge the system. In any hospital where I would practice, I would have to do Caesareans according to the standards of the hospital and the community at large. But what if those standards are wrong? What if the D&C is ridiculous? Unnecessary? Harmful?

I'm on duty now for another twenty-four hours. Heather is staying with Catherine until late this afternoon when Bea gets back, but I am apprehensive about any time they spend together. Friday afternoon there was more difficulty, as Bea cooked food I asked her specifically not to cook, but forgot to put up Heather's hair, which she had promised Heather she would do before she left for the weekend.

I tried to tell Fran that it wasn't going well, but she didn't seem to hear me. I worry constantly about Fran and Laurie blaming me that things are not going well with Bea.

Monday   **Day 169**

A woman who had a hysterectomy last week was complaining yesterday of vaginal pain. She had apparently not been told that her bladder had been punctured during the surgery, so she didn't understand why she was having urinary problems. She also didn't know that in order to remove the uterus and cervix, the vagina must be cut into. She and I had a long talk about the importance of women knowing what is being done to them. I will probably be chastised for talking so frankly to her.

My pager went off at eleven last night as I was hunting for x-rays on the pre-op patients. The ER nurse told me, "It's a bleeder, but I frankly don't see any blood." With obvious irritation at the patient, she added, "I don't think you have to rush down here."

After finishing my search for x-rays, I go down to the ER, and taking the chart from the rack, walk into the GYN room. A woman in her mid-forties sits on the table looking despondent, embarrassed and anxious.

"What brings you here?" I ask routinely, without paying much attention.

"I've been bleeding for a week, and it doesn't stop. I worry about something being wrong."

"How many pads do you use each day?" This is a good way to assess the severity of the bleeding.

"Two or three pads a day, I think, sometimes less." She looks down and away from me. "I mean, I know it isn't a lot of bleeding, but I'm worried."

I wonder if I will discover why she is here tonight. I'm only half listening as I jot down her answers to my questions: "When was your last period?" . . . "How often do you get it?" . . . "How long does it usually last?" . . . "Are you sexually active?" . . . "Do you use birth control?"

She answers them all easily but flatly. Then I ask, "Have you ever been pregnant?" She pauses and then I see that her eyes have filled with tears, her face is flushed and she begins to weep. Putting my paper on the chair where I've been sitting, I walk over to the table and stand next to her. There isn't much I can do except stand there, let her cry, and wait. For a minute I regret my previous distance and remoteness. I had been saving myself for the next ten patients, for the limitless demands on me here. I rest my hand on her shoulder to let her know I am there and that I can wait. Time seems to stop.

"I had a baby," she tells me between sobs as she looks

around for a tissue, which I hand her. "I was fourteen and my family made me give it up and then I had another baby when I was fifteen and I gave that one up too. Every time I think of them I cry. I can't forget."

Handing her more tissue, I say, "Some pains don't go away, do they?"

"I keep trying to forget, but I never do. My babies are grown now, and I still can't forget them."

We then talked at length about adoption, what it is for mothers, for children. I told her about the adoption registry, about which I had recently learned, where women who have given up their children can register their names in case the children want to search for them. I said I would get more information about it for her.

As for her bleeding, I could find nothing on examination. I would guess it's of indeterminate cause and should just be watched for a while. Maybe it's bleeding from loss. Maybe it's the cry of her empty uterus.

Tuesday *Day 170*

Last night Heather cried at bedtime and asked why I don't quit and why I have to work at night. She wants to move back to New Jersey, where I was so much more accessible to her.

I'm on my way in to work for another twenty-four hours, after having seen Heather off to school this morning. I stopped on the way to pick up a tape recorder for her, since recently she has been enjoying a recording I made of a children's story I once wrote. I want to record more stories for her to listen to at bedtime.

I feel terrible entering the institution, facing the silence of my life inside there, my isolation from the others.

Wednesday *Day 171*

Yesterday I spent five hours in the operating room reattaching tubes that had previously been cut. The attending let me do much of the case, using special operating eyeglasses which

magnify the field. The patient was a woman who had her
tubes tied several years ago, partly due to pressure from her
doctor. She is having surgery done because she has remar-
ried but also because she has always regretted the sterilization. There is a 30 to 50 percent chance of success, with an
additional risk of future ectopic pregnancies. Most women
are not informed of these facts before they have their "tubes
tied." Before the surgery she and I spoke of sterilization
abuses, and I told her I was in Washington last year to testify
at HEW on sterilization abuses.

Thursday   *Day 172*

I called in sick today, which is the first time off I've had in
weeks, not preceded by a night in the hospital. I feel disoriented, unsure of the day of the week. My body hurts from
the work I've been doing and the nights without sleep.

Saturday   *Day 174*

Apparently past my initiation with the attendings, I was allowed to do a mini-lap, a laparoscopy, an open laparoscopy
and an abortion yesterday.

Early in the evening I was asked to go in to see a woman
who had a radioactive implant in her vagina. Since I was not
convinced it was safe to go into the room, the nurse called
down to radiology to ask for a lead shield. The radiologist
said, "The shield won't do any good. Tell her to move
quickly." The nurses have been told it is safe for them to
spend half an hour per day in there. At rounds in the morning, I was told by Jackie and Richard that doctors are only
to be in there for five minutes per day.

It is difficult to say "I am afraid." It is part of our training
to deny dangers to ourselves. I knew a radiologist who
boasted of never wearing shielding gloves for x-ray procedures. He died at forty-six of cancer.

Heather came in and stayed with me in the on-call room
last night, so she is feeling better about my being in the

hospital. I took her for a late snack in the cafeteria, and then to the OB floor so she could see where she might be able to stay with me sometimes when I go back on night OB. I was apprehensive about her being on OB because she has such a different view of childbirth from attending home births with me. I didn't want her to see the babies in the nurseries, or hear the women screaming, or even being yelled at. Once last year when she heard about a friend who was going into the hospital to have a baby she asked, "But what's wrong with her? Why does she have to go to a hospital?"

She slept in the morning while I made rounds, waking in time for us to leave.

Tomorrow morning I go on for thirty-six hours and work each day until Thursday, when I go back East to speak at a medical school on "Obstetrics and Gynecology: A Feminist Perspective." It will be a hectic three days back in New Jersey, my first visit since we moved.

This is also the end of the reduced schedule I was granted— late mornings to work things out at home. The crisis with Bea seems to have abated, but now I face the endless days of five o'clock awakenings.

Sunday   *Day 175*

The radiation technician here today refused to do the x-ray on the woman with a radioactive implant because she didn't want to expose herself to the risk. She went on to tell me, "You can't get a chest x-ray on her. By the time the film is carried through the room and put in back of the patient it will have been exposed. The radiation goes through everything."

We talked about technology in general, and she leaned over and in a half whisper told me, "I had a roommate who had a baby at home and the baby was absolutely fine." I "confessed" to having attended home births.

Ultrasound uses radar-type waves to make a picture of organs and cavities within the body. It is currently being widely used on pregnant women to determine the location of the placenta and the size of the baby. It has never been proven safe. Articles have been coming out now for several years about possible hazards, but physicians have ignored the risk and presented this new method as "absolutely safe." It's frightening, because x-rays and DES were also thought to be safe. I talked with the technician about my concerns about ultrasound. She said, "All the radiologists know it does something. Male fetuses all get erections when exposed to the waves." I have read studies showing chromosome damage to cell cultures exposed to ultrasound. And the external fetal monitor, which we use so routinely, also employs ultrasound waves to record the heartbeat.

Ultrasound waves are also used to locate the placenta in order to perform amniocentesis. This is a procedure in which a needle is inserted through a pregnant woman's abdomen and into her uterus. Amniotic fluid, that which surrounds the fetus, is removed. Cells in the fluid are then analyzed for chromosomal abnormalities, as in Down's syndrome and other genetic diseases. This procedure is commonly performed on women over thirty-five years and when there is a familial history of genetic disorders. Both ultrasound and amniocentesis pose possible risks to the fetus.

My call home at six brought the discovery of new hassles with Bea, who insists that Heather is out of control. Bea doesn't want Heather to answer the phone or the door, both of which she has been doing for two years. I said I'd call and talk with her more after eight when Heather was asleep.

Then Heather got on the phone and talked with me about work again, asking me why I am working late at night.

"Someday, Heather, you may have to do something that isn't pleasant just so you can learn."

"I want to be a vet when I grow up," she told me.

"That sounds like fun."

"I want to help animals."

"You know, if you become a vet, you may have to work at night sometimes."

"I don't mind," she told me, "just so I don't have to be alone."

When I called home again after eight, Bea said they had also fought about closing the drapes of the living room. Heather had a friend over playing, and the girls wanted to close the drapes as part of their game. Heather insisted, then Bea exploded. Bea says, "If I can't determine when the drapes get pulled, then I'm not a person." I understand that Bea needs to feel that she and her work are important. Taking care of children in our society is considered such demeaning work that maintaining self-esteem can be difficult.

Even so, this long series of on-call nights, of which tonight is the last, has confirmed that I wasn't foolish in insisting on doing the program part-time. I've decided to leave Heather with my parents for her school-vacation week, since I don't want her home alone with Bea for a week.

It's midnight, and I'm standing in the on-call room looking out at the city and the empty hospital parking lot below. I haven't found a way to make my time here good for me. I have so many questions about the value of what I'm doing. The others in the program don't seem as troubled as I am, and this makes me feel distant from them and leaves me wondering about the years of training still ahead.

Tuesday   *Day 177*

Nanette, an eighteen-year-old, was admitted yesterday to be worked up for laparoscopy today. She has a long history of menstrual cramps and abdominal pain, and went through a laparoscopy before which showed nothing. When I expressed my doubts about another laparoscopy to her attending, he said he had to "do something" because she was calling him constantly. Today, before the surgery, when I raised the possibility of her problem being partly psychosomatic, he said, "But she seems like an honest person. I don't think she's making it up." I couldn't believe he thought psychosomatic means pretending. Psychosomatic pain is real, but it is the pain of the soul taken on by the body.

Today Nanette had needless surgery which showed nothing, while no one attended to the pain in her soul.

Dr. Brucker is a breast surgeon with whom I've been chatting
in the OR lounge. He uses a technique of removing benign
breast lumps under local anesthesia which he has offered to
show me. Today I was able to get out of the laparoscopy in
time to join him, so I have picked up one more skill.

Wednesday　　　　　　　　　　　　　　　　　*Day 178*

Lois Scott came up to me after Grand Rounds this morning
and angrily asked, "Did you listen to Karen Reese's lungs
this morning?" She is the woman whose ovarian cyst Lois
and I removed a couple of days ago. This morning on rounds
I saw that she had run a slight temperature yesterday, although by this morning it was normal. I found no site of
infection.

"No, I examined her carefully," I told Lois, "but I guess
I forgot to listen to her lungs."

Lois was outraged that I hadn't listened to the lungs of a
patient two days post-op. I realized I hadn't listened because
I knew they were fine. I asked Lois, "Did you hear anything
when you listened?"

"No," she said, as I had expected she would.

I can't explain how I know, but sometimes I can just look at
someone and tell if they are sick and where they are sick.
don't think I've ever missed a patient with a post-op lung problem. Usually I have a sense of where infection is, if it is present
and then the exam is to confirm what I already sense.

I agree with Lois, though, that I should have listened.
That's what I'm supposed to be doing here and in any case
I should be monitoring my own instincts by taking all pre-
cautions.

One of my work-ups this afternoon was on a woman patient of Dr. Ingle's scheduled for a hysterectomy and removal
of her ovaries in the morning. I went into her room, intro-

duced myself, and said I would be asking her some questions and then examining her.

"What kind of examination are you talking about?" She seemed tense and apprehensive.

"I'll be doing a pelvic exam."

"No. I won't let you do that. I'll only let Dr. Ingle examine me," she protested defensively. She showed surprise when I said, "That's okay. I still need to ask you some questions."

I settled into a comfortable chair and she sat on the side of her bed while we talked. She was in her late forties, poised, well-dressed and quite open. She told me she had been having irregular bleeding, so Dr. Ingle said she had no alternative but to have her uterus removed. I thought there was a slight question in her statement but I wasn't sure. "I would wear a pad for the rest of my life if I knew I weren't in danger. It's not the bleeding that bothers me but the worry." The big fear for every woman is cancer, although this woman has the kind of irregular bleeding that often comes with menopause.

"Are your ovaries going to be removed too?" I asked, knowing already they were scheduled for removal, but wanting to check on whether she knew or had been included in the decision.

"Yes," she answered, looking at me again with some doubt in her expression. "Is there some question as to whether they should be?" We were discussing some of the pros and cons of ovary removal, of estrogen replacement, and the possibility of ovarian cancer if the ovaries are left in, when Dr. Ingle walked into the room.

"Oh, we were just sitting here talking about her ovaries," I said, looking up at him, hoping there was a chance this issue could really be discussed.

"That's not a question," he said to me sternly. "She decided that in the office and they're being removed, so that's the end of that." He turned to her, adding, "You know you won't let me use hormones on you, so you have no choice about the hysterectomy." His manner was so imposing that this questionable conclusion took on authority.

Dr. Ingle read the "informed consent" statement, which lists all the things that could go wrong, but I had the sense he was only reading it because I was there in the room. For instance, he said, " 'You understand there is the risk of perforation, infection or bowel or bladder problems. . . .' " The patient stopped him, asking, "What, me? From this operation?" sounding shocked. He then reassured her, saying that he just had to read this list, but for her not to worry about any of it.

"How uncomfortable will I be?" she asked, to which he replied, "Oh, not very bad. It's just a little operation."

"Will I be in agony?"

"Of course not. You'll have a day or two when it will hurt and after that you'll be bouncing around and we'll have you out of here in five days."

"Will I be able to do everything?" she asked, and I jokingly responded, "You won't be able to ski the first week."

More seriously, Dr. Ingle told her, "You'll really be able to get around in a week or two. You can drive, for instance."

It was all lies. She *would* be in agony after her surgery and it would be weeks, even months, before she had her strength back. And no one was telling her about the common changes in sexual functioning after hysterectomy, the decrease in vaginal lubrication, difficulty in reaching orgasm, difficulty with arousal.

Dr. Ingle explained to her that I would be doing a pelvic exam on her. She said, "No. I'll only allow you to examine me."

"You have to let Dr. Harrison examine you," he told her, and when it was clear she was going to refuse, Dr. Ingle looked at me apologetically.

After he left, she was apologetic about her refusal. "There's nothing personal about it. I just don't want anyone except my doctor to examine me."

"It's not a problem for me. I respect and appreciate a woman's refusal to have done to her what she doesn't want."

Her eyes were moist and so were mine. I felt moved by

her need to defend the integrity of her body, and by her being apologetic about it.

With Dr. Ingle out of the room, she asked me, "What's the pain really like?"

"Most women have a lot of pain, but we write orders for a lot of medication the first few days, but you must ask for it."

"You mean they don't just bring it?"

"No, you have to ask."

"Then I'd better not just lie here and wait for it," she said, seemingly relieved by this useful information.

"We usually prescribe that it be given every three or four hours as long as you ask for it." I didn't want to scare her about the pain, but if she doesn't expect it, she will think it is because something has gone wrong, not understanding that this is a painful procedure.

She also returned to the question of having the hysterectomy. "Tell me, does the bleeding ever just stop?"

"Sometimes it does, but there is no way of being sure it will." I didn't know what to say because I sensed she had no real choice by then, and she needed to go ahead with her doubts settled. I was also afraid of Dr. Ingle. If the attendings perceived me as someone who interfered with their patients and challenged what they were doing, I would never be able to learn surgery. I thought this hysterectomy was ill-advised. I could see that the woman was still uncertain. But I felt I could say no more than I had already.

Her sister, who had left the room when I first introduced myself, returned. The patient said something about not being sure she wanted to go through with the hysterectomy, whereupon her sister said, "Well, I had a hysterectomy. Aren't I still the same? Don't I look normal?"

It was clear that no one would let this woman consider alternatives to this operation.

Thursday

The days are getting longer again, so there are beautiful pale streaks in the sky and wonderful colors of daylight against the city skyline as I drive to work in the morning.

Barbara came to me in the locker room as I was getting into pinks, saying she wanted to do the hysterectomy I was scheduled to do with Doug Weston.

"Sure, Barb. It's okay with me," I said, much to her astonishment.

"You mean you'd do that for me?" she asked incredulously.

"Mostly I only displease people around here. Here's my chance to do something for you. I'll even cover the clinic for you if the case runs past noon." I remembered seeing Barbara holding the woman's hand in the pre-surgical waiting area, thinking to myself at that time that she should be the one doing the surgery, since she had done the work-up yesterday and was obviously close to the patient.

Jackie initially said yes to the switch, but then came to the OR to tell Barbara she couldn't scrub, and then sent for me. It seems that others had objected to someone of Barbara's first-year rank getting the case. In addition, Richard told Jackie he didn't want to have to work with me in the clinic, as he would if the case ran late.

I started the case with Dr. Weston, who ran into difficulty so that we soon needed another set of hands. Ironically, Barbara was called in to be second assistant, but once she scrubbed in, I moved over and let her be first assistant, which is what she had wanted in the first place.

By afternoon there was rampant anger among the residents. Jackie came to me at four looking tired and despondent, and said, "I suppose *you* hate me too."

"No, I'm not angry with you. I'm sorry everyone else is upset, but I'm not in it." I felt calm and relaxed as I spoke, able to be supportive of her. Being chief resident is a thankless task. Sometimes I think Jackie's cold and strident manner is all a protection against her natural desire to be liked by everyone.

Lloyd Stevens is an infertility specialist who has invited me to spend half a day a week in his office this spring. I'm very excited about doing that, although I certainly don't need extra work. I'll be on night OB then, and I'd go to his office one morning when I got off work.

It's six o'clock when I drive home. Although the sun has gone down, some streaks of light remain in the sky. They complete the day for me when I remember the beautiful pre-sunrise lightening of the sky as I drove to work.

Sunday *Day 182*

Last Friday, speaking at the medical school in New Jersey, talking partly about my residency, I was struck by the youth and innocence of the students. Many came up to me after-ward and asked, "How can we keep from becoming hard-ened?" They see students one year ahead already turning off, closing themselves, becoming dehumanized, so they are afraid. I have few answers for them other than that keeping contact with people outside medicine is important in main-taining values and perspective.

Tuesday *Day 184*

Today I watched Doug Weston do a dilation and evacuation—the removal of a large fetus from the uterus. Richard had said the woman was thirteen weeks pregnant, but after she was under anesthesia Doug found an eighteen-week fetus. The procedure, under such circumstances, is gruesome, and ex-tremely difficult for us as physicians. It is, however, much easier on the woman, who otherwise would have a saline abortion within twenty-four hours of labor before she passed the fetus. This way, she wakes up and it is over.

Doug Weston refuses to give pain medication to abortion patients, as does Jackie. Both of them insist that the pain is not as great as patients say. Weston also refuses to give pain

meds to laparoscopy patients, who have a lot of pain after
the procedure. We argued about medication over the sink
this morning as he tried to justify his practice. Although in
OB I'm the one who questions medication, I see no reason
not to give drugs for surgical pain.

"Pain medication should not be given, because of the possibility of masking a complication," he explained to me.

"I really disagree," I told him. "I don't think codeine
would block the pain of anything serious."

"Michelle, I'm in charge. You have to do what I tell you,"
he said, pulling in his chin and stiffening his back as he
spoke.

"I'm not disputing that, and I certainly won't write an
order for pain meds when you don't want them, but I still
disagree with your not using it."

Deepening his voice, he said, "I have great experience
with such things, Dr. Harrison. You should not disagree with
me."

"But I've practiced many years too, and I think the use of
pain medication comes under the heading of style of practice,
not of what is right and wrong."

Most of the morning he was in his usual bad mood, but
while I was scrubbing a woman and prepping her for the
abortion, I heard strange cooing sounds in back of me. Turning around I found the nurse rubbing Weston's neck and
back.

"Was this a part of your job description?" I asked her
ostensibly as a joke.

She laughed and went on rubbing. I went back to draping
the patient, and then, turning around to them, added, "I
think this comes under the heading of sexual harassment
on the job."

My remarks, although meant seriously, were understandably taken lightly, for it is expected that nurses will do what
they can to improve the disposition of surgeons, who often
behave erratically in the OR and who take out their bad mood
on the nurses.

Dr. Weston was now feeling better, but apparently annoyed with me. He began boasting about his youth and being younger than me, half singing a song about thirty-five being "over the hill." I looked at Gert, one of the nurses who is thirty-six or thirty-seven, about my age, and I said to her in what was to appear light-hearted, "He's such a baby, what does he know at his age?" creating a sense of understanding and sisterhood between us.

Doug Weston retaliated with a diatribe against ERA. "I sure don't believe in it," he said. "I sure won't vote for it in this state."

Gert and I have talked a lot about child-care problems when we've run into each other in the dressing room. She had overheard my telling Jackie about my problems one day, and offered support. She and her children live nearby, and she has offered her two teen-agers as baby-sitters. Gert is divorced with five children. When they were younger and she had to be at work for the early-morning shift, she would wake one child at five and have that child stay awake in case of fire, or any other emergency, because she had to leave for work. She would rotate who had to be up each morning. She said she thought in some ways it was easier with five, because they had each other for company. It may be easier to leave five together, but meeting the needs of five children must be far more complicated and difficult.

Wednesday   *Day 185*

Joan, who will be starting as chief in a week, sat down and discussed the schedule with me. A mother herself, she seemed sympathetic to the problems I am having. I like her a lot. Her lack of anger is a relief here, but I wonder what she'll be like after three months of being chief.

Joan spoke at Grand Rounds about her months working in West Virginia, where she was the only obstetrician in the area. She had packed up her kids and her housekeeper and had gone off to experience rural medicine. After her talk and slide presentation she sat down next to me. Thinking how nice that was, I looked around to see if there were other seats

where she could have sat. I began thinking how nice it wa
that someone would sit next to me even if there were othe
seats, suddenly tearful and aware of how alone and isolate
I feel here. I wondered how the next three months would be
whether Joan would still be sitting next to me after that time
or whether my radicalness, my part-timeness, my genera
differences would bother her too much.

Maybe Joan and I can be friends now because we haven'
yet worked together. In a different context I might be friend
with many people here. In this setting, though, confronte
daily by the institutionalized—though at times well
intentioned—abuse of women's bodies, it is impossible fo
me to "forget it" and be friends.

A psychiatrist friend of mine also spoke at Grand Rounds
During the discussion period I asked about possible long
term effects of ultrasound, which brought laughs from som
of the attendings. Even so, it gave her a chance to talk abou
the issue, which is what I hoped would happen. I hoped they
would listen to an "authority"—as they would not to me.

Thursday   Day 186

Between cases in the OR this morning I went to my locke
and read a few pages from *Woman and Nature* in which
Susan Griffin challenges what our society does to women. I
hear her voice describing the operating room with organs
being removed and women's bodies being "conquered" and
disease being fought. Since I usually feel as if I am on a
battlefield, her voice validates my imagery. I hear different
voices from those around me; in her book I hear my voice
valued.

I was late for sign-out this morning because I spent too
much time taking care of patients on rounds. All Jackie can
do is scream at me, and then scream louder. I'm weary of
six months of trying and that it is still no easier, no more
manageable. Yet it is the loneliness, the isolation that is worst.

Saturday *Day 188*

Bea has had a week of paid vacation, since I had just hired her and hadn't known Heather would be away this week. Not wanting her in the house with me for the week, I decided to pay her, anyway. She called me yesterday at the hospital asking if there was anything she could do in the house before she returns Sunday to take care of Heather. I told her she could come over and do some light housecleaning if she wanted to. Then I added, "I'll tell you what I would like you to do. I'm on for the night, so I'd love to come home to a bed made up with fresh sheets." As I spoke I could feel how inviting that bed would be after a night in the hospital. I saw myself getting into it in the morning, knowing Heather wasn't due back for another day, sleeping as long as I wanted. Bea said "Fine."

The night was very busy. I got only one hour of sleep and arrived home eager to go right to bed. I went upstairs to my room and there saw a bare mattress. The bed had been stripped but not remade. I broke down and wept. I would have been fine with the old sheets, an unmade bed, anything but a stripped bed left for me by the person who had asked how she could help. So I cried. Then I got angry. I made the bed but I couldn't sleep.

Bea came back to the house later in the morning saying she wasn't "into housework." She said I had spoiled the job because I wouldn't let her cook enough. She has given me thirty days' notice, although at the moment she isn't even talking to me.

Monday *Day 190*

Heather arrived at the airport yesterday happy and eager to be home. She cuddled up to me in my arms, suddenly filling for me what had been missing all week. Heather's reaction to Bea's leaving was: "Now we'll have a fourth baby-sitter." I don't think Bea ever liked Heather, so for that reason it will be a relief to have her out of the house.

It is snowing lightly as I drive in for another thirty hours. The street lights have a glow because of the snowy air and the reflection of white on the ground. It is beautiful and quiet with few cars. I always feel a closeness with other drivers at this hour, as though we are the lone partakers of the early morning.

Tuesday   Day 191

I was to work four nights a week on OB, from eight at night to eight in the morning, but Joan and I figured out that I could work only two nights and still have the OB service covered, since the other two nights I was to work there would be overlap with Karen's time. I would then have the breather I need to spend some time at home. Not only do I have to work out child care, I have to work out first what I am doing in the program now and where I want to be in the future.

This evening Heather and I had a grown-up discussion about my being at the hospital so much in which she listed all the times I have been there in the past two weeks, saying "It's not fair to me for you to work so much." I told Heather why I still didn't want to quit, but that I was trying to arrange my schedule so I'd be home more.

My talk with Joan left me feeling more optimistic about being able to stay. I have a meeting with Pierce tomorrow to discuss the change.

Wednesday   Day 192

I told Dr. Pierce about the difficulties I was having.

"And do you have any solutions?" he asked.

"I know I don't want to quit," I told him, and he seemed both pleased and relieved. He said he had gotten some positive feedback both about my skills and my ability to get along with people. But, he added, without any warning, "I am putting you on a leave of absence."

"But, Dr. Pierce, I don't want a leave of absence," I protested. "Joan and I worked out a schedule that keeps the service covered and allows me to cut back to two days." I was fighting tears, not wanting to leave, not wanting this to be happening to me.

"I'm sorry, but you have no choice. It would be too destructive to morale to have you working less than the others." He was wrong. That may have been true in the past, but since Bea has been making so many calls to the hospital, the others have become fully aware of my child-care problems. If I work those two nights, no one would have to cover. If I leave, they will hate me more because someone else will have to do my work.

"Michelle, my only reservation about the leave is the loss of income to you."

He seemed surprised when I said, "It's actually costing me money to be here. I've been paying a hundred dollars a week plus room and board to baby-sitters. I take home five hundred dollars a month from the hospital and have to use my savings to allow me to stay here. If I don't work, I don't need a baby-sitter. It's not the money but the training I want."

Although I managed to hold myself together for the meeting, I spent most of the afternoon crying. Every time I spoke with anyone about leaving, I broke down. I kept going over what happened, trying to figure out how I could have done it differently, but I couldn't find any other solutions.

Joan said this evening at sign-out that she regretted my leaving because I had something unique and different to offer the program. Jackie, who was sitting with us, said, "It's a shame Michelle never had a chance to express her views."

Thursday morning   *Day 193*

There is no humanity in this system, not toward patients, not toward women who both work and care for their children. A part of me is still desperately trying to make it here, but, mostly I begin to realize I cannot mold myself into the kind of person who could. A battle rages within me between fighting to stay and seizing the offer of freedom.

Heather was thrilled when I said I'd be leaving work for a

while. She ran to tell Bea, who then said to me, "If you're going to have kids, you should work at night. I know, because my mother did it." I suddenly felt pity for Bea, and thought about the many years she had harbored anger over the hours her mother had worked. In our society, child care consists of women pitted against other women in the struggle for time, money, recognition and gratification.

Friday morning   *Day 194*

It is possible that I cannot find a new child-care solution because I know I cannot stay in this program and I want relief from the daily battering to my sense of morality and integrity.

Medicine, particularly as it is practiced in the hospital, is a service industry that systematically and impersonally processes sick and healthy people. Physicians are trained and conditioned to see their patients as objects to be assembled and reassembled once they enter the system. If you are sick, or even if you are having a baby, you are presumed to be incapable of intelligent judgment, and therefore—quite properly—under the control of the experts.

The physicians, too, must fit the mold. Their ideas, their techniques, even their demeanor are processed by the system. It is by this same process that the system makes itself invulnerable—even to beneficial change.

Saturday   *Day 195*

I worked on night call with Joan. It was actually pleasurable because, for the first time since I worked with Carol, I wasn't alone. With the affinity I felt for her, it seemed simple: there was a certain amount of work to do, and we did it.

Yesterday morning, however, began with my doing abortions with Doug Weston, who was even more nasty and cutting than usual, but he has apparently been that way with everyone lately.

During one of the abortions he was sitting before the woman's vagina, inserting probes and mumbling half aloud, half to himself, that the residents here don't think they can learn anything from the attendings.

I reflected for a minute and then in a calm way decided to respond honestly. "I don't think that's the problem," I said. "I think you have a lot to teach, but sometimes you are so unpleasant that it's hard to learn anything from you."

He didn't seem offended by what I said, nor did he reply. Actually, he can teach us a lot. He is one of the developers of a new method of examining the inside of the uterus; other attendings come even from other hospitals to learn from him.

My latest fantasy is of taking off about six weeks, and somehow having child care in place by May so I can return—despite everything. On the other hand, when I can stop condemning myself for being a failure, I can enjoy the prospect of time in which to rest, think and write.

Sunday   *Day 196*

After Bea left yesterday—one week early—I spent the day exorcising her from the room she had used. First I cleaned the mess she left, and then I got some yellow paint from the basement and began painting. I hadn't expected to finish, but I did. I put up green gingham curtains I had brought from the New Jersey house and the room didn't seem the same anymore.

I was up on the ladder, feeling terrible about what was happening, wondering how I'd get through the week at the hospital that was still left, when I began to laugh. I suddenly looked at where I was, but instead of feeling the pain of separation and loss, I thought, What an interesting life you lead, Michelle!

Monday   *Day 197*

I made rounds Sunday morning, had about an hour of free time, worked nonstop until one this morning and then slept until five-thirty.

Last night I admitted a woman who came to the ER because of abdominal pain, weakness and fatigue for three weeks, but who is also severely depressed and was thinking of suicide yesterday. She hasn't slept in many nights, and may be hallucinating. I wanted to give her some sedation but my chief, Flo, who functions strictly by protocol, said we couldn't because the woman was admitted as a surgical case, so sedation was contraindicated. I didn't argue with her, but I knew what should have been done. With my impending departure, I find myself synthesizing what I know, and being able to be more certain about what I have learned and what I still need to learn.

I admitted a woman yesterday for hysterectomy who is a poor surgical risk. When I questioned her attending he said, "She can't use birth control because of her religion. I have no choice." I wondered whether she and her husband knew about the risks of the surgery she is about to have.

Wednesday   *Day 199*

Although I woke frequently during the night, I still feel rested this morning. Up at five, I sorted laundry, put away Heather's clothes, and cleaned up after Maggie, whom I forgot to let out last night.

Filled with sadness about leaving, I am also looking forward to time to write, time to myself. I fear I'll never go back because I'm not sure I could put myself through this again. I want to go swimming at the Y, to see my friends, to spend time with Heather. With spring and summer ahead, and some money left to live on, the possibilities seem infinite.

Afternoon

Tara, a neighbor, came to see me Monday because Brenda, her sixteen-year-old, was pregnant. They had been to an abortion clinic where they had been told that Brenda was actually nineteen weeks pregnant, not the eight she had thought. This meant she would have to have a saline abortion done in the hospital. I had hoped to do the procedure Friday morning because I would be on duty Friday night and could be with her when she aborted. I could also do a D&C to remove retained parts, if it was needed in the night. Since the soonest appointment for an admissions work-up was in two weeks—when I would be gone—I arranged to see Brenda today after I went off duty.

Tara and Brenda met me at noon in the clinic. It was officially closed at that hour, so we were free of time pressures. Brenda looked pregnant lying flat on the table with the pear-shaped bulge to her lower abdomen that is characteristic of a pregnancy of five months. I examined her both internally and externally, and although what I saw and felt seemed right for a pregnancy this size, something wasn't quite normal. I took a long time palpating, feeling, trying to imagine a baby inside there swimming around, but I couldn't "see" one in there. I didn't doubt that she was pregnant, but I couldn't find the baby. Although worried that I might upset either Brenda or Tara, I decided to listen for the heartbeat, which should have been present if the fetus was as large as Brenda's abdomen looked. I listened all over her abdomen, trying to hear a fetal heartbeat, trying to convince myself I heard one, but I couldn't hear it.

I told Tara something didn't feel right, so I wanted to establish fetal size by ultrasound examination. I was able to have the procedure done immediately. Watching as the technician made ultrasound pictures of Brenda's abdomen, we could see that she was only nine weeks pregnant. Two huge ovarian cysts had been mistaken for an advanced pregnancy.

I remembered that, some months ago, a woman was injected with saline for an abortion when she'd really had cysts—with almost fatal results.

In the evening

Depression has been with me all afternoon. Taking care of Brenda is what I want to be doing. I don't want to leave. While it's true that I look forward to all the other things I want to do, I want to be at the hospital. I'd like to be taking care of patients.

Thursday   Day 200

I went through the entire winter without ever being chilled, but for the past few days I can't seem to get warm no matter what I wear. It's warm out, but I'm chilled to the bone, in spite of a sweater, a shirt, my white jacket and a poncho. I didn't feel this way when it was six degrees out.

Friday   Day 201

Although yesterday I signed papers requesting the leave of absence, I still cannot believe I will be gone in the morning. A voice inside me wants to scream out in protest: "But you cannot take away my right to this learning, to these skills." They do not have the right to take away my work.

As I drive to the hospital for these final twenty-four hours, I keep looking for a different ending.

Saturday   Day 202

After sign-out, when everyone was leaving for the night except Flo and me, Charlie, who has always been so friendly, walked by and said, "Well, I guess I won't see you. Bye." He suddenly made real what I hadn't fully believed. My fantasies of being rescued were not happening.

Joan said, "I'm sorry it ended this way. Call me if it gets unbearable." I was in tears by now with all my reserve gone.

I kept trying to get myself together. Fortunately I wasn't being paged to go anywhere, so I could hide out in the on-call room. I sat on the bed grieving, not having the energy for one more night of battle in a war that had already been lost. I was to surrender in the morning, but I was ready to give up now. Overwhelmed by a sense of failure, I wanted to be able to slip off to lick my wounds in private. I wanted to go home.

For one of the few times since Heather's birth, I felt incredibly alone with her. I was her only parent, but she was also the person closest to me in the world. I wanted to be holding her.

At eleven I went to the ER, which by now had patients for me to see. As usual, being with a patient put distance between me and my own pain. Alone in the room, working with my hands and my mind, offering comfort, time seems to stop as I become totally immersed in what I am doing.

The first patient I saw was a young pregnant woman, terrified, crying, writhing with abdominal pain, probably as a result of the Chinese dinner she had just eaten. Speaking with her, and then examining her, I felt her begin to relax while the pain seemed to subside.

"I think your hands have healed her," the surgical resident was saying. "I've noticed you doing that before."

Sometimes I can feel my hands making someone better. I also at times "know" in my fingers what is wrong. Flo came down, and after seeing the woman, said, "Michelle, do whatever you think on her. I've learned not to disagree with you about abdominal pain," referring to a disagreement we'd had early this week about another woman.

By three o'clock in the morning, after seeing two more patients in the ER, and then stopping up on L&D, this time ready to say goodbye, I was able to return to the on-call room to sleep.

I dreamed I was sitting at the piano, trying to play, but just as my fingers began to move freely and the notes became music, a giant metronome would begin to tick at a slightly different rate. I kept trying and trying to play, but each time I felt the music begin to flow out of the piano, the metronome would change again, confusing me, stopping my fingers.

Awake at six, I made rounds, then signed out to the people coming on duty for the day.

* * *

Heather threw herself in my arms this morning when I went to pick her up at Catherine's, and then decided to stay and play with her children Alex and Chrissy for the day. I held her, though, for a long time, reassuring myself that she was all right, that she too had survived.

I spent the day grocery shopping, doing laundry, getting my house in order, wondering what I was going to do next, but still engrossed in what seemed like an unfinished dream. I thought of my visit to L&D last night, when I listened to the roar of the galloping fetal monitors, and I understood for the first time why the technology interferes with childbirth: birth is a creative process, not a surgical procedure.

I picture dancers on a stage. Once, doing a pirouette, a woman sustained a cervical fracture as a result of a fall; she is now paralyzed. We try to make the stage safer, to have the dancers better prepared. But can a dancer wear a collar around her neck, just in case she falls? The presence of the collar will inhibit her free motion. We cannot say to her, "This will be entirely natural except for the brace on your neck, just in case." It cannot be "as if" it is not there, because we know that creative movement and creative expression cannot exist with those constraints. The dancer cannot dance with the brace on. In the same way, the birthing woman cannot "dance" with a brace on. The straps around her abdomen, the wires coming from her vagina, change her birth.

The birthing woman plays in an orchestra of her body, her soul, her baby, her loved ones, her past and her future. And we do not know who leads the orchestra.

Doctors cannot lead the orchestra, because they are not within the process. Unable to hear the music, trained only in modalities of power and control, they can only interfere with the music being played.

What should they be able to do? They should stand ready to help the player in trouble to get back into rhythm. Instead, they take over. Instead of supporting the mother, they say, "Okay, you have failed. It's our piece now."

How do you get a 30 percent Caesarean-section rate?

You orchestrate it. You write a piece in which the third movement is a Caesarean, then build the first two with that in mind. You write in a different language; you write in terms of centimeters of dilation, external fetal monitor, internal fetal monitor, pH, scalp electrodes, Caesarean-birth experience, arrest of labor, protracted labor, fetal distress, episiotomy, prolapse, cephalopelvic disproportion, ultrasound waves, amniocentesis, "premium baby," post-mature (when the baby stays too long in utero) and "maternal environment" (formerly known as the mother). Those are the words, the notes, while the piece is played to the rhythm of fear.

Epilogue

I didn't go back. Fran, Laurie and Catherine were ready to help in child care again, while Heather was looking forward to another baby-sitter. Although it was the child-care problems that had precipitated my leaving when I did, I chose not to return to Doctors Hospital. Making that decision was a slow and difficult process.

Initially I was overwhelmed by a sense of defeat and by self-accusations of "not being able to take it." I thought, If only I had tried harder. I had let down the women who had supported me, the midwives who hoped to practice with me, and myself. I had overestimated my strength and underestimated my vulnerability.

In the months that followed my leaving, as I tried to explain what happened, I came to feel that I had been fighting a war which no one else even knew existed. I couldn't face going back to the loneliness of my life on the front line. My friends could only come with me as far as the door of the hospital or be at the other end of the phone—when I could call. I had wanted to be a more sensitive and skilled physician, not a soldier learning to be hard, to distance myself, to attack organs and intact tissues. I didn't want to be in pain. I also didn't want to be creating pain.

When I returned to training more than ten years after my first medical school rotation on OB-GYN, I thought I could more easily accept the compromises that were necessary, and indeed for a while that was true. But the same conflicts were with me. I couldn't say indefinitely, "Well, I'll just do these things for four years and then I won't have to. . . ." I didn't trust myself, because one can always find "reasons" to justify immorality: there are standards, peers, economics. Once justified, they no longer seem so bad. I was afraid that the lures which had caught the others would snare me too—that I couldn't take just a little of the poison.

If we murder we are murderers. If I take out a uterus that need not be removed, if I cut a perineum that need not be cut, then I am committing those crimes. The tissue is no less cut, nor the organs less removed because I, as a woman, am wielding the knife. The poison of OB-GYN is no less lethal when dispensed by a woman.

If I were to have an eye removed, then I would forever be a person with only one eye. If I were to take in poison without spitting it out, I would be a poisoned person. I might survive, but I would be damaged. Medical training is no less violent than surgery or poisoning. It leaves women and men no less scarred or no less without the organs that have been removed.

Medical training works like brainwashing. Two major components are sleep deprivation and isolation from one's support system. Because I was part-time, I was not so cut off from my support nor so deprived of sleep as the other residents. Single-motherhood made it both less desirable and less possible for me to remain separate from my life outside the institution. In addition, my feminism gave me a political context in which to see what was happening to women in the hospital. A combination of both my personal circumstances and my political perspective made it easier for me to challenge what was being told to me, although it took the distance of leaving to be able to see clearly what I was doing and what was being done to me.

Closed off from feeling, I was at times cold as the green walls around me, cold as I had feared before I returned to hospital childbirth. People had become characters in my life. A woman baby-sitting in my home, suffering the pain of her own childhood, was treated by me only in terms of her function in my life. I needed her to take care of Heather, to ask no questions, to insulate me from her needs and those of my child's. Why? So I could take out uteruses and ovaries and wear the uniform of power and acceptance. All day I could perform heroic deeds and be thanked and respected as a humane physician, but in truth I did not function humanely. I was removed from my own gentler self by this ungentle profession.

Would I practice again? At first I thought I had said good-bye to medicine. I sold the house so I would have money to live on, uprooted myself and Heather, again moved back East and concentrated on the writing of this book. For the next two years I wrote, practiced some psychotherapy and studied areas now being called holistic health.

Gradually I have moved back into practice because I remain committed to it as well as to trying to integrate conventional medicine with my visions of how it ought to be.

Women need good health care. The future of women's health care, however, does not lie in the domain of current obstetrics and gynecology, which is founded on certain assumptions about women's bodies and women's lives. Contemporary medicine is based also on the belief that machines are as accurate as humans, that data can be hard, that numbers and statistics and graphs can faithfully represent a human being. This kind of practice excludes intuition, sensitivity and mutuality. It thereby deprives both the physician and the patient of their power to heal and be healed.

I used to have fantasies at Doctors Hospital about women in a state of revolution. I saw them getting up out of their beds and refusing the knife, refusing to be tied down, refusing to submit—whether they are in childbirth or when they were forty and having a hysterectomy for a uterus no longer considered useful. Women's health care will not improve until women reject the present system and begin instead to develop less destructive means of creating and maintaining a state of wellness. It is my hope that this book is a step in that process.

Explanation of Medical Terms Used in This Book

abortion Termination of a pregnancy prior to about twenty weeks gestation. It can be spontaneous (a miscarriage, in lay language) or induced—that is, the result of deliberate interference with the pregnancy.

Stages of abortion
1. Threatened abortion: vaginal bleeding present with little or no cramps, cervix is closed.
2. Inevitable abortion: vaginal bleeding, cramping, with some dilation of the cervix.
3. Incomplete abortion: part of the products of conception (fetus, membranes, placenta) have been expelled through the uterus, but part (usually the placenta) remains in the uterus.
4. Complete abortion: fetus, membranes and placenta have all been expelled.

Types of induced abortion
1. Suction abortion: the cervix is dilated and a suction hose used to remove fetal parts.
2. Saline abortion: saline (salt) solution is injected through the abdomen of the woman and into the uterus, resulting in labor and abortion within about twenty-four hours.
3. Prostaglandin abortion: suppository of prostaglandin, a hormone, is placed in the vagina to induce labor, and abortion then usually occurs within twenty-four to thirty-six hours.

abruptio placenta Premature detachment of the placenta from the uterus which can result in fetal death and maternal hemorrhage.

adhesions Thin bands of tissue like filmy spider webs attaching organs and structures to each other in the abdominal cavity.

amniocentesis Insertion of a needle through the uterus and into the amniotic sac of the fetus to remove amniotic fluid for study.

anterior/posterior repair Repair of the mucosa or wall of the vagina and surrounding tissue for purpose of resuspending bladder (in the case of cystocele) and correcting the loosening of tissue between rectum and vagina. The operation is often performed for purpose of tightening the vaginal opening.

bili-light When a jaundiced newborn is exposed to either artificial or window light, there is a breakdown and excretion of the bilirubin which has caused the jaundice. The light used in hospitals is called a bili-light because it is used in the treatment of excess bilirubin.

breech When fetal position is such that buttocks or feet are in position to be delivered first.

Bartholin cyst Common disorder of Bartholin glands of vagina, often requiring draining and occasionally removal of the entire cyst.

cauterize To burn tissue either with chemicals or electrical heat. Used when cervix is inflamed; used also in surgery to stop bleeding of small vessels instead of tying them with sutures.

cephalopelvic disproportion (CPD), or head-pelvis disproportion. When the fetal head size is estimated to be larger than the pelvic opening through which it must pass. It is usually measured by x-rays.

clinical cephalopelvic disproportion (clinical CPD) When x-rays show there is room for the fetus to pass but because of failure of labor to progress, CPD is judged to be present on clinical grounds, i.e., by observation.

colposcopy Use of portable examining microscope to look at the cells of the surface of the cervix and vagina. It is used to locate abnormal cells, especially in DES daughters.

curettage Scraping of the inside of a cavity. In GYN it is the scraping of the lining of the uterus. *See* D&C.

cystocele A bulging of the bladder into the vagina. May be mild without symptoms and found only on examination, or may produce urinary incontinence.

D&C Dilation, or widening of the cervix, and then curettage, or scraping of the uterus.

DES (diethylstilbesterol) An estrogen that was frequently given to pregnant women twenty to thirty years ago to prevent miscarriage. It has been found to cause cancer and other severe deformities in the reproductive tract of female offspring, as well as deformities in the reproductive tract of male offspring. DES was apparently never effective in preventing or stopping miscarriage. DES is also given to women as the "morning-after" pill.

ectopic pregnancy Pregnancy that occurs outside the uterus, most commonly in the Fallopian tubes. When it ruptures, there can be severe hemorrhage.

epidural anesthesia Anesthetic drug that is injected through a catheter, or tube, which has been inserted in the outer portion of the spinal canal. The tube allows continuous or repetitive doses of the medication, thus extending the duration of the anesthesia effect.

episiotomy Incision of the perineum of a woman in order to enlarge the vaginal opening during childbirth. Two main types are *median*, which extends downward toward the anus, and *mediolateral*, which extends downward but off to one side of the anal sphincter.

fibroids Benign growths in the walls of the uterus, a frequent cause of irregular bleeding. They can grow quite large or be small and without symptoms. They usually regress with menopause.

hydrosalpinx Collection of fluid in a Fallopian tube, often a result of previous infection.

hysterectomy Removal of uterus, done either vaginally, *vaginal hysterectomy*, or abdominally, *abdominal hysterectomy*. Removal of ovaries is *oophorectomy*. Removal of Fallopian tubes is *salpingectomy*. Removal of uterus, tubes and ovaries is *hysterectomy with bilateral* [both] *salpingo-oophorectomy*.

IUD (intrauterine device) Plastic or metal device placed inside the uterus to prevent conception. Frequent complications include perforation through uterus and into the abdomen, increased bleeding, pain and infection.

jaundice A yellow staining of the skin and organs resulting from build-up of bile in the system. It is common in newborns, and depending on the etiology of the jaundice, may or may not be serious.

laparoscopy Surgical procedure in which tubes and light source are inserted into abdomen for purpose of visualizing pelvic organs and for ligating of Fallopian tubes.

laparotomy Surgical incision into the abdominal cavity.

lithotomy Used in GYN to denote a woman's position on a table with her legs up in stirrups and spread apart, giving maximal exposure to her labia and perineum.

meconium The first fetal bowel movement, which is sometimes excreted in utero if the baby is stressed. The amniotic fluid then becomes stained, referred to as *meconium staining*.

mini-lap Modification of a laparotomy involving a very small incision in the abdomen. Used for tubal ligation during sterilization.

myomectomy Surgical removal of fibroids from the walls of the uterus.

pessary A device of rubber, plastic or metal placed in the vagina to push up a uterus that is sagging down.

Pitocin A powerful drug given to begin or stimulate uterine contractions when delivery of a fetus is desired. It is also given after a delivery to help uterus to contract and thus decrease bleeding.

placenta previa Placenta is implanted over the cervix either partly or completely, thus blocking the fetus from being born vaginally. A Caesarean section is then life-saving for both mother and fetus.

premium baby Term used to denote a baby of a woman over thirty-five years of age (considered elderly in OB) or the baby of a woman who has had previous infertility.

prolapsed cord The umbilical cord protrudes through the dilated cervix ahead of the baby so that baby's head descending into the birth canal presses the cord and prevents blood flow to the baby, with subsequent fetal death.

prolapsed uterus Uterus which has lost some of its muscular support and protrudes into the vagina, either moderately with few symptoms or in severe cases actually outside the vagina.

rectocele Protrusion of the rectum into a portion of the vagina. May be mild, without symptoms, or severe, with constipation and difficult defecating.

ruptured membranes When the amniotic membranes surrounding the fetus are broken, thus allowing the amniotic fluid to leak or spill out. Once the membranes are ruptured in labor, both fetus and mother are more susceptible to infection.

true knot When the umbilical cord becomes tied into a knot, which is then pulled tight as the baby descends through the birth canal, thus stopping the blood supply to the baby and resulting in death.

ultrasound The use of sound waves of high intensity to make a picture of internal organs, similar to sonar. No long-term studies have demonstrated its safety. Used in OB to locate placenta and estimate fetal size. It is also used in the external fetal monitor and hand-held amplifying fetal stethoscopes.